EXPERIMENT
IN AUTOBIOGRAPHY

Autobiographical works by H.G. Wells

EXPERIMENT IN AUTOBIOGRAPHY, 2 vols.

H.G. WELLS IN LOVE (edited by G.P. Wells)

EXPERIMENT IN AUTOBIOGRAPHY

DISCOVERIES AND CONCLUSIONS
OF A VERY ORDINARY BRAIN
(SINCE 1866)

BY

H.G. WELLS

VOLUME II

faber and faber
LONDON · BOSTON

First published in 1934
by Victor Gollancz/Cresset Press, London
First published in paperback in 1969
by Jonathan Cape, London
Reissued in this edition in 1984
by Faber and Faber Limited
3 Queen Square London WC1N 3AU

Printed in Great Britain by
Butler & Tanner Ltd, Frome, Somerset
All rights reserved

Copyright H.G. Wells, 1934

British Library Cataloguing in Publication Data

Wells, H.G.
Experiment in autobiography.
Vol. 2
1. Wells, H.G.—Biography   2. Authors,
English—20th century—Biography
I. Title
823'.912   PR5776
ISBN 0-571-13369-X

CONTENTS

Chapter the Seventh
DISSECTION

§1.	Compound Fugue	page 417
§2.	Primary Fixation	421
§3.	*Modus Vivendi*	434
§4.	Writings about Sex	467
§5.	Digression about Novels	487

Chapter the Eighth
FAIRLY LAUNCHED AT LAST

§1.	Duologue in Lodgings (1894–95)	505
§2.	Lynton, Station Road, Woking (1895)	534
§3.	Heatherlea, Worcester Park (1896–97)	557
§4.	New Romney and Sandgate (1898)	581
§5.	Edifying Encounters : Some Types of Persona and Temperamental Attitude (1897–1910)	597
§6.	Building a House (1899–1900)	638

Chapter the Ninth

THE IDEA OF A PLANNED WORLD

§1. Anticipations (1900) and the "New Republic" page 643
§2. The Samurai—in Utopia and in the Fabian Society (1905-9) 656
§3. "Planning" in the *Daily Mail* (1912) 663
§4. The Great War and my Resort to "God" (1914-16) 665
§5. War Experiences of an Outsider 677
§6. World State and League of Nations 693
§7. World Education 715
§8. World Revolution 730
§9. Cerebration at Large and Brains in Key Positions 752
§10. Envoy 822
Index 829

LIST OF ILLUSTRATIONS

Picshua : February 1898	566
Picshua : July 29th, 1898	583
Picshua : October 5th, 1898	587
Picshua : October 8th, 1898. Reminiscences of August 1898	589
Pischua : October 8th, 1898. Reminiscences of New Romney in September	591
Picshua : October 8th, 1898. Bits the Cow Girl. House Hunting	593
Picshua : October 8th, 1898. Reminiscences of September 24th, 1898	595
Picshua : Royal Institution audience	637
Picshua : March 28th, 1901	640, 641
Picshua : June 11th, 1901	642
Picshua : Title page of *Democracy under Revision*	747

VOLUME II
CHAPTERS VII–IX

LIST OF ILLUSTRATIONS

Picshuas : Academic Robes, Four Studies of "It," Reading Glasses, Literary Composition, Frieze Design	440, 441
Picshua : A Satirical Picshua	443
Picshua : Salutary Lesson. Determined behaviour of a Lady Horticulturist	445
Reproduction of Fearful Pome	448, 449
Picshua : Invasion of Table Space	451
Picshua : Tangerines	453
Picshua : Removal to Arnold House	455
Picshua : J.M. Barrie, etc.	456, 457
Picshua : Waiting for the Verdik. *Love and Mr. Lewisham*	459
Picshua : Xmas 1894	531
Picshua : Cycling	544
Picshua : Engaging a Servant	545
Picshua : We cut our first Marrow	554
Picshua : Letter from Authors' Syndicate	555
Picshua : November 1895	556
Picshua : November 18th, 1896	558
Picshua : Letter from *Fortnightly Review*	559
Picshua : New Vagabonds' Club	560
Picshua : Gardening. Publication of *Invisible Man*, September 8th, 1897	562
Picshua : October 1897	564

CHAPTER THE SEVENTH

DISSECTION

§ 1
COMPOUND FUGUE

IF YOU DO NOT WANT to explore an egoism you should not read autobiography. If I did not take an immense interest in life, through the medium of myself, I should not have embarked upon this analysis of memories and records. It is not merely for the benefit of some possible reader, but to satisfy my own curiosity about life and the world, that I am digging down into these obscurities of forty years ago. The reader's rôle, the prospect of publication, is kept in view chiefly to steady and control these operations, by the pervading sense of a critical observer. The egoism is unavoidable. I am being my own rabbit because I find no other specimen so convenient for dissection. Our own lives are all the practical material we have for the scientific study of living ; the rest is hearsay.

The main theme of this book has been exposed in the Introductory Chapter and recalled at intervals. Essentially this autobiography treats of the steady expansion of the interests and activities of a brain, emerging from what I have called a narrow-scope way of living, to a broader and broader outlook and a consequent longer reach of motive. I move from a backyard to Cosmopolis ; from Atlas House to the burthen of Atlas. This theme appears and reappears in varying forms and keys ; in the story of my early reading, in the story of my escape from retail trade, in the story of my student perplexities and my attempts to make my geology scientific and my physics philosophical, and so on. More and more consciously the individual adventurer, as he disentangles himself from the family associations in which he was engendered, is displayed trying to make himself a citizen of the world. As his *persona* becomes lucid it takes that form. He is an individual becoming the conscious Common Man of his time and culture. He is a specimen drop from the changing ocean of general political opinion.

But the making of that world scheme is not the only driving force present in the actual life as it has to be told. In many passages it has not been even the dominant driving force. Other systems of feeling and motive run across or with or against the main theme. Sometimes they seem to have a definite relation to it ; they enhance its colour and interest or they antagonize it, but often there is no possibility of regularizing their intervention. As in all actual fugues the rules are broken and, judged by the strict standard, the composition is irregular.

The second main system of motive in the working out of my personal destiny, has been the sexual system. It is not the only other system of motive by any means. Certain fears and falterings, an undeniable claustrophobia for example, run through the narrative. The phases of disintegration and healing in my right lung, the resentment and slow resignation of my squashed kidney, have interpolated themes of their own, with their own irrelevant developments. Nevertheless the sexual complexes constitute the only other great and continuing system. I suspect the sexual system should be at least the second theme, when it is not the first, in every autobiography, honestly and fully told. It seizes upon the essential egoism for long periods, it insists upon a prominent rôle in the dramatizations of the *persona* and it will not be denied.

I realize how difficult an autobiography that is not an apology for a life but a research into its nature, can become, as I deal with this business of my divorce. I have already emphasised the widening contrast between the mental range of myself and my cousin. I have shown a disposition to simplify out the issue between myself and Catherine Robbins and Isabel to an issue between how shall I put it?—wide-scope lives and narrow-scope lives. That makes a fairly acceptable story of it, with only one fault, that it is untrue. It is all the more untrue because like a bad portrait there is superficial truth in it. The reality was far more complicated. Much more was entangled in the story. I confess that I feel that there are elements in it that I myself apprehend only very imperfectly. Let me take up this fresh chapter, as though I were a portrait painter taking a fresh canvas and beginning over again. Let me alter the pose and the lighting of my experiences so as to bring out in its successive phases the emotional and sensual egoism rather than the intellectual egoism that has hitherto been the focus of attention.

And as I turn over old letters, set date against date, and try and determine the true inter-relation of this vivid memory with that, it grows clearer and clearer to me that my personal unity, the consistency of my present *persona* has been achieved only after a long struggle between distinct strands of motivation, which had no necessary rational relation one to another and that, at the period of which I am writing, this unity was still more apparent than real.

For the normal man, as we have him to-day, his personal unity is a delusion. He is always fighting down the exposure of that delusion. His first impulse is to rationalize his inconsistencies by telling himself fanciful stories of why he did this and that. The tougher job, which all men and women will ultimately be educated to undertake, is to recognize the ultimately irreconcilable quality of these inconsistencies and to make a deal between them.

It is because of this almost universal desire to impose a sort of rational relationship upon the alternation of motives that I (and my biographer Geoffrey West, following my promptings) have represented this early divorce of mine, this first revelation of increasingly powerful strands of sexual force at work in me, as if it were almost entirely a part of my progressive detachment from my world of origin. But it merely chanced to help detach me. Later on, this sexual drive was to hamper and confuse my progress very considerably

The simple attractive story I am half disposed to tell, of myself as an ugly duckling who escaped from the limitations and want of understanding of his cousin and of his family generally, to discover itself a swan in Fleet Street and Paternoster Row, is made impossible by two things: an awkward trick my memory has had of stowing away moments of intense feeling and vivid action quite regardless of the mental embarrassment their preservation may ultimately cause my *persona*, and an analogous disposition already noted, on the part of my friends and family to keep letters I have written. I am astonished at the multitude of my letters that have never been destroyed. I have recovered now some thousand or so of them; as I turn them over past events live again, vanished details are restored, and insist upon a readjustment of the all too plausible values I have long set upon them.

And now let me try to get a little nearer to Isabel's true rôle in my life.

§ 2
Primary Fixation

I HAVE TOLD what I know of my childish and boyish sexual development. It was uncomplicated and I think very normal. There was only a very slight slant towards homosexuality. Less I think than is usual. As a small boy I had adorations for one or two big fellows and as a boy of twelve or thirteen I had affection for one or two little chaps, who obviously played the rôle of girls in my unoriented imagination. These were nothing more than early explorations of my emotional tentacles. All this, as sexual knowledge and discrimination developed, dissolved away to nothing, and by sixteen I was entirely heterosexual in my fantasies. I had a bright strong vision of beautiful women, the sort of women revealed by classical statuary and paintings, reciprocally worshipped and beautifully embraced, which I connected only very remotely with the living feminine personalities I met clothed and difficult, and with whom I " flirted," at times, weakly and formally. I had one or two warning experiences that the hidden happiness of sex was not easy of attainment. My gleams of intimacy at Westbourne Park were not pretty ; plainly my Venus Urania did not live down that frowsty scuffling alley. Later on (I cannot fix the date but it must have been while I was in my twenties and a biological demonstrator) my secret shame at my own virginity became insupportable and I went furtively and discreetly with a prostitute. She was just an unimaginative prostitute. That deepened my wary apprehension that round about the hidden garden of desire was a jungle of very squalid and stupid lairs.

Now my cousin had a real sweetness and loveliness that our closeness did nothing to abolish. All the cloudy drift of desire and romantic imagination in my mind centred more and more upon her. I became so persuaded and satisfied that with her I could get to this fundamental happiness of love which now obsessed me, that for all the years between my student days and our marriage my imagination never wandered very far from her. I played the devoted impatient lover. There was a deep-seated fixation of my mind upon her.

She loved me I knew, but with a more limited and temperate imagination than mine. The jangle of our thoughts and outlooks, that difference in scope, would not have mattered very much if our passions had been in tune. We should have managed then. Our real discord was not mental but temperamental. And she was afraid, and the worldly wisdom of that retouching studio in Regent Street did not help her in the least. My nature protested at having to wait for her so long, protested against having to marry her in church instead of at a registry office. I didn't believe in marriage anyhow, I insisted. The great thing was not marriage but love. I invoked Godwin, Shelley, Socialism.

Streaks of vindictiveness crept into my passion. And I was a very ignorant as well as an impatient lover. I knew nothing of the arts of wooing. I should probably have thought that sort of thing dishonest. My idea was of flame meeting flame. . . . We are so much wiser about that sort of thing nowadays. It is rarer for avid and innocent young bridegrooms to be flung upon shrinking and innocent brides.

It mattered nothing to me, then, that Isabel was manifestly fond of me, cared greatly for me. It was a profound mortification to me, a vast disappointment, that she did not immediately respond to my ardours. She submitted. I had waited so long for this poor climax. " She does not love me," I said in my heart. I put as brave a face as I could upon the business, I dried her tears, blamed my roughness, but it was a secretly very embittered young husband who went on catching trains, correcting correspondence answer books, eviscerating rabbits and frogs and hurrying through the crowded business of every day.

Here was something more organic than any difference in mental scope. And I want to make it quite clear that for a long time my emotional pride, my secret romanticism was still centred quite firmly in my cousin. It is true that I was presently letting my desires wander away from her and that I was making love to other people. I wanted to compensate myself for the humiliation she had so unwittingly put upon me. I was in a phase of aroused liveliness. That did not alter her unpremeditated and unconscious dominance of my imagination, my deep-lying desire for passionate love with her.

Quite soon after my marriage indeed came an adventure, that did much to restore my baffled self-confidence. There was a certain little Miss Kingsmill who came to Haldon Road first as a pupil to learn retouching and then as a helper with the work. She was cheerfully a-moral and already an experienced young woman. She was about the house before and after my marriage; the business stirred her; she may have had confidences from my cousin and a quickening interest became evident in her manner towards me. I found myself alone with her in the house one day; I was working upon a pile of correspondence books, my aunt was out shopping and my wife had gone to London with some retouched negatives. I forget by what excuse Ethel Kingsmill flitted from her retouching desk upstairs, to my study. But she succeeded in dispelling all the gloomy apprehensions I was beginning to entertain, that lovemaking was nothing more than an outrage inflicted upon reluctant womankind and all its loveliness a dream. The sound of my returning aunt's latch-key separated us in a state of flushed and happy accomplishment. I sat down with a quickened vitality to my blottesque red corrections again and Ethel, upstairs, very content with herself, resumed her niggling at her negative. Sentimentally and " morally " this is a quite shocking incident to relate; in truth it was the most natural thing in the world.

After that one adventure I looked the world in the eye again. But it did nothing to change my attachment to Isabel. Our separation did not alter the fact that still for many years she retained the dominant place among my emotional possibilities. I do not know what might have happened if at any time in the course of our estrangement she had awakened and turned upon me with a passionate appeal.

I can see to-day, as I dissect the dead rabbit of my former self, what I never saw before, why it was that after years of complete orientation to my cousin, now that she was my wife, my eye and fancy wandered. Less consciously than instinctively I was trying to undo the knot I had tied and release myself from the strong, unsatisfying bond of habit and affection between us. I still wanted to keep her, if only she would quicken and come alive to me; and quite as strongly I wanted to escape from the pit of disappointment into which I had fallen with her.

As I sit over this specimen of human life, pickled now in correspondence and ineffaceable memories for forty years, I find this replacement, in the course of a few weeks, of a very real simple honesty of sexual purpose by duplicity quite the most interesting fact about my early married life. After six "engagement" years of monogamic sincerity and essential faithfulness, I embarked, as soon as I was married, upon an enterprising promiscuity. The old love wasn't at all dead, but I meant now to get in all the minor and incidental love adventures I could.

I am disposed to think, on the strength I admit, of my one only personal experience, that for the normally constituted human being there must be two contrasted types of phase, fixation upon an individual as one end of the series and complete promiscuity of attention and interest as the other. Anyone, at any time, may be in one or other phase, or moving from one to the other. We are not monogamic by nature, or promiscuous by nature, but some of us happen to get *fixed* for longer or shorter periods. There is a general desire to concentrate. We tend towards attachment but a shock or a mounting subconscious resistance may suddenly interfere. It is like the accumulation of a sediment, in a test-tube which may at any time happen to be heated or shaken. We become dispersed then, perhaps for an indefinite time, until a new trend towards fixation appears. These are matters not within the control of will or foresight, they happen to us before willing begins. That, I think, gives some expression to these alternations of fairly strict loyalty, such as I observed before my marriage, with my subsequent infidelities, which phase again gave place to a second, less powerful, fixation and that to a second discursiveness.

But as I sit and speculate about what really happened to me more than half a life-time ago in 1892 and 1893, I begin to suspect that I am still simplifying too much and that there was another independent strand of motive playing among the others. Is there a strain of evasion in my composition? Does the thought of being bound and settling down, in itself, so soon as it is definitely presented, arouse a recalcitrant stress in me? And how far is that fugitive impulse exceptional, and how far is its presence an ordinary thing in the human make-up? Is this string also tugging at everybody? Is there potential flight as well as attraction in every love affair? I remember clearly how much I desired my cousin to become my mistress before I married her and how much I wished to go on living in lodgings for a time even after we were married, instead of taking a house.

In my case the break between the pull and the drive came to a climax very abruptly. I find I was writing from my home in Sutton in mid-December 1892 as though I intended to live on there indefinitely; and I find myself living in Mornington Place with Catherine Robbins early in the following January! The circumstances of that very abrupt change defeat my memory. Something happened which I cannot recall. I have been inclined to suppose a fit of claustrophobia. Did I perhaps wake up suddenly in the night and say "I must get out of this?" I may have had one of those spasmodic resolutions that do come up sometimes out of the welter of the half-conscious and the subconscious! If so I do not remember it. But I do find indications of precisely the opposite thing, a considerable amount of shilly-shally. Even after I had eloped I was, I know, trying very earnestly to persuade my cousin not to divorce me. Having got away from her I wanted to keep her. It is only now, in this cold and deliberate retrospect, that I admit even to myself how disingenuous, how confused and divided in purpose I was at that time.

Isabel and I paid a visit to the Robbins' household on December 15th and stayed until December 18th. This probably brought on he crisis. Isabel may have given way to a fit of jealousy. My brother Freddy, who was always greatly attached to her and who talked the affair over with her years afterwards, tells me now that she ascribed our separation to her own initiative. She told him she had put it to me that either I must end this continually more intimate and interesting friendship altogether or part from her. She had had a similar phase of possessiveness during my student days at South Kensington. She felt at a disadvantage with these people who could "talk." I do not now recall any such ultimatum, but in the circumstances it was a very natural and probable one and the visit to Putney may have precipitated it. The retort, " Very well, if you can let me go like this, I will go," was equally natural and obvious. There we have exactly the pride and resentment on either side necessary for a sudden separation. She made what is otherwise an unaccountable decision, easy for me.

Brother Freddy comes in very usefully here. Later on, he tells me, she regretted our parting profoundly. I too regretted it. She reproached herself, he says, for failing to " understand " me and for having broken before I was ready to break. She said she had been headstrong and selfish ; she had said her say, I had taken her at her word, and she found there was no going back upon it. There was certainly a deep bond of dearness between us still, we realized that as our anger abated, but, once we were launched upon our several courses, there was no return.

Perhaps it was well that there was no return. There was a superficial volatility and a profound impatience in my make-up that would have taxed her ultimately beyond the limit of her adaptability. We might have gone on dragging out the estrangement. A later breach might have been a less generous one.

My little Aunt Mary, who died two years later, was distressed and perplexed beyond measure by our divorce and, as Isabel told me long afterwards, her opinion of the whole affair expressed itself in a " good scolding " for " losing " me. My mother too was so amazed at Isabel " letting me go," and so near to indignation about it, that she quite forgot to be shocked at the immorality of my situation. I cannot make up my mind how far this disposition on the part of women to make their own sex wholly responsible for the infirmity of purpose of their menfolk is due to deep-seated and ancient traditions, and how far it is innate. But that was how my aunt and my mother behaved.

When my second wife was dying in 1927, she said to me, "I have never destroyed a single letter of yours, I cannot destroy them now. There they are in my bureau, with all my own letters that you have asked me to keep. You must do as you please with them." So that I am able, after a little trouble with some undated letters, to check back every main phase in our reactions throughout our long married life. The record is even fuller than a mere keeping of letters would imply. Not only did we write to each other daily when we were apart, but for all our time when we were together, I had a queer little custom of drawing what we called " picshuas " to amuse her and myself, little sketches of fancy, comment or caricature. I began this in Mornington Place in 1893. These picshuas carried on the tradition of those scratchy odd little drawings with which I used to decorate my letters to my family and friends. Many were destroyed as they were done, but many were thrust into drawers and survived. The growth and changes of tone in our relations is, I say, traceable by means of this accumulation over thirty-five years. And it is quite evident that these letters are those of two loving friends and allies, who are not and never had been passionate lovers. That is the point of importance here.

The earliest of all my letters, the ones written before matters came to a crisis, were the ordinary letters of a self-conscious young man putting his best foot forward in a friendly correspondence. They were letters that might have to be shown to " mother " and eminently discreet. There is no essential change of tone right up to the breach with Isabel. But then came letters written during our crisis, and I find a curiously false and unconvincing note sounding through them. They are plainly the attempts of an extremely perplexed mind to make a fair story out of a muddle of impulses. They are not straightforward, they pose and flatter, they exaggerate. The ring of simple and honest passion is not there ; I would hate to quote a line of them. Fortunately that is not only unnecessary but impossible. They vary so much that no quotations would be really representative.

The resort to heroics in these letters is frequent and facile. I was acting a part. I may have been acting in good faith, to the best of my ability, but I was acting. It is plain that I resolved suddenly at any cost to get my little student to come away and give herself to me, but there is not the slightest indication that I was really possessed by her personality or that at that time I had the smallest apprehension of its sterling quality. Sifting over all my evidence now, not as my apologist but as my scientific historian, I am inclined to think that the most powerful drive at work in me was the longing to relieve my imagination not of the real Isabel but of that Venus Urania, that torment of high and beautiful desire, who had failed to embody herself in Isabel and yet had become so inseparable from her. My mind was seizing upon Amy Catherine Robbins to make her the triumphant rival of that elusive goddess.

On my new mistress, in her turn, I was trying to impose a rôle. Like so many other desperate young love affairs, ours was to be such a love affair as the world had never seen before. Other people were different. We were by mutual agreement two beings of an astonishing genius with an inherent right to turn accepted morality upside down. It was an explosion of moral light. . . .

There was some coming and going between Mornington Place and the Robbins' home in Putney after our first departure. The mother declared herself to be dying of grief, she wept continuously and incredibly, and the daughter went back to her home for some days. Attempts were then made to delay her return to me. Various men friends of the family were invoked to remonstrate and threaten. I stuck to my purpose grimly. Miss Amy Catherine Robbins stuck to my purpose. Vast arguments unfolded about us. She was consumptive; I was consumptive; we were launching on a desperate experiment. We replied magnificently that if we were going to die so soon, the more reason there was that we should spend all that was left of our brief time on earth together. But let her at any rate remain in the shelter of her home until I was divorced, they argued. I answered that I was not sure I wanted to be divorced. We did not believe in the Institution of Marriage and we did not intend to marry. We were both very sure that we did not intend to marry.

The resolve to get the best of an argument may link two people as closely as inherent mutual desire. We hadn't our backs to the wall ; there was indeed nothing in the nature of a wall behind us ; we had only each other. We saw the thing through in spite of immense secret disillusionments. I found this fragile delicate little being of Dresden china, was altogether innocent and ignorant of the material realities of love, it was impossible to be rough or urgent with her and so the deep desired embraces of Venus Urania were now further off from me than ever. But not a soul in the world about us knew anything of that for some years. We stuck to each other stoutly and forged the links of a chain of mutual aid, tolerance and affection that held us close to each other to the day of her death. We got over the worst of our difficulties ; we established a *modus vivendi*. Insensibly the immense pretentiousness of our first beginning evaporated and we began to jest and mock at ourselves very cordially. The " picshuas " began. We worked in close association and sympathy. But there arose no such sexual fixation between us, as still lingered in my mind towards my cousin.

If I am to tell this story at all I must tell here of two illuminating incidents that happen to be known now to no one in the whole world but myself. They seem to me to be profoundly illuminating; but the reader must judge for himself whether I am disposed to exaggerate their significance. They show at any rate how little I had really finished with my cousin when I separated myself from her and how much of that separation was concerned with her and not with her successor. The first of these incidents occurred when I visited her somewhen about 1898 or 99 at a poultry farm she was running, not very profitably, at Twyford between Maidenhead and Reading. I think the pretext of our meeting again was the discussion of some extension of that enterprise. I bicycled to the place and found her amidst green things and swarming creatures depending upon her, in the rustic setting to which by nature she belonged. We spent a day together at Virginia Water, a day without tension, with an easy friendliness we had never known before. We used our old intimate names for each other. Suddenly I found myself overcome by the sense of our separation. I wanted fantastically to recover her. I implored her for the last time in vain Before dawn the house had become unendurable for me. I got up and dressed and went down to find my bicycle and depart. She heard me moving about, perhaps she too had not slept, and she came down, kindly and invincible as ever, and as amazed as ever at my strangeness.

Because you see it was all so unreasonable.

" But you cannot go out at this hour without something to eat," she said, and set about lighting a fire and boiling a kettle.

Her aunt could be heard moving about upstairs, for they occupied adjacent rooms. " It's all right Auntie," she said, and prevented her from coming down to witness my distress.

All our old mingling of intense attraction and baffling reservation was there unchanged. "But how can things like that be, now?" she asked. I gave way to a wild storm of weeping. I wept in her arms like a disappointed child, and then suddenly pulled myself together and went out into the summer dawn and mounted my bicycle and wandered off southward into a sunlit intensity of perplexity and frustration, unable to understand the peculiar keenness of my unhappiness. I felt like an automaton, I felt as though all purpose had been drained out of me and nothing remained worth while. The world was dead and I was dead and I had only just discovered it.

After that I set myself to forget my imaginations about her, by releasing my imaginations for other people. But in that I was unsuccessful for a long time. Five or six years afterwards she married; I do not know the exact date because for more than a year she kept this from me. And then came a still more illuminating incident. When at last I heard of it, I was overwhelmed by a storm of irrational organic jealousy. It took the form of a deliberate effacement of her. I destroyed all her photographs and letters and every souvenir I possessed of her; I would not have her mentioned to me if I could avoid it; I ceased all communications. The portraits I have reproduced here I have had to borrow. That bitterness again is quite incompatible with the plausible and conventional theory that she was nothing more to me than an illiterate young woman whom I "dropped" because she was unequal to a rôle in the literary world. I burnt her photographs. That was a symbolization. If we had lived ten thousand years ago I suppose I should have taken my axe of stone and set out to find and kill her.

And to complete this history here, the still stranger thing is that in another five years all this fixation had vanished. It had been completely swept out of my mind by other disturbances of which I must tell at some later date. The sting had vanished. I was able to meet her again in 1909 in a mood of limitless friendliness, free from all the glittering black magic of sex; and so things remained with us until the end of her life. Some friend we had in common mentioned her to me, brought us into communication again, and we met and continued to meet at intervals after that. Following her marriage, the order for her alimony had been discharged but now, realizing she had to practice many economies, I arranged an income for her, exactly as one might do for a married sister. In quite the same mood of brotherliness I bought a laundry for her when the fancy took her to possess a business of her own. That enterprise was crippled by an operation for appendicitis; she had no great facilities for being nursed in her own house and she came to mine and stayed through her convalescence with my wife and myself until she was well again. No one about us knew her story; she was my cousin and that sufficed; we were in a world far removed from the primitive jealousies, comparisons and recriminations of our early years. We walked about the garden discussing annuals and perennials and roses and trees. When she was growing stronger I took her for my favourite round through the big gardens of Easton Lodge. She was particularly pleased by the lily tank before the house, and by the golden pheasants Lady Warwick had turned loose in the wood behind the ponds.

That was the last walk we ever had together.

She wrote to me in her simple gentle fashion when my wife died, praising and lamenting her. Afterwards she wanted to build a house of her own and asked me to help her. When I saw that her heart was set upon it I agreed to that, though it did not seem to me to be what Americans call a sound proposition. We inspected the site and she showed me the plans. But the house was barely begun before she died and it was abandoned. She died quite unexpectedly. She had been diabetic and making use of insulin for some years. I had just discovered that I too was diabetic and I was looking forward to her coming to a lunch with me, at which I would surprise her by an admirable menu of all the best permissible things I thought it was a cousinly touch that we should share the same diathesis. But something went wrong with her insulin injections and one day in France I got a letter from her husband saying that she was dead. She had been well on Saturday and she became comatose on Monday and died without recovering consciousness.

So ends this history of the rise and fall and sequel of that primary fixation that began when my cousin came downstairs to meet me in that basement tea-party in the Euston Road forty-seven years before. I offer no moral lesson. I have tried to tell things as they happened.

§ 3
Modus Vivendi

THE MIXTURE of high-falutin with sincere determination on the part of this Miss Amy Catherine Robbins and myself in the early stages of our joint adventure, deserves a little more attention. We were both in reality in flight from conditions of intolerably narrow living. But we did not know how to state that properly, we were not altogether clear about it, and we caught at the phrasing of Shelley and the assumption of an imperative passion. She was the only daughter of an extremely timid and conventional mother with no ideas for her future beyond marriage to a safe, uneventful *good* man, and her appearance in my mixed classes was already an expression of her struggle and revolt. My own recalcitrance to the life fate had presented to me I have already dealt with. My intimations of freedom and social and intellectual enterprise (on the noblest scale) went to her head very readily and it was an overwhelming desire for emancipation from consuming everyday obligations for both of us rather than sexual passion, that led to our wild dash at opportunity.

That alliance for escape and self development held throughout our lives. We never broke it. As our heroics evaporated we found ourselves with an immense liking and respect for each other and a great willingness to turn an awkward corner with a jest and a caricature. We discovered a way of doing that. We became and remained the best companions in the world. But our alliance never became an intense sexual companionship, which indeed is why my primary fixation upon my cousin remained so powerful in my mind for ten years or more, and why, later on, as we emerged to success and freedom I was in a phase of imaginative dispersal and began to scandalize the whisperers about us.

Here again it would be easy to dress up my story in a highly logical and creditable manner. But I have never quite succeeded in that sort of dressing-up. A few tactful omissions would smooth out the record beautifully. And if the record is not beautifully smoothed out it is not for want of effort. Between the ages of thirty and forty I devoted a considerable amount of mental energy to the general problem of men and women. And never with any real disinterestedness. I wanted to live a consistent life, I wanted a life that would stand examination, I hated having to fake a front to the world, and yet not only were my thoughts and fancies uncontrollable, but my conduct remained perplexingly disingenuous. I did my best to eliminate my sense of that disingenuousness by candid public theorizing. I spoke out for "Free Love." I suppose I was going through phases roughly parallel with those through which Shelley had passed eighty years before. Hundreds of thousands have passed that way. I did my best to maintain that love-making was a thing in itself, a thing to thank the gods for, but not to be taken too seriously and carried into the larger constructive interests of life.

The spreading knowledge of birth-control,—Neo-Malthusianism was our name for it in those days—seemed to justify my contention that love was now to be taken more lightly than it had been in the past. It was to be refreshment and invigoration, as I set out quite plainly in my *Modern Utopia* (1905), and I could preach these doctrines with no thought of how I would react if presently my wife were to carry them into effect, since she was so plainly not disposed to carry them into effect, and what is much more remarkable, with my recent storm of weeping in that little farm kitchen at Twyford, very conveniently—but quite honestly—forgotten. This again I think is after the common fashion. We are not naturally aware of our two-phase quality. We can all think in the liberal fashion in our phases of dispersal; there is always a Free Love contingent in any community at any time; but its membership varies and at any time any of its members may lapse towards a fixation and towards its attendant exclusiveness and jealous passion. People drop out of the contingent or return to it. At one time love is the happy worship of Venus, the goddess of human loveliness, the graceful mutual compliment of two free bodies and spirits; at another it is the sacred symbol of an intense and mystical personal association, a merging of identities prepared to live and die for one another. It is this variation of phase that plays havoc with every simple dogmatic ruling upon sexual behaviour.

Advocates of free love, in so far as they aim at the liberation of individual sexual conduct from social reproach and from legal controls and penalties, are, I believe, entirely in the right. Nevertheless, with such a liberation, very little is attained. Circumstances are simplified, but the problem itself remains unchanged. We are still confronted with the essential riddle of our own phases of development as we pass from youth to maturity and, as I have already insisted, with this other, more persistent, alternation of phase between dispersal and intensification. The tangle is further complicated by the absolute right of society to intervene directly the existence of children is involved, and by a third mass of difficulties due to the fact that emotionally and physically, and thence to an increasing degree in its secondary associations and implications, love is a different thing for men and women. In a universe of perfect adaptations these differences would reciprocate; in this world they do nothing of the sort.

But here I approach questions and experiences that will be better deferred until I come to that phase of my middle years during which I produced various hesitating yet enterprising love novels. Then, almost in spite of myself, I was forced by my temperament and circumstances to face the possibility that men and women as such, when it comes to planning a greater world order, may be disposed to desire incompatible things. Feminine creativeness and feminine devotion may differ from their masculine parallels and though women radicals and men radicals are members of the same associations and speak to the same meetings, their ends may lie far apart. There may have to be a new treaty of mutual tolerance between the sexes.

But in the early days of my second marriage I did not even suspect the possibility of these fundamental disagreements in the human project. My wife and I had still to win the freedom to think as we liked about our world. What we were then going to think about it, lay some years ahead of us. While we struggled we liked each other personally more and more, we dropped our heroics and laughed and worked together, we made do with our physical and nervous incompatibilities and kept a brave face towards the world.

We dropped our disavowal of the Institution of Marriage and married, as soon as I was free to do so, in 1895. The behaviour of the servants of that period and the landladies and next-door neighbours, forced that upon us anyhow. Directly the unsoundness of our position appeared, servants became impertinent and neighbours rude and strange. How well we came to know the abrupt transition from a friendly greeting " passing the time of day " to a rigid estrangement. Were they really horrified when they " heard about it," or is there a disposition to hate and persecute awaiting release in every homely body? I believe that there has been a great increase in tolerance in the last forty years but in our period, if we had not married, half our energy would have been frittered away in a conflict of garden-wall insults and slights and domestic exactions. We had no disposition for that kind of warfare.

And having got together and found how evanescent were our heroics, and having discovered that our private dreams of some hidden splendour of loving were evaporating, we were nevertheless under both an inner and an outer obligation to stand by one another and pull our adventure through. We refrained from premature discussion and felt our way over our situation with tentatives and careful understatement. We could each wait for the other to take on an idea. She, even less than I, had, that terrible fluidity of speech that can swamp any situation in garrulous justification and headlong ultimatums. And our extraordinary isolation, too, helped us to discover a *modus vivendi*. Neither of us had any confidants to complicate our relations by some potent divergent suggestion, and there was no background of unsympathetic values that either of us respected. Neither of us bothered in the least about what so and so would think. In many matters we were odd and exceptional individuals but in our broad relations to each other and society we may have come much nearer to being absolute and uncomplicated sample man and woman, than do most young couples. The research for a *modus vivendi* is a necessary phase of the normal married life to-day.

Now in this research for a *modus vivendi* certain apparently very trivial things played a really very important part. Although I have published only four lines of verse in my life, I used to be in the habit of making endless doggerel as I got up in the morning, and when we were sitting together in the evening, with my writing things before me I would break off my work to do " picshuas," these silly little sketches about this or that incident which became at last a sort of burlesque diary of our lives and accumulated in boxes until there were hundreds of them. Many—perhaps most—are lost but still there remain hundreds. I invented a queer little device in a couple of strokes to represent her head, and it somehow seemed to us to resemble her ; also a kindred convention, with a large nose and a wreath of laurel suggestive of poetic distinction and incipient baldness, for myself. Like so many couples, we found it necessary to use pet names ; she became Bits or Miss Bits or Snitch or It, with variations, and I was Bins or Mr. Bins. A burlesque description I gave, after a visit to the Zoological Gardens, of the high intelligence and remarkable social life of the gopher, amused us so much that we incorporated a sort of gopher chorus with the picshuas. Whatever we did, whatever was going on in the world, the gophers set about doing after their fashion. Into this parallel world of burlesque and fancy, we transferred a very considerable amount of our every-day life, and there it lost its weight and irksomeness. We transferred our own selves there also. Miss Bits became an active practical imperious little being and Mr. Bins a rather bad, evasive character who went in great awe of her. He was frequently chastised with an umbrella or " Umbler pop." All this funny-silly stuff is so much of the same quality that I find it hard to pick out specimens, but I do not see how I can tell of it without reproducing samples. Here for instance are various " études," some very early sketches of Miss Robbins in her academic gown, done before our elopement, a very characteristic figure of her engaged in literary effort, from about 1896, four later studies of the conventional head of Miss Bits, It usually, It at the slightest hint of impropriety, It sad and It asleep, a treatment of the advent of reading glasses, and a sort of frieze of every-day; the Same, Yesterday, To-day and for Ever. These may seem at the first glance to be the most idle of scribblings but in fact they are acute statements in personal interpretation. Mostly they were done on sheets of manuscript paper, so that here they suffer considerable reduction and compression. This, says my publisher was unavoidable.

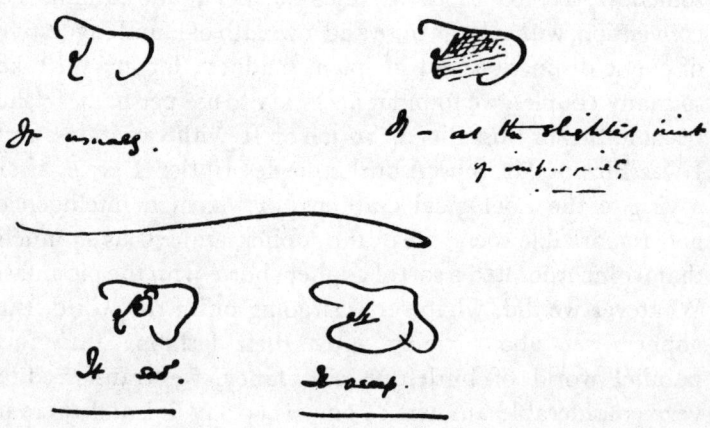

Here is a Satirical Picshua; on one side of the paper is "Bits as she *finks* she is" and on the other, "the real Bits, really a very dear Bits indeed." She writes, sleeps, eats and rides a bicycle with me.

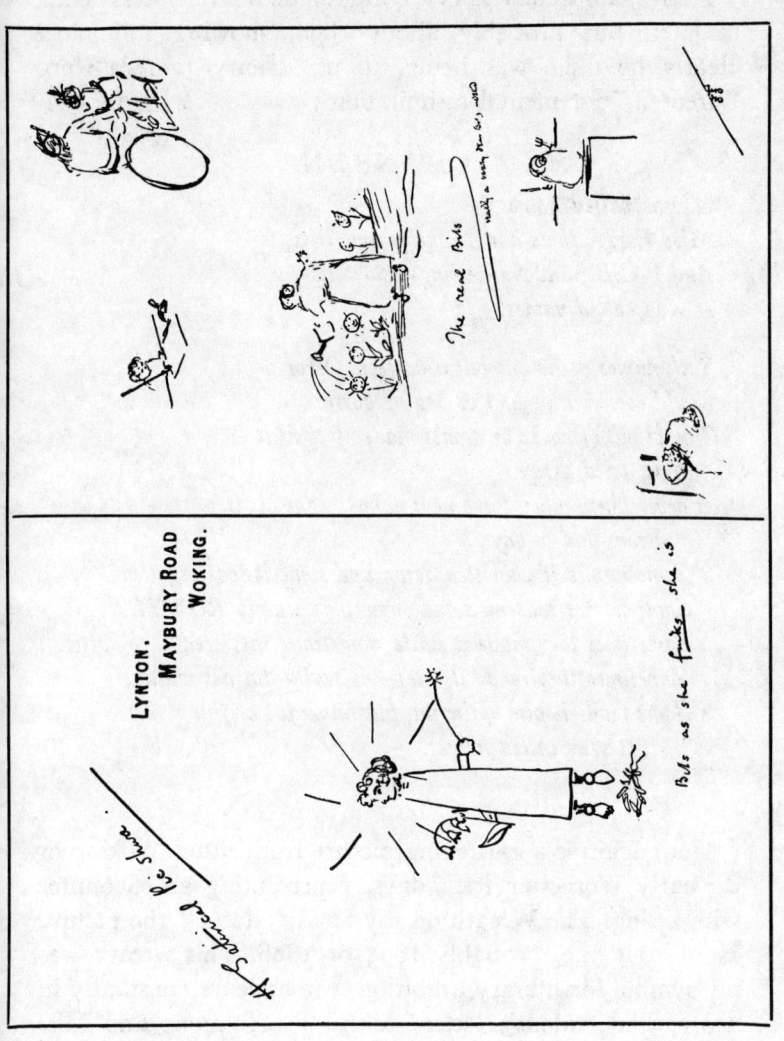

Here again is the text of a sympathetic but relentless poem, undated but probably about 1898, showing still more clearly how she was being, to use Henry James's word " treated," for mental assimilation :

CHANSON

It was *called names*
Miss Furry Boots and Nicketty and Bits,
And P.C.B., and Snitterlings and Snits,
It was *called names.*

Such names as no one but a perfect 'Orror
Could ever fink or find or beg or borrow
Names out of books or names made up to fit it
    In wild array
It never knew when some new name might hit it
    From day to day
    Some names it's written down and some it 'as forgotten
    Some names was nice and some was simply ROTTEN.
    Sometimes they made it smile, sometimes they seemed to flatter
    Sometimes they made it weep—it really did not matter.
    Some made it pine quite fin, but fin or fat or fatter
        It was *called names.*

Here again is a gardening picture from either Woking or the early Worcester Park days, representing an encounter with a slug. The Wreath on my head " dates " the picture as an early one, probably 1895 or 1896. This wreath was my symbol for literary ambitions ; it appears constantly in my earlier student's letters to A. T. Simmons and Miss Healey, and it becomes infrequent after 1898.

Here you have a " Fearful Pome " intended to bring home to an insolent woman her dependence on her lord. This doggerel variant of Lear's nonsense rhyme, brings out the queer little fact that even in these early days at Heatherlea, Worcester Park, the money of the alliance was already under her control. We were living indeed exactly like an honest working-class couple and the man handed over his earnings to his " missus " and was given out his pocket money.

Fearful Pome to Scare and Improve a Bits

The Pobble who has no Toes
Had once as many as Ten
(Now here is a Strange and Horrible Thing
All of his Toes were Men)
Some there are who wrongly hold
His toes did number eleven
But none dare count the Hairs of his Head
(Though the Stars in his Hair are Seven)
Such as would count the Hairs of His Head
Speedily Painfully Die
(Aunt Jobiska he never had
All that tale is a Lie).
All who meet the Pobble abroad
Come to infinite Harm
May you never meet him (Pray the Lord),
Clothed in his Sinister Charm
(Softly (yet dreadfully fast) He goes
That Terrible Pobble who has no Toes)
(It's no good saying you do not care
This Awful Pobble goes everywhere)
Should you meet him, cover your face
Leave your shoes in that Terrible Place
The Pobble—the Foe of the Human Race—and Flee
Your only shelter from his Clutch
Your only Refuge he dare not Touch
The only Being he cares for Much is Me (H.G.)
Me what you fink is simply Fungy
Me what you keep so short of Mungy
Me what you keep so short of Beer
Is your only chance when the Pobble is near
Nex time you go for your Umbler Pop
Fink of that Terrible Pobble and Stop.

~~Your~~ His only Shelter from his Cliob
~~Your~~ His only Refuge ~~from~~ he dare not Touch
The only Being he cares for much
                              is Me. (H.G)

Me what you frank is simply Funny.
Me what you keep so short of Mummy
Me what you keep so short of Beer
'is your only chance when the Piddle is near
They time you go for your Umber Pop.
Funk of that Terrible Piddle & Stop.

Jan Gigoo

Here is a gentle protest against an unfair invasion of table space. The lamp dates it as before 1900 and the spectacles as after 1898.

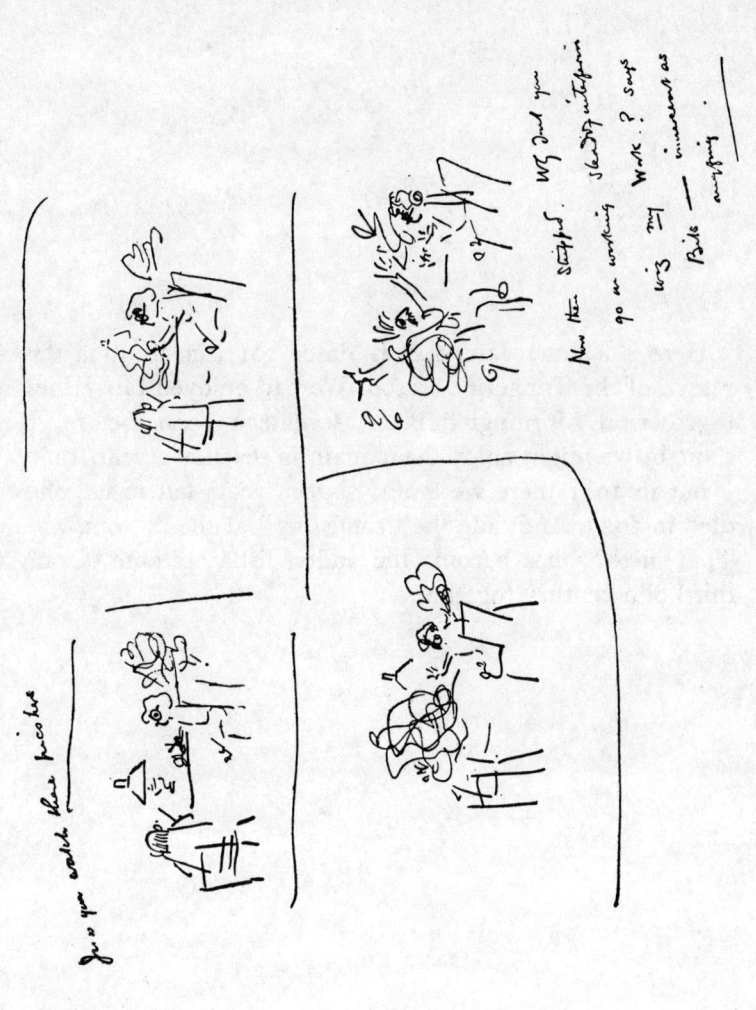

Here is a much later sketch, dated 1911, celebrating the return of the Tangerine season. We had enjoyed tangerines together at Mornington Place, seventeen years before. I thought we might enjoy them again in seventeen years time —but in 1911 there were only sixteen years left to us; she died in 1927. And note the "some day" at the bottom. . . . That picshua has become the oddest little epitome of our third of a century together.

Tangerines
1894

Sweet Seventeen Years.
(with Truffles)

Tangerines.
1911.

Seventeen Years (Props not well Truffles any more).

Tangerines .1928

Snady . o o Tangerines

Here is an earlier picshua again (March 31st, 1899). It commemorates a removal from Beach Cottage, Sandgate, to Arnold House. The helplessness of the male on these occasions of domestic upheaval is contrasted with the ruthless energy of the female. The first thing is "Gup! Movals!", i.e. "Get up—removal!" Then the embarrassed master of the house misses his trousers. He finds himself being carried from house to house and protests, "But Bits why can't I walk like I usually does?" He is crushed by the stern reply "Cos it's Movals." And so on.

On the following two pages is a casual specimen for 1898. The reader may do his best to interpret it. A lens may be needed, but that is due to the unavoidable reduction for printing. By this time the reader has either given up looking at these picshuas or he has learnt their peculiar language. The idea of building a house was already under discussion. We had had a visit from J. M. Barrie (of which a word may be said later) and he and Jane are represented measuring heights (Mezzerinites). There had been trouble over a building site, with a Mr. Toomer. The gophers appear in full cry in pursuit of the said Toomer. The Atom reflects upon her diminutive size. Other points may be guessed at.

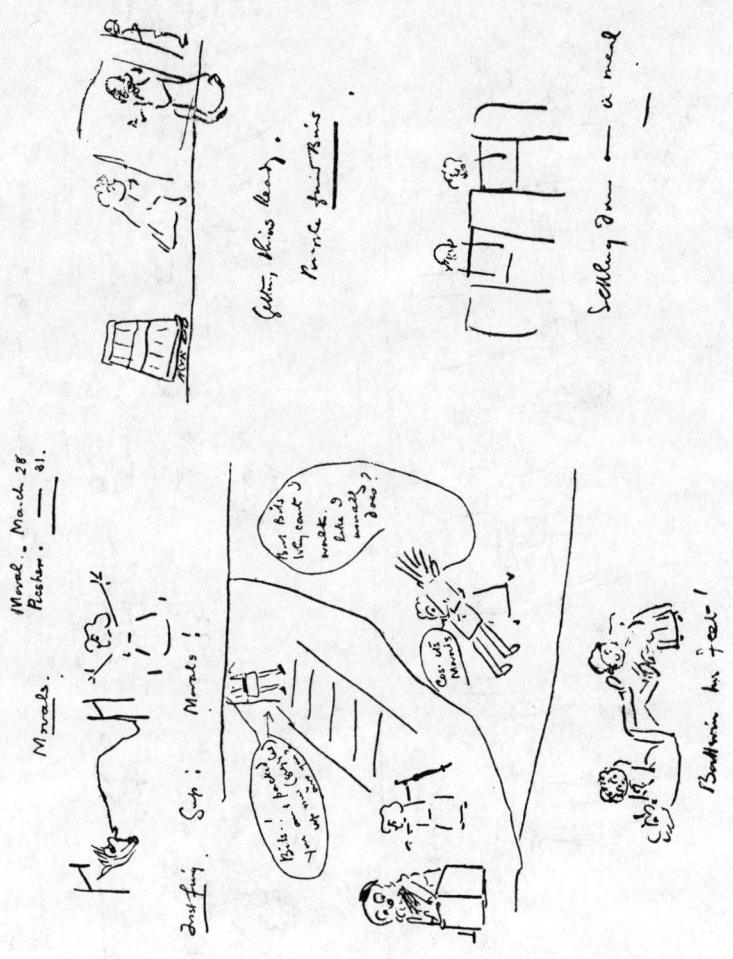

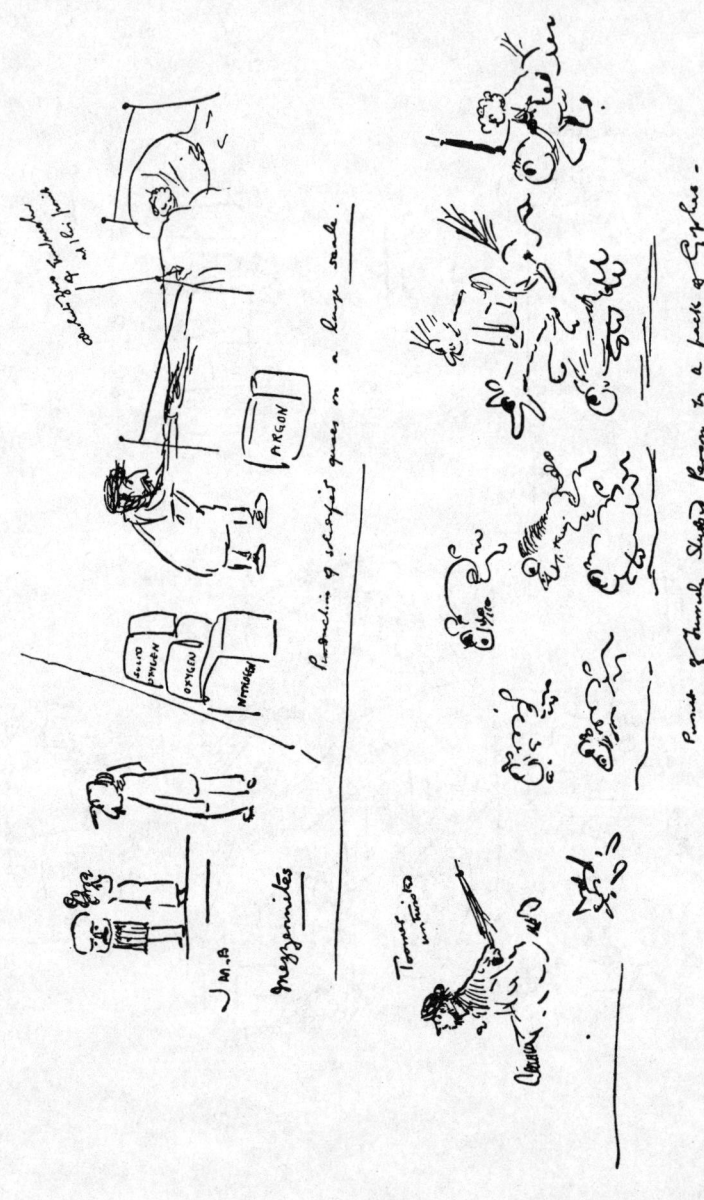

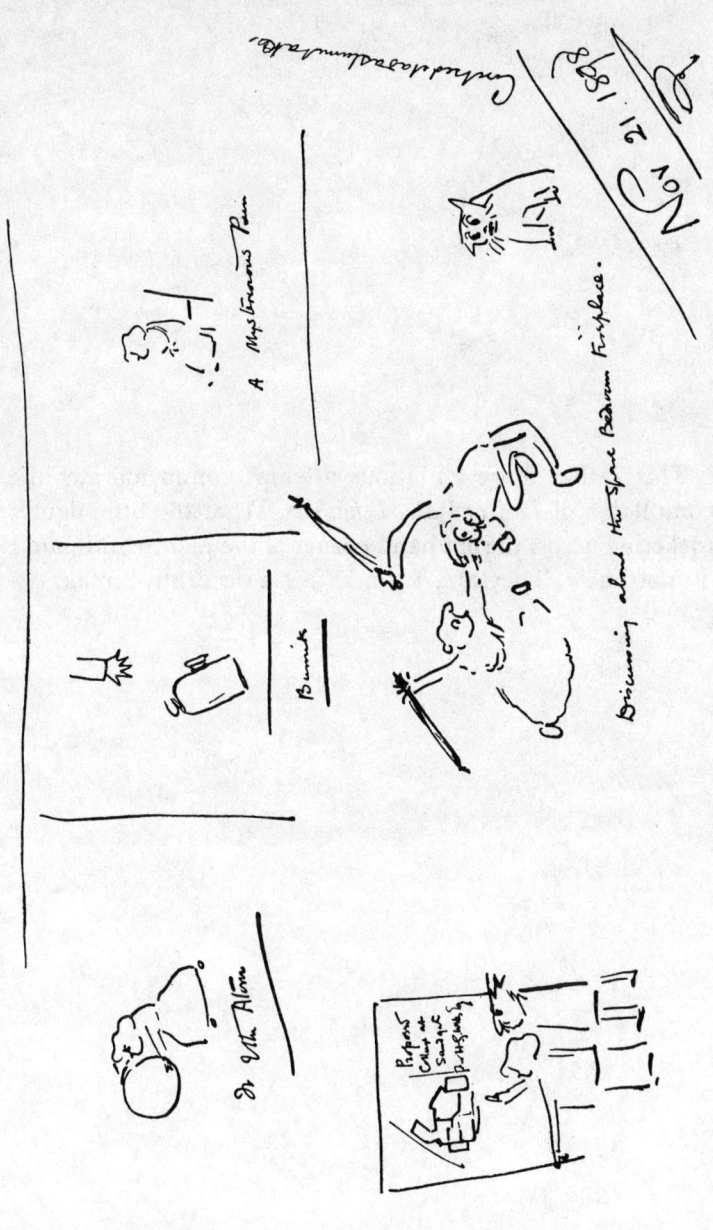

This rather more ambitious attempt commemorates the completion of *Love and Mr. Lewisham*. What the little figures rocketing across the left hand corner of the picture intimate I do not know. They are, I think, just a decorative freak.

Finally let me quote a hymn, celebrating our first seven years together. " Mr. Boo " I may explain was a cat that ran away, and the " Bites " were Harvesters, which we had gathered unwittingly on the Downs behind Folkestone.

Lines written on this piece of paper
Oct. 11th, 1900.

Our God is an Amoosing God. It is His Mercy that
This Bins who formerly was Ill is now quite well and Fat
And isn't going Bald no more nor toofaking and such
For all of which This Bins who writes congratulates Him *much.*

Our God is an Amoosing God, although he let that site,
What first we chose, be Toomerized, he more than made things right
By getting us a better site, a more amoozing chunk
And finding us the Voysey man and Honest Mr. Dunk.

Our God is an Amoosing God. Although he stole our Boo.
(A rather shabby sort of fing for any God to do)
Although he persecuted us for several orful nights
With fings which I can only name by calling of em—Bites.
Although he made me orful ill when I came back from Rome.
Although he keeps the windows back, what's ordered for our mome,
Although, if I aint precious sharp, he gets my socks on odd
And blacks my flangle trowsers. Still—
   He's an Amoosing God.

Yes God is an Amoozing God, and that is why I am
By way of Compliment to Him, so much the Woolly Lamb.
He gives me little woolly Momes and little Furry Bits
He's lately added to my store a Mackintosh that fits.
He gives me Tankards full of Beer and endless pleasant Fings
And so to show my Gratitude to God I sits and sings.
I sits and sings to Lordy God with all my little wits.
(But all the same I don't love 'Im not near what I love Bits.)

But altogether many hundreds of these sketches and scribblings have escaped the dustbin and the fireplace; and they are all at about the same level of skill and humour. There is no need to reproduce more of them. What matters here is the way in which they wrapped about the facts of life and created for us a quaint and softened atmosphere of intercourse. They falsified our relations to the pitch of making them tolerable and workable. The flow of this output was a little interrupted when I took to drawing Good Night Pictures for our children, but it never really ceased. I was drawing picshuas for her within a few weeks of her death, and one day during those last months we had together, we turned the whole collection out and looked them over together, remembering and reminding.

The reader may think I have wandered away from the subject of dispersal and fixation with which I began this section. But indeed it is essential to that subject that I should explain how it was that we two contrived in the absence of a real passionate sexual fixation, a binding net of fantasy and affection that proved in the end as effective as the very closest sexual sympathy could have been in keeping us together. And we were linked together also by our unreserved co-operation in work and business affairs. At first I sent my MSS. to be typed by a cousin (the daughter of that cousin Williams who kept school for a time at Wookey), but later on my wife learnt to typewrite in order to save the delay of posting and waiting to correct copy, which latter process often necessitated retyping. She not only typed, she scrutinized my text, watched after my besetting sin of verbal repetitions, and criticized and advised. Quite early in our life together, so soon as I had any money, I began handing over most of it to her, and for the greater part of our married life, we had a joint and several banking account on which either of us could draw without consulting the other, and she had complete control of my investments. She spent exactly what she thought proper, she made up my income tax returns without troubling me; I ceased more and more to look into things, satisfied when she told me that everything was "all right," and, when she died, I found myself half as much again better off than I had ever imagined myself to be. Another thing between us that seems extremely significant to me as I look back upon it, was this, that I disliked both of her names, Amy and Catherine, and avoided using either. The reader may have noticed that there has been a curious awkwardness hitherto in alluding to her. That is because in actual fact I spoke of her only by the current nickname. Then on the heels of a string of nicknames, I was suddenly moved to call her "Jane" and Jane she became and remained. I do not know exactly when I did this, but very rapidly it became her only name, for me and our friends. "Amy" she dropped altogether; she disliked it as much as I did. Her mother used it abundantly, and perhaps too much, for remonstrance and advice.

But Catherine she liked and as I have told in *The Book of Catherine Wells* she kept it for her literary work. In that volume I have gathered together almost every piece of writing that she completed and in the preface I have given an account of her rather overshadowed but very distinctive literary personality. Her literary initiatives were of a different order and quality from mine, and she insisted upon that and would never avail herself of my name or influence in publishing her own none too abundant writing. We belonged to different schools. Her admiration for Katherine Mansfield, for instance, was unbounded while my appreciation was tempered by a sense of that young woman's limitations; and she had a leaning towards Virginia Woolf, whose lucubrations I have always regarded with a lack-lustre eye. She liked delicate fantasy after the manner of Edith Sitwell, to whom I am as appreciatively indifferent as I am to the quaint patterns of old chintzes, the designs on dinner plates or the charm of nursery rhymes. Again, she found great interest in Proust who for me is far less documentary and entertaining than, let us say, Messrs. Shoolbred's catalogue of twenty years ago, or an old local newspaper, which is truer and leaves the commentary to me.

Catherine Wells was indeed not quite one of us, not quite one with Jane and me, I mean ; she was a quiet, fine spirited stranger in our household ; she was all that had escaped from the rough nicknaming and caricaturing and compromise that would have completely imposed upon her the rôles of Miss Bits and Jane. Our union had never incorporated her. I had glimpses of her at times ; she would look at me out of Jane's brown eyes, and vanish. All I know of her I have let appear in that book. Much later, after the war, when our accumulating means afforded it, Catherine Wells took rooms of her own in Bloomsbury, rooms I never saw ; she explained what she wanted and I fell in with her idea, and in this secret flat, quite away from all the life that centred upon me, she thought and dreamt and wrote and sought continually and fruitlessly for something she felt she had lost of herself or missed or never attained. She worked upon a story in that retreat, a fastidious elusive story that she never brought to any shape or ending ; some of it she polished and retyped many times. It was a dream of an island of beauty and sensuous perfection in which she lived alone and was sometimes happy in her loneliness and sometimes very lonely. In her dream there was a lover who never appeared. He was a voice heard ; he was a trail of footsteps in the dewy grass, or she woke and found a rosebud at her side. . . .

A year or so before her last illness she gave up that flat and ceased to work upon her unfinished book.

It is evident that this marriage of ours had some very distinctive features. Its originality did not end at that perfect business confidence and that queer play of silly humorous fantasy, mental caressing and imposed interpretations already described. At the back of all that, two extremely dissimilar brains were working very intelligently at the peculiar life problem we had created for each other. We came at last to a very explicit understanding about the profound difference in our physical and imaginative responses.

Jane thought I had a right to my own individual disposition and that luck had treated me badly in mating me first to an unresponsive and then to a fragile companion. About that she was extraordinarily dispassionate and logical and much more clearheaded than I was. She faced the matter with the same courage, honesty and self-subordination with which she faced all the practical issues of life. She suppressed any jealous impulse and gave me whatever freedom I desired. She knew as well as I did that for all its elements of artificiality, our alliance was indissoluble; we had intergrown and become parts of each other, and she realized perhaps sooner than I, how little that alliance demanded a monopoly of passionate intimacy. So long as we were in the opening phase of our struggle for a position and worldly freedom, this question was hardly a practical issue between us. There was neither time nor energy to indulge any form of wanderlust. But with the coming of success, increasing leisure and facility of movement, the rapid enlargement of our circle of acquaintance, and contact with unconventional and exciting people, there was no further necessity for the same rigid self-restraint. The craving, in a body that was gathering health and strength, for a complete loveliness of bodily response, was creeping up into my imagination and growing more and more powerful. This craving dominated the work of D. H. Lawrence altogether. For my own part, I could never yield it that importance. I would justify it if I could, but not at the price of that joint attack upon the world to which I was committed with Jane.

My compromise with Jane developed after 1900. The *modus vivendi* we contrived was sound enough to hold us together to the end, but it was by no means a perfect arrangement. That escape of the personality of Catherine Wells from our unison was only one mark of its imperfection. Over against that are to be set the far more frequent escapades of a Don Juan among the intelligentsia. I record our understanding, as I want to record all the material facts of my life; it was an experiment in adjustment, but there was nothing exemplary about it. All life is imperfect: imperfection becomes a condemnation only when it reaches an intolerable level. Our imperfections we made quite tolerable and I do not believe that in making them tolerable we injured anybody else in the world. Compromises of some sort between ill-fitted yet congenial people must, I suppose, become more frequent in our advancing world as individuality intensifies. The more marked the individuality the more difficult is it to discover a complete reciprocity. The more difficult therefore is it to establish an exclusive fixation.

Yet the normal human being gravitates naturally towards an exclusive and complete fixation, with its keen possessiveness and its irrational infinitude of jealousy. What I have called the discursive phase of a human being is the unstable and transitory phase; there is no such thing as complete promiscuity; there is always preference and there is no limit set to the possible swift intensifications of preference; the casual lover loves always on a slippery slope. The French with their absurd logicality distinguish between the *passade*, a stroke of mutual attraction that may happen to any couple, and a real love affair. In theory, I was now to have *passades*.

But life and Latin logic have always been at variance, and it did not work out like that. There is no such distinction to be drawn. There are not small preferences that do not matter and big ones that do; there are all sizes and grades of preferences. For women even more than for men, the frequent *passade* seems unattractive. A woman understands much more than a man the undesirability of inconsequent discursive bodily love. She gives her Self, there is personality as well as her person in the gift; she may reckon on a greater return than she gets, but indeed it is a poor sort of love-making on either side in which, at the time at any rate, there is not the feeling that selves are being given Otherwise it would be the easiest thing in the world to solve all this riddle of incompatible temperaments by skilled prostitution.

Clearly Jane and I were persuaded of the possibility of some such solution, though presumably in terms rather less brutally simple. I do not think we could have made our treaty if we had not thought so. On either side, we supposed, there were men and women with an excess of sexual energy and imagination. On either side there were restless spirits with a craving for variety. What could be more rational than for such super-animated men and women to find out and assuage one another?

And everything else would remain as it was before.

But as a matter of fact, short of some rare miracle of flatness, nothing does remain as it was before. Two worlds are altered every time a man and woman associate. The alterations may vary widely in extent but an alteration is always there. It would indeed be a very remarkable thing if Nature, for all her general looseness and extravagance, had contrived it otherwise. Jane's humour and charity, and the fundamental human love between us, were to be tried out very severely in the years that lay ahead. Suffice it here to say that they stood the test.

§4
WRITINGS ABOUT SEX

AND HERE, I think, and not later, is the place for a compact account of my writings so far as they concern the relations of men and women. These books and papers arose very directly out of my own personal difficulties. They were essentially an eversion, a generalization, an attempt to put my case in the character of Everyman.

In my earlier writings the topic of sex is conspicuously absent, I felt then that I knew nothing about it that could possibly be communicated. I muddled with my own problems in my own fashion, shamefacedly. Then, because I still felt I knew nothing about it, I began asking questions.

I think that as the waters of oblivion swallow up my writings bulk by bulk, the essays and booklets and stories and novels I wrote about love and sex-reactions will be the first section to go right out of sight and memory. If any survive they will survive as a citation or so, as historical sidelights for the industrious student. They had their function in their time but their time has already gone by. They were essentially negative enquiries, statements of unsolved difficulties, protests against rigid restraints and suppressions; variations of " Why not ? " They helped to release a generation from restriction and that is about all they achieved. Aesthetically they have no great value. No one will ever read them for delight.

Love and Mr. Lewisham was published in 1900. The " love " in it is the most naïve response of youth and maiden imaginable, and the story is really the story of the " Schema " of a career and how it was torn up. The conflict and disharmony between the two main strands in what I have called, my "Compound Fugue," was troubling my mind. Mr. Lewisham was a teacher and science student as I had been, and his entanglement is quite on all fours with mine. But he has a child. Because he loved his Ethel, Mr. Lewisham had to tear up his Schema and settle down. Domestic claustrophobia, the fear of being caught in a household, which I have suggested may have played a part in my departure from Sutton, is evident in this book. At the time of writing it (1898-99), I did not consciously apply the story of Mr. Lewisham to my own circumstances, but down below the threshold of my consciousness the phobia must have been there. Later on, in 1910, it had come to the surface and I sold Spade House deliberately, because I felt that otherwise it would become the final setting of my life.

The *Sea Lady* (published in 1902 and planned two years earlier) is a parallel story of the same two main strands of motive, but it is told under quite a different scheme of values. Something new comes to light ; a sensuous demand. There is an element of confession in the tale but it is a confession in motley. And love, instead of leading to any settling down, breaks things up. But the defeat of the disinterested career is just as complete. Chatteris, the lover, plunges not into domesticity but into the sea, glittering under a full moon. A craving for some lovelier experience than life had yet given me, is the burthen in this second phase. Not only Catherine Wells but I too could long at times for impossible magic islands. Chatteris is a promising young politician, a sort of mixture of Harry Cust and any hero in any novel by Mrs. Humphry Ward, and he is engaged to be married to a heroine, quite deliberately and confessedly lifted, gestures, little speeches and all, from that lady's *Marcella*. All the hopes of this heroine are shattered by a mermaid who comes ashore as the Bunting family, the heroine's hosts, are bathing from the end of their garden at Sandgate. For at Sandgate people's gardens go right down to the beach. The mermaid is—beauty. And the magic of beauty. She drives Chatteris into a madness of desire for "other dreams," for a life beyond reason and possibility. The book ends as lightly as it began—in a "supreme moment"—of moonshine.

The next book of mine in which unsolved sexual perplexities appear is *A Modern Utopia* (1905). Plato ruled over the making of that book, and in it I followed him in disposing of the sexual distraction, by minimizing the differences between men and women and ignoring the fact of personal fixation altogether. That is and always has been the intellectual's way out. My Samurai are of both sexes, a hardy bare-limbed race, free lovers among themselves—and mutually obliging. Like the people of the original Oneida community in New York State they constituted one comprehensive "group marriage." Possibly among such people fixations would not be serious; that is hypothetical psychology. I may have stressed the mutual civility of the order. The book was popular among the young of our universities; it launched many of them into cheerful adventures that speedily brought them up against the facts of fixation, jealousy and resentment. It played a considerable part in the general movement of release from the rigid technical chastity of women during the Victorian period.

So far as there can be any general theory of sexual conduct and law, the *Modern Utopia* remains my last word. Within that comprehensive freedom, individuals, I believe, must work out their problems of fixation and co-operation, monopolization, loyalty and charity, each for himself and herself. For everyone and every couple there is a distinctive discord and perhaps in most cases a solution. The key to the progressive thought of our time is the frank realization of this immense variety in reaction and the repudiation of the rigid universal solutions of the past. We do not solve anything by this realization, but we liberate and individualize the problem. It is an interesting paradox that Socialism should involve extreme sexual individualism and Competitive Individualism clip the individual into the rigid relationships of the family.

A Modern Utopia was leading up to *Ann Veronica* (1909) in which the youthful heroine was allowed a frankness of desire and sexual enterprise, hitherto unknown in English popular fiction. That book created a scandal at the time, though it seems mild enough reading to the young of to-day. It is rather badly constructed, there is an excessive use of soliloquy, but Ann Veronica came as near to being a living character as anyone in my earlier love stories. This was so because in some particulars she was drawn from life. And for that and other reasons she made a great fuss in the world.

The particular offence was that Ann Veronica was a virgin who fell in love and showed it, instead of waiting as all popular heroines had hitherto done, for someone to make love to her. It was held to be an unspeakable offence that an adolescent female should be sex-conscious before the thing was forced upon her attention. But Ann Veronica wanted a particular man who excited her and she pursued him and got him. With gusto. It was only a slight reflection of anything that had actually occurred, but there was something convincing about the behaviour of the young woman in the story, something sufficiently convincing to impose the illusion of reality upon her; and from the outset Ann Veronica was assailed as though she was an actual living person.

It was a strenuous and long sustained fuss. The book was banned by libraries and preached against by earnest clergymen. The spirit of denunciation, latent in every human society, was aroused and let loose against me. I have turned over my memories and records of that fuss and I find it so abundant and formless an accumulation of pettiness that I cannot put it together into a narrative. It is a jumble of

DISSECTION

slights, injustices and hasty condemnations, plus a considerable amount of exacerbated resentment and ineffective reprisal on my own part. I do not make a good or dignified martyr. There was not only a "bad press" and a great deal of public denunciation of me but there was an attempt, mainly on the part of people who did not know me, to ostracize me socially. The head and front of the public attack was Mr. St. Loe Strachey, the proprietor of the *Spectator*. A reviewer in his columns rallied the last resources of our noble language, made no bones about it, pulled himself together as men must do when the fundamentals of life are at stake, and said in so many words that Ann Veronica was a whore. It was I think an illegitimate extension of the term.

He was a fine fellow, that reviewer. "The muddy world of Mr. Wells's imaginings," said he, was "a community of scuffling stoats and ferrets, unenlightened by a ray of duty and abnegation." That was rough on the Samurai of my Modern Utopia. He writhed with "loathing and indignation" and so on and so on, mounting and shouting, up to that last great manly word.

That denotes the quality of the fuss and gives the clue to my resentment. Strachey's hostility, if a little clumsy and heavy, was perfectly honest, and before he died we met—as witnesses in defence of a birth-control pamphlet—and became very good friends. I was indignant and expostulatory at the time, but on the whole I really had very little to complain of. The social attack did me no harm. It made no perceptible difference in my life that we two were sent to Coventry by people we had never met. The people who had met us did not send us to Coventry. Most of my friends stood the proof very delightfully; people as various as G. K. Chesterton, C. F. G. Masterman, Sydney Olivier and his family, Ray Lankester, Shaw, Harry Cust, and Lady Mary Elcho, came out stoutly for me and would have nothing to do with any social boycott. Altogether it was no sort of martyrdom, as martyrdoms go nowadays, and its general ineffectiveness amounted to a victory. My ostracism had its use as a filter to save me from many dull and dreary people. And my ultimate victory was no mere personal one. Mr. Fisher Unwin had bought the book outright and did very well by it. It sold and went on selling in a variety of editions. After *Ann Veronica*, things were never quite the same again in the world of popular English fiction; young heroines with a temperamental zest for illicit love-making and no sense of an inevitable Nemesis, increased and multiplied not only in novels but in real life.

But for a time the uproar about *Ann Veronica* put me quite out of focus with the public and the literary world. The fact that the great bulk of my work displayed an exceptional want of reference to sex or love-making, or the position of woman, was ignored; and if I had been a D. H. Lawrence, with every fig leaf pinned aside, I could not have been considered more improper than I was. This brought me a quite new type of reader, and books like *Kipps*, *The War of the Worlds*, *The First Men in the Moon* and *The Wonderful Visit* were bought by eager seekers after obscenity—to their extreme disillusionment. They decided after a baffled perusal that I was dreadfully overrated and superficial, and my brief reputation in the cloacal recesses of the bookish world evaporated speedily enough.

In 1911 this conflict was revived upon a broader basis, if with less intensity, over my *New Machiavelli*. I would not drop the subject of the passionate daughter, and there was, I admit, considerable defiance of manner if not of matter, both in the *New Machiavelli* and in *Marriage* which followed it. Quite manifestly I had refused to learn my lesson and, this time, I was to be squashed for good. But this final attack was delivered two years too late. Many people were beginning to be ashamed of the violence of their reactions to *Ann Veronica* and others were plainly bored by the demands of my more persistent antagonists for a fresh effort to erase me, and the result of this second attempt to end Wells was on the whole distinction rather than destruction. Instead of being made an outcast, finally and conclusively, I was made a sort of champion.

The *New Machiavelli* was first printed as a serial in Ford Madox Hueffer's *English Review* and persistent rumours that no publisher would consent to issue it led to a considerable sale of the back numbers of that periodical at enhanced prices—with the usual disappointment for the purchasers. " What is all the fuss about ? " the poor dears demanded. " There is nothing in it ! " There was indeed furtive work with the publishers on the part of what are called influential people, but I neither know nor care who were these influential people, and I do not know what was said and done. The respectable firm of Macmillan was already under contract to publish the book and could not legally or honourably back out, but it presently appealed to me in a state of great embarrassment, for permission to publish in this particular case under the imprint of John Lane, who was less squeamish about his reputation for decorum. I consented to that, and so the gentility of Macmillans, or whatever else was threatened by those influential people, was preserved.

The *New Machiavelli* is all the world away from overt eroticism. The theme is simply a fresh variant upon the theme of *Love and Mr. Lewisham* and the *Sea Lady* ; it stressed the harsh incompatibility of wide public interests with the high, swift rush of imaginative passion—with considerable sympathy for the passion. The Marcella-like heroine of the *Sea Lady* is repeated, but the mermaid has become a much more credible young woman, and it is to exile in Italy and literary effort, and not to moonshine and death, that the lovers go. There is some good characterization in it, one or two well-written passages and an amusing description of a fire at an actual dinner-party, given by Cust, at which I was present. But it is nothing outstanding in the way of a novel.

I was not indulging myself and the world in artistic pornography or making an attack upon anything I considered moral. I found nothing for self-reproach in my private conduct, I did not know for some time that the imaginations of the back benches of the Fabian Society and the riff-raff of the literary world were adorning my unwitting and undeserving head with a rakish halo. I did not realize how readily my simple questionings could be interpreted as the half confessions of a sort of Fabian Casanova, an inky Lovelace, the satyr-Cupid of Socialism. I was asking a " Why not ? " that had been accumulating in my mind all my life, and the intensity of my questioning had no doubt been greatly enhanced by the peculiar inhibitions of my first wife and the innocent fragility of my second. I was releasing, in these books, a long accumulation of suppression. So far as I can remember my phases, however, the influence of my particular experiences was quite subconscious at the time and I think I should have come to that particular " Why not ? " in some fashion—anyhow. I was asking my question in perfect good faith and I went on asking it.

I was working out the collateral problems with an ingenuous completeness, and I did not mean to relinquish that enquiry. I had come to the conclusion that sex-life began with adolescence, which after all was only discovering what " adolescence " means, and that when it began—it ought to begin. I thought it preposterous that any young people should be distressed by unexplained desires, thwarted by arbitrary prohibitions and blunder into sexual experiences, blindfold. The stories of Isabel and my wife and myself were plainly stories of an excessive, artificial innocence. I contemned that " chastity " which is mere abstinence and concealment more and more plainly. I believed and said that a normal human being was not properly balanced, physically and mentally, without an active sexual life ; that this was as necessary and almost as urgently necessary, as fresh air and free movement, and I have never found any reason to change that opinion.

But a propaganda of more and franker and healthier love-making was not, I found—as Plato found before me—a simple proposition. It carried with it certain qualifying conditions. Some of these, but not all of them, I brought into the discussion. In a world where pressure upon the means of subsistence was a normal condition of life, it was necessary to compensate for the removal of traditional sexual restraints, and so my advocacy of simple and easy love-making had to be supplemented by an adhesion to the propaganda of the Neo-Malthusians. This I made in my *Anticipations* (1900) and I continued to write plainly on that subject in a period when Neo-Malthusianism was by no means the respectable movement it has since become.

In some of these earlier essays on sexual liberation, I seem now to be skirmishing about on the marginal conventions of the business and failing to come to grips with its more intimate realities. I was condemning a great system of suppressions and prohibitions as unreasonable; but at first I did not face up steadily to the fact that they were as natural as they were unreasonable. I was giving a fair hearing to one set of instincts and not allowing another set to come into court. I had not examined by what necessary processes the net of restraints I was denouncing had been woven to entangle pleasure and happiness. In spite of my own acute experience, I was ignoring that gravitation towards fixation in love, with its intense possessiveness, dominance, jealousy and hatred of irresponsible indulgence, which lies at the heart of the problem. I had been suppressing it in myself and I was ignoring it in my arguments.

Gradually as my disputes and controversies went on, my attention was forced back, almost in spite of myself, towards these profounder elements in the human make-up which stand in the way of a cheerful healthy sexual go-as-you-please for mankind. I was obliged to look jealousy in the face. All this tangle of restriction, restraint, opposition and anger, could be explained as so much expansion, complication and organization of jealousy. Jealousy may not be a reasonable thing, but it lies at least as close to the springs of human action as sexual desire. Jealousy was not merely a trouble between competitive lovers. Parents, onlookers, society could be jealous.

I set myself to examine the credentials of jealousy. At some time I had read Lang and Atkinson's *Human Origins*, probably under the influence of Grant Allen, and the book illuminated me very greatly. I realized the rôle played by the primitive taboos in disciplining and canalizing the dominant jealousy of the more powerful males so as to make possible the development of tribal societies. I saw the history of expanding human associations as essentially a successive subjugation of the patriarchal group to wider collective needs, by jealousy-regulating arrangements. Continually civilization had been developing, by buying off or generalizing, socializing and legalizing jealousy and possessiveness, in sex as in property. We were debarred from sexual ease, just as we were debarred from economic ease, by this excessive fostering in our institutions of the already sufficiently strong instinct of ownership. The Family, I declared, was the inseparable correlative of private proprietorship. It embodied jealousy in sexual life as private ownership embodied jealousy in economic life. And to the very great dismay of the strategists and tacticians of the Fabian Society, and to the immense embarrassment of the Labour Party socialists, I began to blurt out these ideas and attempt to sexualise socialism.

I should naturally like to present my mental process in this matter as completely lucid, consistent and far-seeing from the beginning, and if it were not for that family habit of filing letters and accumulating records to which I have already alluded, I think I should have been able to do that. Nobody now would remember my tergiversation if my files did not. But it is clear that though my association with Labour Socialism had very little effect upon my stories and romances, it did affect various pamphlets, discussions and letters I wrote upon the subject.

Let me deal with the novels first. They do follow a fairly consistent line. The topic of jealousy dominated *In the Days of the Comet* (1906). The swish of a comet's tail cools and cleanses the human atmosphere, and jealousy, and with it war and poverty, vanish from the world. Jealousy is also the dominant trouble in the *Passionate Friends* (1913) and *The Wife of Sir Isaac Harman* (1914), while *Marriage* (1912), once more presents the old conflict between broad intentions and passionate urgencies, that had furnished the motif of three earlier tales, *Love and Mr. Lewisham*, *The New Machiavelli* and the *Sea Lady*. In all these novels the interest centres not upon individual character, but upon the struggles of common and rational motives and frank enquiry against social conditions and stereotyped ideas. The actors in them are types, therefore, rather than acutely individualized persons. They could not be other than types. For reasons that will become plainer as I proceed, my output of this " discussion-fiction " between men and women became relatively much less important after the outbreak of the war. Christina Alberta in *Christina Alberta's Father* (1925) is a much more living figure than Ann

Veronica and her morals are far easier; but times had changed and not a voice was raised against her. That *Spectator* reviewer, and much else, had died since 1909. That particular liberation had been achieved.

Apart from these, only three of my stories can be put into the category of sex-discussion,—*The Secret Places of the Heart* (1922) in which I was thinking not so much of the problem of jealousy, as of love-making considered as a source or waste of energy, and, to a lesser degree and interwoven with quite other ideas, *Meanwhile* (1927) which betrays a similar trend. I may be able to return later to the rather different issue of these more recent books. They are raising the question whether after all a woman can be a good citizen and if she can, in what way, a problem also appearing *inter alia* in *The World of William Clissold* (1926). In the last " book " of the latter, there is also a sketch of a feminine personality " Clementina " which stands by itself, an incidental lark, because it is so manifestly objective and interrogative.

Turning from my novels to the various papers, pamphlets and letters I was putting out through this same period, I discover a much less candid display of view and attitude. I began well, but I found I was speedily entangled and bemused by various political and propagandist issues. I find a quite straightforward statement of my ideas in a paper I read to the Fabian Society in October 1906, under the title of *Socialism and the Middle Classes*. Therein I say plainly that I " no more regard the institution of marriage as a permanent thing than I regard a state of competitive industrialism as a permanent thing " and the whole paper sustains this attitude. But subsequently I published this, bound-up with a second article which had appeared in the *Independent Review* (*Socialism and the Family*, 1906) and, in this last, the phrasing is, to say the least of it, more discreet. I am advocating in both what is plainly a correlative of the break-up of the family, the public endowment of motherhood. But the question as to whether this endowment is to be confined to women under some sort of marriage contract recognized by the state, or extended to all mothers indiscriminately is not distinctly stated. The issue was vague in my own mind; there were questions of fatherly influence and of eugenics to consider, and I had still to think them out. It is regrettable that those perplexities still clouded my attitude; otherwise I find the record satisfactory up to this point.

But then came an ingenious mis-statement by Mr. Joynson-Hicks (as he was then) while campaigning against Labour Socialism in the Altrincham division (Cheshire), and a more or less deliberate misquotation by Mr. J. H. Bottomley, a conservative election agent for the Newton division, which lured me into an excess of repudiation. Joynson-Hicks had declared that Socialists would part husband and wife, and subject every woman to a sort of communal prostitution. Challenged to justify this statement, which greatly shocked the rank and file of the Labour battalions, he defended himself by an appeal to my works. "He was not in the habit of making a statement without some kind of justification, and one had only to read Mr. Wells' book, where it clearly stated that 'Wives no less than goods, were to be held in common'; and 'Every infant would be taken away from the mother and father and placed in a State nursery.' (*Daily Dispatch*, Oct. 12th, 1906.)"

Mr. Bottomley had put it in this way, in a pamphlet for local circulation: "Essentially the Socialist position is a denial of property in human beings; not only must land and the means of production be liberated, but women and children, just as men and things must cease to be owned. *So in future it will be not my wife or your wife, but our wife.*" The words in italics were his own addition but, somehow, they got inside the quotation marks.

Two quotations, one from *The Times Literary Supplement*, in a review of *In the Days of the Comet*, and one from the *Spectator* for October 19th, 1907, in an article on *Socialism and Sex Relations*, also got into the dispute. *The Times Literary Supplement* said : " Socialistic men's wives, we gather, are, no less than their goods, to be held in common. Free love, according to Mr. Wells, is to be of the essence of the new social contract." And the words of the *Spectator* were as follows : " For example we find Mr. Wells in his novel, *In the Days of the Comet*, making Free Love the dominant principle for the regulation of sexual ties in his regenerated State. The romantic difficulty as to which of the two lovers of the heroine is to be the happy man is solved by their both being accepted. Polyandry is ' the way out ' in this case, as polygamy might be in another."

Now the proper reply to this sort of attack was to stick to the phrase Free Love, insist that this did not mean indiscriminate love, point out that the words supposed to be quoted had not been used, and explain with patience and lucidity, that personal sexual freedom and collective responsibility for the family, did not mean " having wives in common " or taking children away from their parents or practising polyandry or polygamy or anything of that sort. But instead of explaining, I spluttered into exaggerated indignation at the dishonesty of those misplaced inverted commas of Mr. Bottomley's, I repudiated " Free Love," which was obviously wrong of me, simply because, like the word atheist, the phrase had acquired an unpopular flavour, and unsaid, more or less distinctly, much that I had been saying during the previous half a dozen years. I was entangling myself with politics, and I found my socialistic associates were embarrassed by my speculations. I did not want them to reproach me.

In *New Worlds for Old* (1908) first published as a serial in the *Grand Magazine* in 1907, I went still further along the line of self-repudiation, and I read with contrition to-day, this dreadful passage of quite Fabian understatement :

" Socialism has not even worked out what are the reasonable conditions of a State marriage contract, and it would be ridiculous to pretend it had. This is not a defect in Socialism particularly, but a defect in human knowledge. At countless points in the tangle of questions involved, the facts are not clearly known. Socialism offers no theory whatever as to the duration of marriage, as to whether, as among the Roman Catholics, it should be absolutely for life, or, as some hold, for ever ; or, as among the various divorce-permitting Protestant bodies, until this or that eventuality ; or even, as Mr. George Meredith suggested some years ago, for a term of ten years. In these matters Socialism does not decide, and it is quite reasonable to argue that Socialism need not decide. Socialism maintains an attitude of neutrality."

This is a false attitude. Socialism, if it is anything more than a petty tinkering with economic relationships is a renucleation of society. The family can remain only as a biological fact. Its economic and educational autonomy are inevitably doomed. The modern state is bound to be the ultimate guardian of all children and it must assist, replace, or subordinate the parent as supporter, guardian and educator ; it must release all human beings from the obligation of mutual proprietorship, and it must refuse absolutely to recognize or enforce any kind of sexual ownership. It cannot therefore remain neutral when such claims come before it. It must disallow them. But in these incriminatory documents I find myself being as vague, tactful and reassuring about sentimental interpretations— as if I had set out in life to become a Nationalist Prime Minister.

These skirmishes with politicians and pamphleteers occurred in 1906-7 and 8 and I touched my nadir of compromise and understatement in that last year. Later on, when I tell of my relations to accepted religious forms and beliefs I shall have to deal again with this politic, conciliatory strain in me. It can be excused. It can be explained as the deference of modesty and as a civilized inclination to conformity; it has its amiable aspects. But whatever may be possible in larger brains, mine is not clever and subtle enough to be disingenuous to that extent; my proper rôle is to say things plainly and still more plainly, to be aggressive and derisive and let persuasion go hang. It is better to offend rather than mislead. When I am diplomatic I am lost. It was really an extraordinarily good thing for me that circumstances conspired with my innate impulse, when I am at the writing desk, to let statement and story rip, to put me quite openly where I was, with the *Ann Veronica* shindy in 1909 and the subsequent campaign, in 1910 and 1911, against the *New Machiavelli*. After that it was plain where I stood, and that in spite of our pretty, orderly home and the general decorum of our industrious lives, Jane and I were not to be too hastily accepted as a nice, deserving young couple respectfully climbing the pleasant stairway of English life from quite modest beginnings, to social recognition, prosperity, and even perhaps " honours."

It was not only that the Fabian and Labour politician found my persistent development of "Why not?" in regard to the family and marriage, inconvenient, but also that I was at cross purposes upon the same score with the feminist movement in the new century. My realization of how far away I was to the left of the official left movements of my time had something to do, I think, with these lapses towards compromise I am now deploring.

The old feminist movement of the early nineteenth

century had undergone a sort of rejuvenation in the eighties and nineties. It had given up its bloomers and become smart, energetic and ambitious. There was a growing demand on the part of women for economic and political independence, and at first it seemed to me that here at last advancing upon me was that great-hearted free companionship of noble women of which I had dreamed from my earliest years.

As the hosts of liberation came nearer and could be inspected more accurately I found reason to qualify these bright expectations. If women wanted to be free, the first thing was surely for them to have complete control of their persons, and how could that happen unless Free Love and Neo-Malthusianism replaced directed and obligatory love and involuntary child-bearing, in the forefront of their programme. Their inferiority was a necessary aspect of the proprietary, patriarchal family, and there was no way of equalizing the economic disadvantage imposed upon them by the bearing and care of children, short of the public endowment of motherhood. These things and not any petty political enfranchisement, I reasoned, must surely constitute the real Magna Charta of Women, and I set myself to explain this with the same tactless simplicity and lucidity that had already caused such inconvenience to the politicians of the Labour Party.

But the leaders of the feminist revival were no more willing than were the socialists to realize where they were going. They were alive to the wrongs that set them moving but not to the ends towards which their movement would take them. Confronted by the plain statement of the Free Citizen Woman as opposed to the Domesticated Woman their hearts failed them. It became increasingly evident that a large part of the woman's suffrage movement was animated less by the desire for freedom and fullness of life, than by a passionate jealousy and hatred of the relative liberties of men. For one woman in the resuscitated movement who wanted to live generously and nobly, a score were desirous merely of making things uncomfortable for the insolent, embarrassing, oblivious male. They did not want more life; their main impulse was vindictive.

They wanted to remain generally where they were and what they were, but to have it conceded that they were infinitely brighter and better and finer than men, that potentially they were finer poets, musicians, artists, social organizers, scientific investigators and philosophers than men could ever be, that a man owed everything to his mother and nothing to his father and so forth and so on; that women therefore ought to be given unlimited control over the goods and actions of their lawful partners, be empowered to impose upon these gross creatures complete chastity, or otherwise, as the fancy might take them, and, instead of establishing a free and liberal equality, entirely reverse the ascendency of the sexes. This was a very wholesome *tu quoque* for ages of arrogant masculine bad manners, but it was not practical politics and it did not penetrate to the more fundamental realities of the sexual stress.

That feminism had anything to do with sexual health and happiness, was repudiated by these ladies with flushed indignation so soon as the suggestion was made plain to them. Their modesty was as great as their boldness. Sex—what was sex? Get thee behind me Satan! They were not thinking of it. They were good pure women rightly struggling for a Vote, and that was all they wanted. The Vote was to be their instrument of dominance. They concentrated all the energy of their growing movement upon that claim. The new Feminist Movement had no more use for me therefore than the Labour Socialists. To both these organizations I was an *enfant terrible* and not to be talked about.

It is no part of the plan of this book to tell the tale of that nagging, ignoble campaign which ended abruptly with the Declaration of War in 1914, to detail once again the window-smashing, the burning of country houses, churches and the contents of letter boxes, the squawking at meetings, " votes for women " until the discussion of public affairs became impossible, the consequent expulsion of the struggling heroines with all kinds of ignoble and indelicate reprisals, the ensuing discovery by indignant young women of good family, of the unexpected dirtiness and nastiness of police cells and prisons—one good by-product anyhow—and all the rest of it. In *The Wife of Sir Isaac Harman* (1914) I tried to explain to myself and my readers the suppressions and resentments that might lead a gentle woman to smash a plate-glass window. I studied my model carefully and I think the figure lives, but no suffragette saw herself in my mirror. Nor will I relate here how as Europe collapsed into war, the Vote was flung to women simply to keep them quiet, and how the only traceable consequence has been the further enfeeblement of the waning powers of Democracy.

In those gentler days before the return towards primitive violence began, it was possible for girls and women to pester mankind and presume upon the large protective tolerance of civilization. Since then, the progressive disintegration of social order, the increasing amount of gangsterism and terrorism in political life, has made the atmosphere too grim and heavy for the definite organization of women as such, for social and political aggression. Their understanding of the disintegrative forces at work seems to be a feeble one, and in the conscious constructive effort of to-day they count *as a sex* for remarkably little. There has been no perceptible woman's movement to resist the practical obliteration of their freedoms by Fascists or Nazis. The sex war has died away and in England only the gentle sarcasms and grumblings of Lady Rhondda and her group of clever ladies in *Time and*

Tide remain to remind us of it. Over most of the world it has died down altogether.

I can look back now with sympathetic amusement upon the encounter of my former self, that rising and decidedly over-confident young writer of half my age with this new and transitory being : the Militant Suffragette. What a surprise and perplexity she was ! The young man's disposition to lump all the feminity in the world, in its infinite variety, into a class, to indict it and judge it as a class, after having felt a strong disposition to adore it—as a class, was perfectly natural, superficially reasonable and fundamentally absurd. Still heavily under the sway of organic illusion he prepared to welcome these goddesses, at last in splendid revolt, and to do his utmost for them, and, instead of goddesses escaping, he encountered a fluttering swarm of disillusioned and wildly exasperated human beings, all a little frightened at what they were doing, and with no clearer conception than any other angry crowd of what had set them going and what was to be done about it. Helpfully and with the brightest hopes he produced his carefully reasoned diagnosis of their grievances ; he spread his ingenious arrangement of Neo-Malthusianism, Free Love (" ton corps est à toi "), economic independence, the endowment of motherhood and the systematic suppression of jealousy as an animal vice, and he found his lucid and complete statement thrust aside, while the riot passed on, after the manner of riots, vehemently loudly and vacuously, to a purely symbolic end—the Vote in this case—and essential frustration and dispersal.

Slowly as the blaze of antagonism created by the open sex-war of 1900–14 has died down, men and women under an inexorable need for each other and an imperative necessity for co-operation, have returned again to the commanding and infinitely varied problems of mutual adjustment, to the million and one perennial problems of man and woman.

I do not know how far the main attack and the capture of the actual Vote was of value to humanity but I have no doubt of the service done by that slower and wider campaign of "Why not?" in which I played my little part. A tiresome and obstructive accumulation of obsolete restraints, conventions and pretences, was cleared out of the way for a new generation. That did not put an end to the facile self-deceptions of sex because these are of the very stuff of life, nor could it abolish the see-saw between the chronic mutual need and the chronic resistance to entanglement, but it did clear the way for an individual management of the glamour and its ensuing centrifugal strain. It put the glamour in its place and made the fugitive impulse controllable and tolerable. When goddesses and Sea Ladies vanish and a flash back to the ancestral chimpanzee abolishes the magic caverns of Venus, human beings arrive. Instead of a rigid system of obligations and restrictions which would solve, for everyone, the Woman Problem, in one simple universal fashion, we are left with an almost infinite series of variations of the problem of association between men and women, and an infinitude of opportunities for mutual charity.

§ 5
Digression about Novels

I FIND BEFORE ME a considerable accumulation of material, first assembled together in a folder labelled "Whether I am a Novelist." It has been extremely difficult to digest this material into a presentable form. It refuses to be simplified. It is like a mental shunting yard in which several trains of thought have come into collision and I feel now that the utmost I can do with it is not so much to set these trains going again as to salvage some few fragmentary observations from the wreckage.

One of these trains comes in from the previous section. It is an insistence upon the importance of individuality and individual adjustment in life; " Problems of association between men and women and an infinitude of opportunities for mutual charity." That carries on very obviously towards the idea of the novel as an expanding discussion of " How did they treat each other? How might they have treated each other? How should they treat each other? " I set out to write novels, as distinguished from those pseudo-scientific stories in which imaginative experience rather than personal conduct was the matter in hand, on the assumption that problems of adjustment were the essential matter for novel-writing. *Love and Mr. Lewisham* was entirely a story about a dislocation and an adjustment.

But across the track of that train of thought came another in which the novel presented itself not as an ethical enquiry but as the rendering of a system of impressions. In this distended and irregularly interesting folder, which I find so hard to reduce to straightforward explicitness, I find myself worrying round various talks and discussions I had with Henry James a third of a century ago. He was a very important figure in the literary world of that time and a shrewd and penetrating critic of the technique by which he lived. He liked me and he found my work respectable enough to be greatly distressed about it. I bothered him and he bothered me. We were at cross purposes based as I shall show later on very fundamental differences, not only of temperament but training. He had no idea of the possible use of the novel as a help to conduct. His mind has turned away from any such idea. From his point of view there were not so much "novels" as The Novel, and it was a very high and important achievement. He thought of it as an Art Form and of novelists as artists of a very special and exalted type. He was concerned about their greatness and repute. He saw us all as Masters or would-be Masters, little Masters and great Masters, and he was plainly sorry that " Cher Maître " was not an English expression. One could not be in a room with him for ten minutes without realizing the importance he attached to the dignity of this art of his. I was by nature and education unsympathetic with this mental disposition. But I was disposed to regard a novel as about as much an art form as a market place or a boulevard. It had not even necessarily to get anywhere. You went by it on your various occasions.

That was entirely out of key with James's assumptions. I recall a talk I had with him soon after the publication of *Marriage*. With tact and circumlocution, James broke it to me, that he found a remarkable deficiency in that story. It was a deficiency that he had also observed in a vast proportion of contemporary fiction, it had exercised him very fruitfully, and his illuminating comments spread out from that starting point to a far-reaching tentacular discussion of what a novel should do and be.

The point he was stressing was this : *Marriage* is the story of a young man of science, Trafford, who, apparently without much previous experience, pilots a friend's aeroplane (in 1912 !) and crashes, he and the friend together, into a croquet party and the Pope family and the life of Marjorie Pope. Thereupon there is bandaging, ambulance work and much coming and going and Marjorie, who is already engaged to a Mr. Magnet, falls deeply in love with Trafford. She drives to the village in a donkey cart to do some shopping and meets the lamed Trafford, also driving a donkey cart and their wheels interlock and they fall talking. All that—except for the writing of it—was tolerable according to James. But then, in order to avoid the traffic in the high road the two young people take their respective donkey carts into a side lane and remain there talking for three hours. And this is where James's objection came in. Of the three hours of intercourse in the lane the novel tells nothing, except that the young people emerged in open and declared love with each other. This, said James, wasn't playing the game. I had cut out an essential, after a feast of irrelevant particulars. Gently but firmly he insisted that I did not myself know what had happened and what was said in that lane; that there was even a touch of improbability about their staying there so long and that this lack of information and probability at a crucial point was due to the fact that I had not thought out the individualities concerned with sufficient care and thoroughness. I had not cared enough about these individualities. Moreover in the conversations between the two principals, the man in particular supplied information about himself and his position in life in such a way as to talk at the reader instead of to the girl. The talk was in fact more for the benefit of the former. Trafford had to supply this information because I had been too inept or hasty to convey it in any other way. Or because there was too much to convey in any other way. Henry James was quite right in saying that I had not thought out these two people to the pitch of saturation and that they did not behave unconsciously and naturally. But my defence is that that did not matter, or at least that for the purposes of the book it did not matter very much.

Now I do not exactly remember the several other points he made in that elaborate critical excursion, nor did I attempt any reprisals upon his own work, but his gist was plain. If the Novel was properly a presentation of real people as real people, in absolutely natural reaction in a story, then my characters were not simply sketchy, they were eked out by wires and pads of non-living matter and they stood condemned. His discourse, which had evidently been maturing against my visit, covered not only my work but that of several of my contemporaries whom he had also read with interest and distaste. And the only point upon which I might have argued but which I did not then argue, was this, that the Novel was not necessarily, as he assumed, this real through and through and absolutely true treatment of people more living than life. It might be more and less than that and still be a novel.

To illustrate with what lovely complication of veracity and disingenuousness, with what curious intricate suavity of intimation he could develop his point I will quote from a letter of his, also bearing upon the same book *Marriage*. His intricate mind, as persistent and edentate as a pseudopodium, was still worrying round and about the question raised by that story. " I have read you," he says, " as I always read you, and as I read no one else, with a complete abdication of all those 'principles of criticism,' canons of form, preconceptions of felicity, references to the idea of method or the sacred laws of composition, with which I roam, with which I totter, through the pages of others attended in some dim degree by the fond yet feeble theory of, but which I shake off, as I advance under your spell, with the most cynical inconsistency. For under your spell I do advance—save when I pull myself up stock still in order not to break it even with so much as the breath of appreciation ; I live with you and in you and (almost cannibal-like) *on* you, on you H. G. W., to the sacrifice of your Marjories and your Traffords, and whoever may be of their company ; not your treatment of them, at all, but, much more, their be-fooling of you (pass me the merely scientific expression—I mean your fine high action in view of the red herring of lively interest they trail for you at their heels) becoming thus of the essence of the spectacle for me, and nothing in it all 'happening' so much as these attestations of your character and behaviour, these reactions of yours as you more or less follow them, affect me as vividly happening. I see you ' behave ' all along much more than I see them even when they behave (as I'm not sure they behave *most* in *Marriage*), with whatever charged intensity or accomplished effect ; so that the ground of the drama is somehow most of all in the adventure for *you*—not to say *of* you, the moral, temperamental, personal, expressional, of your setting it forth ; an adventure in fine more appreciable to me than any of those you are by way of letting *them* in for. I don't say that those you let them in for don't interest me too, and don't ' come off ' and people the scene and lead on the attention, about as much as I can do with ; but only, and always, that you beat them on their own ground and that your ' story,' through the five hundred pages, says more to me than theirs. You'll find this perhaps a queer rigmarole of a statement ; but I ask of you to allow for it just now as the mumble, at best, of an invalid ; and wait a little till I can put more of my hand on my sense. Mind you that the restriction I may seem to you to lay on my view of your work, still leaves that work more convulsed with life and more brimming with blood than any it is given me nowadays to meet. The point I have wanted to make is that I find myself absolutely unable, and still more unwilling, to approach you, or to take leave of you, in any projected light of criticism, in any judging or concluding, any comparing, in fact in any aesthetic or ' literary ' relation at all. . . ."

Tried by Henry James's standards I doubt if any of my novels can be taken in any other fashion. There are flashes and veins of character duly " treated " and living individuals in many of them, but none that satisfy his requirements fully. A lot of *Kipps* may pass, some of *Tono Bungay*, *Mr. Britling Sees it Through* and *Joan and Peter* and let me add, I have a weakness for Lady Harman and for Theodore Bulpington and——. But I will not run on. These are pleas in extenuation. The main indictment is sound, that I sketch out scenes and individuals, often quite crudely, and resort even to conventional types and symbols, in order to get on to a discussion of relationships. The important point which I tried to argue with Henry James was that the novel of completely consistent characterization arranged beautifully in a story and painted deep and round and solid, no more exhausts the possibilities of the novel, than the art of Velazquez exhausts the possibilities of the painted picture.

The issue exercised my mind considerably. I had a queer feeling that we were both incompatably right. I wrote one or two lectures and critical papers on the scope of the novel, and I argued with myself and others, that realism and exhaustive presentation were not its only objectives. I think I might have gone further and maintained that they were not even its proper objectives but at best only graces by the way, but at the time I was not clear enough to say that. I might have made a good case by asserting that fiction was necessarily fictitious through and through, and that the real analogy to Velazquez who painted straight from dwarfs and kings, would be biography, character drawn straight from life and not an invented story. James was very much against the idea that there was a biographical element in any good novel, and he and his brother William were very severe upon Vernon Lee when she produced a character in a short story (*Lady Tal*, 1892) markedly like Henry. But it is beyond the power of man to "create" individuals absolutely. If we do not write from models then we compile and fabricate. Every "living" character in a novel is drawn, frankly or furtively, from life—is filched from biography whole or in scraps, a portrait or a patch-up, and its actions are a reflection upon moral conduct. At whatever number of "removes" from facts we may be, we are still imputing motives to somebody. That is the conclusion I am coming to now, but I did not have it ready at that time. I allowed it to be taken for granted that there was such a thing as The Novel, a great and stately addendum to reality, a sort of super-reality with " created " persons in it, and by implication I admitted that my so-called novels were artless self-revelatory stuff, falling far away from a stately ideal by which they had to be judged.

But now I ask when and where has that great ideal been realized—or can it ever be realized?

Competent critics have since examined this supreme importance of individualities, in other words of " character " in the fiction of the nineteenth century and early twentieth century. Throughout that period character-interest did its best to take the place of adjustment-interest in fiction. With a certain justice these authorities ascribe the predominance of individuation to the example of Sir Walter Scott. But more generally it was a consequence of the prevalent sense of social stability, and he was not so much a primary influence as an exponent. He was a man of intensely conservative quality; he accepted, he accepted wilfully, the established social values about him; he had hardly a doubt in him of what was right or wrong, handsome or ungracious, just or mean. He saw events therefore as a play of individualities in a rigid frame of values never more to be questioned or permanently changed. His lawless, romantic past was the picturesque prelude to stability; our current values were already potentially there. Throughout the broad smooth flow of nineteenth-century life in Great Britain, the art of fiction floated on this same assumption of social fixity. The Novel in English was produced in an atmosphere of security for the entertainment of secure people who liked to feel established and safe for good. Its standards were established within that apparently permanent frame and the criticism of it began to be irritated and perplexed when, through a new instability, the splintering frame began to get into the picture.

I suppose for a time I was the outstanding instance among writers of fiction in English of the frame getting into the picture.

I did not see this clearly in those opening years of this century, but in 1912 I made a sort of pronouncement against the " character " obsession and the refusal to discuss values, in a paper on *The Contemporary Novel* delivered to *The Times* Book Club, in which I argued for an enlarging scope for the novel. My attack upon the creation-of-character idea was oblique and subconscious rather than direct. " We (novelists) are going to deal with political questions and religious questions and social questions. We cannot present people unless we have this free hand, this unrestricted field. What is the good of telling stories about people's lives if one may not deal freely with the religious beliefs and organizations that have controlled or failed to control them ? What is the good of pretending to write about love, and the loyalties and treacheries and quarrels of men and women, if one must not glance at those varieties of physical temperament and organic quality, those deeply passionate needs and distresses, from which half the storms of human life are brewed ? We mean to deal with all these things, and it will need very much more than the disapproval of provincial librarians, the hostility of a few influential people in London, the scurrility of one paper " (one for St. Loe Strachey and that bold bad word), " and the deep and obstinate silences of another, to stop the incoming tide of aggressive novel-writing. We are going to write about it all. We are going to write about business and finance and politics and precedence and pretentiousness and decorum and indecorum, until a thousand pretences and ten thousand impostures shrivel in the cold, clear draught of our elucidations. We are going to write of wasted opportunities and latent beauties until a thousand new ways of living open to men and women. We are going to appeal to the young and the hopeful and the curious, against the established, the dignified, and defensive. Before we have done, we will have all life within the scope of the novel."

These are brave trumpetings. In effect in my hands the Novel proved like a blanket too small for the bed and when I tried to pull it over to cover my tossing conflict of ideas, I found I had to abandon questions of individuation. I never got "all life within the scope of the novel." (What a phrase! Who could?)

In the criticism of that time there was a certain confusion between this new spreading out of the interest of the novel to issues of custom and political and social change, and the entirely more limited "Novel with a Purpose" of the earlier nineteenth century. This examined no essential ideas; its values were established values, it merely assailed some particular evil, exposed some little-known abuse. It kept well within the frame. The majority of the Dickens novels were novels with a purpose, but they never deal with any inner confusion, any conflicts of opinion within the individual characters, any subjective essential change. A much closer approximation to the spread-out novel I was advocating is the propaganda novel. But I have always resented having my novels called propaganda novels, because it seems to me the word propaganda should be confined to the definite service of some organized party, church or doctrine. It implies direction from outside. If at times I have been inclined to thrust views upon my readers, they were at any rate my own views and put forward without any strategic aim.

To return to this novel *Marriage*, the story tells how

masculine intellectual interest met feminine spending and what ensued. Trafford is not so much a solid man as a scientific intelligence caught in the meshes of love, and Marjorie Pope's zest in buying and arrangement is emphasized to the exclusion of any minor tricks and turns. But the argument of the book would not have stood out, if there had been any such tricks and turns. Marjorie's father is an intrusion of character drawing who really had no business in the book at all. Mr. Magnet also is a slightly malicious irrelevance; the humourless speech he makes in London on humour is, for example, transcribed verbatim from a reported speech by a distinguished contemporary.

Indisputably the writing is scamped in places. It could have been just as light and much better done. But that would have taken more time than I could afford. I do not mean by that I could have earned less money and been a more conscientious writer, though that consideration very probably came in, but I mean that I had very many things to say and that if I could say one of them in such a way as to get my point over to the reader I did not worry much about finish. The fastidious critic might object, but the general reader to whom I addressed myself cared no more for finish and fundamental veracity about the secondary things of behaviour than I. I did not want to sweep under the mat for crumbs of characterization, nor did he want me to do so. What we wanted was a ventilation of the point at issue.

It required some years and a number of such experiments and essays in statement as the one I have quoted, before I got it really clear in my own mind that I was feeling my way towards something outside any established formula for the novel altogether. In the established novel, objective through and through, the characteristic exterior reactions of the character were everything and the conflicts and changes of ideas within his brain were ignored. (That according to the jargon of the time would have been to "introduce controversial matter.") But I was becoming more and more interested in the interior conflict, this controversial matter stewing and fermenting in all our brains, and its ventilation in action. There is no satisfactory device I knew for exhibiting a train of reasoning in a character unless a set of ideas similar to those upon which the character thinks exists already in the reader's mind. Galsworthy's Soames Forsyte *thinks* for pages, but he thinks along recognized British lines. He does not grapple with ideas new and difficult both for the reader and himself. I could not see how, if we were to grapple with new ideas, a sort of argument with the reader, an explanation of the theory that is being exhibited, could be avoided. I began therefore to make my characters indulge in impossibly explicit monologues and duologues. As early as 1902, Chatteris in the *Sea Lady* talks a good deal more than is natural. *Ann Veronica* soliloquizes continually. In *Marriage* (1912), Trafford and Marjorie go off to Labrador for a good honest six months talk about their mutual reactions and argue at the reader all the time. Mr. Brumley in *The Wife of Sir Isaac Harman* (1914) exercises a garrulous pressure upon the flow of the story throughout. *The Research Magnificent* (1915) is largely talk and monologue. I try in that book the device of making the ostensible writer speculate about the chief character in the story he is telling. The ostensible writer becomes a sort of enveloping character, himself in discussion with the reader Still more expository is the *Soul of a Bishop* (1917).

Incidentally I may complain that *The Research Magnificent* is a book deserving to be remembered and yet seems to be largely forgotten. I liked it when I re-read it and I find it remarkably up to date with my present opinions. It was blotted out by the war. But Amanda is alive and Benham has his moments of vitality.

By 1919, in *The Undying Fire*, I was at last fully aware of what I was doing and I took a new line. I realized I had been trying to revive the Dialogue in a narrative form. I was not so much expanding the novel as getting right out of it. *The Undying Fire* is that great Hebrew imitation of the Platonic Dialogue, the Book of Job, frankly modernized. The arrangement of the ancient book is followed very closely; the speakers even to their names are recognizably the same. The man of Uz is Mr. Job Huss; Eliphaz the Temanite becomes Sir · Eliphaz Burrows, manufacturer of a new building material called Temanite, Bildad is Mr. William Dad and Elihu becomes Dr. Elihu Barrack. They parallel their ancient arguments; even their speeches in their order correspond closely with the pattern of the ancient book. In many ways I think *The Undying Fire* one of the best pieces of work I ever did. I set great store by it still.

But after all these protests of the excellence and intelligence of my intentions, I have to admit that the larger part of my fiction was written lightly and with a certain haste. Only one or two of my novels deal primarily with personality, and then rather in the spirit of what David Low calls the caricature-portrait, than for the purpose of such exhaustive rendering as Henry James had in mind. Such caricature-individualities are Hoopdriver in *The Wheels of Chance* (1896), *Kipps* (1905) and Mr. Polly in *The History of Mr. Polly* (1910). My uncle and aunt in *Tono Bungay* (1909), one or two minor characters in *The Dream* (1924), *Christina Alberta's Father* (1925) and *The Bulpington of Blup* (1932), are also caricature-individualities of which I am not ashamed. Theodore Bulpington is as good as Kipps. Please. But I doubt if any of these persons have that sort of vitality which endures into new social phases. In the course of a few decades they may become incomprehensible; the snobbery of Kipps for example or the bookish illiteracy of Mr. Polly may be altogether inexplicable. *The Dream* is an attempt to show how our lives to-day may look to our happier descendants. It is in the same class as *In the Days of the Comet*.

My experimentation with what I may call the Dialogue Novel was only one of the directions in which I have wandered away from the uncongenial limitations of the novel proper. The plain fact is that I have never been willing to respect these limitations or to accept the Novel as an art form. *Mr. Britling Sees it Through* is a circumstantial story, but it ends in Dialogue and Monologue. *Joan and Peter* (1918) again starts respectably in large novel form and becomes dialogue only towards the end. It is as shamelessly unfinished as a Gothic cathedral. It was to have been a great novel about Education but it grew so large that Peter's public-school experiences, among other things, had to be left out. He just jumps from the preparatory school to the War and the flying corps. The missing public-school stage is to be found in *The Story of a Great Schoolmaster*. Joan I like as a character; A. A. Milne has said nice things about her, but nobody else has had a good word for her—or indeed a bad one. *The Dream* (1924) has some good minor characters, but it is plainly a social criticism from a new angle, rather than a novel proper. A young man of the great world of the future on a holiday walk in the mountains, injures his hand, falls into a fever and dreams " through a whole life " of our present world. *The World of William Clissold* (1926) again is quite unorthodox in shape and approach. It is an attempt to present a thesis upon contemporary life and social development, in the form of a fictitious autobiography. A young chemist, like Trafford in *Marriage*, gives up pure research for industrial organization, grows rich, finds his successful life boring and retires to a house in Provence to think things out and find a better use for himself. He writes the one book that every man has it in him to write. The main strand of the earlier novels reappears in this, the perplexity of the man with general ideas and a strong constructive impulse when he finds that the women he meets do not enter into this stream of motive, but, except for the odd concluding "book," this obsession of so much of my fiction sits lightly here because of the predominance of economic and political questioning. I shall return to *The World of William Clissold* when I deal with my political ideas and later on I may be free to discuss its autobiographical significance. It anticipated a more serious attempt at social analysis, *The Work, Wealth and Happiness of Mankind* (1931), *The Open Conspiracy* (1928) and *The Shape of Things to Come* (1933).

The Autocracy of Mr. Parham (1930) is a rather boisterous caricature not of the personality but of the imaginations of a modern British imperialist of the university type. It might have been dedicated to Mr. L. S. Amery. It amuses me still, but few people share my liking. Reality has outdone fiction since and Mosley fooling it in the Albert Hall with his black shirts (1934) makes Parham's great dream-meeting there seem preposterously sane and sound. *Men Like Gods* frankly caricatures some prominent contemporaries. Another breach of established literary standards with which, in spite of its very tepid reception, I am mainly content, was *Mr. Blettsworthy on Rampole Island* (1928). I laughed when writing both it and *Men Like Gods* and *The Autocracy of Mr. Parham.* The gist of Rampole Island is a caricature-portrait of the whole human world. I wish I could hear at times of people still reading these three stories. They got, I think, a dull press.

Exhaustive character study is an adult occupation, a philosophical occupation. So much of my life has been a prolonged and enlarged adolescence, an encounter with the world in general, that the observation of character began to play a leading part in it only in my later years. It was necessary for me to reconstruct the frame in which individual lives as a whole had to be lived, before I could concentrate upon any of the individual problems of fitting them into this frame. I am taking more interest now in individuality than ever I did before. As mankind settles down into the security of that modern world-state with which contemporary life is in labour, as men's minds escape more and more from the harsh urgencies and feelings of a primary struggle, as the conception of the modern world-state becomes the common basis of their education and the frame of their conduct, the discussion of primary issues will abate and the analysis of individual difference again become a dominating interest. But then surely people will be less round-about in their approach to expression and the subterfuge of fiction will not be so imperative as it is to-day.

Our restraints upon the written discussion of living people are antiquated. Why should David Low say practically what he likes about actual people with his pencil, while I must declare every character in a novel is fictitious? So I am disposed to question whether the Novel will have any great importance in the intellectual life of the future because I believe we are moving towards a greater freedom of truthful comment upon individuals ; if it survives I think it will become more frankly caricature-comment upon personalities and social phases than it is at present, but it seems equally probable to me that it will dwindle and die altogether and be replaced by more searching and outspoken biography and autobiography. Stories, parables, parodies of fact will still be told, but that is a different matter. The race of silly young men who announce that they are going to write The Novel may follow the race of silly young men who used to proclaim their intention of writing The Epic, to limbo. In my time The Novel, as projected, was usually a "Trilogy." Perhaps in 1965 the foolish young men will all be trailing in the wake of Lytton Strachey and Philip Guedalla and announcing colossal biography-sequences. They will produce vast mosaics of pseudo-reality, galleries of portraits, presenting contemporary history in a state of exaltation.

Who would read a novel if we were permitted to write biography—all out? Here in this autobiography I am experimenting—though still very mildly, with biographical and auto-biographical matter. Although it has many restraints, which are from the artistic point of view vexatious, I still find it so much more real and interesting and satisfying that I doubt if I shall ever again turn back towards The Novel. I may write a story or so more—a dialogue, an adventure or an anecdote. But I shall never come as near to a deliberate attempt upon The Novel again as I did in *Tono Bungay* (1909).

Next to *Tono Bungay*, *Mr. Britling Sees it Through* and *Joan and Peter* come as near to being full-dress novels as anything I have written. They are both fairly sound pictures of contemporary conditions. *Mr. Britling Sees it Through* was a huge success more particularly in America, where it earned about £20,000 ; *Tono Bungay* did well ; but *Joan and Peter* never won the recognition I think it deserved. To me it seems a far finer piece of work than *Mr. Britling Sees it Through*.

Even *Tono Bungay* was not much of a concession to Henry James and his conception of an intensified rendering of feeling and characterization as the proper business of the novelist. It was an indisputable Novel, but it was extensive rather than intensive. That is to say it presented characters only as part of a *scene*. It was planned as a social panorama in the vein of Balzac. That vein has produced some physically and mentally great books, and it continues to this day to produce evidences of the nervous endurance of ambitious writers, vast canvasses, too often crude or conventional in interpretation, superficial in motivation and smeary and wholesale in treatment. I cannot imagine it holding out against a literature of competent historical and contemporary studies. *The Forsyte Saga*, as a broadly conceived picture of prosperous British Philistia by one of its indigenes, is not so good and convincing as a group of untrammelled biographical studies of genteel successful types, might be. An industrious treatment of early nineteenth century records again would make Balzac's *Comédie Humaine* seem flighty stuff. Yet in *War and Peace* one may perhaps find a justification for the enhancement and animation of history by fictitious moods and scenes.

I will confess that I find life too short for many things I would like to do. I do not think I am afraid of death but I wish it had not to come so soon. In the natural course of things I shall be lucky, I suppose, if I live a dozen years more, and beyond measure fortunate if I last as a fully living brain for another twenty years. This is barely time to turn round in. Good biography requires more time than that—let alone that I have other things to do. Yet I have known some intensely interesting people whom it would be delightful and rewarding to treat! It is a pity. If I could have forty good years or so more of vigour, I could find a use for every day of it, and then I would write those copious intimate character studies, character in relation to changing values and conditions, that now I fear I shall never be able to do. They would have to be copious. Impermanent realities are not to be rendered without an abundance of matter. In a changing world there cannot be portraits without backgrounds and the source of the shifting reflected light upon the face has to be shown. Here at page 504 of this experiment in autobiography I have to assure the possibly incredulous reader that my attempt to compress it and reduce it to a quintessence, has been strenuous and continual.

CHAPTER THE EIGHTH

FAIRLY LAUNCHED AT LAST

§ 1

Duologue in Lodgings 1894-95

THIS IS AN EXPERIMENT in autobiography and again, I insist, I am writing for myself quite as much as for my reader. In turning over my memories of my early marriage and divorce and the documents that preserve the facts of the case, I learned in the sight of the reader, a great deal about myself and I found it natural to carry on from those early and determining thoughts and experiences to their reflection in my novels and my public discussion of personal relationships. I brought that account of my novels and pseudo-novels down to the present time. These discursive sections have served a useful purpose, they have functioned as a siding, so to speak, into which it has been possible to shunt a number of things that would otherwise have turned up later to complicate the main story of this brain with which I am dealing. That main story, is the development, the steady progressive growth of a modern vision of the world, and the way in which the planned reconstruction of human relationships in the form of a world-state became at last the frame and test of my activities. It is as much the frame and test of my activities as the spread of Islam was the frame and test of an early believing Moslem and the kingdom of God and salvation, of a sincere Christian. My life in the fact that it has evolved a general sustaining idea has become, at least psychologically a religious life ; its *persona* is deoriented from the ego. My essential purpose is that world-vision. I shall try to express it, as fully and effectively as I can, in a last culminating chapter, a sort of testamentary chapter, which I shall call *The Idea of a Planned World*.

But before I can get on to this a further amount of anecdotage and incident is needed to make this development clear. My struggle for a footing is still only half told. I come back now to the point from which I launched out into a dissection of my sexual impulses and conduct, when at the beginning of 1894, at the age of twenty-seven and a half, I left my house, 4 Cumnor Place, Sutton, and went to live in sin and social rebellion first at Mornington Place and then in Mornington Road.

The last decade of the nineteenth century was an extraordinarily favourable time for new writers and my individual good luck was set in the luck of a whole generation of aspirants. Quite a lot of us from nowhere were " getting on." The predominance of Dickens and Thackeray and the successors and imitators they had inspired was passing. In a way they had exhausted the soil for the type of novel they had brought to a culmination, just as Lord Tennyson (who died as late as 1892), Tennyson of the Arthurian cycle, had extracted every poetical possibility from the contemporary prosperous bourgeoisie. For a generation the prestige of the great Victorians remained like the shadow of vast trees in a forest, but now that it was lifting, every weed and sapling had its chance, provided only that it was of a different species from its predecessors. When woods are burnt, it is a different tree which reconstitutes the forest. The habit of reading was spreading to new classes with distinctive needs and curiosities. They did not understand and enjoy the conventions and phrases of Trollope or Jane Austen, or the

FAIRLY LAUNCHED AT LAST

genteel satire of Thackeray, they were outside the "governing class" of Mrs. Humphry Ward's imagination, the sombre passions and inhibitions of the Brontë country or of Wessex or Devonshire had never stirred them, and even the humours of Dickens no longer fitted into their everyday experiences.

The Education Act of 1871 had not only enlarged the reading public very greatly but it had stimulated the middle class by a sense of possible competition from below. And quite apart from that, progress was producing a considerable fermentation of ideas. An exceptional wave of intellectual enterprise had affected the British "governing class." Under the influence of such brilliant Tories as Arthur Balfour and George Wyndham, a number of people in society were taking notice of writing and were on the alert for any signs of literary freshness. Such happy minor accidents as the invasion of England by the Astor family with a taste for running periodicals at a handsome loss, contributed also in their measure to the general expansion of opportunity for new writers. New books were being demanded and fresh authors were in request. Below and above alike there was opportunity, more public, more publicity, more publishers and more patronage. Nowadays it is relatively hard for a young writer to get a hearing. He (or she) plunges into a congested scramble. Here as everywhere production has outrun consuming capacity. But in the nineties young writers were looked for. Even publishers were looking for them.

For a time the need to be actually new was not clearly realized. Literary criticism in those days had some odd conventions. It was still either scholarly or with scholarly pretensions. It was dominated by the mediaeval assumption that whatever is worth knowing is already known and whatever is worth doing has already been done. Astonishment is unbecoming in scholarly men and their attitude to newcomers is best expressed by the word "recognition." Anybody fresh who turned up was treated as an aspirant Dalai Lama is treated, and scrutinized for evidence of his predecessor's soul. So it came about that every one of us who started writing in the nineties, was discovered to be "a second"—somebody or other. In the course of two or three years I was welcomed as a second Dickens, a second Bulwer Lytton and a second Jules Verne. But also I was a second Barrie, though J. M. B. was hardly more than my contemporary, and, when I turned to short stories, I became a second Kipling. I certainly, on occasion, imitated both these excellent masters. Later on I figured also as a second Diderot, a second Carlyle and a second Rousseau. . . .

Until recently this was the common lot. Literature "broadened down from precedent to precedent." The influence of the publisher who wanted us to be new but did not want us to be *strange*, worked in the same direction as educated criticism. A sheaf of second-hand tickets to literary distinction was thrust into our hands and hardly anyone could get a straight ticket on his own. These second-hand tickets were very convenient as admission tickets. It was however unwise to sit down in the vacant chairs, because if one did so, one rarely got up again. Pett Ridge for instance pinned himself down as a second Dickens to the end of his days. I was saved from a parallel fate by the perplexing variety of my early attributions.

Of course Jane and I, starting life afresh in our guinea-a-week ground floor apartments in Mornington Place, had no suspicion how wise we had been in getting born exactly when we did. We did not realize we were like two respectable little new ordinary shares in a stock-exchange boom. We believed very gravely in the general sanity of things and we took the tide of easy success which had caught us up, as the due reward of our activity and efforts. We thought this was how things had always been and were always going to be. It was all delightfully simple. We were as bright and witty as we knew how, and acceptance, proofs and a cheque followed as a matter of course. I was doing my best to write as other writers wrote, and it was long before I realized that my exceptional origins and training gave me an almost unavoidable freshness of approach and that I was being original in spite of my sedulous efforts to justify my discursive secondariness.

Our life in 1894 and 95 was an almost continuous duologue. In Mornington Place and in Mornington Road we occupied a bedroom with a double bed and came through folding doors to our living-room. All our clothing was in a small chest of drawers and a wardrobe and I did my work at a little table with a shaded paraffin lamp in the corner or, when it was not needed for a meal, at the table in the middle of the living-room. All my notes and manuscripts were in a green cardboard box of four drawers. Our first landlady in Mornington Place was a German woman, Madame Reinach, and her cooking was so emphatic, her sympathy with our romantically unmarried state so liberally expressed, her eagerness for intimate mutual confidences so pressing, and her own confidences so extraordinary, that presently Jane went off by herself to Mornington Road and found another lodging for us.

Here our landlady, whose name by some queer turn I have forgotten, mothered us very agreeably. She was a tall, strong-faced, Scotswoman. For a London landlady she was an exceptionally clean, capable, silent and stoical woman. She had been housemaid, if I remember rightly, in the household of the Duke of Fife, and she began to approve of me when she found I worked continuously and never drank. I think that somewhere between the housemaid stage and this lodging house of hers, someone may have figured who lacked my simple virtues. (An old friend with a better memory than mine tells me her name was Mrs. Lewis. But I still do not remember.)

We would wake cheerfully and get up and I would invent rhymes and " pomes " of which I have already given sufficient samples, as we washed and dressed and avoided collisions with each other. We had no bathroom and our limited floor space was further restricted by a " tub," a shallow tin bird-bath in which we sponged and splashed. Perhaps we would peep through the folding doors and if the living room was empty, one of us, I in trousers and nightshirt—those were pre-pyjama days—or Jane in her little blue dressing-gown and her two blonde pigtails reaching below her waist, would make a dash for the letters. Usually they were cheering letters. Perhaps there was a cheque ; perhaps there was an invitation to contribute an article or maybe there was a book for review. As we read these, a firm tread on the stairs, a clatter and an appetizing smell and at last a rap-rap on the folding doors announced our coffee and eggs and bacon.

How vividly I remember the cheerfulness of that front room ; Jane in her wrapper on the hearthrug toasting a slice of bread ; the grey London day a little misty perhaps outside and the bright animation of the coal-fire reflected on the fire-irons and the fender !

After breakfast I would set to work upon a review or one of the two or three articles I always kept in hand, working them up very carefully from rough notes until I was satisfied with them. Jane would make a fair copy of what I had done, or write on her own account, or go out to supplement our landlady's catering, or read biology for her final B.Sc. degree examination. After the morning's work we might raid out into Regent's Park or up among the interesting shops and stalls of the Hampstead Road, for a breath of air and a gleam of amusement before our one o'clock dinner. After dinner we would prowl out to look for articles.

This article hunt was a very important business. We sought unlikely places at unlikely times in order to get queer impressions of them. We went to Highgate Cemetery in the afternoon and protested at the conventionality of the monumental mason, or we were gravely critical, with a lapse into enthusiasm in the best art-critic manner, of the Parkes Museum (sanitary science), or we went on a cold windy day to Epping Forest to write " Bleak March in Epping Forest." We nosed the Bond Street windows and the West End art and picture shows to furbish forth an Uncle I had invented to suit the taste of the *Pall Mall Gazette*—a tremendous man of the world he was, the sort of man who might live in the Albany. (*Select Conversations with an Uncle*, is the pick of what we got for him.) I was still a fellow of the Zoological Society (afterwards my subscription went into abeyance) and we sought articles and apt allusions from cage to cage. Whenever we hit upon an idea for an article that I did not immediately write, it was put into the topmost of my nest of green drawers for future use.

On wet afternoons or after supper when we could work no more we played chess (which yielded an article) and bézique, which defied even my article extracting powers. Bézique was introduced to us by my old fellow student Morley Davies, who had taken on my Correspondence Classes and was working for his B.Sc. He lodged near by and he would come in after supper and gravely take down a triple pack with us.

We went very little to concerts, theatres or music-halls for the very sound reason that we could not afford it. Our only exercise was " going for a walk." And for a time except for occasional after-supper visitors like Davies, or my distant cousin Owen Thomas, who was arranging my divorce upon the most economical lines, or a tea at Walter Low's, we had no social life at all. But then I never had had any social life and Jane's experience had been chiefly of little dances, tea parties, croquet parties and lawn tennis in the villadom of Putney, formal entertainments of which she was now disposed to be very scornful.

It is perhaps not surprising that as the spring came on, Jane and I, in spite of our encouraging successfulness, displayed signs of being run down. I had something wrong with a lymphatic gland under my jaw and when I called in a Camden Town doctor to clean it up for me, he insisted that Jane was in a worse state than I and that she ought to be much more in the fresh air and better nourished if she was not to become tuberculous. He ordered her Burgundy and we went out and bought an entire bottle at once,—Gilbey's Burgundy, Number—something or other—and Jane consumed it medicinally, one glass per meal. We decided to transfer ourselves to country lodgings for the summer. Except for the facilities of getting books and the advisability of being near one's editors, there seemed to be no particular reason why we should be tied to London. Moreover Jane's mother, Mrs. Robbins, had let her house at Putney; she had been lodging with some friends in North London and she too was ailing and in need of the open air. She had accepted our irregular situation by this time and was quite ready to join us. And while we were hesitating on the verge of this necessity came an accession of work that seemed to make an abandonment of London altogether justifiable.

I was invited one day to go and see my editor, Cust of the *Pall Mall Gazette*—either that or I had asked to see him, I forget which. I went down to the office for my second encounter with an editor but this time I wore no wetted top-hat to shame me by its misbehaviour and no tail coat. I was evidently wearing quite reasonable clothes because I have forgotten them. I was learning my world. The *Pall Mall Gazette* was installed in magnificent offices in the position now occupied by the Garrick Theatre. I was sent up to the editor's room. I remember it as a magnificent drawing-room; Fleet Street hath not its like to-day. There was certainly one grand piano in it, and my memory is inclined to put in another. There was a vast editor's desk, marvellously equipped, like a desk out of Hollywood. There were chairs and sofas. But for the moment I saw nobody amidst these splendours. I advanced slowly across a space of noiseless carpet. Then I became aware of a sound of sobbing and realized that someone almost completely hidden from me lay prostrate on a sofa indulging in paroxysms of grief.

In the circumstances a cough seemed to be the best thing.

Thereupon the sound from the sofa ceased abruptly and a tall blond man sat up, stared and then stood up, put away his pocket handkerchief and became entirely friendly and self-possessed. Whatever emotional crisis was going on had nothing to do with the business between us and was suspended. Yes, he wanted to see me. He liked my stuff and it was perfectly reasonable that I should want to make up my income by doing reviewing. There wasn't any job he could give me on the staff just now. So soon as there was he would think of me. Did I know W. E. Henley? I ought to go and see him.

He asked me where I got my knowledge and how I had learnt to write and what I was and I told him to the best of my ability. He put me at my ease from the beginning. There was none of the Olympian balderdash of Frank Harris about him. He combined the agreeable manners of an elder brother with those of a fellow adventurer. It wasn't at all Fleet Street to which he made me welcome but a Great

Lark in journalism. I suppose he knew hardly more of Fleet Street than I did. I must certainly go and see Henley, but just now there was someone else I must meet.

He touched a bell and presently across the large spaces of the room appeared Mr. Lewis Hind. Hind was a contrast to Cust in every way, except that he too was an outsider in the journalistic world. He was tall, dark and sallow, with a reserved manner and an impediment in his speech. He had begun life in the textile trade and at one time he had gone about London with samples of lace. He had been an industrious student, with Clement K. Shorter and W. Pett Ridge, at the Birkbeck Institute and he had adventured with them into the expanding field of journalism. He had been taken up and influenced in the direction of catholicism by Mrs. Alice Meynell and he had found a permanent job as sub-editor of the *Magazine of Art* under Henley and, through his introduction and that of Mrs. Meynell he had come aboard Mr. Astor's *Pall Mall* adventure. The *Gazette* had thrown off a weekly satellite, the *Pall Mall Budget*, which was at first merely a bale of the less newsy material in the *Gazette*. My *Man of the Year Million* had appeared in it, with some amusing illustrations, and had made a little eddy of success for me. Hind edited this budget and it was proposed to expand it presently into an independent illustrated weekly with original matter, all its own. He was looking for "features." He carried me off from Cust's room to his own less palatial quarters and there he broached the idea of utilizing my special knowledge of science in the expanded weekly, in a series of short stories to be called "single sitting" stories. I was to have five guineas for each story. It seemed quite good pay, then, and I set my mind to imagining possible stories of the kind he demanded.

We left Cust in his office. Whether he went on with his crisis or forgot about it I cannot say, but from my later acquaintance with him, I think he most probably forgot about it.

The first of the single sitting stories I ground out was the *Stolen Bacillus* and after a time I became quite dexterous in evolving incidents and anecdotes from little possibilities of a scientific or quasi-scientific sort. I presently broadened my market and found higher prices were to be got from the *Strand Magazine* and the *Pall Mall Magazine*. Many of these stories, forty perhaps altogether, have been reprinted again and again in a variety of collections and they still appear and reappear in newspapers and magazines. Hind paid me £5 for them, but the normal fee I get nowadays for republication in a newspaper, is £20, and many have still undeveloped dramatic and film possibilities. I had no idea in those energetic needy days of these little tips I was putting aside for my declining years.

At about the same time that Hind set me writing short stories, I had a request from the mighty William Ernest Henley himself for a contribution to the *National Observer*. I went to see the old giant whose " head was bloody but unbowed " at his house upon the riverside at Putney. He was a magnificent torso set upon shrunken withered legs. When I met President Franklin Roosevelt this spring I found the same big chest and the same infirmity. He talked very richly and agreeably and, as he talked, he emphasized his remarks by clutching an agate paper weight in his big freckled paw and banging it on his writing table. Years afterwards when he died his wife gave me that slab of agate and it is on my desk before me as I write. I resolved to do my very best for him and I dug up my peculiar treasure, my old idea of " time-travelling," from the *Science Schools Journal* and sent him in a couple of papers. He liked them and asked me to carry on the idea so as to give glimpses of the world of the future. This I was only too pleased to do, and altogether I developed the notion into seven papers between March and June. This was the second launching of the story that had begun in the *Science Schools Journal* as the *Chronic Argonauts*, but now nearly all the traces of Hawthorne and English Babu classicism had disappeared. I had realized that the more impossible the story I had to tell, the more ordinary must be the setting, and the circumstances in which I now set the Time Traveller were all that I could imagine of solid upper-middle-class comfort.

With these *Time Traveller* papers running, with quite a number of stories for Hind germinating in my head, with a supply of books to review and what seemed a steady market for my occasional, my frequent occasional, articles in the *Gazette*, it seemed no sort of risk to leave London for a lodging at Sevenoaks, and thither we went, all three of us, as London grew hot and dusty and tiring. For awhile things were very pleasant at Sevenoaks. We went for long walks and Jane recovered rapidly in health and energy. We explored Knole Park and down the long hill to Tunbridge and away to the haunts of my grandfather, Penshurst Park. Jane was still working for her final degree, though she never actually sat for the examination; botany was to be one of her three subjects and we gathered and brought home big and various bunches of flowers so that she might learn the natural orders.

At first Mrs. Robbins was not with us. When she joined us she was in ill health; she had recovered only very partially from her disapproval of our unmarried state, and her presence was a considerable restraint upon our jests and "picshuas" and daily ease. At times the tension of her unspoken feelings would oblige her to take to her room and eat her meals there. This slight and retreating shadow upon our contentment was presently supplemented by graver troubles. There was a sudden fall in my income. Abruptly the *National Observer* changed hands. This was quite a sudden transaction; the paper had never paid its expenses and its chief supporter decided to sell it to a Mr. Vincent who also took over the editorial control from Henley. Mr. Vincent thought my articles queer wild ramblings and wound them up at once. At the same time the *Pall Mall Gazette* stopped using my articles. The literary editor, Marriott Watson, always a firm friend of mine, was away on holiday and his temporary successor did not think very much of my stuff. I did not know of this, and I was quite at a loss to account for this sudden withdrawal of support. I thought it might be a permanent withdrawal. For the first time we found our monthly expenditure exceeding our income. A certain dismay pervaded our hitherto cheerful walks. And then an equally unexpected decision by Mr. Astor announced an approaching end to the brief bright career of the *Pall Mall Budget* and with it my sure and certain market and prompt pay for a single-sitting story.

Just then came an emissary from the divorce court with a writ, couched in stern uncompromising phrases, and instead of locking this securely away, Jane put it in a drawer accessible to the curiosity of our landlady. There had been some little trouble with her already; she wanted to charge an extra sixpence for every meal Mrs. Robbins took in her own room, she said we littered up the place with our wild flowers, and she thought I consumed an unconscionable amount of lamp-oil by writing so late. She was faintly irritated about Jane's disinclination for womanly gossiping with her, she felt we were " stuck-up " in some way, and when she realized that we had no marriage lines, her indignation flared. She could not immediately tax us with our flagrant immorality, for that would have been to admit her own prying, but she became extremely truculent in her bearing and negligent in her services. Dark allusions foreshadowed the coming row. We were not the sort of people everybody would want to take in. There were people who were right and you could tell it, and people who were not. Life assumed a harsh and careworn visage.

It seemed rather useless to go on writing articles. All the periodicals to which I contributed were holding stuff of mine in proof and it might be indiscreet to pour in fresh matter to such a point that the tanks overflowed and returned it. But I had one thing in the back of my mind. Henley had told me that it was just possible he would presently find backing for a monthly. If so, he thought I might rewrite the *Time Traveller* articles as a serial story. Anyhow that was something to do and I set to work on the *Time Machine* and rewrote it from end to end.

I still remember writing that part of the story in which the *Time Traveller* returns to find his machine removed and his retreat cut off. I sat alone at the round table downstairs writing steadily in the luminous circle cast by a shaded paraffin lamp. Jane had gone to bed and her mother had been ill in bed all day. It was a very warm blue August night and the window was wide open. The best part of my mind fled through the story in a state of concentration before the Morlocks but some outlying regions of my brain were recording other things. Moths were fluttering in ever and again and though I was unconscious of them at the time, one must have flopped near me and left some trace in my marginal consciousness that became a short story I presently wrote, *A Moth, Genus Novo*. And outside in the summer night a voice went on and on, a feminine voice that rose and fell. It was Mrs.—— I forget her name—our landlady in open rebellion at last, talking to a sympathetic neighbour in the next garden and talking through the window at me. I was aware of her and heeded her not, and she lacked the courage to beard me in my parlour. " Would I *never* go to bed ? How could she lock up with that window staring open? Never had she had such people in her house before,—never. A nice lot if everything was known about them. Often when you didn't actually know about things you could feel them. What she let her rooms to was summer visitors who walked about all day and went to bed at night. And she hated meanness and there were some who could be mean about sixpences. People with lodgings to let in Sevenoaks ought to know the sort of people who might take them. . . ."

It went on and on. I wrote on grimly to that accompaniment. I wrote her out and she made her last comment with the front door well and truly slammed. I finished my chapter before I shut the window and turned down and blew out the lamp. And somehow amidst the gathering disturbance of those days the *Time Machine* got itself finished. Jane kept up a valiant front and fended off from me as much as she could of the trouble that was assailing her on both sides. But a certain gay elasticity disappeared. It was a disagreeable time for her. She went and looked at other apartments and was asked unusual questions.

It was a retreat rather than a return we made to London, with the tart reproaches of the social system echoing in our ears. But before our ultimate flight I had had a letter from Henley telling me it was all right about that monthly of his. He was to start *The New Review* in January and he would pay me £100 for the *Time Machine* as his first serial story. One hundred pounds! And at the same time the mills of the *Pall Mall Gazette* began to go round and consume my work again. Mrs. Robbins went back to stay with friends in North London and Jane and I found our old rooms with our Scotch landlady at 12 Mornington Road, still free for us.

We seem to have stuck it in London for the rest of the year. Somewhen that autumn Frank Harris, who was no longer editing the *Fortnightly Review*, obtained possession of the weekly *Saturday Review*. He proceeded to a drastic reconstruction of what was then a dull and dignified periodical. He was mindful of those two early articles of mine, the one he had published and the one he had destroyed, and he sent for me at once. He sent also for Walter Low and a number of other comparatively unknown people. The office was in Southampton Street, off the Strand, and it occupied the first and second floors. I found people ascending and descending and the roar of a remembered voice told me that Harris was on the higher level. I found Blanchamp in a large room on the drawing-room floor amidst a great confusion of books and papers and greatly amused. Harris was having a glorious time of it above. He had summoned most of the former staff to his presence in order to read out scraps from their recent contributions to them and to demand, in the presence of his " Dear Gahd " and his faithful henchman Silk, why the hell they wrote like that? It was a Revolution,—the twilight of the Academic. But Professor Saintsbury, chief of that anonymous staff, had been warned in time by Edmund Gosse and so escaped the crowning humiliation.

Clergymen, Oxford dons, respectable but strictly anonymous men of learning and standing, came hustling downstairs in various phases of indignation and protest, while odd newcomers in strange garments as redolent of individuality as their signatures, waited their turn to ascend. I came late on the list and by that time Harris was ready for lunch and took Blanchamp, Low and myself as his guests and audience to the Café Royal, where I made the acquaintance of Camembert of the ripest and a sort of Burgundy quite different from the bottle I had bought for Jane in her extremity. I don't think we talked much about my prospective contributions. But I gathered that our fortunes were made, that

Oxford and the Stuffy and the Genteel and Mr. Gladstone were to be destroyed and that under Harris the *Saturday Review* was to become a weekly unprecedented in literary history.

It did in fact become a very lively, readable and remarkable publication. It was never so consciously and consistently " written " as Henley's defunct *National Observer*, but it had a broader liveliness and a far more vigorous circulation. Among other rising writers Harris presently had at work upon it was a lean, red-haired Irishman named Shaw, already known as a music critic and a Socialist speaker, who so far broke through its traditional anonymity as to insist upon his initials appearing after his dramatic criticisms, D. S. Maccoll (also presently initialled), J. F. Runciman (ditto), Cunninghame Graham (full signature), Max Beerbohm, Chalmers Mitchell, Arthur Symons, J. T. Grein.... I cannot remember half of them. Signed articles increased and multiplied and all sorts of prominent and interesting people made occasional contributions. A " Feature," a series of articles on " The Best Scenery I know " was begun and a " Correspondence " section broke out. No man, it seems, had ever been stirred to write letters to the old " Saturday " or he had been snubbed when he did. Now some were invited and others were stung to contribute the most interesting letters. What Saintsbury thought of it all has never, I think, been recorded. But then Saintsbury very rarely brought his critical acumen to bear upon contemporary writing.

Our City articles also, I gathered, were developing a vigour all their own under the immediate direction of Harris. " I'm a blackmailer," he announced, time and again, and represented himself as a terrible wolf among financiers. Possibly he did something to justify his boasts; in later life he seems to have told Hugh Kingsmill some remarkable stories of cheques extorted and bundles of notes passing from hand to hand but manifestly in the long run it came to very little and he died a year or so ago at Nice in anything but wealthy circumstances.

England in my time has been very liable to adventurous outsiders; Bottomley and Birkenhead, Ramsay MacDonald and Loewenstein, Shaw and Zaharoff, Maundy Gregory and me—a host of others; men with no legitimate and predetermined rôles, men who have behaved at all levels of behaviour but whose common characteristic it has been to fly across the social confusion quite unaccountably, scattering a train of interrogations in their wake. Only the Court, the army and navy, banking and the civil service have been secure against this invasion. Such men are inevitable in a period of obsolete educational ideas and decaying social traditions. Whatever else they are they are not dull and formal. They quicken, if it is only quickening to destroy. Harris was certainly a superlative example of the outside adventurer. He was altogether meteoric.

Nobody seemed to know whence Harris had come. He was supposed to be either a Welsh Jew or a Spanish Irishman; he spoke with an accent, but he had done so much to his accent that I doubt whether Shaw could place it precisely. It had a sort of " mega-celtic " flavour—if I may coin a word. His entirely untrustworthy reminiscences give Galway as his birth-place. The meticulous student may find these matters fully discussed in the *Life* by A. I. Tobin and Elmer Gertz and in Hugh Kingsmill's *Frank Harris*. He emerged as a bright pressman in Chicago, made his way to London, pushed into journalism, and when he was sent to write up the bad treatment of the tenants on the Cecil estates, achieved a reputation for vigour and mental integrity by praising instead of cursing. He was taken notice of. He clambered to the editorship of the *Evening News*. From that, before it fell

FAIRLY LAUNCHED AT LAST

away from him, he leapt still higher. Legend has it that he went to Chapman, the proprietor of the *Fortnightly Review*, and told him his paper was dull because he did not know enough prominent people, and then to one or two outstanding people and pointed out the value of publicity in this democratic age, and particularly the value of the publicity to be got through a personal acquaintance with Mr. Chapman; that he invited him to meet them and them to meet him, to the great social gratification of Mr. Chapman, and emerged triumphantly from the resultant party as editor of the *Fortnightly Review*. He infused a certain amount of new life into it and challenged the established ascendency of the *Nineteenth Century*. He married a wealthy widow, a Mrs. Clayton, who had a small but charming house in the then socially exalted region of Park Lane. There he reached his zenith. He saw himself entering parliament; he cultivated the constituency of Hackney, he aspired, he told Hugh Kingsmill, to become the "British Bismarck" (whatever he imagined that to mean. He may have been thinking of his moustache) and all sorts of prominent and interesting people went to the dinner parties at Park Lane. But he could not stay the course. His sexual vanity was overpowering, he not only became a discursive amorist but he talked about it, and there ensued an estrangement and separation from his wife and her income and Park Lane. His dominating way in conversation startled, amused and then irritated people, and he felt his grip slipping. The directors of the *Fortnightly* became restive and interfering. He began to drink heavily and to shout still louder as the penalties of loud shouting closed in on him. When I met him for the second time as the editor with a controlling interest in the *Saturday Review*, he had already left his wife and lost her monetary support, but he was still high in the London sky. He was still a star of the magnitude of Whistler or Henley or Oscar Wilde and we, his younger contributors, were little chaps below him.

I think his blackmailing in the *Saturday Review* period was almost pure romancing, for he achieved neither the wealth nor the jail that are the alternatives facing the serious blackmailer. He was far too loud and vain, far too eager to create an immediate impression to be a proper scoundrel. I have been hearing about him all my life and I have never heard convincing particulars of any actual monetary frauds ; the *Saturday Review*, I can witness, paid punctually to the end of his proprietorship. His claims to literary flair, if not to literary distinction, were better founded. He read widely and confusedly but often with vivid appreciation, and he pretended to great learning. He was the sort of man who will prepare a long quotation in Greek for a dinner party. Kingsmill says he sported an Eton tie at times and talked of the " old days " at Rugby. Also he insisted that he had been a cowboy, a foremast hand and a great number of other fine romantic things, as occasion seemed to demand. I never saw him do anything more adventurous than sit and talk exuberantly in imminent danger of unanswerable contradiction.

That was what he lived for, talking, writing that was also loud talk in ink, and editing. He was a brilliant editor for a time and then the impetus gave out and he flagged rapidly. So soon as he ceased to work vehemently he became unable to work. He could not attend to things without excitement. As his confidence went he became clumsily loud.

His talk was most effective at the first hearing ; after some experience of it, it began to bore me so excessively that I avoided the office when I knew he was there. There was no variety in his posing and no fancy in his falsehoods. I do not remember that he said a single good thing in all that uproar ; his praise, his condemnations, his assertions, his pretensions to an excessive villainy and virility, have all dissolved in my memory into a rich muddy noise. Always he was proclaiming himself the journalistic Robin Hood, bold yet strangely sensitive and tender-hearted—with the full volume of his voice. The reader may get the quality of it best in his book *The Man Shakespeare*.

I went on writing for him until 1898, but with diminishing frequency. Throughout that period he shrank in my mind from his original dimensions of Olympian terror to something in retreating perspective that kept on barking. Sometimes I relented towards him and did my best to restore him to his original position in my esteem as a Great Character, or at least a Great Lark. But really he had not the versatility and detachment for the Great Lark. He could never get sufficiently away from his ugly self. He had nothing of the fresh gaiety of Harry Cust who was everything a Great Lark should be.

After 1898 I saw Harris only intermittently. He left London. Something obscure happened to the *Saturday Review* and he sold his interest in it and went to France.

Thereafter I heard him rumbling about, for the most part below the horizon of my world, a distant thunder. He came up to visibility again for a time as the editor of an old and long respectable monthly called *Hearth and Home*. He desecrated the Hearth and got rid of the Homelike quality very rapidly and thoroughly. Before or after that (I forget which) he was editor of a periodical with menace even in the title, *The Candid Friend*, which was abusive rather than candid, and faded out. Afterwards he worked his mischief upon *Vanity Fair* and then upon a publication called *Modern Society*. But he did nothing extraordinarily or gallantly wicked though he did much that was noisily offensive.

We had a quarrel during the *Vanity Fair* phase. He sent me a book called *The Bomb*. I thought the first part good and the second tawdry and bad and I asked him which part of it was really his. I had touched a tender spot. His idea of a retort was to publish terrific " slatings " of my *Tono Bungay*, which for reasons still obscure to me he called Tono-the-Bungay. That did not alter the fact that *The Bomb* is curiously unequal.

Modern Society got him into prison but only on the score of contempt of court. He commented on the private character of the defendant in a divorce case that was *sub judice*. His "martyrdom," as he called it later, lasted a month. Then for a time I heard no more of him.

One morning in war time, somewhen in 1915, my neighbour Lady Warwick came sailing down from Easton Lodge to Easton Glebe, my house on the edge of her park. It is not her way to beat about the bush. " Why does Frank Harris say I am not to tell you he is here ? " she asked.

Was he here ? He was at Brook End with his wife—in fear of prosecution. He had found reason for bolting from Paris and he had thrown himself upon her never-failing generosity. Brook End was a furnished house just beyond the far gates of the park which she was in the habit of lending to all and sundry who appealed to her. He had been boasting too much in Paris about his German sympathies and his influence with the Indian princes, and the French who are a logical people and take things said far too seriously, made themselves disagreeable and inquisitive. They are quite capable of shooting a man on his own confession. He gave way to panic. He fled to England with Mrs. Harris and a couple of valises. He still saw denunciation in every tree and the rustle of the summer leaves outside the windows at Brook End seemed the prelude to arrest.

I explained that he and I had been exchanging abusive letters and I supposed that he was expecting me to behave as he would have behaved if our positions had been reversed. Jane came in and we agreed that it was a case for cordial and even effusive hospitality. Mrs. Harris is a very pleasant and loyal lady and there was little need for effort in our welcome to her. Harris—a very subdued Harris it was—brightened up and we did what we could to make his stay in Essex pleasant until he could get a passage to America. He sat at my table and talked of Shakespeare, Dryden, Carlyle, Jesus Christ, Confucius, me and other great figures; of poetry and his own divine sensitiveness and the execrable cooking in Brixton jail.

Presently they got a passage for America and departed.

He had been gone some days when I had another visit from Lady Warwick. This time she did not come to the point so directly. As we walked in my rose garden she asked me what I really thought of Frank Harris. Didn't she know?

You see, she had had a number of letters—quite interesting letters from a certain royal personage.

" And you gave them to him? "

" Oh *no* ! But he asked to look through them. He thought he might advise me about them. One doesn't *care* to destroy things like that. They have historical importance."

"And they are now in his valise on their way to America? "

" Yes. How did you know that? "

It seemed to me, I am afraid, an altogether amusing situation. " Even if the ship is torpedoed," I said, " Harris will stick to those letters."

It was a lengthy and costly business to recover and place those carelessly written and very private documents in the hands most likely to hold them discreetly. Meanwhile Harris took over *Pearson's Magazine* in America and ran it as a pro-German organ until America came into the war. He reduced a circulation of 200,000 to 10,000. He published a hostile and quite imaginary interview with me to show

how entirely ignorant and foolish was my attitude in the struggle.

But this is my autobiography and not a biography of Harris. I never saw him again. I found myself very near him when I made a winter home for myself near Grasse, but I kept any craving I had to hear his voice once more, well under control. Messages passed between us and I promised to go and see him—when I could manage it. But I never did manage and I am rather sorry now. He died in 1932 and after all, by that time, he was an old man of seventy-seven or seventy-eight, and it would have done me no harm to have gone over and listened to him for an hour or so.

Shaw was far kinder to him. When he was staying at Antibes in the summer of 1928 he went over to Nice on several occasions, and renewed the old acquaintance. It was an odd friendship. Harris never wearied and bored Shaw as he wearied and bored me. Shaw found something attractive in all those boastings of sentimentalized villainy and passionate virility. And moreover he could hold his own with Harris in a way that I could not do. In his earlier years he had been wont to face and sway the uproar of excited public meetings. Talking to Harris must have seemed almost like old times come again. But Harris in talk went over me like a steam roller and flattened me out completely.

Very generously Shaw allowed Harris to write a *Life* of himself. It is the work of an ego-centred, sex-crazy old man. And it reveals more than anything else the profound resentment of Harris at the relative success of his former contributor. Shaw, he says, was a miracle of impotence in art, in affairs and in love. That is the main thesis. The analysis is pseudo-physiological throughout. Shaw took these outpourings with an admirable good humour and helped the book greatly by adding elucidatory contributions of his own. But so far as I and my autobiography are concerned, the latter years of Harris at Nice are no more than " noises heard off." I know nothing of that redoubtable suppressed *Life and Loves* of his, in four volumes, which is sought after by collectors of " curious " books, except that it must certainly be tumultuous and unveracious.

So much for that hot, vehement brain which went roaring past my own less audible hemispheres of grey matter on their way through this world. I am told that *The Life and Loves of Frank Harris* is a warning to all autobiographers, and I can quite believe it. Apparently it is a hotchpotch of lies, self-pity, vain pretensions and exhibitionism and the end is unhappiness and despair. Nevertheless I do not feel urged, even for my own good, to go to the pains needed to procure and read a surreptitious copy of it. I do not think I should learn anything more about this awful example of undisciplined egoism than I know and have told already. The core of the matter is this, that this man drank and shouted and had to go on drinking and shouting all through his life because the tireless pursuit of self-discovery upon his heels gave him no peace ; he never had the courage to face round at his reality and he was never sufficiently stupefied to forget it. He was already in flight before the horror of The Man Frank Harris, before ever he came to London. And yet, perhaps, if he had turned, he might have made something quite tolerable of his repudiated and falsified self. I cannot tell. It would have been a stiff job anyhow with that dwarfish ill-proportioned body, that ugly dark face and with lust-entangled vanity and greediness of overpowering strength.

I return from this digression to the years 1894–95 and my visits to Southampton Street to get books for review from Frank Harris and Blanchamp and to carry them off, whole armfuls, in a hansom cab to 12 Mornington Road. There I sat down and Jane and I mugged up our reviews of them, whenever the light of invention burnt low and an original article seemed out of the question.

I was now in a very hopeful and enterprising mood. Henley had accepted the *Time Machine*, agreed to pay £100 for it, and had recommended it to Heinemann, the publisher. This would bring in at least another £50. I should have a book out in the spring and I should pass from the status of journalist—" occasional journalist " at that, and anonymous —to authorship under my own name. And there was talk of a book of short stories with Methuen. Furthermore John Lane was proposing to make a book out of some of my articles, though for that I was to get only £10 down. The point was that my chance was plainly coming fast. I should get a press— and I felt I might get a good press—for the *Time Machine* anyhow. If I could get another book out before that amount of publicity died away I should be fairly launched as an author and then I might be able to go on writing books. This incessant hunt for " ideas " for anonymous articles might be relaxed and the grind of book-reviewing abated.

I find in my archives a " picshua " commemorating my Christmas dinner for 1894. Very few picshuas survive from the first year of my life with Jane. I did not draw so very many then, and she did not begin methodically to save what I drew until we had a house and storage. The early pictures were not nearly so neat and dexterous as the later. But this one shows our tall landlady (bless her !) giving a last glance at the table she has laid for myself and Jane and Mrs. Robbins. The fare is recognizably a turkey. Detail however is hasty and inadequate. The interested reader will note the folding doors. He will note too a queer black object on the table to the left of Jane. That represents, however inadequately, a black glass flagon. In this flagon there was a wine—I do not know if it is still sold by grocers—a golden wine, called

"Canary Sack." I am not at all sure if it was the same as Falstaff's sack; it was a sweetish thin sherry-like wine.

That wine on the table, even more than the turkey and the presence of Mrs. Robbins, marks the fact that already in the first year Jane and I felt we were winning our queer little joint fight against the world, for the liberty of our lives and the freedom of our brains. We had had a serious talk about our social outlook. People, often strange people, were beginning to ask us out. All sorts of unfamiliar food and drink might be sprung upon us, for the dietary Jane had been brought up upon was scarcely less restricted than my own. We knew no wines but port and sherry. Accordingly we decided to experiment with food and drink so far as the resources of the Camden Town and Tottenham Court Road luxury trade permitted. We tried a bottle of claret and a bottle of hock and so forth and so on, and that is why we "washed down" our Christmas fare with Canary Sack. So that if anyone asked us to take Canary Sack we should know what we were in for. But nobody ever did ask us to take Canary Sack. My knowledge of Canary Sack is still waste knowledge.

And we discussed whether we would go out to a dinner or so in a restaurant in preparation for our social emergence. There was the Holborn Restaurant and there were restaurants in Soho which offered dinners from 1s. 6d. upwards, where we might acquire the elements of gastronomic *savoir faire*.

I had already been to one formidable dinner party, the "Wake" of Henley's *National Observer*. It was perhaps not in the best possible taste to call it a wake, seeing that the new editor proprietor who had undertaken to carry on the life of the deceased, was present as a guest. George Wyndham, Nathaniel Curzon, Walter Sickert, Edgar Vincent (better known nowadays as Lord D'Abernon), G. S. Street, Arthur

Morrison, Bob Stevenson, Charles Baxter (R. L. S.'s business manager), H. B. Marriott Watson and other contributors to the paper were present. I am not sure whether J. M. Barrie and Rudyard Kipling were there, but both had been among Henley's men. I sat at the tail of a table, rather proud and scared, latest adherent to this gallant band. And because I was there at the end I was first to be served with a strange black blobby substance altogether unknown to me. I was there to enjoy myself and I helped myself to a generous portion. My next door neighbour—I rather fancy it was Basil Thomson—eyed the black mound upon my plate.

"I see you *like* caviar," he remarked.

"Love it," I said.

I didn't, but I ate it all. I had my proper pride.

That dinner was at Verrey's in Regent Street and I remember walking very gravely and carefully along the kerb of the pavement at a later hour, to convince myself that the exalted swimming in my head which had ensued upon the festival, was not in the nature of intoxication. If there had been a tight-rope handy leading straight out over the bottomless pit I suppose that in that mood of grave investigation I should have tried it. I decided that I was not drunk, but that I was "under the influence of alcohol." My literary ambitions were bringing me into a quite unanticipated world, full of strange sorts of food and still more various sorts of drink. A certain discretion might, I decided with a wary eye on the kerb, be necessary.

It was a good thing for me that behind the folding doors at 12 Mornington Road slept a fine and valiant little being, so delicate and clean and so credulous of my pretensions, that it would have been intolerable to appear before her unshaven or squalid or drunken or base. I lived through my Bohemian days as sober as Shaw if not nearly so teetotally.

Which reminds me of a bitter complaint I once heard in

the *Saturday Review* office from one of Harris's satellites. "When we're here'n the'vning all com'fly tight tha' fella Shaw comes in—dishgrashful shtate shobriety—talks and *talks* . . . AND TALKS."

§ 2
LYNTON, STATION ROAD, WOKING (1895)

I BEGAN THE NEW YEAR with my first and only regular job on a London daily. Cust had promised that I should have the next vacancy, whatever it was, on the *Pall Mall*, and the lot fell upon the dramatic criticism. I was summoned by telegram. " Here," said Cust and thrust two small pieces of coloured paper into my hand.

" What are these ? " I asked.

" Theatres. Go and do 'em."

" Yes," I said and reflected. " I'm willing to have a shot at it, but I ought to warn you that so far, not counting the Crystal Palace Pantomime and Gilbert and Sullivan, I've been only twice to a theatre."

" Exactly what I want," said Cust. " You won't be in the gang. You'll make a break."

" One wears evening dress ? "

It was not in Cust's code of manners to betray astonishment. " Oh yes. To-morrow night especially. The Haymarket."

We regarded each other thoughtfully for a moment. "Right oh," said I and hurried round to a tailor named Millar in Charles Street who knew me to be solvent. " Can you make me evening clothes by to-morrow night ? " I asked, " Or must I hire them ? "

The clothes were made in time but in the foyer I met Cust and George Steevens ready to supply a criticism if I failed them and nothing came to hand from me. But I did the job in a fashion and posted my copy fairly written out in its bright red envelope before two o'clock in the morning in the Mornington Road pillar box. The play was "*An Ideal Husband*, a new and original play of modern life by Oscar Wilde."

That was on the third of January 1895, and all went well. On the fifth I had to do *Guy Domville*, a play by Henry James at the St. James's Theatre. This was a more memorable experience. It was an extremely weak drama. James was a strange unnatural human being, a sensitive man lost in an immensely abundant brain, which had had neither a scientific nor a philosophical training, but which was by education and natural aptitude alike, formal, formally eesthetic, conscientiously fastidious and delicate. Wrapped about in elaborations of gesture and speech, James regarded his fellow creatures with a face of distress and a remote effort at intercourse, like some victim of enchantment placed in the centre of an immense bladder. His life was unbelievably correct and his home at Rye one of the most perfect pieces of suitably furnished Georgian architecture imaginable. He was an unspotted bachelor. He had always been well off and devoted to artistic ambitions; he had experienced no tragedy and he shunned the hoarse laughter of comedy; and yet he was consumed by a gnawing hunger for dramatic success. In this performance he had his first and last actual encounter with the theatre.

Guy Domville was one of those rare ripe exquisite Catholic Englishmen of ancient family conceivable only by an American mind, who gave up the woman he loved to an altogether coarser cousin, because his religious vocation was stronger than his passion. I forget the details of the action. There was a drinking scene in which Guy and the cousin, for some obscure purpose of discovery, pretended to drink and, instead, poured their wine furtively into a convenient bowl of flowers upon the table between them. Guy was played by George Alexander, at first in a mood of refined solemnity and then as the intimations of gathering disapproval from pit and gallery increased, with stiffening desperation. Alexander at the close had an incredibly awkward exit. He had to stand at a door in the middle of the stage, say slowly "Be keynd to Her. . . . *Be* keynd to Her" and depart. By nature Alexander had a long face, but at that moment with audible defeat before him, he seemed the longest and dismallest face, all face, that I have ever seen. The slowly closing door reduced him to a strip, to a line, of perpendicular gloom. The uproar burst like a thunderstorm as the door closed and the stalls responded with feeble applause. Then the tumult was mysteriously allayed. There were some minutes of uneasy apprehension. "Author" cried voices. "Au-thor!" The stalls, not understanding, redoubled their clapping.

Disaster was too much for Alexander that night. A spasm of hate for the writer of those fatal lines must surely have seized him. With incredible cruelty he led the doomed James, still not understanding clearly how things were with him, to the middle of the stage, and there the pit and gallery had him. James bowed; he knew it was the proper thing to bow. Perhaps he had selected a few words to say, but if so they went unsaid. I have never heard any sound more devastating than the crescendo of booing that ensued. The gentle applause of the stalls was altogether overwhelmed. For a moment or so James faced the storm, his round face white, his mouth opening and shutting and then Alexander, I hope in a contrite mood, snatched him back into the wings.

That was my first sight of Henry James with whom I was later to have a sincere yet troubled friendship. We were by nature and training profoundly unsympathetic. He was the most consciously and elaborately artistic and refined human being I ever encountered, and I swam in the common thought and feeling of my period, with an irregular abundance of rude knowledge, aggressive judgments and a disposition to get to close quarters with Madame Fact even if it meant a scuffle with her. James never scuffled with Fact; he treated her as a perfect and unchallengable lady; he never questioned a single stitch or flounce of the conventions and interpretations in which she presented herself. He thought that for every social occasion a correct costume could be prescribed and a correct behaviour defined. On the table (an excellent piece) in his hall at Rye lay a number of caps and hats, each with its appropriate gloves and sticks, a tweed cap and a stout stick for the Marsh, a soft comfortable deerstalker if he were to turn aside to the Golf Club, a light-brown felt hat and a cane for a morning walk down to the Harbour, a grey felt with a black band and a gold-headed cane of greater importance, if afternoon calling in the town was afoot. He retired at set times to a charming room in his beautiful walled garden and there he worked, dictating with a slow but not unhappy circumspection, the novels that were to establish his position in the world of discriminating readers. They are novels from which all the fiercer experiences are excluded; even their passions are so polite that one feels that they were gratified, even at their utmost intimacy, by a few seemly gestures; and yet the stories are woven with a peculiar humorous, faintly fussy, delicacy, that gives them a flavour like nothing else in the language. When you want to read and find reality too real, and hard storytelling tiresome, you may find Henry James good company. For generations to come a select type of reader will brighten appreciatively to the *Spoils of Poynton*, *The Ambassadors*, *The Tragic Muse*, *The Golden Bowl* and many of the stories.

I once saw James quarrelling with his brother William James, the psychologist. He had lost his calm; he was terribly unnerved. He appealed to me, to me of all people, to adjudicate on what was and what was not permissible behaviour in England. William was arguing about it in an indisputably American accent, with an indecently naked reasonableness. I had come to Rye with a car to fetch William James and his daughter to my home at Sandgate. William had none of Henry's passionate regard for the polish upon the surfaces of life and he was immensely excited by the fact that in the little Rye inn, which had its garden just over the high brick wall of the garden of Lamb House, G. K. Chesterton was staying. William James had corresponded with our vast contemporary and he sorely wanted to see him. So with a scandalous directness he had put the gardener's ladder against that ripe red wall and clambered up and peeped over!

Henry had caught him at it.

It was the sort of thing that isn't done. It was most emphatically the sort of thing that isn't done. . . . Henry had instructed the gardener to put away that ladder and William was looking thoroughly naughty about it.

To Henry's manifest relief, I carried William off and in the road just outside the town we ran against the Chestertons who had been for a drive in Romney Marsh; Chesterton was heated and I think rather swollen by the sunshine; he seemed to overhang his one-horse fly; he descended slowly but firmly; he was moist and steamy but cordial; we chatted in the road for a time and William got his coveted impression.

But reminiscence is running away with me. I return to the raw young dramatic critic standing amidst the astonished uneasy stallites under the storm that greeted *Guy Domville*. That hissing and booing may have contributed something to the disinclination I have always felt from any adventure into The Theatre.

On that eventful evening I scraped acquaintance with another interesting contemporary, Bernard Shaw. I had known him by sight since the Hammersmith days but I had never spoken to him before. Fires and civil commotions loosen tongues. I accosted him as a *Saturday Review* colleague and we walked back to our respective lodgings northward while he talked very interestingly about the uproar we had left behind us and the place of the fashionable three-act play amidst the eternal verities. He laid particular stress on the fact that nobody in the audience and hardly any of the caste, had realized the grace of Henry James's language.

Shaw was then a slender young man of thirty-five or so, very hard-up, and he broke the ranks of the boiled shirts and black and white ties in the stalls, with a modest brown jacket suit, a very white face and very red whiskers. (Now he has a very red face and very white whiskers, but it is still the same Shaw.) He talked like an elder brother to me in that agreeable Dublin English of his. I liked him with a liking that has lasted a life-time. In those days he was just a brilliant essayist and critic and an exasperating speaker in Socialist gatherings. He had written some novels that no one thought anything of, and his plays were still a secret between himself and his God.

From that time onward I saw him intermittently, but I did not see very much of him until I went into the Fabian Society, six or seven years later. Then he was a man in the forties and a much more important figure. He was married and he was no longer impecunious. His opinions and attitudes had developed and matured and so had mine. We found ourselves antagonistic on a number of issues and though we were not quite enough in the same field nor near enough in age to be rivals, there was from my side at any rate, a certain emulation between us.

We were both atheists and socialists; we were both attacking an apparently fixed and invincible social system from the outside; but this much resemblance did not prevent our carrying ourselves with a certain sustained defensiveness towards each other that remains to this day. In conversational intercourse a man's conclusions are of less importance than his training and the way he gets to them, and in this respect chasms of difference yawned between Shaw and myself, wider even than those that separated me from Henry James. I have tried to set out my own formal and informal education in a previous chapter. Shaw had had no such sustained and constructive mental training as I had been through, but on the other hand he had been saturated from his youth up in good music, brilliant conversation and the appreciative treatment of life. Extreme physical sensibility had forced him to adopt an austere teetotal and vegetarian way of living, and early circumstances, of which Ireland was not the least, had inclined him to rebellion and social protest; but otherwise he was as distinctly over against me and on the aesthetic side of life as Henry James. To him, I guess, I have always appeared heavily and sometimes formidably facty and close-set; to me his judgments, arrived at by feeling and expression, have always had a flimsiness. I want to get hold of Fact, strip off her inessentials and, if she behaves badly put her in stays and irons; but Shaw dances round her and weaves a wilful veil of confident assurances about her as her true presentment. He thinks one can " put things over " on Fact and I do not. He philanders with her. I have no delusions about the natural goodness and wisdom of human beings and at bottom I am grimly and desperately educational. But Shaw's conception of education is to let dear old Nature rip. He has got no further in that respect than Rousseau. Then I know, fundamentally, the heartless impartiality of natural causation, but Shaw makes Evolution something brighter and softer, by endowing it with an ultimately benevolent Life Force, acquired, quite uncritically I feel, from his friend and adviser Samuel Butler. We have been fighting this battle with each other all our lives. We had a brisk exchange of letters after the publication of the *Science of Life*.

But let me return to those theatrical first nights of mine. None of the criticism I wrote was ever anything but dull. I did not understand the theatre. I was out of my place there. I do not think I am made to understand the theatre, but at any rate I never sat down to ask myself, " What is all this stage stuff about ? What is the gist of this complex unreality ? " If I had done so, then I should have emerged with a point of view and data for adequate critical writing— even if that writing had turned out to be only a denunciation of all the existing methods and machinery.

Shaw like James and like his still more consciously cultivated disciple, Granville Barker, believed firmly in The Theatre as a finished and definite something demanding devotion ; offering great opportunities to the human mind. He perceived indeed there was something very wrong with it, he demanded an endowed theatre, a different criticism, a different audience than the common " Theatre-goer " we knew, but in the end he could imagine this gathering of several hundred people for three hours entertainment on a stage becoming something very fine and important and even primary in the general life. I had no such belief. I was forming a conception of a new sort of human community with an unprecedented way of life, and it seemed to me to be a minor detail whether this boxed-up performance of plays, would occur at all in that ampler existence I anticipated. "Shows" there will certainly be, in great variety in the modern civilization ahead, very wonderful blendings of thought, music and vision ; but except by way of archaeological revival, I can see no footlights, proscenium, prompter's box, playwright and painted players there.

Of course this wasn't clear in my mind in the nineties, but I did fail to find The Theatre sufficiently important adequately to stir my wits and so if for no other reason my work as a dramatic critic was flat and spiritless. Yet I saw some good plays. In Wilde's *Importance of Being Earnest* Alexander did a magnificent piece of work that completely effaced his Guy Domville from my mind, and in Pinero's *Notorious Mrs. Ebbsmith* I saw and heard young Mrs. Pat Campbell, with her flexible body and her delightful voice, for the first time.

After the wear of a month or so for my new dress clothes my rough but essentially benevolent personal Providence appreciated the listlessness of this forced uncongenial work and intervened to stop it. I caught a bad cold, streaks of blood appeared again, and once more the impossibility of my moving about in London in all weather was demonstrated. I resigned The Theatre into better hands, those of G. S. Street, who was later to be a gentle and understanding Censor of Plays, and I set about finding a little house in the country, where I could follow up with another book the success that I felt was coming to the *Time Machine* and my short-story volume.

Our withdrawal to Woking was a fairly cheerful adventure. Woking was the site of the first crematorium but few of our friends made more than five or six jokes about that. We borrowed a hundred pounds by a mortgage on Mrs. Robbins' house in Putney and with that hundred pounds, believe it or not, we furnished a small resolute semi-detached villa with a minute greenhouse in the Maybury Road facing the railway line, where all night long the goods trains shunted and bumped and clattered—without serious effect

FAIRLY LAUNCHED AT LAST

upon our healthy slumbers. Close at hand in those days was a pretty and rarely used canal amidst pine woods, a weedy canal, beset with loosestrife, spiræa, forget-me-nots and yellow water lilies, upon which one could be happy for hours in a hired canoe, and in all directions stretched open and undeveloped heath land, so that we could walk and presently learn to ride bicycles and restore our broken contact with the open air. There I planned and wrote the *War of the Worlds*, the *Wheels of Chance* and the *Invisible Man*. I learnt to ride my bicycle upon sandy tracks with none but God to help me; he chastened me considerably in the process, and after a fall one day I wrote down a description of the state of my legs which became the opening chapter of the *Wheels of Chance*. I rode wherever Mr. Hoopdrive rode in that story. Later on I wheeled about the district marking down suitable places and people for destruction by my Martians. The bicycle in those days was still very primitive. The diamond frame had appeared but there was no free-wheel. You could only stop and jump off when the treadle was at its lowest point, and the brake was an uncertain plunger upon the front wheel. Consequently you were often carried on beyond your intentions, as when Mr. Polly upset the zinc dust-bins outside the shop of Mr. Rusper. Nevertheless the bicycle was the swiftest thing upon the roads in those days, there were as yet no automobiles and the cyclist had a lordliness, a sense of masterful adventure, that has gone from him altogether now.

Jane was still a very fragile little being and as soon as I had sufficiently mastered the art of wheeling I got a tandem bicycle of a peculiar shape made for us by the Humber people and we began to wander about the south of England, very agreeably. But here I think a photograph and a selection of picshuas may take up the story again. The first picshua shows us starting out upon an expedition that

carried us at last across Dartmoor to Cornwall and the second shows Jane engaging her first domestic servant.

We lived very happily and industriously in the Woking home for a year and a half and then my mother-in-law fell ill and for a time it was necessary that she should live with us, so that we had to move to a larger house at Worcester Park. We had married as soon as I was free to do so. By the time of our removal, our circle of acquaintances and friends had increased very considerably. I will not catalogue names but one friendly figure stands out amidst much other friendliness, that once much reviled and now rather too much forgotten writer, Grant Allen. I do not think I have ever made a fair acknowledgement of a certain mental indebtedness to him. Better thirty-five years late than never.

He was about twenty years older than I. He had been a science teacher in the West Indies and he was full of the new wine of aggressive Darwinism. He came back to England and, in that fresh illumination, began writing books for the general reader and essays in natural history. He was a successful popularizer and he had a very pronounced streak of speculative originality. But he had the schoolmaster trick of dogmatism and a rash confidence in every new idea that seized upon him. In these days no editor paid very much for scientific contributions and James Payne, the editor of the *Cornhill Magazine*, showed him that the better way to prosperity was to travel abroad and write conventional novels about places of interest to British tourists. The middle-class British and Americans who were beginning to travel very freely in Europe were delighted to read easy stories of sentiment and behaviour introducing just the places they had visited and the sights they had seen. With this work Grant Allen achieved a reasonable popularity and prosperity. But he was uneasy in his prosperity. He had had an earlier infection of that same ferment of biology and socialism that was working in my blood. He wanted not merely to enjoy life but to do something to it. Social injustice and sexual limitation bothered his mind, and he was critical of current ideas and accepted opinions. I myself was destined to go through roughly parallel phases of uneasiness and to fall even more definitely under the advancing intimations of the different life of the coming world-state.

Like myself Grant Allen had never found a footing in the professional scientific world and he had none of the patience, deliberation—and discretion—of the established scientific worker, who must live with a wholesome fear of the Royal Society and its inhibitions before his eyes. Grant Allen's semi-popular original scientific works such as his *Origin of the Idea of God* (1897) and his *Physiological Aesthetics* (1877) were at once bold and sketchy, unsupported by properly verified quotations and collated references, and regardless or manifestly ignorant of much other contemporary work. They were too original to be fair popularization and too unsubstantiated to be taken seriously by serious specialists, and what was good in them has been long since appropriated, generally without acknowledgement, by sounder workers, while the flimsy bulk of them moulders on a few dusty and forgotten shelves. His anthropology became an easy butt for the fuller scholarship and livelier style of Andrew Lang.

His attempt to change himself over from a regularly selling, proper English "purveyor of fiction" to the novelist with ideas and initiative and so contribute materially to vital literature was equally unfortunate. In that also he was, so to speak, an undecided amphibian, an Amblystoma, never quite sure whether he had come out of the water for good or not. He had always to earn a living, and the time left over from that, just as it had not been enough either for the patient and finished research needed to win respect in the scientific world, was now not enough for the thorough and well thought-out novel of aggressive reality.

Later on I was to be in much the same case. In his spare time, so to speak, and unaware that the devices and methods of the ordinary trade novel are exactly what cannot be used for fresh matter, he wrote what was really a sentimental novelette, *The Woman Who Did*. He tried (I am sure with a hurried pen) to present a woman who deliberately broke the rigid social conventions of the period and bore an illegitimate child as "her very own," and, without any intensive effort to conceive her personality, he tried to tell the story so that she should be sympathetic for the common-place reader. That was a most dangerous and difficult thing to attempt, and since, later on, I was to try out something of a kindred sort in *Ann Veronica*, *The New Machiavelli* and *The Wife of Sir Isaac Harman*, I can bear my expert witness to the difficulty of the technical miracle he was so glibly setting about to perform. My mature persuasion is that the distance a novel can carry a reader out of his or her moral and social preconceptions is a very short one. I think a novel can do more than a play in this way; I don't believe an audience in a theatre has ever budged a bit from its established standards of conduct for anything that has been put on the stage; but in either case what principally occurs is recognition and response. The most fatal thing that can be done is to "assume" the rightness of the new standard you are putting over. This was done excessively in *The Woman Who Did*. Stupid people will never read anything with which they do not agree, so what is the good of trying to write down to them? And even quite intelligent people will read and consider an account of strange defiant behaviour only if it is neither glorified nor extenuated but put before them simply as a vitalized statement. "Look here!" you must say, "What do you think of this?" So

FAIRLY LAUNCHED AT LAST 549

long as they are interested, judging freely, and not bristling with resentful resistance, you are doing the job. But everybody bristled at *The Woman Who Did*.

I bristled. I was infuriated. I was the more infuriated because I was so nearly in agreement with Grant Allen's ideas, that this hasty, headlong, incompetent book seemed like a treason to a great cause. It was, I felt, opening a breach to the enemy. So I slated him with care and intensity, in this style :

" We have endeavoured to piece this character together, and we cannot conceive the living woman. She is, he assures us with a certain pathos, a ' real woman.' But one doubts it from the outset. ' A living proof of the doctrine of heredity ' is her own idea, but that is scarcely the right effect of her. Mr. Grant Allen seems nearer the truth when he describes her as ' a solid rock of ethical resolution.' Her solidity is witnessed to by allusions to her ' opulent form ' and the ' lissom grace of her rounded figure.' Fancy a girl with an ' opulent ' form ! Her ' face was, above all things, the face of a free woman,' a ' statuesque ' face, and upon this Mr. Grant Allen has chiselled certain inappropriate ' dimples,' which mar but do not modify that statuesque quality. ' She was too stately of mien ever to grant a favour without granting it of pure grace and with a queenly munificence '—when Alan kissed her. She dresses in a ' sleeveless sack embroidered with arabesques,' and such-like symbolic garments. So much goes to convey her visible presence. The reader must figure her sackful of lissom opulence and her dimpled, statuesque features for himself—the picture eludes us. She had a ' silvery voice.' The physical expression of her emotions was of two kinds, a blush, and a ' thrill to the finger-tips.' This last phrase is always cropping up, though we must confess we can attach no meaning to it ourselves and cannot imagine Mr. Grant Allen doing so. Her soul is ' spotless.' Never did she do anything wrong. (And this is a ' real woman ' !) When Alan called to see her on some trivial business ' she sat a lonely soul, enthroned amid the halo of her own perfect purity '—a curious way of receiving visitors. She is ' pure ' and ' pellucid ' and ' noble,' and so forth on every page almost.

And at the crisis she 'would have flaunted the open expression of her supreme moral faith before the eyes of all London,' had not Alan, the father of the baby in question, with 'virile self-assertion' restrained her.

"Clearly this is not a human being. No more a human being than the women twelve hands tall of the fashion magazines. Had her author respected her less he might have drawn her better. Surely Mr. Grant Allen has lived long enough to know that real women do not have spotless souls and a physical beauty that is invariably overpowering. Real women are things of dietary and secretions, of subtle desires and mental intricacy; even the purest among them have at least beauty spots upon their souls. This monstrous Herminia—where did he get her? Assuredly not of observation and insight. She seems to us to be a kind of plaster-cast of 'Pure Womanhood' in a halo, with a soul of abstractions, a machine to carry out a purely sentimental principle to its logical conclusion. Alan, her lover, is a kind of ideal prig, 'a pure soul in his way, and mixed of the finer paste' from which the heroes of inferior novels are made. The Dean, her father, is the sympathetic but prejudiced cleric of modern comedy. The source of Ethel Waterton is acknowledged: she 'was a most insipid blonde from the cover of a chocolate-box.' Dolores, for whom Mr. Grant Allen feels least, for or against, is far and away the best character in the book. She is so, we think, for that very reason.

"Now the book professes to be something more than an artistic story, true to life. It is, we are led to infer, an ethical discussion. But is it? The problem of marriage concerns terrestrial human beings, and the ingratitude of the offspring of a plaster-cast, though wonderful enough, bears no more on our moral difficulties than the incubation of Semele, or the birth of the Minotaur. In these problem novels at least, truth is absolutely essential. But to handle the relation of the sexes truly needs a Jean Paul Richter, or a George Meredith. It is not to be done by desiring.

"And the gospel Mr. Grant Allen—who surely knows that life is one broad battlefield—is preaching: what is it? It is the emancipation of women. He does not propose to emancipate them from the narrowness, the sexual savagery, the want of charity, that are the sole causes of the miseries of the illegitimate and the unfortunate. Instead he wishes to emancipate them from monogamy, which we have hitherto regarded as being more of a fetter

FAIRLY LAUNCHED AT LAST

upon virile instincts. His proposal is to abolish cohabitation, to abolish the family—that school of all human gentleness—and to provide support for women who may have children at the expense of the State. We are all to be foundlings together, and it will be an inquisitive child who knows its own father. Now Mr. Grant Allen must know perfectly well that amorous desires and the desire to bear children are anything but overpowering impulses in many of the very noblest women. The women, who would inevitably have numerous children under the conditions he hopes for, would be the hysterically erotic, the sexually incontinent. *Why* he should make proposals to cultivate humanity in this direction is not apparent. We find fine handsome sayings about Truth and Freedom, but any establishment for his proposition a reviewer much in sympathy with him on many of his opinions fails altogether to discover in his book. A fellowship of two based on cohabitation and protected by jealousy, with or without the marriage ceremony, seems as much the natural destiny of the average man as of the eagle or the tiger.

" And we have a quarrel, too, with the style of the book. Had Mr. Grant Allen really cared, as he intimates he cared, for truth and beauty, had he really loved this Herminia of his creation, would he have put her forth in such style as he has done? ' Ordinary,' ' stereotyped,' ' sordid,' ' ignoble,' are among the adjectives he applies to the respectable villadom he identifies with the English people. Yet every one of them fits the workmanship he has considered worthy of his heroine."

And so on. Twenty years later I was, by the bye, to find myself in a position almost parallel to that of Grant Allen with my *Passionate Friends*, which in its turn was slated furiously and in much the same spirit by the younger generation in the person of Rebecca West. But I have never been able to persuade myself that I deserved that trouncing quite as much as Grant Allen merited his.

He behaved charmingly. He wrote me a very pleasant invitation to come and talk to him and I ran down by train one Sunday, walked up from Haslemere station and lunched with him in Hindhead. In these days Hindhead was a lonely place in a great black, purple and golden wilderness of heath ; there was an old inn called The Huts and a score of partly hidden houses. Tyndall had built a house there, Conan Doyle was close by, Richard Le Gallienne occupied a cottage as tenant, motor-cars and suburbanism were still a dozen years away. Le Gallienne came in after lunch. His sister was staying in the house with her husband, James Welsh, the actor. We sat about in deck chairs through a long sunny summer afternoon under the pines in the garden on the edge of the Devil's Punch Bowl.

Across the interval of years I do not recall that wandering conversation with any precision. Probably we talked a lot about writing and getting on in the world of books. I was a new and aggressive beginner in that world and I was being welcomed very generously. And also I suppose we must have talked of the subject of *The Woman Who Did* and its related issues. Grant Allen and I were in the tradition of Godwin and Shelley. Its trend was to force a high heroic independence on women—even on quite young women. But Grant Allen who had something in him—I will not say like a Faun or a Satyr, but rather like the earnest Uncle of these woodland folk, was all for the girls' showing spirit. I was rather enwrapped then in my private situation. Le Gallienne was an Amorist and he trailed a flavour of Swinburne and Renascence Italy—Browning's Renascence Italy, across our talk.

When history is properly written, it will be interesting to trace the Amorist through the ages. There have been phases when the Amorist has dominated manners and costume and decoration and phases when he has been rather shamefaced and occasional in the twilight and the bushes and the staircase to the ballroom. The Amorist just then was in the ascendant phase, and Richard Le Gallienne was the chief of our Amorists. He was busy then with prose fancies in

FAIRLY LAUNCHED AT LAST

which roses and raptures and restaurants were very attractively combined, and he was inciting the youth of our period to set out upon the Quest of the Golden Girl. He was long and slender with a handsome white half-feminine face, expressive hands and a vast shock of black hair. I found him an entertaining contrast to myself and we got on very well together until suddenly he went out of the literary world of London to America.

I add three other picshuas from the Woking period here. They will amuse some readers. Others will find them detestable, but after all, this is my autobiography. One records a horticultural triumph not uncommon in suburban gardens. The other two are vain-glorious to the ultimate degree. The last of the three reeks with the " shop " of authorship ; one observes also the pride of Jane, the author's family in a state of wonder, the envious hostile reviewer with a forked tail, press cutting (from Romeike), much sordid exultation about royalties and cheques. But we were very young still, we had had a hard and risky time and it was exciting to succeed.

September 9th 1895

We cut our first Manord.

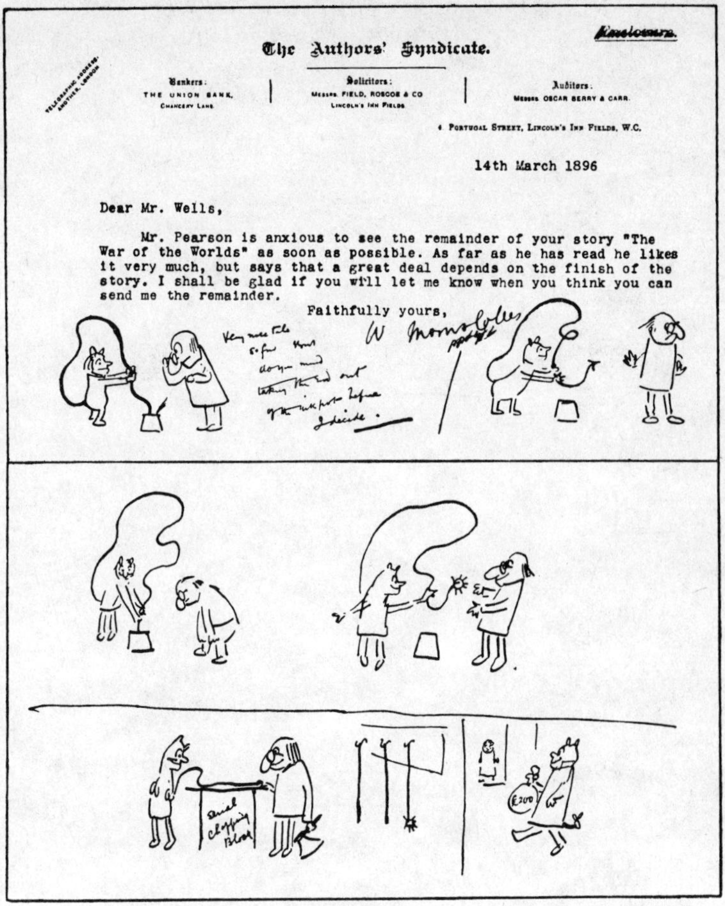

The Authors' Syndicate.

Bankers:
THE UNION BANK,
Chancery Lane

Solicitors:
Messrs. FIELD, ROSCOE & CO
Lincoln's Inn Fields

Auditors:
Messrs. OSCAR BERRY & CARR.

4 Portugal Street, Lincoln's Inn Fields, W.C.

14th March 1896

Dear Mr. Wells,

Mr. Pearson is anxious to see the remainder of your story "The War of the Worlds" as soon as possible. As far as he has read he likes it very much, but says that a great deal depends on the finish of the story. I shall be glad if you will let me know when you think you can send me the remainder.

Faithfully yours,

W Morris Colles

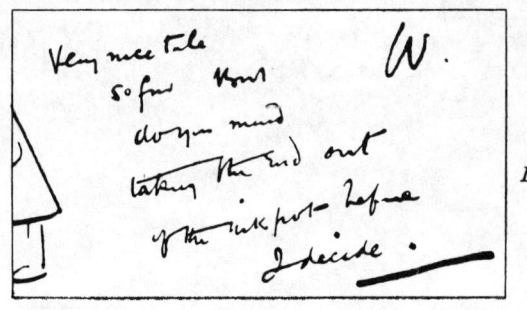

Detail

§ 3
Heatherlea, Worcester Park (1896–1897)

I THINK I HAVE sufficiently conveyed now the flavour of my new way of life and I will not go with any great particularity into the details of my history after we had moved to Worcester Park. I will trust a few picshuas to carry on the tale. This Worcester Park house had two fairly big rooms downstairs, a visitor's room and a reasonably large garden and we started a practice of keeping open house on Saturday afternoons which improved our knowledge of the many new friends we were making. Among others who stayed with us was Dorothy Richardson, a schoolmate of Jane's. Dorothy has a very distinctive literary gift, acute intensity of expression and an astonishingly vivid memory; her "*Pilgrimage*" books are a very curious essay in autobiography; they still lack their due meed of general appreciation; and in one of them, *The Tunnel*, she has described our Worcester Park life with astonishing accuracy. I figure as Hypo in that description and Jane is Alma.

The first picshua here shows our daily routine and our domestic humour in full swing. This is documentary evidence of Jane's participation in my early work and of the punishments and discipline alleged to prevail during the writing of *When the Sleeper Awakes* and *Love and Mr. Lewisham*. The next records my return to the *Fortnightly Review* and what I think must have been a dinner at the *New Vagabonds Club* at which I seem to have been the guest of honour. The third records details of this glorious occasion. The waiter seems to have missed me for ice pudding; the figures who bow before Jane are J. K. Jerome, Sidney Low, Douglas Sladen and Kenneth Grahame (of the immortal *Wind in the Willows*). Vain-glory is again offensively evident.

Nov 18/96.

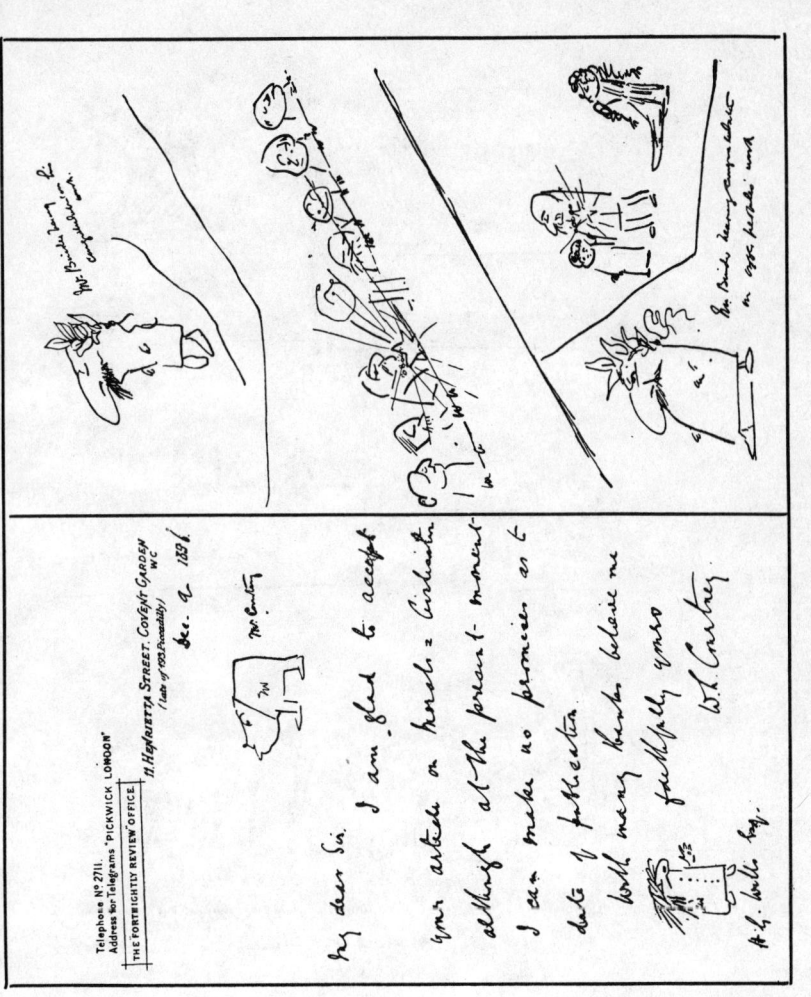

Telephone No 2711.
Address for Telegrams "PICKWICK, LONDON"
THE FORTNIGHTLY REVIEW OFFICE.
11, Henrietta Street, Covent Garden WC
(late of 193 Piccadilly)

Dec. 2. 1891.

My dear Sir,

I am glad to accept your article on Herald & Lichtenstein although at the present moment I can make no promise as to date of publication.

With many thanks believe me
faithfully yours
W. L. Courtney

H. L. Wells Esq.

The next picshua records our industry in our Heatherlea garden under the direction of our jobbing gardener (one day a week) Mr. Tilbury. The date of this particular picshua, as the small figure in the corner indicates, was the day of publication of the *Invisible Man*, a tale, that thanks largely to the excellent film recently produced by James Whale, is still read as much as ever it was. To many young people nowadays I am just the author of the *Invisible Man*. The writing on Jane's foot, by the bye, is " gloshers," which is, so to speak, idiotic for galosh. But why I wrote that word in that fashion, is—like the mating cry of the pterodactyl and the hunting habits of the labyrinthodon—lost in the mist of the past.

Next comes a picshua full of self-congratulations. " The improvement of a certain person's mind " has been resumed. Jane made a brief attempt to take up her B.Sc. degree work again, but that was presently abandoned. The shelf of our books is filling up. At an Omar Khayyám dinner I had met George Gissing and he was very anxious for us to go with him to Italy in the spring. We study a guide to Italy.

The next picshua shows the Italian project maturing. Jane was still far from strong and she had been ordered an iron tonic. We brace ourselves to face the danger of malaria and the austerities of a Roman breakfast. Neither of us had ever been across the channel before; Jane had some French and German, but my knowledge of languages was limited to the decaying remains of my swift matriculation cramming of exceptions. All that had been written work and I did not so much pronounce as block out rude masses of misconceived sound. " Abroad " was a slightly terrifying world of adventure for us. And we were not going to just nibble at the continent. We were going straight through, at one bite, to Rome.

FAIRLY LAUNCHED AT LAST

We did go to Rome in the spring of 1898. We spent a month there with Gissing and then went on by ourselves to Naples, Capri, Pompeii, Amalfi and Paestum. Capri and Paestum cropped up a little later in a short story, *A Vision of Armageddon*. We acquired a traveller's smattering of Italian, a number of photographs, some glowing memories and brighter ideas about diet and wine. We returned by way of Switzerland and Ostend. The uneasy social life of nineteenth century Europe was in a phase of inflammation. In Naples people were rioting for " Pane e Lavoro ! " and in the square outside our hotel in Brussels there was a demonstration, and the crowd was singing the Marseillaise and fired a revolver or so.

George Gissing was a strange tragic figure, a figure of internal tragedy, and it is only slowly that I have realized the complex of his misfortunes. There is a novel about him by Morley Roberts *The Private Life of Henry Maitland* (1912) which tells the substance of his tale with considerable inaccuracy, and there is an admirable study of his life and work by Frank Swinnerton, so good that it would be officious and impertinent for me to parallel it, however briefly, here. The portrait by Sir William Rothenstein which figures in Swinnerton's book could hardly be bettered. I had read and admired Gissing's *In the Year of Jubilee* and his *New Grub Street* before I met him and I began our first conversation by remarking upon the coincidence that Reardon, in the latter book, lived like myself as a struggling writer in Mornington Road with a wife named Amy. This was at an Omar Khayyám dinner whither I had gone as the guest of either Grant Allen or Edmund Clodd (I forget which). Gissing was then an extremely good-looking, well-built man, slightly on the lean side, blond, with a good profile and a splendid leonine head; his appearance betraying little then of the poison that had crept into his blood to distress, depress and undermine his vitality and at last to destroy him. He spoke in a rotund Johnsonian manner, but what he had to say was reasonable and friendly. I asked him to come over to us at Worcester Park and his visit was the beginning of a long intimacy.

He talked very much of ill health and I tried to make him a cyclist, for he took no exercise at all except walking, and I thought it might be pleasant to explore Surrey and Sussex with him, but he was far too nervous and excitable to ride. It was curious to see this well-built Viking, blowing and funking as he hopped behind his machine. " Get on to your ironmongery," said I. He mounted, wabbled a few yards, and fell off shrieking with laughter. " Ironmongery ! " he gasped. " Oh ! riding on ironmongery ! " and lay in the grass at the roadside, helpless with mirth. He loved laughter and that was a great link between us—I liked to explode him with some slight twist of phrase. He could be very easily surprised and shocked to mirth, because he had a scholar's disposition to avoid novel constructions and unusual applications of words. In the summer of 1897, Jane and I spent some weeks or so at Budleigh Salterton near to a lodging he had taken and then it was that our daring adventure " abroad " was conceived.

I knew nothing in those days of his early life, of how in his precocious teens he had wrecked his career as a scholar by a liaison with a young street-walker, a liaison which had led to some difficulties about money and a police court. Friends appeared to rescue him but nobody seems to have troubled about her. He was sent to America for a fresh start and the effect of a fresh start under conditions of sexual deprivation in Boston, had been to send him in flight to Chicago and then bring him back in a recoil to England, to hunt out and marry his mistress. They lived dismally in lodgings while he tried to write great novels. For her it was an intolerable life. She left him and died in hospital.

Clearly there was for him something about this woman, of which no record remains, some charm, some illusion or at any rate some specific attraction, for which he never had words. She was his Primary Fixation. For him she had been Woman. All this was past, but he had created a new situation for himself by picking up a servant girl in Regent's Park one Sunday afternoon and marrying her. Told thus baldly the thing is almost incredible, and an analysis of his motives here would take an extravagant amount of space. His home training had made him repressive to the explosive pitch; he felt that to make love to any woman he could regard as a social equal would be too elaborate, restrained and tedious for his urgencies, he could not answer questions he supposed he would be asked about his health and means, and so, for the second time, he flung himself at a social inferior whom he expected to be easy and grateful. This second marriage was also a failure; failure was inevitable; the new wife became a resentful, jealous scold. But we never saw her and I cannot judge between them. To us Gissing was just himself. " I cannot ask you to my home," he said. " Impossible—quite impossible. Oh quite impossible. I have to dismiss any such ideas. I have no home."

He did not always keep such ideas dismissed, but for the most part they were out of the picture. He kept his own family also, the custodians of those strangling early standards, out of our way, just as he kept his wife out of our way. He was terrified at the prospect of incompatibility. His sensitiveness to reactions made every relationship a pose, and he had no natural customary *persona* for miscellaneous use.

The Gissing I knew, therefore, was essentially a specially posed mentality, a personal response, and his effect upon me was an extraordinary blend of a damaged joy-loving human being hampered by inherited gentility and a classical education. He craved to laugh, jest, enjoy, stride along against the wind, shout, "quaff mighty flagons." But his upbringing behind the chemist's shop in Wakefield had been one of repressive gentility, where "what will the neighbours *think* of us?" was more terrible than the thunder of God. The insanity of our educational organization had planted down in that Yorkshire town, a grammar school dominated by the idea of classical scholarship. The head was an enthusiastic pedant who poured into that fresh and vigorous young brain nothing but classics and a "scorn" for non-classical things. Gissing's imagination therefore escaped from the cramping gentilities and respectability of home to find its compensations in the rhetorical swagger, the rotundities and the pompous grossness of Rome. He walked about Wakefield in love with goddesses and nymphs and excited by ideas of patrician freedoms in a world of untouchable women. Classics men according to their natures are all either "Latins" or "Hellenes." Gissing was a Latin, oratorical and not scientific, unanalytical, unsubtle and secretly haughty. He accepted and identified himself with all the pretensions of Rome's triumphal arches.

His knowledge of classical Rome was extraordinarily full. We found him, there, an unsparing enthusiastic guide. With a sort of a shamed hostility indeed he recognized the vestiges of mediaevalism and the Renascence that cumbered the spectacle. But that was just a subsequent defilement, like mud on the marble of a submerged palace. At the back of his mind, a splendid Olympus to our Roman excursions, stood noble senators in togas, marvellous matrons like Lucrece, gladiators proud to die, Horatiuses ready to leap into gulfs *pro patria*, the finest fruit of humanity, unjudged, accepted, speaking like epitaphs and epics, and by these standards also he measured the mundane swarm he pictured *In the Year of Jubilee*. For that thin yet penetrating juice of shrewd humour, of kindly stoicisms, of ready trustfulness, of fitful indignations and fantastic and often grotesque generosities, which this dear London life of ours exudes, he had no palate. I have never been able to decide how much that defect of taste was innate or how far it was a consequence partly of the timid pretentiousness of his home circumstances, and partly of that pompous grammatical training to which his brain was subjected just in his formative years. I favour the latter alternative. I favour it because of his ready abundant fits of laughter. You do not get laughter without release, and you must have something suppressed to release. " Preposterous ! " was a favourite word with him. He told me once of how he was awakened at three in the morning in a London hotel by a clatter of milk cans under his window. He lay in bed helpless with laughter that civilization should produce this marvel of a chamber designed for sleeping, just over a yard where the rattling of milk cans was an inevitable nightly event.

At the back of my mind I thought him horribly miseducated and he hardly troubled to hide from me his opinion that I was absolutely illiterate. Each of us had his secret amusement in the other's company. He knew the Greek epics and plays to a level of frequent quotation but I think he took his classical philosophers as read and their finality for granted ; he assumed that modern science and thought were merely degenerate recapitulations of their lofty and inaccessible wisdom. The transforming forces of the world about us he ascribed to a certain rather regrettable " mechanical ingenuity " in our people. He thought that a classical scholar need only turn over a few books to master all that scientific work and modern philosophy had made of the world, and it did not disillusion him in the least that he had no mastery of himself or any living fact in existence. He was entirely enclosed in a defensive phraseology and a conscious " scorn " of the " baser " orders and " ignoble " types. When he laughed he called the world "Preposterous," but when he could not break through to reality and laughter then his word was "Sordid." That readiness to call common people "base" "sordid" "mean," "the vulgar sort" and so forth was less evident in the man's nature than in his writings. Some of his books will be read for many generations, but because of this warping of his mind they will find fewer lovers than readers. In Swinnerton's book one can see that kindly writer starting out with a real admiration and sympathy for his subject and gradually beinge stranged by the injustice, the faint cruelty of this mannered ungraciousness towards disadvantaged people.

Through Gissing I was confirmed in my suspicion that this orthodox classical training which was once so powerful an antiseptic against Egyptian dogma and natural superstitions, is now no longer a city of refuge from barbaric predispositions. It has become a vast collection of monumental masonry, a pale cemetery in a twilight, through which new conceptions hurry apologetically on their way to town, finding neither home nor sustenance there. It is a cemetery, which like that churchyard behind Atlas House, Bromley, can give little to life but a certain sparkle in the water and breed nothing any more but ghosts, *ignes fatui* and infections. It has ceased to be a field of education and become a proper hunting ground for the archaeologist and social psychologist.

So, full of friendly antagonisms, Gissing, Jane and I went about Rome together, our brains reacting and exchanging very abundantly. It was Rome before the mischiefs of Mayor Nathan, before the vast vulgarity of the Vittorio Emmanuele monument had ruined the Piazza Venezia, and when the only main thoroughfare was the Corso. The Etruscan tombs still slept undiscovered in the Forum and instead of Boni's flower beds there were weeds and wild flowers. Walking through some fields near Tivoli the *Story of Miss Winchelsea's Heart* came into my head—and I remember telling it to Gissing.

Gissing, like Gibbon, regarded Christianity as a deplorable disaster for the proud gentilities of classicism and left us to " do " the Vatican and St. Peter's by ourselves. In many of the darkened, incense-saturated churches, I felt old Egypt and its mysteries still living and muttering, but the papal city and its swarming pilgrims, its libraries and galleries, its observatory, its Renascence architecture, filled me with perplexing impressions. Much more than pomp, tradition and decay was manifest in these activities. The Scarlet Woman of my youthful prejudices was not in evidence. Protestantism, I perceived, had not done justice to Renascence Rome.

Here, quite plainly, was a great mental system engaged in a vital effort to comprehend its expanding universe and sustain a co-ordinating conception of human activities. That easy word " superstition " did not cover a tithe of it.

It dawned upon me that there had been a Catholic Reformation as drastic as and perhaps profounder than the Protestant Reformation, and that the mentality of clerical Rome, instead of being an unchanged system *in saecula saeculorum* had been stirred to its foundations at that time and was still struggling—like everything else alive—in the grip of adaptive necessity. In spite of my anti-Christian bias I found something congenial in the far flung cosmopolitanism of the Catholic proposition. Notwithstanding its synthesis of decaying ancient theologies and its strong taint of otherworldishness, the Catholic Church continues to be, in its own half-hearted fashion, an Open Conspiracy to reorganize the whole life of man. If the papal system had achieved the ambitions of its most vigorous period, it would have been much more in the nature of that competent receiver for human affairs, the research for which has occupied my mind so largely throughout my life, than that planless Providentialism which characterized almost all the political and social thought of the nineteenth century. Catholicism is something greater in scope and spirit than any nationalist protestantism and immeasurably above such loutish reversions to hate as Hitlerism or the Ku-Klux-Klan. I should even hesitate to call it " reactionary " without some qualification.

I have lived for many years in open controversy with Catholicism and though, naturally enough, I have sometimes been insulted by indignant zealots, I have found the ordinary Catholic controversialist a fair fighter and a civilized man—worthy of that great cultural system within which such minds as Leonardo and Michael Angelo could develop and find expression. He has an antiquated realist philosophy which too often gives him a sort of pert hardness, but that is another matter. It is a question too fine for me to discuss whether I am an outright atheist or an extreme heretic on the furthest verge of Christendom—beyond the Aryans, beyond the Manichaeans. But certainly I branch from the Catholic stem.

Let me however return from this Vatican excursion to George Gissing. That disposition to get away from entangling conditions which is manifest in almost every type of imaginative worker, accumulated in his case to quite desperate fugitive drives. In Italy with us he was in flight from his second wife. The dreadful intimacy of that isolated life at Ewell, without a thought in common, an intimacy of perpetual recrimination, had become intolerable. A well-known educationist, a woman who had evidently a very great admiration for Gissing, had proposed to take in Mrs. Gissing and the children and try to establish tolerable relations with her, to " educate " her in fact, while Gissing recovered his mental peace in his beloved Italy. But the

FAIRLY LAUNCHED AT LAST

experiment was not working well; the helpful lady was meddling with things beyond her experience and the poor wife, perplexed and indignant beyond measure by this strange man who had possessed himself of her life, was progressing through scenes and screams towards a complete mental breakdown; she was behaving very badly indeed, and letters would arrive at the Hotel Aliberti in Rome, that left Gissing white and shaking between anger and dismay for the better part of a day. The best thing then was to go off with him outside Rome to some wayside albergo, to the Milvian bridge, or towards Tivoli or along the Appian Way, drink rough red wine, get him talking Italian to peasants, launch out upon wild social, historical and ethnological discussions, and gradually push the gnawing trouble into the background again.

This poor vexed brain—so competent for learning and aesthetic reception, so incompetent, so impulsive and weakly yielding under the real stresses of life—went on from us into Calabria and produced there *By the Ionian Sea* and, later on, after returning to England, *The Private Papers of Henry Ryecroft*. The interest of these books, with their halting effort to pose as a cultivated leisurely eighteenth century intelligence, is, I think, greatly intensified by the realization that beneath the struggle to sustain that *persona*, the pitiless hunt of consequences, the pursuit of the monstrous penalties exacted for a false start and a foolish and inconsiderate decision or so, was incessant. Perhaps Gissing was made to be hunted by Fate. He never turned and fought. He always hid or fled.

Presently we were back at Worcester Park and he was established with a " worthy housekeeper," a cook general in fact, in a cottage in Dorking. The wife was still being hushed up by the friend in London and did not know of his whereabouts. He was intensely solitary and miserable at Dorking.

One day he came to us with a request. There was a proposal from a Frenchwoman to translate his novels into French. He wished to confer with her. Impossible for a lone man to entertain a strange lady at Dorking; would we arrange a meeting?

They lunched with us and afterwards they walked in our garden confabulating. She was a woman of the intellectual bourgeoisie, with neat black hair and a trim black dress, her voice was carefully musical, she was well read, slightly voluble and over-explicit by our English standards, and consciously refined and intelligent. To Gissing she came as the first breath of continental recognition, and she seemed to embody all those possiblities of fine intercourse and one-sided understanding for which he was craving. For Gissing carried the normal expectancy of the male, which I have already dealt with in my own dissection, to an extravagant degree. Never did a man need mothering more and never was there a less sacrificial lover.

Presently we learnt from a chance remark that the lady had visited him one day at Dorking. She had become "Thérèse." He made no further confidences. Then he broke up his Dorking establishment and left for Switzerland, where he was joined by Thérèse and her mother. He confided that there was to be a joint ménage and to ease things with the French relations, the mother carried the relationship so far towards a pseudo-marriage as to circulate cards with the surname of Thérèse erased in favour of "Gissing." All this had, of course, to be carried out with absolute secrecy towards his actual wife and most of his English friends. Those of us who knew, thought that if he could be put into such circumstances as would at last give his very fine brain a fair chance to do good work, connivance in so petty a deception was a negligible price to pay.

Presently he published a novel called *The Crown of*

Life. It is the very poorest of his novels but it is illuminating as regards himself. The "crown of life" was love—in a frock-coat. This was what Gissing thought of love or at any rate it was as much as he dared to think of love. But after all, we argued, something of the sort had to happen and now perhaps he would write that great romance of the days of Cassiodorus.

But things did not work out as we hoped. When, a year or so later, Jane and I, returning from an excursion to Switzerland, visited him in Paris, we found him in a state of profound discontent. The apartment was bleakly elegant in the polished French way. He was doing no effective work, he was thin and ailing, and he complained bitterly that his pseudo mother-in-law, who was in complete control of his domestic affairs, was starving him. The sight of us stirred him to an unwonted Anglo-mania, a stomachic nostalgia, and presently he fled to us in England. An old school friend of his, Henry Hick, a New Romney doctor, of whom I shall have a word or so to say later, came over to look at him, and declared he was indeed starved, and Jane set to work and fed him up—weighing him carefully at regular intervals—with marvellous results.

I was glad to have him in our house, but it carried a penalty. For suddenly Thérèse began to write me long, long, wonderfully phrased letters—on thin paper and crossed—informing me that she could not bring herself to write to him directly and demanding my intervention. I had still to realize the peculiar Latin capacity for making copious infusions of simple situations. Presently when Gissing went off for some days to Hick, he too began to write at Thérèse to me—long letters in his small fine handwriting.

But I was busy upon work of my own and after one or two rather hasty attempts at diplomacy I brutalized the situation. I declared that the best thing for Gissing to do would be to decide never to return to France, since there was an evident incompatibility of appetite between him and the lady, or alternatively if there was any sort of living affection still between them, which I doubted, he must stipulate as a condition of his return that the catering should be taken out of the hands of the mother and put in those of the daughter under his own direction, and finally I announced that in no circumstances would I read through, much less paraphrase, consider or answer any further letters from Thérèse. Whatever she wrote to me, I should send to him for him to deal with directly. And with that I washed my hands of their immediate troubles.

He went back to her on the terms I had suggested, so I suppose there was still some sort of tenderness between them. Then these three poor troubled things full of the spirit of mute recrimination, perplexed and baffled by each other's differences, went down to a furnished house at St. Jean-de-Luz and, afterwards, to St. Jean-Pied-de-Port in the mountains above, and there he set to work writing what was to have been, what might have been under happier circumstances, a great historical picture of Italy under the Gothic kings, *Veranilda*. He had had this book in mind almost all the time I had known him. He had been reading Cassiodorus for it in 1898. Towards Christmas 1903 some of Thérèse's relations came to visit them. On some excursion with them he caught a cold, which settled on his chest. Neither Thérèse nor her mother was the nursing type of woman. A sudden hatred seized him of the comfortless house he was in, of the misty mountain village, of economized French food and everything about him and a sudden fear fell upon him of the crackling trouble in his lungs and the fever that was gathering in his veins. He had been writing with deepening distress to Morley Roberts in November. Just on the eve of Christmas came telegrams to both of us:

"George is dying. Entreat you to come. In greatest haste."

I had private bothers of my own and I was supposed to be nursing a cold, but as Roberts did not seem to be available and made no reply to a telegram I sent him, I decided to go. It was Christmas Eve. I had no time to change out of my garden clothes and I threw some things into a handbag and went off in a fly to Folkestone Pier to catch the afternoon boat. I made my Christmas dinner of ham at Bayonne station.

I found the house a cheerless one. I saw nothing, or at least I remember seeing nothing of Thérèse's mother; I think she had retired to her own room. Thérèse was in a state of distress and I thought her extremely incompetent. The visitors were still visiting but I insisted upon their departure. There was however a good little Anglican parson about, with his wife, and they helped me to get in a nurse (or rather a "religieuse," which is by no means the same thing) and made some beef-tea before they departed for their home in St. Jean-de-Luz.

Gissing was dying of double pneumonia and quite delirious all the time I was there. There was no ice available and his chest had to be kept cool by continually dipping handkerchiefs in methylated spirit and putting them on him. Also his mouth was slimy and needed constant wiping. I kept by him, nursing him until far into the small hours while the weary religieuse recuperated, dozing by the fire. Then I found my way back to my inn at the other end of the place through a thick fog. St.-Jean-Pied-de-Port is a lonely frontier town and at night its deserted streets abound in howling great dogs to whom the belated wayfarer is an occasion for the fiercest demonstrations. I felt like a flitting soul hurrying past Anubis and hesitating at strange misleading turnings on the lonely Pathway of the Dead. I forget every detail of the inn but I still remember that sick-room acutely.

It is one of the many oddities of my sheltered life that until the death of Gissing I had never watched a brain passing through disorganization into a final stillness. I had never yet seen anyone dying or delirious. I had expected to find him enfeebled and anxious and I had already planned how we could get a civil list pension from Mr. Balfour, to educate his boys and how I would tell him of that and what other reassurances I might give him. But Gissing aflame with fever had dropped all these anxieties out of his mind. Only once did the old Gissing reappear for a moment, when abruptly he entreated me to take him back to England. For the rest of the time this gaunt, dishevelled, unshaven, flushed, bright-eyed being who sat up in bed and gestured weakly with his lean hand, was exalted. He had passed over altogether into that fantastic pseudo-Roman world of which Wakefield Grammar School had laid the foundations.

"What are these magnificent beings!" he would say. "Who are these magnificent beings advancing upon us?" Or again, "What is all this splendour? What does it portend?" He babbled in Latin; he chanted fragments of Gregorian music. All the accumulation of material that he had made for *Veranilda* and more also, was hurrying faster and brighter across the mirrors of his brain before the lights went out for ever.

The Anglican chaplain, whose wife had helped with the beef-tea, heard of that chanting. He allowed his impression to develop in his memory and it was proclaimed later in a newspaper that Gissing had died " in the fear of God's holy name, and with the comfort and strength of the Catholic faith." This led to some bitter recriminations. Edward Clodd and Morley Roberts were particularly enraged at this " body-snatching " as they called it, and among other verbal missiles that hit that kindly little man in the full publicity of print were " crow," " vulture " and " ecclesiastical buzzard." But he did not deserve to be called such names. He did quite honestly think Gissing's " Te Deums " had some sort of spiritual significance.

Another distressful human being in the sick chamber that night was Thérèse. I treated her harshly. She annoyed me because I found a handkerchief was being used to wipe his mouth that had been dipped in methylated spirit, and her thrifty soul resisted me when I demanded every clean handkerchief he possessed. Her sense of proportion was inadequate and her need for sympathy untimely. As I was hurrying across the room to do him some small service, I found her in my way. She clasped her hands and spoke in her beautifully modulated voice. " Figure to yourself, Mr. Wells, what it must mean to me, to see my poor Georges like this ! "

I restrained myself by an effort. " You are tired out," I said. " You must go to bed. He will be safe now with the nurse and me."

And I put her gently but firmly out of the room. . . .

So ended all that flimsy inordinate stir of grey matter that was George Gissing. He was a pessimistic writer. He spent his big fine brain depreciating life, because he would not and perhaps could not look life squarely in the eyes,— neither his circumstances nor the conventions about him nor the adverse things about him nor the limitations of his personal character. But whether it was nature or education that made this tragedy I cannot tell.

§ 4
New Romney and Sandgate (1898)

I CAME BACK from Italy to Worcester Park in the summer of 1898, on the verge of the last bout of illness in my life before my health cleared up, quite unaware of the collapse that hung over me. I ascribed a general sense of malaise, an inability to stick to my work—I was then writing *Love and Mr. Lewisham*—to want of exercise and so the greater my lassitude the more I forced myself to exertion. What was happening was a sort of break-up of the scars and old clotted accumulations about my crushed kidney, and nothing could have been worse for me than to start, as we did, upon a cycling journey to the south coast. I was ashamed of my bodily discomfort—until I was over forty the sense of physical inferiority was a constant acute distress to me which no philosophy could mitigate—and I plugged along with a head that seemed filled with wool and a skin that felt like a misfit. Somewhere on the road I caught a cold.

We struggled to Lewes and then on to Seaford. We decided I must really be overdoing this exercise and we went into lodgings for a rest. All this is brought back to me by the hieroglyphics of the picshuas. Here under date of July 29th is one of them. Our sitting-room was evidently furnished with unrestrained piety. We were physically unhappy and our discomfort breaks out in hatred of our fellow visitors to Seaford. Jane has complained that she is dull. Some forgotten joke about a hat is traceable; I fancy I may have used her hat as a waste-paper basket; and noises (buniks) upstairs are afflicting me. By way of rest I am struggling to complete *Love and Mr. Lewisham*. Whenever I felt ill I became urgent to finish whatever book I was working on, because while a book unfinished would have been worth nothing, a finished book now meant several hundred pounds. Before going to Rome I had already scamped the finish of *When the Sleeper Wakes* (which afterwards I rechristened in better English *When the Sleeper Awakes*) and I came near to scamping *Love and Mr. Lewisham*. But the suppuration that was going on in my now aching side, was too rapid to allow that. *Love and Mr. Lewisham* was finished with much care and elaboration

some months later. My erring kidney began apparently to secrete ink. Jane, after brooding over my condition, was struck by an idea and went out and bought a clinical thermometer. We found my temperature had mounted to 102 F.

We had no established doctor but I had met a friend of Gissing's, Henry Hick, who was medical officer of health for Romney Marsh and who had asked us to stay a night with him in the course of our cycling tour. New Romney seemed close at hand, we exchanged telegrams and I went to him at once by little cross country lines and several changes of train. I was now in considerable pain, the jolting carriages seemed malignantly uncomfortable, I suffered from intense thirst, I could get nothing to drink and the journey was interminable. With an unfaltering gentleness and no sign of dismay, Jane steered this peevish bundle of suffering that had once been her " Mr. Binder " to its destination. Hick was a good man at diagnosis and he did me well. An operation seemed indicated and he put me to bed and starved me down to make the trouble more accessible to the scalpel, but when the surgeon came from London it was decided that the offending kidney had practically taken itself off and that there was nothing left to remove. Thereupon I began to recover and after a few years of interrogative suspense and occasional pain not even a reminiscent twinge remained of my left kidney.

I find the picshuas resume after a couple of months. Before October I did some little drawings as I lay in bed, and amused myself by colouring them and these I think prevented the immediate resumption of the picshua diary. Mrs. Hick had just presented the world with a daughter ; I became her godfather and began an elaborate illustrated story dedicated to this young lady called *The Story of Tommy and the Elephant*. This little book was preserved, and years afterwards when my god-daughter needed some money to set up as a medical practitioner she sold it and the copyright with my assent, and it was published in facsimile. It had an artless quaintness that pleased people and it did well and still sells as a Christmas present book.

On October 5th the picshuas testify that I hatched out a new project called *Kipps*, and completed *Love and Mr. Lewisham*. By this time I had left Hick's helpful home and was, in a rather invalidish fashion, taking up my work again. I had been driven in a comfortable carriage to Sandgate and after a week or so in a boarding house we had installed ourselves in a little furnished house called Beach Cottage. Hick did not think it advisable for me to go back to Worcester Park and I never entered that house again.

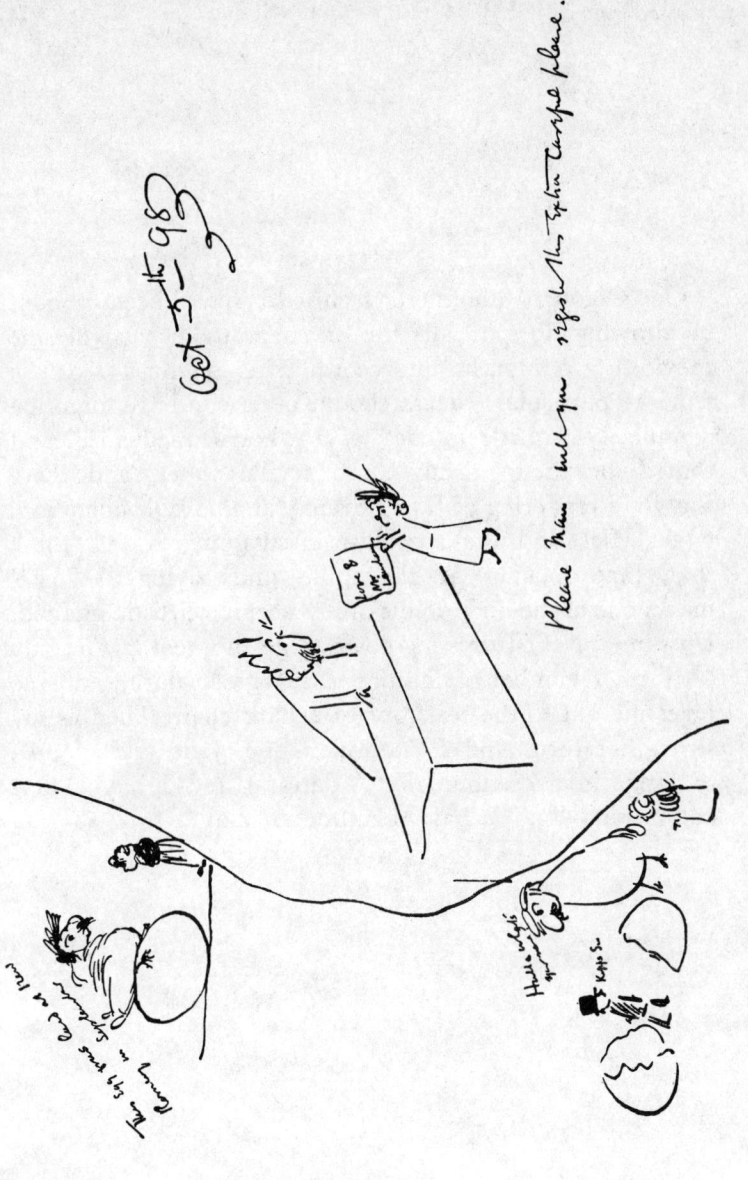

On October 8th there seems to have been a bout of drawing to put all the momentous events of the previous two months on record. The picshuas recall a score of particulars that I should otherwise have forgotten completely. I am reminded of a "horrid medicine," and that I began to drink Contrexeville water, and there is a vivid rendering of Jane's dismay at a possible operation, while Hick and the specialist discuss my case. I think that Jane looking at the knife and saying "Wow" marks one of the high points of my peculiar artistic method. I assume my first dressing-gown, I get up, leaning heavily on Jane, I gambol (galumph) to her great alarm, and she takes me out to the sea front in a Bath chair. Then as my strength returns and I can run alone, Jane takes to sea bathing (in a costume that "dates") and I buy a new cotton hat—"not a halo this time after all."

The next drawing records merely the interruption of a picnic by intrusive cows during the period of recovery. Jane was never afraid of death. I have seen her twice when she thought she would be killed and she was quite steady, but she was town bred and she did not like cows. She distrusted these kind fragrant animals.

The next picshua records that we amused ourselves by shooting with an air gun, and then there began the serious business of finding a new home. According to the best advice available, a long period of invalidism was before me. I had to reconcile myself to complete exile from London, and contrive to live in dry air with no damp in the subsoil and in as much sunshine as possible.

Beach Cottage was a temporary refuge and so close to the sea that in rough weather the waves broke over the roof. Jane planted me there and then went off to pack up the furniture in Heatherlea and bring it down to an unfurnished house, Arnold House, into which we presently moved on a short lease, until we could find something better suited to our needs. That was difficult. Already in the picshuas given we are manifestly thinking of having to build a house and at last we decided to set about that adventure. I have already given a picshua of our removal from Beach Cottage to Arnold House in § 3 of Chapter Seven.

A queer little incident in my illness which it would be ungrateful to omit, was the sudden appearance of Henry James and Edmund Gosse at New Romney, riding upon bicycles from the direction of Rye. They took tea with Dr. Hick and us and were very charming and friendly, and Jane and I were greatly flattered by their visit. It never dawned upon me that they had any but sociable motives in coming over to see me. And later on, when I was in Beach Cottage, J. M. Barrie came in to see me. I gathered he had taken it into his head to spend a day at the seaside and visit me. (There is a picshua in § 3 of Chapter Seven commemorating his visit.) Barrie talked slowly and wisely of this and that, but particularly of his early struggles and the difficulties of young writers. There were times when a little help might do much for a man who was down. It never entered my head that I myself might be considered " down " just then, and I argued the matter with him. Once a man borrowed or was subsidized, I said, the " go " went out of his work. It was a dangerous and perhaps a fatal thing to deprive a man's cheques of the sharp freshness of an unencumbered gain. " Perhaps you're right," meditated Barrie, and went on after a pause to tell of how when he first came to London he did not understand the nature of a cheque. " I just put them in a drawer and waited for the fellow to send me the real money," he said. " I didn't see the sense of them."

He helped himself to a buttered bun. " When first I came to London," he remarked, " I lived almost entirely on boons. . . . "

The experience of later years has made me realize that in this way the Royal Literary Fund was making its enquiries about me, and that I was not so completely outside the range of assistance as I imagined. But I never had any assistance of that kind and at that time I did not want it. I was now some hundreds of pounds on the solvent side and thinking of building a house with my balance. I knew nothing of investment and having a house of my own seemed as good a use for savings as I could imagine.

§ 5
EDIFYING ENCOUNTERS: SOME TYPES OF PERSONA AND TEMPERAMENTAL ATTITUDE (1897–1910)

I HAD A three years agreement for Arnold House and I stayed out my full time in it, gradually rebuilding my overstrained body and recovering resisting power to colds and suchlike infections. It was a semi-detached villa and it had a long narrow strip of grass which ended in a hedge of tamarisk along the sea wall. Upon the beach one day the *Sea Lady* appeared, very lovely in a close fitting bathing dress and with the sunlight in her hair, and took possession of my writing desk.

Our next door neighbours were a very pleasant couple named Popham, small rentiers with cultivated tastes who read well and thought of doing something to mend the world. They were the children of that serious Noncomformity which founded so many sound businesses in the mid-Victorian epoch, turned them into honest joint-stock companies and left its children just independent enough to travel, trifle with the Arts and supply the backbone of the new British intelligentsia. The Pophams were always handy to play with. They taught me to swim, so far as I have ever learnt to swim, we moored a raft twenty or thirty yards from shore and I struggled out to it, and I found Popham as good a companion as Bowkett for long bicycle rides into Kent. Mrs. Popham was a sister-in-law of Graham Wallas whom I had already heard speaking in the old days in William

Morris's greenhouse meetings. Presently he came down to Sandgate with his wife and we found we had a lot to talk about together.

Wallas was a rather slovenly, slightly pedantic, noble-spirited man and I cannot measure justly the influence of the disinterested life he led on my own. It was I think very considerable. The Wallases, the Oliviers and the Webbs were quite the best of the leading Fabians—Shaw I refuse to count as a typical Fabian; they lived lives devoted to the Res Publica right out to the end of their days. They took the idea of getting a living as something by the way; a sort of living was there for them anyhow; and the real business of life began for them only after that had been settled and put on one side.

From what I have told of myself it must be plain that in those days I was full of mercenary *go*; " price per thousand " and " saleable copy " were as present in my mind as they are in the picshuas I have shown. My commercialism is not, I think, innate, but my fight with the world for Jane and myself and my family, had set a premium upon money making. I was beginning to like the sport. I was beginning to enjoy being able to pay for things. I was getting rather keen on my literary reputation as a saleable asset. It was as good for my mind as uninfected mountain air in an early case of tuberculosis to go for walks with Wallas, worlds away from any thought of prices, agents, serializations, " rights." We even went off to Switzerland together for a couple of weeks and walked among the passes of Valais, over the Gemmi, over the Aletsch Glacier to Bel Alp, up to Zermatt, up the Furka, over the St. Gotthard, talking.

Essentially Wallas was a talker and a lecturer. He liked picking a case to pieces with a quiet fastidious deliberation far more than he liked the labour of putting things together. My journalistic experiences since my student days had bitten into me the primary need of sending in copy in time or even a little in advance of time. All my life I have been " delivering the goods " even if the packing has been hasty and the execution scampered at any rate, if not actually *scamped*. The habit is ingrained. I had meant to loiter over this autobiography for years—and perhaps not publish it in the end. I sketched an opening for it two years ago. And here it is being pressed to a finish. But the bad side of Wallas's rentier unworldliness was that he was under no inner compulsion to get things positively done. If he had not had very definite academic ambitions and a real joy in answering questions, he might have sunken altogether into sterile erudite wisdom. As it is, the London School of Economics will testify how much the personal Graham Wallas outdid the published Graham Wallas. Alfred Zimmern and Walter Lippmann were among his particular pupils and there is scarcely any considerable figure among the younger generation of publicists who does not owe something to his slow, fussy, mannered, penetrating and inspiring counsels. He was a classical scholar, but Hellenic rather than Roman—in contrast to Gissing—a Platonist and not a Homerist. His grasp upon modern scientific philosophy was a firm one.

Our Swiss conversations centred upon our common feeling that there had to be some firmer basis, a better thought-out system of ideas, for social and political activities than was available at that time. He had been greatly impressed by the book of Professor Ostrogorski on *Democracy and the Organization of Political Parties* (1902). It was an early break towards realism in political science. It swept aside legist conceptions of government by a frank treatment of parliamentary actuality. It was plain to Wallas that realistic acid might be made to bite still deeper into political conventionality. He wanted to make a psychological examination of mass-political reactions the new basis for a revision of governmental theory, and he thought of calling this study "A Prolegomenon to Politics." Finally he produced it as *Human Nature in Politics* (1908). Walter Lippmann, under his inspiration, produced *A Preface to Politics*, and the Alpine sunlight of that mental hike of ours is also very evident in my own *Modern Utopia* (1905). We were all branching out in characteristic directions from the Ostrogorski stimulus.

Wallas and I never lost contact completely. Within a few months of his death (1932) he was in my study reading and commenting very illuminatingly and usefully upon the political chapters of my *Work, Wealth and Happiness of Mankind*. He had been reading a good deal of Bentham at that time, digging out long forgotten books, and I remember his glasses gleaming appreciatively as he squatted in my lowest easy chair and dilated on the " old boy's " abundance and breadth of range. Bentham, too, had been a sort of encyclopædist. I do not think Wallas wrote anything about this aspect of Bentham, though I know he dealt with him largely in his lectures on local government ; he was just going over him for pleasure, gathering a bright nosegay of characteristic ideas—to be presently dropped by the wayside.

Somewhere between my own tendency to push on to conclusions and Wallas's interminable deliberation, lies I suppose the ideal method of the perfect student working " without haste and without delay."

My opinion of the texture and mental forms of the brain of Graham Wallas was very high, and I formed an almost equal respect for the intelligence of another of those early Fabians, Sydney Olivier who became Lord Olivier. Both the Webbs also I found very good, if antagonistic, stuff. Beatrice had (and has) a delightful way that is all her own, of throwing out bold general propositions about things in the most aggressive manner possible. I should call her style of talk experimental dogmatism. If you disagree, you say "Oh Nonsense!" and restate her proposition in a corrected form. Then she fights with unscrupulous candour and invincible good temper. Sidney is not nearly so exploratory; his convictions are less vivid and plastic; his aim is rather persuasion than truth, he is politic rather than philosophical. Of Shaw's mind I have already given an impression.

In my account of *fin-de-siècle* socialism I have criticized the peculiar limitations of pseudo " practicality " and anti-Utopianism that went with the academic and civil-service associations of the Fabian group. In particular I have shown how they shirked and delayed the problem of the competent receiver. Here I am dealing not so much with these ideological limitations with which I presently fell foul, as with their pervading sense of the importance of social service as the frame of life, and the way in which Jane and I were probably influenced by them. We may have had that in us from the beginning, Jane particularly, but they brought it out in us. They may have done much to deflect me from the drift towards a successful, merely literary career into which I was manifestly falling in those early Sandgate days. I might have become entirely an artist and a literary careerist and possibly a distinguished one, and then my old friend Osborn of the *National Observer*, the *Morning Post* and "Boon" would never have had occasion to call my books "sociological cocktails."

A much more tawdry brain in the Fabian constellation which played its part in teaching me about human reactions was that of Hubert Bland. As my personal acquaintances with the Fabians extended we found the Blands had a house at Dymchurch, within an easy bicycle ride of us, to which they came in summer-time. They were the strangest of couples and they played a large part in the Fabian comedy. Doris Langley Moore has recently given a very frank account of them in her excellent life of Mrs. Bland (*E. Nesbit* 1933), to which I make my acknowledgements. E. Nesbit was a tall, whimsical, restless, able woman who had been very beautiful and was still very good-looking; and Bland was a thick-set, broad-faced aggressive man, a sort of Tom-cat man, with a tenoring voice and a black-ribboned monocle and a general disposition to dress and live up to that. The two of them dramatized life and I had as yet met few people who did that. They loved scenes and " situations." They really enjoyed strong emotion. There was no such persistent pursuit of truth and constructive ends in them as in their finer associates. It was not in their imaginative scheme.

Much of her activity went into the writing of verse, rather insincere verse, rather sentimental stories for adults and quite admirable tales for children. The Bastable family she created is still a joy to little people between ten and seventeen. She earned the greater part of the joint income. She ran a great easy-going hospitable Bohemian household at Well Hall, Eltham, an old moated house with a walled garden. Those who loved her and those who wished to please her called her royally " Madame " or " Duchess," and she had a touch of aloof authority which justified that. A miscellany of people came and went there and to lodgings handy-by the smaller house at Dymchurch; the Chesterton brothers, Laurence Housman, Enid Bagnold, Horace Horsnell, Arthur Watts, Oswald Barron, Edgar Jepson, Alfred Sutro, Berta Ruck, Jack Squire, Clifford Sharp, Monseigneur Benson, Frederick Rolfe (Baron Corvo), a multitude of young writers, actors and aspirants in an atmosphere of talk, charades, mystifications and disputes. And there also I and Jane visited and learnt to play Badminton and gossip and discuss endlessly.

At first it seemed to be a simple agreeable multitudinousness from which literary buds and flowers sprang abundantly, presided over by this tall, engaging, restless, moody, humorous woman. Then gradually the visitor began to perceive at first unsuspected trends and threads of relationship and scented, as if from the moat, a more disturbing flavour. People came to Well Hall and went, and some of them went for good. There had been " misunderstandings."

I thought at first that Well Hall was a new group for us and now in the retrospect I realize that it was a new sort of world. It was a world of rôles and not of realities. Perhaps that is the more usual type of world, the sort of world in which people do not say " I am thus and thus," but " I will be thus and thus." From what I have told in the earlier part of this autobiography it is plain that my own people, my parents, brothers, aunt, cousin and so forth, and the people with whom I came in contact, were either very simple-minded people indeed or else they were people with the sustained and developed simplicity and coherence of a scientific training or people with whom my contacts were simple and unrevealing. But the Blands were almost the first people I met at all intimately, who were fundamentally intricate, who had no primary simple idea. They had brains as active and powerful as most other brains in my world, but—as I began to realize only after some disconcerting experiences—they had never taken them down to any sort of philosophy; they had never focused them on any single objective, and they started off at all sorts of levels from arbitrarily adopted fantasies and poses.

The incongruity of Bland's costume with his Bohemian setting, the costume of a city swell, top-hat, tail-coat, greys and blacks, white slips, spatterdashes and that black-ribboned monocle, might have told me, had I had the ability then to read such signs, of the general imagination at work in his *persona*, the myth of a great Man of the World, a Business Man (he had no gleam of business ability) invading for his own sage strong purposes this assembly of long-haired intellectuals. This myth had, I think, been developed and sustained in him, by the struggle of his egoism against the manifest fact that his wife had a brighter and fresher mind than himself, and had subtler and livelier friends. For many years, says Miss Moore, she carried on a long correspondence with Laurence Housman and I guess that Bland had had to protect his self-esteem against many such intimations of insufficiency in his own equipment. He could not pervade her. That particular correspondence, the biographer relates, was ended when E. Nesbit, against her character and disposition, followed Bland on the anti-feminist side of the suffrage dispute.

In the end she became rather a long-suffering lady, but her restless needle of a mind, her quick response, kept her always an exacting and elusive lady. It was I am convinced because she, in her general drift, was radical and anarchistic, that the pose of Bland's self-protection hardened into this form of gentlemanly conservatism. He presented himself as a Tory in grain, he became—I know of no confirmation—a man of good old family; he entered the dear old Roman Catholic church. These were all insistencies upon soundness and solidity as against her quickness and whim. He was publicly emphatic for social decorum, punctilio, the natural dependence of women and the purity of the family. None of your modern stuff for *him*. All this socialism he assured you, so far as it was any good, was a reaction from nineteenth-century liberalism to the good old social organization that flourished in England before the days of Adam Smith.

She acquiesced in these posturings. If she had not, I suppose he would have argued with her until she did, and he was a man of unfaltering voice and great determination. But a gay holiday spirit bubbled beneath her verbal orthodoxies and escaped into her work. The Bastables are an anarchistic lot. Her soul was against the government all the time.

This discordance of form and spirit lay on the surface of their lives. Most of us who went to them were from the first on the side of the quicksilver wife against the more commonplace, argumentative, cast-iron husband. Then gradually something else came into the *ensemble*. It came first to the visitor at Well Hall as chance whisperings, as flashes of conflict and fierce resentment, as raised voices in another room, a rush of feet down a passage and the banging of a door.

Mrs. Langley Moore in her careful and well informed book lays the whole story bare with many particulars I never knew before. There was a more primitive strand in Bland's make-up. He was under an inner compulsion to be a Seducer—on the best eighteenth-century lines. That, and not Tory-Socialism, was his essential preoccupation; that was what he talked to himself about when he was in his own company. His imaginations may have been running into this mould before he met her, it is not a very rare mould, but the clash of their personalities confirmed the tendency. That I suppose was where he really got even with her wit and freaks and fantasies and with a certain essential physical coldness in her. And in return he gave her some romantically difficult situations. The astonished visitor came to realize that most of the children of the household were not E. Nesbit's but the results of Bland's conquests, that the friend and companion who ran the household was the mother of one of these young people, that young Miss So-and-so, who played Badminton with a preoccupied air was the last capture of Hubert's accomplished sex appeal. All this E. Nesbit not only detested and mitigated and tolerated, but presided over and I think found exceedingly interesting.

Everywhere fantastic concealments and conventions had been arranged to adjust these irregularities to Hubert's pose of ripe old gentility. You found after a time that Well Hall was not so much an atmosphere as a web.

In company, in public, Bland talked and wrote of social and political problems and debated with a barrister-like effectiveness, but when I was alone with him, the fundamental interest insisted upon coming to the surface. He felt my unspoken criticisms and I could not check his assertive apologetics. He would talk about it. He would give hints of his exceptional prowess. He would boast. He would discuss the social laxities of Woolwich and Blackheath, breaking into anecdotes, " simply for the purpose of illustration." Or he would produce a pocket-worn letter and read choice bits of it—" purely because of its psychological interest." He did his utmost to give this perpetual pursuit of furtive gratification, the dignity of a purpose. He was, he claimed to me at least, not so much Don Juan as Professor Juan. " I am a student, an experimentalist," he announced, " in illicit love."

" Illicit love " ! It had to be " illicit " and that was the very gist of it for him. It had to be the centre of a system of jealousies, concealments, hidings, exposures, confrontations, sacrifices, incredible generosities—in a word, drama. What he seemed most to value was the glory of a passionate triumph over openness, reason and loyalty—and getting the better of the other fellow. The more complex the situation was, the better it was fitted for Bland's atmosphere.

It is curious how opposed this mentality of what I may call the seventeenth and eighteenth century " Buck," is to the newer, rationalist, go-as-you-please of the Shelley type, to which my own mind was being attracted in those days. I wanted to abolish barriers between the sexes and Bland loved to get under or over or through them. The more barriers the better. In those days I would have made illicit love impossible —by making almost all love-making *licit*. There was no real inconsistency therefore between Bland's private life and his enthusiasm for formal conventionality and it was perfectly logical that though we were both disposed to great freedoms by the accepted standards, we were in diametrically antagonistic schools. He thought it made a love affair more exciting and important if one might be damned for it and I could not believe these pleasant intimacies could ever bring real damnation to anyone. He exalted chastity because so it meant a greater sacrifice, and I suppose he would have thought it a crowning achievement to commit incest or elope with a nun. He was sincerely disgusted at my disposition to take the moral fuss out of his darling sins. My impulses were all to get rid of the repressions of sexual love, minimize its importance and subordinate this stress between men and women as agreeably as possible to the business of mankind.

So now, with the detachment of half a lifetime, I define the forces that first attracted me to Well Hall and then made Well Hall jar upon me; but at that time I did not see so clearly and I found these two people and their atmosphere and their household of children and those who were entangled with them, baffling to an extreme degree. At the first encounter it had seemed so extraordinarily open and jolly. Then suddenly you encountered fierce resentments, you found Mrs. Bland inexplicably malignant; doors became walls so to speak and floors pitfalls. In that atmosphere you surprised yourself. It was like Alice through the Looking Glass; not only were there Mock Turtles and White Queens and Mad Hatters about, but you discovered with amazement that you were changing your own shape and stature.

The web of concealments and intrigue that radiated from the Bland ménage and met many other kindred if less intricate strands among that miscellany of enquiring and experimenting people which constituted the Fabian Society, spread like the mycelium of a fungus throughout that organization. The Blands were among the earliest founders of that " Fellowship of the New Life " from which the Fabian

Society sprang. They were original members of the latter, and Bland, because he was neither the chief bread winner of his family nor restrained by any fundamental mental consistency nor preoccupied with any really ordered creative aims, was able to devote all the time and energy that could be spared from fluttering the Blackheath dovecotes, to Fabian manœuvres. He was always there, just as dry old Quaker-trained Edward Pease, the salaried trustworthy secretary, was always there, and Pease was by nature a very honest desiccating pedant and Bland by nature a politician. Bland was as loose internally as Pease was rigid and they were inspired by a natural antagonism. The little society was setting out upon the most gigantic enterprise that humanity has ever attempted, a New Life (Think of it!) and even if that new life was restricted by subsequent provisos to economic reconstruction only, it still meant a vast long trying game of waiting and preparation; the society was not only poor, small and with everything to learn about its job, but from the very beginning it had these two personalities, like the germs of a congenital disease, vitiating and diverting its energies.

Long before my innocence came into the society, some deep feud between Pease and the Blands had established itself when Pease and not Bland became the salaried secretary; and the mysterious concealments, reservations, alliances, imputations, schemes and tactics of these obscure issues played havoc with the affairs of our middle-class socialist propaganda. The larger purposes of the Wallases, Webbs and Shaw had to defer continually to the dark riddle of "what the Blands will do about it." There was no reckoning without them for they turned up, excited and energetic, with satellites, dependents, confederates and new associates at every meeting. In the dusty confusion of personalities and secondary issues created by them, rumour moved darkly and anonymous letters flittered about like bats at twilight. By the time I came into the society Bland, the able politician, was established in the mind of Shaw, for example, as a necessary evil and Pease as an unavoidable ally. When Shaw faced towards social and political problems, this implacable animosity loomed so large for him that at times it blotted out the stars.

The topic of *Human Nature in Politics* (to borrow a title from Graham Wallas) is a vast one, and here was a hard specimen for my frustration and education. Following Ostrogorski, Wallas dealt with this trouble from the point of view of mass reactions, but now here I am approaching it —or rather blundering into it—from the opposite direction, by way of biography. What are we to do with these energetic vital types who will not subdue themselves to a broad and consistent aim ; who choose a pose, stage situations, fly off at a tangent and never table their objectives ? Shall we never be able to keep secondary issues and idiosyncrasies in their place ? How far is it inevitable that we should live in a world of personal " misunderstandings " ? How far is directive simplicity possible ? What can be done to keep our public and social objectives untangled and simple and clear ?

Before it had existed half a dozen years, the Fabian Society was in urgent need of a searching psycho-analysis, and there has never yet been a government or party, an educational directorate, or a religion that has not presently diverged into morasses of complication and self-contradiction. How far is that to be the case with us for ever ?

How far might some more universal and more efficient education, more penetrating, better planned and better administered, have started and sustained our Fabian Society —every one of us well meaning—in a better understanding and a less wasteful co-operation ? Were the complexities of

Bland and his wife, the intellectual freakishness of Shaw, the intricate cross-purposes of that bunch of animated folk, unavoidable and incurable?

The Federation of the New Life passed like a dreamer's sigh, but within some fated term of years, unless mankind is to perish, there must be a real Federation of the New Life. I find myself on the verge here of slipping away from my already sufficiently copious autobiographical purpose into what might prove a limitless dissertation on human behaviour, a sort of outline, a digest, of all available biography. It is time to recall my enquiring pen—as one calls a roving dog to heel—and return to my personal story, to return from cosmo-biography to autobiography, and to go on telling how I, at any rate, in spite of all those deflections and entanglements, found at last a satisfactory simplification and orientation of my own existence in the idea of an educational, political and economic world unification.

Of that mental and moral consolidation my last chapter must tell. In the early Sandgate days not only was I being attracted more and more powerfully towards the civil service conception of a life framed in devotion to constructive public ends *à la Webb*, but I was also being tugged, though with less force, in a quite opposite direction, towards the artistic attitude. I have never been able to find the artistic attitude fundamentally justifiable but I understand and sympathize with the case for it. It was expressed in varying modes and very engagingly by a number of brains through whose orbits my own was travelling. Professor York Powell had come to know me, through the Marriott Watsons and the *Pall Mall Gazette* group, and he was very strong in his assertion that the " artist " lived in a class apart, having a primary and overriding duty to his " gift." He might be solvent if he liked and political in his off time, but his primary duty was to express the divine juice that was in him.

York Powell, a big bearded man with a deep abundant chuckle, came very frequently to Sandgate, where he had an old gnarled boatman friend, who was something of a character, Jim Payne. I did my best to be initiated by York Powell into the charms of sea-fishing and a sort of tarry wisdom peculiar to Jim Payne, but the inoculation never really took. York Powell was always trying to draw Jim out for my benefit and Jim was harder to draw out than a badger. I never saw him drawn.

To a lodging in Sandgate also came Bob Stevenson, the " Spring-Heeled Jack " of his cousin Robert Louis' *Talk and Talkers*, after a stroke, for the ending of his days. I had known him before his illness and had heard him do some marvellous talks ; a dissertation upon how he would behave if he was left nearly two millions, still lingers in my mind. One million was just to keep—one could never bear to break a single million—but all the rest was to be spent and distributed magnificently. He described his dinner before his benefactions began. He was particular about a large deed-box full of cheque books to be brought to him by bank messengers " in scarlet coats with *new* gold bands round their top-hats." He chose among his friends those whose presence and advice would be most conducive to wise and generous giving. He planned the most ingenious gifts and the most remarkable endowments. I have tried to give a faint impression of his style of imaginative talking in Ewart's talk about the City of Women in *Tono Bungay*. But Ewart is not even a caricature of Bob ; only Bob's style of talk was grafted on to him. Bob Stevenson, like York Powell, was all on the side of aesthetic concentration and letting the rest go hang. He could not imagine what these Fabians were up to. They were not real in his universe.

Henry James, too, had developed expressionism into an elaborate philosophy ; it is a great loss to the science of criticism that he should have died before his slowly unfolding autobiography reached a point where he could state his mature attitude. In several talks we hovered on the abundant verge of it but even the evenings at Lamb House were too short for anything but intimations and preliminaries.

Another very important acquaintance of my early Sandgate time, now too little appreciated in the world, was the American Stephen Crane. He was one of the earliest of those stark American writers who broke away from the genteel literary traditions of Victorian England and he wrote an admirable bare prose. One or two of his short stories, *The Open Boat*, for example, seem to me imperishable gems. He made his reputation with a short book about the civil war, *The Red Badge of Courage*. It was an amazing feat of imaginative understanding. It was written, as Ambrose Bierce said, not with ink but blood. And forthwith the American newspapers pounced upon him to make him a war correspondent. He was commissioned to go to Cuba, to the Spanish-American war and to the Turko-Greek war of 1897. He was a lean, blond, slow-speaking, perceptive, fragile, tuberculous being, too adventurous to be temperate with anything and impracticable to an extreme degree. He liked to sit and talk, sagely and deeply. How he managed ever to get to the seats of war to which he was sent I cannot imagine. I don't think he got very deeply into them. But he got deeply enough into them to shatter his health completely.

In Greece he met and married an energetic lady who had been sent out by some American newspaper as the first woman war correspondent. With, perhaps, excessive vigour she set out to give her ailing young husband a real good time. Morton Frewen (the wealthy father of Clare Sheridan) lent them a very old and beautiful house, Brede House near Rye and there they inaugurated a life of gay extravagance and open hospitality. I forget the exact circumstances of our first meeting but I remember very vividly a marvellous Christmas Party in which Jane and I participated. We were urged to come over and, in a postscript, to bring any bedding and blankets we could spare. We arrived in a heaped-up Sandgate cab, rather in advance of the guests from London. We were given a room over the main gateway in which there was a portcullis and an owl's nest, but at least we got a room. Nobody else did—because although some thirty or forty invitations had been issued, there were not as a matter of fact more than three or four bedrooms available. One of them however was large and its normal furniture had been supplemented by a number of hired truckle-beds and christened the Girls' Dormitory, and in the attic an array of shake-downs was provided for the men. Husbands and wives were torn apart.

Later on we realized that the sanitary equipment of Brede House dated from the seventeenth century, an interesting historical detail, and such as there was indoors, was accessible only through the Girls' Dormitory. Consequently the wintry countryside next morning was dotted with wandering melancholy, preoccupied, men guests.

Anyhow there were good open fires in the great fireplaces and I remember that party as an extraordinary lark—but shot, at the close, with red intimations of a coming tragedy. We danced in a big oak-panelled room downstairs, lit by candles stuck upon iron sconces that Cora Crane had improvised with the help of the Brede blacksmith. Unfortunately she had not improvised grease guards and after a time everybody's back showed a patch of composite candle-wax, like the flash on the coat of a Welsh Fusilier. When we were not dancing or romping we were waxing the floor or rehearsing a play vamped up by A. E. W. Mason, Crane, myself and others. It was a ghost play, and very allusive and fragmentary, and we gave it in the School Room at Brede. It amused its authors and caste vastly. What the Brede people made of it is not on record.

We revelled until two or three every night and came down towards mid-day to breakfasts of eggs and bacon, sweet potatoes from America and beer. Crane had a transient impulse to teach some of the men poker, in the small hours, but we would not take it seriously. Mason I found knew my old schoolfellow Sidney Bowkett and had some anecdotes to tell me about him. " In any decent saloon in America," said Crane, " you'd be shot for talking like that at poker," and abandoned our instruction in a pet.

That was the setting in which I remember Crane. He was profoundly weary and ill, if I had been wise enough to see it, but I thought him sulky and reserved. He was essentially the helpless artist; he wasn't the master of his party, he wasn't the master of his home; his life was altogether out of control; he was being carried along. What he was still clinging to, but with a dwindling zest, was artistry. He had an intense receptiveness to vivid work; he had an inevitably right instinct for the word in his stories; but he had no critical chatter. We compared our impressions of various contemporaries. "That's Great," he'd say or simply "*Gaw!*" Was So-and-so " any good " ? So-and-so was " no good."

Was he writing anything now ?

His response was joyless. Pinker the agent had *fixed* some stories for him. " I got to do them," he said, " I got to do them."

The tragic entanglement of the highly specialized artist had come to him. Sensation and expression—and with him it had been well nigh perfect expression—was the supreme joy of his life and the justification of existence for him. And here he was, in a medley of impulsive disproportionate expenditure, being pursued by the worthy Pinker with enquiries of when he could " deliver copy " and warnings not to overrun his length. The good thing in his life had slipped by him.

In the night after the play Mrs. Crane came to us. He had had a haemorrhage from his lungs and he had tried to conceal it from her. He " didn't want anyone to bother." Would I help get a doctor?

There was a bicycle in the place and my last clear memory of that fantastic Brede House party is riding out of the cold skirts of a wintry night into a drizzling dawn along a wet road to call up a doctor in Rye.

That crisis passed, but he died later in the new year, 1900. He did his utmost to conceal his symptoms and get on with his dying. Only at the end did his wife wake up to what was coming. She made a great effort to get him to Baden-Baden. She conveyed him silent and sunken and stoical to Folkestone by car, regardless of expense, she had chartered a special train to wait for him at Boulogne and he died almost as soon as he arrived in Germany.

Two other important men of letters were also close at hand to present the ideal of pure artistry to me rather less congenially. These were Ford Madox Hueffer and Joseph Conrad, of whom the former—through certain defects of character and a copious carelessness of reminiscence—is, I think, too much neglected, and the latter still placed too high in the scale of literary achievement. Joseph Conrad was really Teodor Jozef Konrad Korzeniowski. He had very wisely dropped his surname and was content to be Joseph Conrad to English readers. He had been excited by a review I wrote of his *Almayer's Folly* in the *Saturday Review*; it was his first " important " recognition and he became anxious to make my acquaintance.

At first he impressed me, as he impressed Henry James, as the strangest of creatures. He was rather short and round-shouldered with his head as it were sunken into his body. He had a dark retreating face with a very carefully trimmed and pointed beard, a trouble-wrinkled forehead and very troubled dark eyes, and the gestures of his hands and arms were from the shoulders and very Oriental indeed. He reminded people of Du Maurier's Svengali and, in the nautical trimness of his costume, of Cutliffe Hyne's Captain Kettle. He spoke English strangely. Not badly altogether; he would supplement his vocabulary—especially if he were discussing cultural or political matters—with French words; but with certain oddities. He had learnt to read English long before he spoke it and he had formed wrong sound impressions of many familiar words; he had for example acquired an incurable tendency to pronounce the last *e* in these and those. He would say, " *Wat* shall we do with *thesa* things? " And he was always incalculable about the use of " shall " and " will." When he talked of seafaring his terminology was excellent but when he turned to less familiar topics he was often at a loss for phrases.

Yet he wove an extraordinarily rich descriptive English prose, a new sort of English of his own, conspicuously and almost necessarily free from stereotyped expressions and hack phrases, in which foreign turns and phrases interlaced with unusual native words unusually used. And I think it was this fine, fresh, careful, slightly exotic quality about his prose, that " foreign " flavour which the normal Anglo-Saxon mind habitually associates with culture, that blinded criticism to the essentially sentimental and melodramatic character of the stories he told. His deepest theme is the simple terror of strange places, of the jungle, of night, of the incalculable sea; as a mariner his life was surely a perpetual anxiety about miscalculations, about the hidden structural vices of his ship, about shifting cargo and untrustworthy men; he laid bare with an air of discovery what most adventurers, travellers and sailors habitually suppress. Another primary topic with him—best treated in that amazingly good story *Amy Foster*, a sort of caricature autobiography, was the feeling of being incurably " foreign." He pursued a phantom " honour "—in *Lord Jim* for instance ; his humour in *The Nigger of the Narcissus*, is dismal, and you may search his work from end to end and find little tenderness and no trace of experienced love or affection. But he had set himself to be a great writer, an artist in words, and to achieve all the recognition and distinction that he imagined should go with that ambition, he had gone literary with a singleness and intensity of purpose that made the kindred concentration of Henry James seem lax and large and pale. *The Mirror of the Sea* was his favourite among his own writings, and I think that in that he showed a sound critical judgment.

He came into my ken in association with Ford Madox Hueffer and they remain together, contrasted and inseparable, in my memory. Ford is a long blond with a drawling manner, the very spit of his brother Oliver, and oddly resembling George Moore the novelist in pose and person. What he is really or if he is really, nobody knows now and he least of all ; he has become a great system of assumed personas and dramatized selves. His brain is an exceptionally good one and when first he came along, he had cast himself for the rôle of a very gifted scion of the Pre-Raphaelite stem, given over to artisic purposes and a little undecided between music, poetry, criticism, The Novel, Thoreau-istic horticulture and the simple appreciation of life. He has written some admirable verse, some very good historical romances, two or three books in conjunction with Conrad, and a considerable bulk of more or less autobiographical— unreality. As a sort of heir to Pre-Raphaelitism, he owned among other things a farm called the Pent at the foot of the

Downs above Hythe; it had been occupied previously by Christina Rossetti and Walter Crane the artist; and he had let it to Conrad; Conrad wrote about *The Heart of Darkness* and *The Secret Agent* on a desk that may have creaked to the creative effort of *Goblin Market*; and thither Hueffer and I walked to our meeting.

One goes downhill to the Pent, the windows of the house are low and my first impression of Conrad, was of a swarthy face peering out and up through the little window panes.

He talked with me mostly of adventure and dangers, Hueffer talked criticism and style and words, and our encounter was the beginning of a long, fairly friendly but always rather strained acquaintance. Conrad with Mrs. Conrad and his small blond-haired bright-eyed boy, would come over to Sandgate, cracking a whip along the road, driving a little black pony carriage as though it was a droshky and encouraging a puzzled little Kentish pony with loud cries and endearments in Polish, to the dismay of all beholders. We never really " got on " together. I was perhaps more unsympathetic and incomprehensible to Conrad than he was to me. I think he found me Philistine, stupid and intensely English; he was incredulous that I could take social and political issues seriously; he was always trying to penetrate below my foundations, discover my imaginative obsessions and see what I was really up to. The frequent carelessness of my writing, my scientific qualifications of statement and provisional inconclusiveness, and my indifference to intensity of effect, perplexed and irritated him. Why didn't I *write*? Why had I no care for my reputation?

" My dear Wells, what is this *Love and Mr. Lewisham about*? " he would ask. But then he would ask also, wringing his hands and wrinkling his forehead, " What is all this about Jane Austen? What is there *in* her? What is it all *about*? "

I remember a dispute we had one day as we lay on the Sandgate beach and looked out to sea. How, he demanded, would I describe how that boat out there, sat or rode or danced or quivered on the water? I said that in nineteen cases out of twenty I would just let the boat be there in the commonest phrases possible. Unless I wanted the boat to be important I would not give it an outstanding phrase and if I wanted to make it important then the phrase to use would depend on the angle at which the boat became significant. But it was all against Conrad's over-sensitized receptivity that a boat could ever be just a boat. He wanted to see it with a definite vividness of his own. But I wanted to see it and to see it only in relation to something else—a story, a thesis. And I suppose if I had been pressed about it I would have betrayed a disposition to link that story or thesis to something still more extensive and that to something still more extensive and so ultimately to link it up to my philosophy and my world outlook.

Now here perhaps—if I may deal with Conrad and others and myself as hand specimens—is something rather fundamental for the educationist. I have told in my account of my school days (Ch. 3 §1) how I differed from my schoolmate Sidney Bowkett, in that he felt and heard and saw so much more vividly, so much more emotionally, than I did. That gave him superiorities in many directions, but the very coldness and flatness of my perceptions, gave me a readier apprehension of relationships, put me ahead of him in mathematics and drawing (which after all is a sort of abstraction of form) and made it easier for me later on to grasp general ideas in biology and physics. My education at Kensington was very broad and rapid, I suggest, because I was not dealing with burning and glowing impressions—and when I came to a course where sense impressions were of primary importance, as they were in the course in mineralogy (see Ch. 5 §3), I gave way to irrepressible boredom and fell down. My mind became what I call an educated mind, that is to say a mind systematically unified, because of my relative defect in brightness of response. I was easy to educate.

These vivid writers I was now beginning to encounter were, on the contrary, hard to educate—as I use the word educate. They were at an opposite pole to me as regards strength of reception. Their abundant, luminous impressions were vastly more difficult to subdue to a disciplined and co-ordinating relationship than mine. They remained therefore abundant but uneducated brains. Instead of being based on a central philosophy, they started off at a dozen points; they were impulsive, unco-ordinated, wilful. Conrad, you see, I count uneducated, Stephen Crane, Henry James, the larger part of the world of literary artistry. Shaw's education I have already impugned. The science and art of education was not adequate for the taming and full utilization of these more powerfully receptive types and they lapsed into arbitrary inconsistent and dramatized ways of thinking and living. With a more expert and scientific educational process all that might have been different. They lapsed—though retaining their distinctive scale and quality—towards the inner arbitrariness and unreality of the untrained common man.

Not only was I relatively equipped with a strong bias for rational associations but, also, accident threw me in my receptive years mostly among non-dramatizing systematic-minded people. My mother dramatized herself, indeed, but so artlessly that I rebelled against that. My scientific training and teaching confirmed and equipped all my inherent tendency to get things ruthlessly mapped out and consistent. I suspected any imaginative romancing in conduct. I defended myself against romancing by my continual self-mockery and caricature—what you see in this book therefore as a sort of bloom of little sketches is not really an efflorescence but something very fundamental to this brain-story. I am holding myself down from pretentious impersonations. But they were there, trying to get me. A man is revealed by the nature of his mockeries.

Such mentalities as my wife, Graham Wallas and the Webbs, and the general Socialist proposition, did much to sustain the educational consolidation that was going on in me. So that by the time I encountered such vigorously dramatizing people as the Blands and such vivid impressionists as Conrad I was already built up and set in the most refractory and comprehensive forms of conviction. I had struggled with a considerable measure of success against the common vice of self-protective assumptions. I had, I have, few " complexes." I would almost define education as the prevention of complexes. I was seeing myself as far as possible without pretences, my *persona* was under constant scrutiny, even at the price of private and secret sessions of humiliation, and not only was I trying to avoid posing to myself but I kept up as little pose as possible to the world. I eschewed dignity. I found therefore something as ridiculous in Conrad's *persona* of a romantic adventurous un-mercenary intensely artistic European gentleman carrying an exquisite code of unblemished honour through a universe of baseness as I did in Hubert Bland's man-of-affairs costume and simple Catholic piety.

When Conrad first met Shaw in my house, Shaw talked with his customary freedoms. " You know, my dear fellow, your books won't *do* "—for some Shavian reason I have forgotten—and so forth.

I went out of the room and suddenly found Conrad on my heels, swift and white-faced. " Does that man want to *insult* me ? " he demanded.

The provocation to say " Yes " and assist at the subsequent duel was very great, but I overcame it. " It's humour," I said, and took Conrad out into the garden to cool. One could always baffle Conrad by saying " humour." It was one of our damned English tricks he had never learnt to tackle.

Later on he wanted Ford Madox Hueffer to challenge me. If Conrad had had his way, either Hueffer's blood or mine would have reddened Dymchurch sands. I thought an article Hueffer had written about Hall Caine was undignified and I said that he had written it as if he was a discharged valet —or something equally pungent. Hueffer came over to tell me about it. " I tried to explain to him that duelling isn't done," said Hueffer.

In those days Hueffer was very much on the rational side of life ; his extraordinary drift towards self-dramatization— when he even changed his name to Captain Ford—became conspicuous only later, after the stresses of the war. In the light of that his last book, *It was the Nightingale*, is well worth reading. I think Conrad owed a very great deal to their early association ; Hueffer helped greatly to " English " him and his idiom, threw remarkable lights on the English literary world for him, collaborated with him on two occasions, and conversed interminably with him about the precise word and about perfection in writing.

They forced me to consider and define my own position in such matters. Did I really care for these things ? I like turning a phrase as well as any man, I try my utmost to achieve precision of statement where precision is important, and some passages of mine, the opening sections (§§ 1–4) in the chapter on " How Man has Learnt to Think " in the *Work, Wealth and Happiness of Mankind* for instance, I rewrote a dozen times. But I have a feeling that the happy word is the gift, the momentary capricious gift of the gods a flash of mother-wit. You cannot *train* for it ; you cannot write well and forcibly without at times writing flatly, and the real quality of a writer is, like divinity, inalienable. This incessant endeavour to keep prose bristling up and have it "vivid" all the time defeats its end. I find very much of Conrad oppressive, as overwrought as an Indian tracery, and it is only in chosen passages and some of his short stories that I would put his work on a level with the naked vigour of Stephen Crane. I think Tomlinson's more loosely written *By Sea and Jungle* is more finely felt and conveys an intenser vision than most of Conrad's sea and jungle pieces.

All this talk that I had with Conrad and Hueffer and James about the just word, the perfect expression, about this or that being "written" or not written, bothered me, set me interrogating myself, threw me into a heart-searching defensive attitude. I will not pretend that I got it clear all at once, that I was not deflected by their criticisms and that I did not fluctuate and make attempts to come up to their unsystematized, mysterious and elusive standards. But in the end I revolted altogether and refused to play their game. "I am a journalist," I declared, "I refuse to play the 'artist.' If sometimes I am an artist it is a freak of the gods. I am journalist all the time and what I write *goes now*—and will presently die."

I have stuck to that declaration ever since. I write as I walk because I want to get somewhere and I write as straight as I can, just as I walk as straight as I can, because that is the best way to get there. So I came down off the fence between Conrad and Wallas and I remain definitely on the side opposed to the aesthetic valuation of literature. That valuation is at best a personal response, a floating and indefinable judgment. All these receptive critics pose for their work. They dress their souls before the glass, add a few final touches of make-up and sally forth like old bucks for fresh "adventures among masterpieces." I come upon masterpieces by pure chance; they happen to me and I do not worry about what I miss.

Throughout my life, a main strand of interest has been the endeavour to anchor *personas* to a common conception of reality. That is the structural idea of my *Research Magnificent*. I shall tell more of that endeavour in the next chapter. But this theme of the floating *persona*, the dramatized self, recurs at various levels of complexity and self-deception, in Mr. Hoopdriver in *The Wheels of Chance*, in the dreams of Mr. Parham, in *Christina Alberta's Father*, and most elaborately of all, in *The Bulpington of Blup*. This last is a very direct caricature study of the irresponsible disconnected aesthetic mentality. It is friendship's offering to the world of letters from the scientific side. E. Nesbit, by the bye, did some short stories in which she dealt with this same unreality in the world as she knew it. She saw through herself enough for that. They are collected together under the title of *The Literary Sense*.

So far in this section I have tried to show the pull of two main groups of divergent personalities and two main sets of tendency upon my character, during those still plastic days at Sandgate, and to indicate something of the quality of my response. These brains passed so to speak to the right of me and the left of me ; I felt their gravitational attraction. The scientific pull was the earlier and stronger. I moved more and more away from conscious artistry and its exaltations and chagrins ; I was strengthened against self-dramatization and confirmed in my disposition to social purposiveness. This definition and confirmation of my mind was the principal thing that was happening to me in those early Sandgate years. But I should be simplifying my story over much if I left that chapter in my life merely as a sort of straightforward tug-of-war in my brain, in which the systematizing, politically directed impulse won. There were other thrusts and drifts, interests and attractions, quite outside this particular conflict as to whether I should keep my mental effort based on an objective or float off into cloudland.

For instance at an entirely different level from these issues of poise and aim in my development, something else was going on,—I was busy " getting on in the world." One does not get on without giving a considerable amount of one's waking time to it. It is plain from the letters home already quoted and the " picshuas " here reproduced, that this was a very constant and lively interest in our early days. Jane and I were concerned in questions of " rights " and royalties and " price per thou " in a manner that was altogether ungenteel. We affected no innocence about " publicity " and we welcomed a large bundle of press-cuttings and felt anxious if the little blue packets were unpunctual and meagre. And somehow it is here and not in relation to whether writing was an end or an implement that the figure of Arnold Bennett with his bright and busy brain seething in a fashion all its own, comes in. We two, he and I, got on in the world abreast—and it was extremely good fun for both of us. Later on we diverged.

He wrote to me first, in September 1897, on the notepaper of a little periodical he edited, called *Woman*, to ask how I came to know about the Potteries, which I had mentioned in the *Time Machine* and in a short story, and after that we corresponded. In a second letter he says he is " glad to find the Potteries made such an impression " on me, so I suppose I had enlarged upon their scenic interest, and adds " only during the last few years have I begun to see its possibilities." In a further letter he thanks me for telling him of Conrad. He had missed *Almayer's Folly* in a batch of other novels for his paper and I had discovered it. That was one up for me. Now under my injunction he is rejoicing over *The Nigger of the Narcissus*. " Where did the man pick up that style and that synthetic way of gathering up a general impression and flinging it at you ? . . . He is so consciously an artist. Now

Kipling isn't an artist a bit. Kipling doesn't know what art is—I mean the art of words ; *il ne se préoccupe que de la chose racontée.*" Follow praises of George Moore. That unnecessary scrap of French is very Bennett. He was already deliberately heading for France and culture, learning French, learning to play the piano, filling up the gaps of a commonplace middle-class education with these accomplishments—and all with the brightest efficiency. Presently he came to Sandgate to see us and his swimming and diving roused my envy.

Never have I known anyone else so cheerfully objective as Bennett. His world was as bright and hard surfaced as crockery—his *persona* was, as it were, a hard, definite china figurine. What was not precise, factual and contemporary, could not enter into his consciousness. He was friendly and self-assured ; he knew quite clearly that we were both on our way to social distinction and incomes of several thousands a year. I had not thought of it like that. I was still only getting something between one and two thousand a year, and I did not feel at all secure about getting more. But Bennett knew we couldn't stop there. He had a through ticket and a time-table—and he proved to be right.

Our success was to be attained straightforwardly by writing sound clear stories, lucidly reasonable articles and well constructed plays. His pride was in craftsmanship rather than in artistic expression, mystically intensified and passionately pursued, after the manner of Conrad. Possibly his ancestors had had just the same feel about their work, when they spun the clay of pots and bowls finely and precisely. He was ready to turn his pen to anything, provided it could be done well. He wrote much of the little weekly paper, *Woman*, he was editing—including answers to correspondents—often upon the most delicate subjects—over the signature, if I remember rightly, of " Aunt Ellen." He did it as well as he knew how. He declared he did it as well as it could be done. His ancestors on the potbanks had made vessels for honour or for dishonour. Why should not he turn out whatever was required? Some years ago he and Shaw and I were all invited by an ingenious advertisement manager to write advertisements for Harrods' Stores, for large fees. We all fell into the trap and wrote him letters (which he used for his purposes) for nothing. Shaw and I took the high attitude. We were priests and prophets; we could not be paid for our opinions. Bennett frankly lamented the thing could not be done because it " wasn't *done*." But he could see no reason why a writer should not write an advertisement as an architect builds a shop.

We were both about of an age; to be exact he was six months younger than I; we were both hard workers, both pushing up by way of writing from lower middle-class surroundings, where we had little prospect of anything but a restricted salaried life, and we found we were pushing with quite surprising ease; we were learning much the same business, tackling much the same obstacles, encountering similar prejudices and antagonisms and facing similar social occasions. We both had a natural zest for life and we both came out of a good old English radical tradition. We were liberal, sceptical and republican. But beyond this we were very different animals indeed. While I was becoming more and more set upon changing my world and making it something entirely different and while Conrad was equally set upon wringing an unprecedented intensity of phrasing out of his, Bennett was taking the thing that is, for what it was, with a naïve and eager zest. He saw it brighter than it was; he did not see into it and he did not see beyond it. He was like a child at a fair. His only trouble was how to get everything in in the time at his disposal, music, pictures, books, shows, eating, drinking, display, the remarkable clothes one could wear, the remarkable stunts one could do, the unexpected persons, the incessant fresh oddities of people; the whole adorable, incessant, multitudinous lark of it.

There it was. What more could you want?

Since I have just been writing about educated and uneducated types I perceive I am exposed to the question whether Bennett was an educated type? I would say that in my sense of the word he was absolutely immune to education and that he did not need it. He was impermeable. He learnt with extraordinary rapidity and precision. He was full of skills and information. The bright clear mosaic of impressions was continually being added to and all the pieces stayed in their places. He did not feel the need for a philosophy or for a faith or for anything to hold them together. One of the most characteristic, if not the best of his books, is *Imperial Palace*, a most competent assemblage of facts, but told with an exultation, a slight magnification. His self-explanation —explanation rather than analysis—is the *Card*. In that book he shows that he could see himself as plainly and directly as he saw anything else. It is not a self dramatization; it is pleased recognition, even of his own absurdities. *A Great Man* again is delighted self-caricature—even to his youthful bilious attacks. If there was any element of self-deception in his *persona* it was a belief in the luck that comes to men who are " Cards "—Regular Cards. His investments for example were too hopeful. When he died— and he died a well spent man—he left a holding of Russian securities, which he had bought for a rise that never came.

His work was extraordinarily unequal. Working with cultivated and conscious craftsmanship upon things intimately known to him, he produced indubitable masterpieces. There are few novels in our period to put beside *The Old Wives' Tale* and *Riceyman Steps* and few stories to equal *The Matador of the Five Towns*. And yet he could write a book about death and eternity like *The Glimpse*—a glimpse into an empty cavern in his mind. He wrote a vast amount of efficient yet lifeless fiction from which his essential work is slowly being disinterred.

After his first visit to Sandgate, we never lost touch with each other. We never quarrelled, we never let our very lively resolve to " get on " betray our mutual generosity ; we were continually interested in one another and continually comparing ourselves with each other. He thought me an odd card ; I thought him an odd card. I became more and more involved in the social and political issues I shall describe in the next chapter, I made all sorts of contacts outside literary circles, I broadened and spread myself ; and maybe I spread myself thin ; while he retracted and concentrated. The boundaries of my personality became less definite and his more and more firmly drawn. I have told already how I put my banking account under the control of my wife, did not know of my own investments, allowed matters of furnishing, house-building, invitations and so forth to go right out of my control. I have never had any household in which my rôle has not been essentially that of the paying guest. But Bennett's control of the particulars of his life remained always (the word was one of his favourite ones) meticulous. He loved the direction of organization ; the thing breaks out in his *Imperial Palace*. His home at Thorpe le Soken ; his home in Cadogan Square were beautifully managed—by himself. His clothes were carefully studied. At the Reform Club we used to note with all respect the accordance of shirt and tie and sock and handkerchief, and draw him out upon the advisability of sending our laundry to Paris. I would ask him where to buy a watch or a hat. " Do you mind," he would say to me, " if I just arrange that tie of yours."

The difference between Bennett and myself, particularly in our later developments, is perhaps interesting from a psychological point of view, though I do not know how to put it in psychological language. We contrasted more and more in our contact with the external world as our work unfolded. He developed his relation to the external world and I developed the relation of the external world to myself. He increased in precision and his generalizations weakened; I lost precision and my generalizations grew wider and stronger. This is something superficially parallel but certainly not identical with the comparison I have been making between the systematized mental life of those who are both scientifically disposed and trained and those who are moved to the unco-ordinated vivid expressiveness of the artist.

I will venture here to throw out a wild suggestion to the brain specialist. The artistic type relative to the systematizing type may have a more vigorous innervation of the cortex, rather more volume in the arteries, a richer or more easily oxygenated blood supply. But the difference between the meticulous brain and the loose *sweeping* brain may be due not to any cortical difference at all, but to some more central ganglionic difference. Somewhere sorting and critical operations are in progress, concepts and associations are called up and passed upon, links are made or rejected, and I doubt if these are cortical operations. The discussion of mind working is still in the stage of metaphor, and so I have to put it that this " bureau " of co-ordination and censorship, is roomy, generous and easy going in the Bennett type, and narrow, centralized, economical and exacting in my own. I believe that, corresponding to these mental differences, there was a real difference in our cerebral anatomy.

It was perhaps a part of his competent autonomy that Bennett was so remarkably free from the normal infantilism of the human male. He was not so dependant upon women for his comfort and self-respect as most of us are; he was not very deeply interested in them from that point of view. And he had not that capacity for illusion about them which is proper to our sex. The women in his books are for the most part good hard Staffordshire ware, capable, sisterly persons with a tang to their tongues. He seemed always to regard them as curious, wilful creatures—to be treated with a kind of humorous wariness. There were pleasures in love but they had their place among other pleasures. To have a mistress in France was, he felt, part of the *ensemble* of a literary artist, and afterwards it seemed to him right that the household of a rapidly rising novelist should have a smart, attractive wife, a really well-dressed wife. So that he set about marrying rather as he set about house-hunting. For him it was as objective a business as everything else. Marriage wasn't by any means that organic life association at once accidental and inevitable, that ingrowing intimacy, that it is for less lucidly constituted minds.

Yet he was not cold-hearted ; he was a very affectionate man. Indeed he radiated and evoked affection to an unusual degree, but in some way that I find obscure and perplexing his sexual life did not flood into his general life. His personality never, so to speak, fused with a woman's. He never gave the effect of being welded, even temporarily, with the woman he was with. They did not seem really to have got together.

I think there was some obscure hitch in his make-up here, some early scar that robbed him of the easy self-forgetfulness, that " egoism expanded out of sight," of a real lover. I associate that hitch with the stammer that ran through his life. Very far back in his early years something may have happened, something that has escaped any record, which robbed him of normal confidence and set up a lifelong awkwardness.

He experienced certain chagrins in that search for a wife, he was not able to carry it through with complete detachment, and when he came to the English home he had chosen at Thorpe le Soken, he brought with him a French wife who had previously been his close friend, a lady of charm and lucidity but with a very marked personality which failed to accord in every particular with his realization of what the wife of a successful London novelist should be. I will not go into the particulars of their gradual disagreement and legal separation, his abandonment of Thorpe le Soken for Cadogan Square, nor of his subsequent pseudo-marriage, at which " all London " connived, to the mother of his one child. I think these affairs bothered him a lot but they did not trouble him fundamentally. He reflected on this and that, and laughed abruptly. And anyhow this part of his story is outside this present autobiography.

He left a tangle behind him full of possibilities of recrimination and misadjustment. There have been posttestamentary proceedings, and one lady has taken to journalistic reminiscences about him, reminiscences which, it seems to me, show chiefly how little a woman may understand a man in spite of having lived with him. But perhaps I am prejudiced in this matter. The real Arnold Bennett who is cherished in the memories of his friends, was remarkably detached from this matrimonial and quasi-matrimonial bye-play.

Having been more than a little frustrated in his ambitions to run a well-managed wife in two brilliantly conducted establishments in London and the country, he fell back upon the deliberate development of his own personality. It was no self-dramatization he attempted; no covering up of defects by compensatory assumptions; it was a cool and systematic exploitation of his own oddities. He was as objective about himself and as amused about himself as about anything else in the world. He improved a certain swing in his movements to a grave deliberate swagger; he enriched his gestures. He brushed up his abundant whitening hair to a delightful cockscomb. The stammer he had never been able to conquer was utilized for a conversational method of pauses and explosions. He invented a sort of preliminary noise like the neigh of a penny trumpet. He dressed to the conception of an opulent and important presence. He wore a fob. He made his entry into a club or a restaurant an event. It pleased his vanity no doubt, but why should pleasing one's vanity by evoking an effusive reception in a room or restaurant be any different from pleasing one's palate with a wine? It was done with a humour all his own. Deep within him the invincible Card rejoiced. He knew just how far to carry his mannerisms so that they never bored. They delighted most people and offended none.

I wish Frank Swinnerton who was his frequent associate during his last phase would Boswellize a little about him before the memories fade. Only Swinnerton could describe Bennett calling up the chef at the Savoy to announce the invention of a new dish, or describe him dressing a salad. And Swinnerton could tell of his water-colour painting and his yacht. He ran a yacht but he never let me see it. It was a bright and lovely toy for him, and I think he felt I might just look at it and then at him, with the wrong expression. He was a member of the Yacht Club. I have it on my conscience that I said an unkind thing about his water colours. " Arnold," I said, " you paint like Royalty."

Let me return from Arnold Bennett to the tale of how Jane and I " got on " in the years between 1895 and 1900. In the beginning of this Chapter I brought the history of our social education up to my first encounter with caviar and our tentative experiments with Canary Sack and the various vintages of Messrs. Gilbey available in Camden Town. We soon got beyond such elementary investigations. The enlargement of our lives, once it began, was very rapid indeed, but we found the amount of *savoir-faire* needed to meet the new demands upon us, not nearly so great as we had supposed.

I think my glimpses of life below stairs at Up Park helped me to meet fresh social occasions with a certain ease. A servant in a big household becomes either an abject snob or an extreme equalitarian. At Up Park there was a footman who kept a diary of the bad English and the " ignorance " he heard while he was waiting at table ; he would read out his choice items with the names and dates exactly given, and he may have helped importantly to dispel any delusion that social superiority is more than an advantage of position. I never shared the belief, which peeps out through the novels of George Meredith, Henry James, Gissing and others, that " up there somewhere " there are Great Ladies, of a knowledge, understanding and refinement, passing the wit of common men. The better type of social climbers seek these Great Ladies as the Spaniards sought El Dorado. And failing to find them, invent them.

Jane and I never started with that preoccupation. We did not so much climb as wander into the region of Society. We found ourselves lunching, dining and week-ending occasionally with a very healthy and easy-minded sort of people, living less urgently and more abundantly than any of the other people we knew ; with more sport, exercise, travel and leisure than the run of mankind ; the women were never under any compulsion to wear an unbecoming garment, and struck Jane as terribly expensive ; and everybody was " looked after " to an enviable degree. They had on the whole easier manners than we had encountered before. But they had very little to show us or tell us. The last thing they wanted to do was to penetrate below the surface of things on which they lived so agreeably.

Among the interesting parties I remember in those early days, were several at Lady Desborough's at Taplow Court, and Lady Mary Elcho's at Stanway. There I used to meet people like Arthur Balfour, various Cecils and Sedgwicks, George Curzon, George Wyndham, Sir Walter Raleigh, Judge Holmes, Lady Crewe, Mrs. Macguire, Maurice Baring. . . . But never mind all that. Samples must serve for a catalogue. There was sometimes good talk at dinner and after dinner, but mostly the talk was allusive and gossipy. Balfour for the most part played the rôle of the receptive, enquiring intelligence. " Tell me," was a sort of colloquial habit with him. He rarely ventured opinions to be shot at. He had the lazy man's habit of interrogative discussion. Close at hand to us at Sandgate was the house of Sir Edward Sassoon. Lady Sassoon was a tall witty woman, a Rothschild, very much preoccupied with speculations about a Future Life and the writings of Frederic W. H. Myers. Philosophers like McTaggart, who were expected to throw light on her curiosity about the Future Life, mingled with politicians like Winston Churchill, trying over perorations at dinner, and Edwardians like the Marquis de Soveral. Most of these week-end visits and dinner parties were as unbracing mentally, and as pleasant, as going to a flower show and seeing what space and care can do with favoured strains of some familiar species. In these days there were also such persistent lunch givers as Mrs. Colefax (now Lady Colefax) and Sir Henry Lucy (Toby M.P.) of *Punch*, who gathered large confused tables of twenty or thirty people. There one met " celebrities " rather than people in positions ; the celebrities anyhow were the salt of the feast ; and as Jane and I were much preoccupied with our own game against life, the chief point of our conversation was usually to find out as unobtrusively as possible who we were talking to and why. And by the time we were beginning to place our neighbours, the lunch party would break up and sweep them away.

We would compare notes afterwards " I met old So-and-so." " And what did he say? " " Oh, just old nothing."

None of these social experiences had anything like the same formative impressions upon my mind as the encounters with the politico-social workers and with the writers in earnest, and the artists, upon which I have enlarged. The best thing that these friendly glimpses of the prosperous and influential did for us was to remove any lurking feeling of our being " underneath " and to confirm my natural disposition to behave as though I was just as good as anybody and just as responsible for our national behaviour and outlook.

We were " getting on." At first it was very exciting and then it became less marvellous. We still found ourselves rising. I remember about this time—to be exact in January 24th, 1902—I was asked to read a paper to the Royal Institution and I wrote and read *The Discovery of the Future*, about which I shall have more to say in my concluding chapter. An impression I sketched at the time of a Royal Institution audience may very fitly conclude this chapter. I regard this picshua as a masterpiece only to be compared to the Palaeolithic drawings in the Caves of Altamira. It marks our steady invasion of the world of influential and authoritative people. I remember that Sir James Crichton-Browne (who was about as young then as he is now; he was born in 1840) was very kind and polite to us on this occasion and that after the lecture was delivered I met Mrs. Alfred and Mrs. Emile Mond, long before there was any Lord Melchett, when Brunner Mond & Co. was only the

638   EXPERIMENT IN AUTOBIOGRAPHY

embryo of I.C.I. They wanted to collect us socially, and it was suddenly borne in upon us that we had become worth collecting—eight years from our desperate start in Mornington Place.

§ 6
BUILDING A HOUSE (1899-1900)

IN THE PRESENT SECTION there is little need for writing. A few photographs[1] and two picshuas will serve to tell the tale. We found a site for the house we contemplated, we found an architect in C. F. A. Voysey, that pioneer in the escape from the small snobbish villa residence to the bright and comfortable pseudo-cottage. Presently we found ourselves with all the money we needed for the house and a surplus of over £1,000. And my health was getting better and better. The house was still being built when it dawned upon us as a novel and delightful idea that we were now justified in starting a family. A picture of the pretty little study in which I was to work for ten years finishing *Kipps*, producing *Anticipations*, *A Modern Utopia*, *Mankind in the Making*, *Tono Bungay*, *Ann Veronica*, *The New Machiavelli* and various other novels, may very well be included in this picture chapter.

Voysey wanted to put a large heart-shaped letter plate on my front door, but I protested at wearing my heart so conspicuously outside and we compromised on a spade. We called the house Spade House. The men on the lift beside my garden, which used to ascend and descend between Folkestone and Sandgate, confused my name with that of another Wells, " the Man who Broke the Bank at Monte

---

[1] In this volume one of the photographs faces p. 652.

Carlo "—and they told their passengers that it was " on the ace of spades " that the trick was done. I was no longer lean and hungry-looking, I was " putting on weight " (as the second picshua shows) and in order to keep it down I pulled a roller about my nascent garden in the sight of the promenaders on the Leas, unconscious at first of my sporting fame. But soon I went about Sandgate and Folkestone like a Wagnerian hero with a motif of my own—whenever there was a whistling errand boy within earshot.

Spade House faced the south with a loggia that was a suntrap. The living-rooms were on one level with the bedrooms so that if presently I had to live in a wheeled chair I could be moved easily from room to room. But things did not turn out in that fashion. Before the house was finished, Voysey had revised his plans so as to have a night and day nursery upstairs, and presently I was finishing *Kipps* and making notes for what I meant to be a real full-length novel at last, *Tono Bungay*, a novel, as I imagined it, on Dickens-Thackeray lines, and I had got a bicycle again and was beginning the exploration of Kent. I became a Borough magistrate and stability and respectability loomed straight ahead of us. I might have been knighted ; I might have known the glories of the O.M. ; I might have faced the photographer in the scarlet of an honorary degree. Such things have nestled in the jungle beside my path. But Ann Veronica (bless her !) and my outspoken republicanism saved me from all that. There is only one honour I covet, and I will say nothing about it because it will never come my way, and there is only one disappointment I have ever had in this field, and that was when Jane was not put upon the Essex county bench—for which she was all too good.

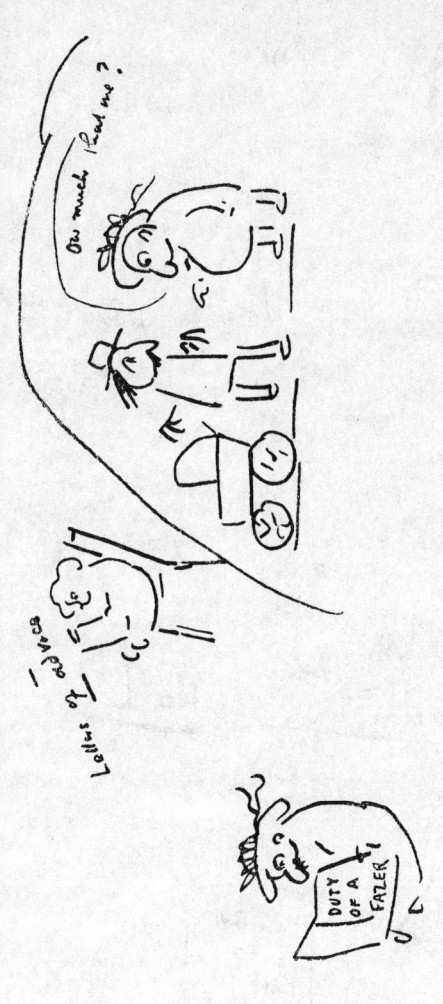

CHAPTER THE NINTH

THE IDEA OF A PLANNED WORLD

§ 1
ANTICIPATIONS (1900) AND THE "NEW REPUBLIC"

IN THIS NEWLY BUILT Spade House I began a book *Anticipations* which can be considered as the keystone to the main arch of my work. That arch rises naturally from my first creative imaginations, *The Man of the Year Million* (written first in 1887) and *The Chronic Argonauts* (in the *Science Schools Journal* 1888), and it leads on by a logical development to *The Shape of Things to Come* (1933) and to the efforts I am still making to define and arrange for myself and for a few other people who inhabit my world, the actual factors necessary to give a concrete working expression to a world-wide " Open Conspiracy " to rescue human society from the net of tradition in which it is entangled and to reconstruct it upon planetary lines.

Necessarily this main arch, the structural frame of my life, is of supreme importance to me, and naturally it is of supreme importance in this picture of my world. It is unavoidable therefore that at times I should write as if I imagined that —like that figure of Atlas which stood in my father's shop window—I sustained the whole world upon my shoulders.

That is the necessary effect of an autobiographical perspective. Every man who has grown out of his infantile faith in the sanity of things about him and developed a social consciousness, carries his whole world upon his shoulders. In an autobiography he is bound to tell about that. He cannot pretend to be unaware of what his mind is doing. He becomes perforce the judge of all the world. He cannot add, "in my opinion" or, "though it is not for me to judge," to every sentence. If he is afraid to appear self-important and an arrogant prig, he had better leave out the story of his brain altogether. But then, what will remain?

I once met a very eminent American who regaled me with an anecdote. He said, "I once saw Abraham Lincoln."

"Yes?" I said eagerly.

"He was as close to me as you are. Closer."

"Well?"

"I saw him."

"And *what* did you see?"

"Abraham Lincoln of course. Surely you've heard of Abraham Lincoln?"

That was really modest autobiography, a *locus* and, beyond that, nothing. But the alternative would have been to pronounce a judgment on Abraham Lincoln.

I should probably romance about it, fill in gaps and simplify unduly, if I tried to give an orderly account of how preoccupation with the future became dominant in my conscious life. But I think my contact with evolutionary speculation at my most receptive age played a large part in the matter. I cannot judge, I do not know how to judge, whether the accident of writing those two early pieces about the remote future and mankind and time-travelling gave me a bias in this matter, and whether, having once made a little success in forecasting, it seemed natural to give the public more from the same tap, or whether on the other hand there was an innate disposition to approach things in general from that unusual side. The idea of treating time as a fourth

THE IDEA OF A PLANNED WORLD

dimension was, I think, due to an original impulse ; I do not remember picking that up. But I may have picked it up, because it was in the air. If I did not then the bias was innate.

The future depicted in the *Time Machine* (1894) was a mere fantasy based on the idea of the human species developing about divergent lines, but the future in *When the Sleeper Awakes* (1898) was essentially an exaggeration of contemporary tendencies: higher buildings, bigger towns, wickeder capitalists and labour more downtrodden than ever and more desperate. Everything was bigger, quicker and more crowded ; there was more and more flying and the wildest financial speculation. It was our contemporary world in a state of highly inflamed distension. Very much the same picture is given in *A Story of the Days to Come* (1899) and *A Dream of Armageddon* (1903). I suppose that is the natural line for an imaginative writer to take, in an age of material progress and political sterility. Until he thinks better of it. Michael Arlen betrayed the same tendency in his *Man's Mortality* as recently as 1932. But in 1899 I was already beginning to realize there might be better guessing about the trend of things.

Along came the end of the century, just apt to my thoughts, and I arranged with W. L. Courtney, who had succeeded Frank Harris as editor of the *Fortnightly Review*, to publish a series of papers discussing what was likely to happen in the new century.

Now *Anticipations* was not only a new start for me, but, it presently became clear, a new thing in general thought. It may have been a feeble and vulnerable innovation, but it was as new as a new-laid egg. It was the first attempt to forecast the human future as a whole and to estimate the relative power of this and that great systems of influence. Partial forecasts and forebodings existed in abundance already; we had estimates for instance, of the length of time it would take to exhaust the world's coal supply, of the prospects of population congestion if the birth-rate remained stable, of the outlook for this planet as the solar system cooled, as it was then supposed to be doing, very rapidly; but most of these conclusions were based on such narrowly conditioned calculations that they could be dismissed quite easily by challenging the validity of the assumptions. A comprehensive attempt to state and weigh and work out a general resultant for the chief forces of social change throughout the world, sober forecasting, that is to say, without propaganda, satire or extravaganza, was so much a novelty that my book, crude though it was and smudgily vague, excited quite a number of people. Macmillan's, my English publishers, were caught unawares by the demand and had sold out the first edition before they reprinted. It sold as well as a novel.

Among other people who were excited by *Anticipations* was myself. I became my own first disciple. Perhaps at the outset of this series I was inspired chiefly by the idea of producing some timely interesting articles. But before I was half way through the series I realized that this sort of thing could not remain simply journalistic. If I was not doing something widely and profoundly important I was at least sketching out something widely and profoundly important. I was carrying on the curves instead of the tangents of history. I was indicating, even if I was not to some extent providing, new data of quite primary importance for rationalized social political and economic effort. I was writing the human prospectus.

One of the things I would like to see done in the world is the foundation of a number of chairs for the teaching of an old subject in a new spirit. If I belonged to the now rapidly vanishing class of benevolent multi-millionaires I would create Professorships of Analytical History. Instead of presenting the clotted masses of un-digested or ill-digested fact which still encumber academic history to-day, my Professors would be doing fully, systematically and soundly, just what I did, though in the flimsiest way, in these *Anticipations*. From the biological point of view my Professors would be human ecologists ; indeed Human Ecology would be a good alternative name for this new history as I conceive it. Then there need be no challenge to those who are still in endowed possession of " history " as such. My new men and the students under them would be working out strands of biological, intellectual, economic consequences. Periods, nations and races they would consider only in so far as these provided them with material facts. They would be related to the older school of historians much as vegetable physiologists ecologists and morphologists are related to the old plant-flattening, specimen-hunting, stamen-counting botanists. The end of all intelligent analysis is to clear the way for synthesis. The clearer their new history became the nearer they would be to efficient world-planning. All this is very obvious to-day but it was by no means clear in 1900. It took me some years to grasp the magnitude of my own realization.

Sooner or later Human Ecology under some name or other, will win its way to academic recognition and to its proper place in general education—in America sooner than in Europe, I guess—but the old history made up of time-worn gossip and stale and falsified politics, is deeply embedded in literature and usage. The invasion of the field of history by the scientific spirit is belated and slow. The old history, barbarically copious and classically fruitless, is strongly entrenched in the centres of learning throughout the world ; it is closely interwoven with the legal profession and the current politico-social organization, and has all the resistant vigour of hierarchic dignity on the defensive. For years yet, I am afraid, the young will still have to learn the more significant facts about Queen Elizabeth's doubtful virginity, memorize such legal documents as the Constitutions of Clarendon and the Bill of Rights and discuss those marvellous world policies invented for examination purposes by dons addicted to self-identification with Julius Caesar or Napoleon Bonaparte or Charles the Fifth or Disraeli or some other of the many exaggerated and inflammatory figures about which history has festered. But this material has no more educational value than the reading of detective stories, until a sound analytical treatment brings it right into the texture of contemporary affairs and points on through their confusion to the broad lines of probability ahead.

I made a first attempt to formulate this idea in my Royal Institution lecture in January 1902. I called this lecture the *Discovery of the Future* and I drew a hard distinction between what I called the legal (past-regarding) and the creative (future-regarding) mind. I insisted that we overrated the darkness of the future, that by adequate analysis of contemporary processes its conditions could be brought within the range of our knowledge and its form controlled, and that mankind was at the dawn of a great change-over from life regarded as a system of consequences to life regarded as a system of constructive effort. I did not say that the future could be foretold but I said that its conditions could be foretold. We should be less and less bound by the engagements of the past and more and more ruled by a realization of the creative effect of our acts. We should release ourselves more and more from the stranglehold of past things.

An attack upon the assumption that history is made by " Great Men " is clearly implied in this view. Napoleon and Caesar were typical " Great Men." I hold they were as much an outcome of systemic processes as are the pustules that break out through the skin of many growing

THE IDEA OF A PLANNED WORLD

young people. Just now we are living in a world where such boils are breaking out everywhere; everywhere there are dictators and "leaders"; everywhere there are "movements" festering about anything from the highly distended Mussolini to our own little black-head, Mosley. It is a spotty stage in the adolescence of mankind, a spotty stage that will pass. It is the Great Man idea and method in final pathological decay.

My lecture was printed in *Nature* (February 6th, 1902) and afterwards reprinted as a pamphlet. I find it, when I re-read it now and measure it by the present certainties of my mind, vague, inexact and rhetorical, but that is the measure of the progress in definition that has been going on in the intervening third of a century. When it was read, that lecture was well abreast of its time.

In 1902 I returned to the *Fortnightly Review* in which *Anticipations* had appeared and contributed a second series of papers under the general title of *Mankind in the Making*, which was published as a book in 1903. This is less in the vein of Analytical History and more in the nature of a general prospectus for the human enterprise. In 1905, I published *A Modern Utopia*, also after a serialization in the *Fortnightly*, and in this I presented not so much my expectations for mankind as my desires.

Let me however return to *Anticipations* for a while. The full title of the book is *Anticipations of the Reaction of Mechanical and Scientific Progress upon Human Life and Thought*. It begins with a statement of what is now a matter of world-wide recognition, the fundamental change in the scale of human relationships and human enterprises brought about by increased facilities of communication. It goes on to apply this generalization to one after another of the fundamental human interests, to show how it affects the boundaries of political divisions, the scope and nature of collective organisations, working loyalties and educational necessities.

I had discovered no new principle here. It was too obvious a thing to be a discovery, and it had already been applied most illuminatingly by Grant Allen in an unpretending essay on the distances between country towns. I never read anything more germinal in my life, unless it was Lang and Atkinson's *Primal Law and Social Origins*, than this particular magazine article. It woke me up to the reciprocal relationship between facilities of locomotion and community-size, and so to a realization of what was happening to the world. I was, I think, the first to apply this relationship comprehensively to historical analysis. If I did not discover this principle I was certainly among the first to call attention to its far-reaching implications.

Anticipations begins with two papers on land-traction and the redistribution of population through the evolution of transport. Then follows an examination of the way in which the change of scale is destroying a long established social order and creating a social confusion in which no new classifications are yet apparent. Here again I was in a region of possible knowledge which was then immensely unexplored. There are two chapters on this social flux, and some guessing at its possible recrystallization, and these lead on naturally to a " Life History of Democracy." Modern Democracy is shown to be not an organic method of social organization but the political expression of a phase of social liquefaction. This chapter on Democracy, the chapter called the " Greater Synthesis " and the concluding chapter on "Faith, Morals and Public Policy in the Twentieth Century " are, from my present point of view, the most imperfect and the most interesting parts of *Anticipations*. The forecasts of modern war, striking as their partial fulfilment has been, of the interplay of languages, of the probability of defeat for Germany in the war that was then already threatening us, the renascence of Poland and the

THE IDEA OF A PLANNED WORLD

prospective movements of boundaries and predominances, though they show a considerable amount of shrewdness, have now been so much overtaken by events and proved or disproved, that they need not concern me here. My great miss in these early shots at forecasting was that I never guessed at the possibility of a modernized planning régime arising in Russia—of all countries. I saw the approaching decivilization of Ireland but I wrote that Russia would be only another and vaster Ireland. I was quite out about Russia.

The fact that in 1900 I had already grasped the inevitability of a World State and the complete insufficiency of the current parliamentary methods of democratic government is of more than merely autobiographical interest. Everybody in 1900 was shirking the necessity for great political reconstructions everywhere. Even the raising of the question carried my book outside the sphere of " practical politics " as they were then understood.

At that early date I was somehow already alive to the incompatibility of the great world order fore-shadowed by scientific and industrial progress, with existing political and social structures. I was already searching about in my mind, and in the facts about me, for ideas about the political and social will and mentality that were demanded by these inevitable material developments. The fact that I regarded myself as a complete outsider in public affairs, and that I felt debarred from any such conformity as would have given me a career within the established political and educational machinery, probably helped importantly in the liberation of my mind to these realizations, and supplied the disinterested vigour with which I worked them out. I could attack electoral and parliamentary methods, the prestige of the universities and the ruling class, the monarchy and patriotism, because I had not the slightest hope or intention of ever using any of these established systems for my own advancement or protection. For a scientific treatment of the theory of government my political handicap was a release. I had the liberty of that irresponsible child in the fable of the Emperor's Clothes. I could say exactly what I thought because it was inconceivable that I could ever be a successful courtier.

In *Anticipations*, I take up the contemporary pretensions of democracy and state the widely unspoken thought of the late Victorians : " This will not work." I then consider existing governments and ruling influences and say as plainly, " These do not work." What most active people were saying was, " They will work well enough for a few years more." And so, through circumstances and simplicity rather than through any exceptional intelligence, I arrived ahead of everyone at the naked essential question, which everyone about me was putting off for to-morrow, " What, then, will work ? " And the attempt to answer that has been the cardinal reality of my thought and writing ever since.

The first tentative answer, as I made it in *Anticipations*, was something I called " The New Republic." It was an answer in the most general terms and it was given in a thoroughly Nineteenth Century spirit. I have written already, in Chapter the Fifth, § 5 of the peculiar fatuous hopefulness of the Nineteenth Century and here I am—true to my period.

This New Republic was to consist of all those people throughout the world whose minds were adapted to the demands of the big scale conditions of the new time.

" I have sought to show," I wrote, " that in peace and war alike a process has been and is at work, a process with all the inevitableness and all the patience of a natural force, whereby the great swollen, shapeless, hypertrophied social mass of to-day must give birth at last to a naturally and informally organized, educated class, an unprecedented sort of people, a New Republic dominating the world. It will be none of our ostensible governments that will effect this great clearing up ; it will be the mass of power and intelligence altogether outside the official state systems of to-day that will make this great clearance, a new social Hercules that will strangle the serpents of war and national animosity in his cradle. . . . It will appear first, I believe, as a conscious organization of intelligent and quite possibly in some cases wealthy men, as a movement having distinct social and political aims, confessedly ignoring most of the existing apparatus of political control, or using it only as an incidental implement in the attainment of these aims. It will be very loosely organized in its earlier stages, a mere movement of a number of people in a certain direction, who will presently discover with a sort of surprise the common object towards which they are all moving."

After the fatalistic optimistic fashion of the time, you see, I assumed that this " New Republic " would appear of its own accord, would " emerge." This was Liberalism—after the Tennysonian pattern. But even then some doubt was lurking at the back of my mind whether it might not prove necessary to *assist* the process of emergence. That there was something to be done about it, and that waiting for the great civilization of the future to arrive was not enough, grew clearer and clearer in my mind, year after year. Destiny, like the God of the Jews, gives no unconditional promises.

In § 5 of Chapter Five of this book I have already made a general criticism of the Socialism of the opening century and told, as one of the newer generation at that time, of my reactions to the assumptions and limitations of the Socialist movement. In several of my books my dawning sense that both Marxism and Fabian Socialism were failing to complete their first intentions and beginning to " date," found expression. Here I have to touch again upon the issues of that section, but from a new angle. What concerns me now is the story of my own disentanglement and the curious way in which I was using my prestige and possibilities as an imaginative writer, to do the thinking-out of this problem of human will and government, under fantastic forms. Just as Pope found it easier to discuss natural theology in verse, so at this stage, I found it more convenient to discuss sociology in fable. While in the Fabian Society I was raising *The Question of Scientific Administrative Areas* (1903), I was also writing a story based on exactly the same idea, *The Food of the Gods* (serialized in 1903 and published as a book in 1904), which began with a wild burlesque of the change of scale produced by scientific men and ended in the heroic struggle of the rare new big-scale way of living against the teeming small-scale life of the earth. Nobody saw the significance of it, but it left some of its readers faintly puzzled. They were vastly amused and thrilled by my giant wasps and rats, but young Caddles was beyond them. And later on in the same way the research for some means of changing the collective drive of human motives threw off the fable of *In the Days of the Comet* (1906), when an impalpable gas from a comet's tail sweeps into our atmosphere, does the work of centuries of moral education in the twinkling of an eye, and makes mankind sane, understanding and infinitely tolerant.

The more formal research for the realization of the New Republic was pursued in *Mankind in the Making*. I was realizing that the correlative of a new republic was a new education and this book is a discursive examination, an all too discursive examination, of the formative elements in the social magma. The best part is the criticism and the rejection of selective breeding as giving any immediate hope of human improvement. Much of the rest shirks the harder task of scrutinizing the " man-making forces in society," in favour of a series of sketchy suggestions and rhetorical passages. Sometimes the text degenerates into mere scolding. Here is the conclusion of this, the most completely forgotten of my books. This stuff, you will observe, is not really getting on with the business at all ; it is revivalism, field preaching. It is the exhortation of a man who has not yet been able to establish, at any point, working contacts for the realization of his ideas. Plainly he is exhorting himself as well as others. Just to keep going.

" Assuredly youth will come to us, if this is indeed to be the dawn of a new time. Without the high resolve of youth, without the constant accession of youth, without recuperative power, no sustained forward movement is possible in the world. It is to youth, therefore, that this book is finally addressed, to the adolescents, to the students, to those who are yet in the schools and who will presently come to read it, to those who, being still plastic, can understand the infinite plasticity of the world. It is those who are yet unmade who must become the makers. . . . After thirty there are few conversions and fewer fine beginnings ; men and women go on in the path they have marked out for themselves. Their imaginations have become firm and rigid, even if they have not withered, and there is no turning them from the conviction of their brief experience that almost all that is, is inexorably so. Accomplished things obsess us more and more. . . .

" With each year of their lives they come more distinctly into conscious participation with our efforts. Those soft little creatures that we have figured grotesquely as dropping from an inexorable spout into our world ; those weak and wailing lumps of pink flesh, more helpless than any animal, for whom we have planned better care, a better chance of life, better conditions of all sorts ; those larval souls, who are at first helpless clay in our hands, presently, insensibly, have become helpers beside us in the struggle. In a little while they are beautiful children, they are boys and girls and youths and maidens, full of the zest of new life, full of an abundant, joyful receptivity. In a little while they are walking with us, seeking to know whither we go, and whither we lead them, and why. . . . In a little while they are young men and women, and then men and women, save for a fresher vigour, like ourselves. For us it comes at last to fellowship and resignation. For them it comes at last to responsibility, to freedom, and to introspection and the searching of hearts. . . .

To know all one can of one's self in relation to the world about one, to think out all one can, to take nothing for granted except by reason of one's unavoidable limitations, to be swift, indeed, but not hasty, to be strong but not violent, to be as watchful of one's self as it is given one to be, is the manifest duty of all who would subserve the New Republic. For the New Republican, as for his forerunner the Puritan, conscience and discipline must saturate life. He must be ruled by duties and a certain ritual in life. Every day and every week he must set aside time to read and think, to commune with others and himself; he must be as jealous of his health and strength as the Levites of old. Can we in this generation make but a few thousands of such men and women, men and women who are not afraid to live, men and women with a common faith and a common understanding, then, indeed, our work will be done. They will in their own time take this world as a sculptor takes his marble, and shape it better than all our dreams."

That I think is my style at its worst and my matter at its thinnest, and quoting it makes me feel very sympathetic with those critics who, to put it mildly, restrain their admiration for me. But it is a proper part of the story to record a phase when I did come to the surface and spout like that, before I took breath and went down into things again.

§ 2
The Samurai—in Utopia and in the Fabian Society (1905–1909)

A Modern Utopia goes half way towards the fantastic story for its form, in a fresh attack upon the problem of bringing the New Republic into existence. It is fairly plain to me that I felt I was going ineffectively nowhere, in those discursive utterances in *Mankind in the Making*, where the only tolerable stuff was the plain and simple squashing of " Positive Eugenics." But I had still to discover how to get at a fruitful presentation of New Republican organization. I now tried an attack upon my difficulties, so to speak, from the rear, by dropping the study of existing conditions and asking first, " What is it that has to be done ? What sort of world do we want ? " I took a leaf; in fact I took a number of pages; from Plato in that. Only after the answer to that question had begun to appear, would it be possible to take up the consideration of how to get there with any hope of success.

Of course, as I have already explained in my criticism of Fabian Socialism and classical Marxism, this was flying in the face of potent and sacred dogmas. Both schools were so ignorant of the use of the imagination in scientific exploration, that they thought Utopianism " unscientific "—and their snobbish terror of that word " unscientific " had no limits. That does not alter the fact that my Utopian attack upon the problem of socialist administration was thoroughly worth the making.

In February 1906, I find that I was defending my method of approach to the problem of administration, at a meeting of the Sociological Society, in a paper entitled " The so-called Science of Sociology." This was afterwards reprinted in *An Englishman Looks at the World* (1914). In this paper I insisted that in sociology there were no units for treatment, but only one single unit which was human society, and that in consequence the normal scientific method of classification and generalization breaks down. " We cannot put Humanity into a museum, or dry it for examination ; our one, single, still living specimen is all history, all anthropology, and the fluctuating world of men. There is no satisfactory means of dividing it, and nothing else in the real world with which to compare it. We have only the remotest ideas of its 'life-cycle' and a few relics of its origin and dreams of its destiny. . . . Sociology must be neither art simply, nor science in the narrow meaning of the word at all, but knowledge rendered imaginatively and with an element of personality, that is to say, in the highest sense of the term, literature."

There were, I argued, two literary forms through which valid sociological work may be carried on; the first, the fitting of "schemes of interpretation" to history and the second, smaller in bulk and "altogether under-rated and neglected," the creation and criticism of Utopias. This I maintained should be the main business of a sociological society. This essay was a little excursion by the way and the subsequent discussion was entirely inconclusive. Mr. Wilfred Trotter thought it was an "Attack on Science" and Mr. Swinny defended Comte from my ingratitude.

(Probably I am unjust to Comte and grudge to acknowledge a sort of priority he had in sketching the modern outlook. But for him, as for Marx, I have a real personal dislike, a genuine reluctance to concede him any sort of leadership. It is I think part of an inherent dislike of leadership and a still profounder objection to the subsequent deification of leaders. Leaders I feel should guide as far as they can—and then vanish. Their ashes should not choke the fire they have lit.)

Although it has never had any great popular sale, *A Modern Utopia* remains to this day one of the most vital and successful of my books. It is as alive to-day as *Mankind in the Making* is dead. It was the first approach I made to the dialogue form, and I am almost as satisfied with its literary quality as I am with that of *The Undying Fire*. The trend towards dialogue like the basal notion of the Samurai, marks my debt to Plato. *A Modern Utopia*, quite as much as that of More, derives frankly from the *Republic*.

In this *Modern Utopia* I made a suggestion for a temperamental classification of citizens as citizens. For the purposes of the state I proposed a division into four types of character, the poietic, the kinetic, the dull and the base. A primary

THE IDEA OF A PLANNED WORLD

problem of government was to vest all the executive and administrative work in the kinetic class, while leaving the poietic an adequate share in suggestion, criticism and legislation, controlling the base and giving the dull an incentive to kinetic effort.

The device of the order of the Samurai, as I worked it out in this book, does I think solve this problem better than any other method that has ever been suggested. Membership of the Samurai was voluntary, but was made difficult by qualifications and severe disciplinary tests and, on the principle that the bow need not always be strung, could be abandoned and resumed, under proper safeguards, according to the way of living desired by the individual at any time. In the Utopian constitution, free-speech and great fields of initiative were jealously guarded from repressive controls. The kinetic were trained to respect them. The " base " were merely those who had given evidence of a strong anti-social disposition and were the only individuals inalterably excluded from the Samurai. Membership of either of these four classes, was regulated by the filtering processes of education and of the tests of social life, and was never hereditary.

The experience of the thirty years that have passed since I launched this scheme, and particularly the appearance of such successful organizations as the Communist Party and the Italian Fascists has greatly strengthened my belief in the essential soundness of this conception of the governing order of the future. A Samurai Order educated in such an ideology as I have since tried to shape out, is inevitable if the modern world-state is ever to be fully realized. We want the world ruled, not by everybody, but by a politically-minded organization open, with proper safeguards, to everybody. The problem of world revolution and world civilization becomes the problem of crystallizing, as soon as possible, as many as possible of the right sort of individuals from the social magma, and getting them into effective, conscious co-operation.

Before working out my sketch *A Modern Utopia*, I was disposed to think that this ruling order, which I had called at first The New Republic, would appear of its own accord. After I had published and seen something of the effect of *A Modern Utopia*, I realized that an Order of the Samurai was not a thing that comes about of itself and that if ever it were to exist, it must be realized as the result of very deliberate effort. After publishing *A Modern Utopia* in 1906, I went to America and wrote a series of impressions, *The Future in America* in which I dwelt upon the casual and chaotic elements in American development, noted the apparent absence of any "sense of the State" and speculated on the possibility of supplying that deficiency. Then I returned to begin a confused, tedious, ill-conceived and ineffectual campaign to turn the little Fabian Society, wizened already though not old, into the beginnings of an order, akin to these Samurai in *A Modern Utopia*, which should embody for mankind a sense of the State.

I envisaged that reconditioned Fabian Society as becoming, by means of vigorous propaganda, mainly carried on by young people, the directive element of a reorganized socialist party. We would attack the coming generation at the high school, technical college and university stage, and our organization would quicken into a constructive social stratum.

The idea was as good as the attempt to realize it was futile. On various occasions in my life it has been borne in on me, in spite of a stout internal defence, that I can be quite remarkably silly and inept; but no part of my career rankles so acutely in my memory with the conviction of bad judgment, gusty impulse and real inexcusable vanity, as that storm in the Fabian tea-cup. From the first my motives were misunderstood, and it should have been my business to make them understandable. I antagonized Shaw and Beatrice Webb for example, by my ill-aimed aggressiveness, yet both these people have since shown by their behaviour towards Fascism and Communism respectively, that their trend of mind is all towards just such a qualification of crude democracy as in 1906 I was so clumsily seeking. I was fundamentally right and I was wrong-headed and I left the Society, at last, if possible more politically parliamentary and ineffective than I found it. If I were to recount the comings and goings of that petty, dusty conflict beginning with my paper *The Faults of the Fabian* (February 1906) and ending with my resignation in September 1908, the reader would be intolerably bored. Fortunately for him it would bore me far more to disinter the documents, fight my battles over again and write it all down. And nobody else will ever do it.

I can but mention in passing the crowded meetings in Cliffords Inn, the gathered " intelligentsia "—then so new in English life—the old radical veterans and the bubbling new young people; the fine speeches of Shaw; Sidney Webb, with his head down talking fast with a slight lisp, terribly like a Civil Servant dispensing information; the magnificent Bland in a frock-coat and a black-ribboned monocle, debating, really debating Sir, in a rococo variation of the front bench parliamentary manner; red-haired Haden Guest, being mercurial, and Edward Pease, the secretary, invincibly dry; myself speaking haltingly on the verge of the inaudible, addressing my tie through a cascade moustache that was no sort of help at all, correcting myself as though I were a manuscript under treatment, making ill-judged departures into parenthesis; the motions, the amendments, the disputes with the chairman, the shows of hands, the storms of applause; the excited Socialists disgorging at last, still disputing, into philistine Fleet Street and the Strand, swirling into little eddies in Appenrodt's, talking a mixture of politics and personalities. Our seriousness was intense. We typed and printed and issued Reports and Replies and Committee Election Appeals and Personal Statements, and my original intentions were buried at last beneath a steaming heap of hot secondary issues.

The order of the Fabian Samurai perished unborn. I went, discoursing to undergraduate branches and local branches, to Oxford, Cambridge, Glasgow, Manchester and elsewhere pursuing the lengthening threads of our disputes. The society would neither give itself to me to do what I wished with it, nor cast me out. It liked the entertainment of its lively evenings. And at last I suddenly became aware of the disproportionate waste of my energy in these disputes and abandoned my attack. Not there was the New Republic to be discovered. By me at any rate.

Reflections of that queer conflict are to be found in *The New Machiavelli* (1911). For some time I was a baffled revolutionary. I did not know what to do next. My Theory of Revolution by Samurai hung in the air and I could not discover any way of bringing it down to the level of reality. At the very time when I was failing, Lenin, under the stresses of a more pressing reality, was steadily evolving an extraordinarily similar scheme, the reconstructed Communist Party. Whether there was any genetic connection between his scheme and mine I have never been able to ascertain. But the in-and-out arrangement whereby a man or woman could be a militant member of the organization and then drop out of its obligations and privileges, the imposition of special disciplines and restrictions upon the active members and the recognition that there are types of good citizens who will live best and work best outside the responsible

THE IDEA OF A PLANNED WORLD 663

administrative organization, are common alike to my project and the Russian reality. Moreover they resemble each other in insisting upon a training in directive ideas as part of the militant qualification. If Russia has done nothing else for mankind, the experiment of the Communist Party is alone sufficient to justify her revolution and place it upon an altogether higher level than that chaotic emotional release, the first French Revolution.

§ 3
"Planning" in the "Daily Mail" (1912)

If for a time I could not get on with the project of an organized "New Republic" as such, this did not prevent my making an occasional attack upon the general problem of social reconstruction. In 1912 Northcliffe asked me to write a series of articles for his *Daily Mail* on the Labour Unrest. Here again I displayed a certain prophetic quality. I got a year or so ahead of the general movement. " Planning " is a world-wide idea nowadays, but in 1912 this that follows was strange stuff for the readers of the leading half-penny daily to find upon their breakfast tables :

" No community has ever yet had the will and the imagination to recast and radically alter its social methods as a whole. The idea of such a reconstruction has never been absent from human thought since the days of Plato, and it has been enormously reinforced by the spreading material successes of modern science, successes due always to the substitution of analysis and reasoned planning for trial and the rule of thumb. But it has never yet been so believed in and understood as to render any real endeavour to reconstruct possible. The experiment has always been too gigantic for the available faith behind it, and there have been against it the fear of presumption, the interests of all advantaged people, and the natural sloth of humanity. We do but emerge now from a period of deliberate happy-go-lucky and the influence of Herbert Spencer, who came near raising public shiftlessness to the dignity of a national philosophy. Everything would adjust itself—if only it was left alone.

"Yet some things there are that cannot be done by small adjustments, such as leaping chasms or killing an ox or escaping from the roof of a burning house. You have to decide upon a certain course on such occasions and maintain a continuous movement. If you wait on the burning house until you scorch and then turn round a bit or move away a yard or so, or if on the verge of a chasm you move a little in the way in which you wish to go, disaster will punish your moderation. And it seems to me that the establishment of the world's work upon a new basis —and that and no less is what this Labour Unrest demands for its pacification—is just one of those large alterations which will never be made by the collectively unconscious activities of men, by competitions and survival and the higgling of the market. Humanity is rebelling against the continuing existence of a labour class as such, and I can see no way by which our present method of weekly wages employment can change by imperceptible increments into a method of salary and pension—for it is quite evident that only by reaching that shall we reach the end of these present discontents. The change has to be made on a comprehensive scale or not at all. We need nothing less than a national plan of social development if the thing is to be achieved.

"Now that, I admit, is, as the Americans say, a large proposition. But we are living in a time of more and more comprehensive plans, and the mere fact that no scheme so extensive has ever been tried before is no reason at all why we should not consider one. We think nowadays quite serenely of schemes for the treatment of the nation's health as one whole, while our fathers considered illness as a blend of accident with special providences; we have systematized the community's water supply, education, and all sorts of once chaotic services, and Germany and our own infinite higgledy-piggledy discomfort and ugliness have brought home to us at last even the possibility of planning the extension of our towns and cities. It is only another step upward in scale to plan out new, more tolerable conditions of employment for every sort of worker and to organize the transition from our present disorder."

And again :

"I have attempted a diagnosis of this aspect of our national situation. I have pointed out that nearly all the social forces of our time seem to be in conspiracy to bring about the disappearance of a labour class as such and the rearrangement of our work and industry upon a new basis. That rearrangement demands an unprecedented national effort and the production of an adequate National Plan. Failing that, we seem doomed to a period of chronic social conflict and possibly even of frankly revolutionary outbreaks that may destroy us altogether or leave us only a dwarfed and enfeebled nation. ..."

(But all this was complicated with an advocacy of "proportional representation" and one or two other minor reforms which I now find myself less willing to revive. Not so much because I have lost faith in them as because I realize that they are of such secondary importance that any insistence upon them distorts the proportions of the general proposition. If ever they are mentioned people say : "So *that's* your panacea ! " and everything else is ignored.)

§ 4
THE GREAT WAR AND MY RESORT TO "GOD"
(1914–1916)

THE ONSET of the Great War hung portentously over us all throughout the three years between the Agadir incident (July 1911) and the invasion of Belgium in August 1914. The inevitability of a crash was more and more manifest, and my reluctant attention was swung round to this continually more immediate threat to the structure of civilization. In 1913, in a short series of articles in the *Daily Mail*, I was writing about the modernization of warfare. (They are reprinted together with the Labour Unrest series and other articles in *An Englishman Looks at the World*, 1914) and early in 1914 I published a futuristic story *The World Set Free*, in which I described the collapse of the social order through the use of " atomic bombs " in a war that began, prophetically and obviously enough, with a German invasion of France by way of Belgium.

After this collapse there was to be a wave of sanity—a disposition to believe in these spontaneous waves of sanity may be one of my besetting weaknesses—and a wonderful council at Brissago (near Locarno !) was to set up the new world order. Yet, after all, the popular reception of President Wilson in 1919 was more like a wave of sanity than anything that had ever occurred in history before. Already in 1908 in *The War in the Air*, written before any practicable flying had occurred, I had reasoned that air warfare, by making warfare three dimensional, would abolish the war front and with that the possibility of distinguishing between civilian and combatant or of bringing a war to a conclusive end. This I argued, must not only intensify but must alter the ordinary man's attitude to warfare. He can no longer regard it as we did the Boer War for example as a vivid spectacle in which his participation is that of a paying spectator at a cricket or base-ball match.

No intelligent brain that passed through the experience of the Great War emerged without being profoundly changed. Our vision of life was revised in outline and detail alike. To me, as to most people, it was a revelation of the profound instability of the social order. It was also a revelation of the possibilities of fundamental reorganization that were now open to mankind—and of certain extraordinary weaknesses in the collective mentality. I was intensely indignant at the militarist drive in Germany and, as a convinced Republican, I saw in its onslaught the culminating expression of the monarchist idea. This, said I, in shrill jets of journalism, is the logical outcome of your parades and uniforms! Now to fight the fighters!

People forget nowadays how the personal imperialism of the Hohenzollerns dominated the opening phase of the war. I shouted various newspaper articles of an extremely belligerent type. But my estimate of the moral and intellectual forces at large in the world, was out. I would not face the frightful truth. I anticipated an explosion of indignant common sense that would sweep not simply the Hohenzollerns but the whole of the current political system, the militant state and its symbols, out of existence, leaving the whole planet a confederated system of socialist republics. Even in *In the Fourth Year* (1918) I denounced the "Krupp-Kaiser" combination and took it almost as a matter of course that such a thing as a private-profit armament industry could not survive the war. Perhaps in the long run its cessation may be the tardy outcome of the cataclysm, but that outcome, I must admit, is still being most tragically delayed. It is being delayed by the general inability to realize that a "sovereign state" is essentially and incurably a war-making state. My own behaviour in 1914–15 is an excellent example of that inability.

The fount of sanguine exhortation in me swamped my warier disposition towards critical analysis and swept me along. I wrote a pamphlet, that weighed, I think, with some of those who were hesitating between participation and war resistance, *The War that will end War*. The title has become proverbial. The broken promise of the phrase is still used as a taunt by the out-and-out pacifist against anyone who does not accept the dogma of non-resistance in its entirety. But in some fashion armed forces that take action have to be disarmed and I remain persuaded that there will have to be a last conflict to inaugurate the peace of mankind. Rather than a war between sovereign governments, however, it is far more likely to be a war to suppress these wherever they are found.

Anatole France in regard to the war was in much the same case as myself. We had met several times before 1914 and formed a very friendly estimate of each other, and when *The Book of France* was compiled and published, for relief funds in the devastated regions, he contributed an article *Debout pour la Dernière Guerre*, which he insisted I should translate. I did so under the title of *Let us Arise and End War*.

As I reassemble all that I can of my hasty, discursive and copious writings during the early stages of the war, and do my utmost to recover my actual states of mind, it becomes plain to me that for a time—in spite of my intellectual previsions—the world disaster, now that it had come, so overwhelmed my mind that I was obliged to thrust this false interpretation upon it, and assert, in spite of my deep and at first unformulated misgivings, that here and now, the new world order was in conflict with the old. Progress was arrested, its front was shattered under my eyes, so shattered that even to this day (1934) it has not reformed, and I convinced myself that on the contrary it was the old traditional system falling to pieces, and the world state coming into being (as the world alliance) under my eyes. The return to complete sanity took the greater part of two years. My mind did not get an effective consistent grip upon the war until 1916.

I remember distinctly when the first effectual destructive tap came to my delusion. It was a queer and a very little but, at the same time, very arresting incident. For some British readers there will be a shock, when they read of it, quite different in its nature from the shock that came to me. But I have given fair warning in this book that I am a Republican, and that the essential disavowals of my soul go deeper than the merely theological beliefs of my fellow countrymen. Perhaps they do not get enough of this sort of shock.

I was walking from my flat in St. James's Court to lunch and talk at the Reform Club. Upon the wall at the corner of Marlborough House as it was then, I saw a large bill; it was an unusual place for an advertisement and I stopped to read it. It was a Royal Proclamation. I forget what matter it concerned; what struck me was the individual manner of the wording. King George was addressing " my people." There was no official " we " and " our " about it.

I had been so busy with the idea of civilization fighting against tradition, I had become so habituated to the liberal explanation of the monarchy as a picturesque and harmless vestigial structure, that this abrupt realization that the King was placing himself personally at the head of his people, was like a bomb bursting under my nose. My mind hung over that fact for a moment or so.

" Good God ! " I said in the greatest indignation, " what has *he* got to do with our war ? "

I went my way digesting it.

" *My* people "—me and my sort were *his* people !

So long as you suffer any man to call himself your shepherd sooner or later you will find a crook round your ankle. We were not making war against Germany; we were being ordered about in the King's war with Germany.

It took me some months of reluctant realization to bring my mind to face the unpalatable truth that this " war for civilization," this " war to end war " of mine was in fact no better than a consoling fantasy, and that the flaming actuality was simply this, that France, Great Britain and their allied Powers were, in pursuance of their established policies, interests, treaties and secret understandings, after the accepted manner of history and under the direction of their duly constituted military authorities, engaged in war with the allied central powers, and that under contemporary conditions no other war was possible. The World-State of my imaginations and desires was presented hardly more by one side in the conflict than by the other. We were fighting for " King and Country " and over there they were fighting for " Kaiser and Fatherland " ; it was six of one and half a dozen of the other, so far as the World-State was concerned.

The efforts of my brain to grasp the vast possibilities of human violence, feebleness and docility that I had neglected and ignored so long in my eagerness to push forward to the modern State, and further to adjust my guiding *persona* to these reluctant realizations, were, I suppose, paralleled in hundreds of thousands of brains. We couldn't get out of it for a time and think it out—and the young men particularly were given no time to think. They thought it out in the trenches—and in No Man's Land. And I, exempt from service and free to express myself, had offered them nothing better than the *War to end War!*

Naturally, in my autobiography, my mind must occupy the central position of this story of disillusionment, as a rabbit on the table represents its species, but the conscious and subconscious conflicts I tell on my own behalf were general and not particular to me. I documented the process with exceptional abundance ; that is my only distinction. Before the end of 1914, I had already set to work upon a record of my mental phases, elaborated in a novel, *Mr. Britling Sees it Through*. It is only in the most general sense autobiographical—and I lost no son. But the story of Mr. Britling's son and Mr. Britling's grey matter could be repeated with ten thousand variations. Mr. Britling is not so much a representation of myself as of my type and class, and I think I have contrived in that book to give not only

THE IDEA OF A PLANNED WORLD

the astonishment and the sense of tragic disillusionment in a civilized mind as the cruel facts of war rose steadily to dominate everything else in life, but also the passionate desire to find some immediate reassurance amidst that whirlwind of disaster.

Mr. Britling after much tribulation "found God." He has lost his son and he sits in his study late at night trying to write to the parents of his boy's German tutor who is also among the dead.

" ' *These boys, these hopes, this war has killed.*'
" The words hung for a time in his mind.
" ' No ! ' said Mr. Britling stoutly. ' They live ! '
" And suddenly it was borne in upon his mind that he was not alone. There were thousands and tens of thousands of men and women like himself, desiring with all their hearts to say, as he desired to say, the reconciling word. It was not only his hand that thrust against the obstacles. . . . Frenchmen and Russians sat in the same stillness, facing the same perplexities ; there were Germans seeking a way through to him. Even as he sat and wrote. And for the first time clearly he felt a Presence of which he had thought very many times in the last few weeks, a Presence so close to him that it was behind his eyes and in his brain and hands. It was no trick of his vision ; it was a feeling of immediate reality. And it was Hugh, Hugh that he had thought was dead, it was young Heinrich living also, it was himself, it was those others that sought, it was all these and it was more, it was the Master, the Captain of Mankind, it was God, there present with him, and he knew that it was God. It was as if he had been groping all this time in the darkness, thinking himself alone amidst rocks and pitfalls and pitiless things, and suddenly a hand, a firm strong hand, had touched his own. And a voice within him bade him be of good courage. There was no magic trickery in that moment ; he was still weak and weary, a discouraged rhetorician, a good intentioned ill-equipped writer ; but he was no longer lonely and wretched, no longer in the same world with despair. God was beside him and within him and about him. . . . It was the crucial moment of Mr. Britling's life. It was a thing as light

as the passing of a cloud on an April morning; it was a thing as great as the first day of creation. For some moments he still sat back with his chin upon his chest and his hands dropping from the arms of his chair. Then he sat up and drew a deep breath. . . .

"For weeks his mind had been playing about this idea. He had talked to Letty of this Finite God, who is the king of man's adventure in space and time. But hitherto God had been for him a thing of the intelligence, a theory, a report, something told about but not realised. . . . Mr. Britling's thinking about God hitherto had been like some one who has found an empty house, very beautiful and pleasant, full of the promise of a fine personality. And then as the discoverer makes his lonely, curious explorations, he hears downstairs, dear and friendly, the voice of the Master coming in. . . .

"There was no need to despair because he himself was one of the feeble folk. God was with him indeed, and he was with God. The King was coming to his own. Amidst the darknesses and confusions, the nightmare cruelties and the hideous stupidities of the great war, God, the Captain of the World Republic, fought his way to empire. So long as one did one's best and utmost in a cause so mighty, did it matter though the thing one did was little and poor?

"'I have thought too much of myself,' said Mr. Britling, 'and of what I would do by myself. I have forgotten *that which was with me*. . . .'"

But the exact truth of the matter is that he had forgotten that which was *in* him, the impersonal, the man in general, which is as much our inheritance as our human frame. He was trying to project his own innate courage so as to feel it external to himself, independent of himself and eternal. Multitudes were doing the same thing at this time.

I went to considerable lengths with this attempt to deify human courage. I shocked many old friends and provoked William Archer's effective pamphlet *God and Mr. Wells*. In the long run I came to admit that by all preceding definitions of God, this God of Mr. Britling was no God at all.

But before I returned to that completeness of sincerity, there had to be some ingenious theological contortions. I was perhaps too aware of the numbers of fine-minded people who were still clinging not so much to religion as to the comfort of religious habits and phrases. Some lingering quality of childish dependence in them answered to this lapse towards a "sustaining faith" in myself. What we have here is really a falling back of the mind towards immaturity under the stress of dismay and anxiety. It is a very good thing at times to hear such words as " Let not your Heart be troubled ; neither let it be afraid " spoken as if with authority. It is a good thing to imagine the still companionship of an understanding Presence on a sleepless night. Then one can get to sleep again with something of the reassurance of a child in its cot. Everywhere in those first years of disaster men were looking for some lodestar for their loyalty. I thought it was pitiful that they should pin their minds to " King and Country " and suchlike clap-trap, when they might live and die for greater ends, and I did my utmost to personify and animate a greater, remoter objective in *God the Invisible King*. So by a sort of *coup d'état* I turned my New Republic for a time into a divine monarchy.

I cannot disentangle now, perhaps at no time could I have disentangled, what was simple and direct in this theocratic phase in my life, from what was—*politic*. I do not know how far I was being perfectly straightforward in this phase, how far I was—as the vulgar have it—"codding myself," and how far I was trying to make my New Republicanism acceptable in a different guise to that multitude which could not, it seemed, dispense with kingship. But what these God-needing people require is the sense of a Father on whom they can have the most perfect reliance. They are straining back to the instinctive faith of " little children," that ultimately everything is all right. They are frightened people who want to be told that they need not brace up to the grimness before them. With all the will in the world I could not bring myself to present my God as that sort of God. I could invent a heartening God but not a palliating God. At his best my deity was far less like the Heavenly Father of a devout Catholic or a devout Moslem or Jew than he was like a personification of, let us say, the Five Year Plan. A Communist might have accepted him as a metaphor. No mystic could have used him because of the complete lack of miraculous aid or distinctive and flattering personal response. As he is presented in *God the Invisible King* he is no better than an inspiring but extremely preoccupied comrade, a thoroughly hard leader.

At no time did my deistic phrasing make any concessions to doctrinal Christianity. If my gestures were pious, my hands were clean. I never sold myself to organized orthodoxy. At its most artificial my religiosity was a flaming heresy and not a time-serving compromise. I never came nearer to Christianity than Manicheism—as Sir John Squire pointed out long ago.

I followed up *God the Invisible King*, with *The Soul of a Bishop* (also 1917)—in which I distinguish very clearly between the God of the Anglican Church and this new personification of human progressiveness—and both *Joan and Peter* (1918) and *The Undying Fire* (1919) are strongly flavoured with deified humanism. Another God indeed, God the Creator, appears for a brief interview with Peter in the hospital—and a very strange untidy God he is. He is evidently the male equivalent, humorous and self exculpatory, of what I have called elsewhere "that old harridan, Dame Nature." And in the last meditation of Joan and Peter's Uncle Oswald, "God," he feels, is "a name battered out of all value and meaning."

The Undying Fire is artistically conceived and rather brilliantly coloured ; I have already expressed my satisfaction with it as the best of my Dialogue-Novels ; and it crowns and ends my theology. It is the sunset of my divinity. Here is what Mr. Huss got from his God when at last he met him face to face.

" It was as if the dreamer pushed his way through the outskirts of a great forest and approached the open, but it was not through trees that he thrust his way but through bars and nets and interlacing curves of blinding, many-coloured light towards the clear promise beyond. He had grown now to an incredible vastness so that it was no longer earth upon which he set his feet but that crystalline pavement whose translucent depths contain the stars. Yet though he approached the open he never reached the open ; the iridescent net that had seemed to grow thin, grew dense again ; he was still struggling, and the black doubts that had lifted for a moment swept down upon his soul. And he realized he was in a dream, a dream that was drawing swiftly now to its close.

" ' Oh God ! ' he cried, ' answer me ! For Satan has mocked me sorely. Answer me before I lose sight of you again. Am I right to fight ? Am I right to come out of my little earth, here above the stars ? '

" ' Right if you dare.'

" ' Shall I conquer and prevail ? Give me your promise ! '

" ' Everlastingly you may conquer and find fresh worlds to conquer.'

" ' *May*—but *shall* I ? '

" It was as if the torrent of molten thoughts stopped suddenly. It was as if everything stopped.

" ' Answer me,' he cried.

" Slowly the shining thoughts moved on again.

" ' So long as your courage endures you will conquer . . .

" ' If you have courage, although the night be dark, although the present battle be bloody and cruel and end in a strange and evil fashion, nevertheless victory shall be yours—in a way you will understand—when victory comes. Only have courage. On the courage in your heart all things depend. By courage it is that the stars continue in their courses, day by day. It is the courage of life alone that keeps sky and earth apart. . . . If that courage fail, if that sacred fire go out, then all things fail and all things go out, all things—good and evil, space and time.'

" ' Leaving nothing ? '

" ' *Nothing.*'

" ' Nothing,' he echoed, and the word spread like a dark and darkening mask across the face of all things."

But before that, Mr. Huss following in the footsteps of Job had said :

" ' I will not pretend to explain what I cannot explain. It may be that God is as yet only foreshadowed in life. You may reason, Doctor Barrack, that this fire in the heart that I call God, is as much the outcome of your Process as all the other things in life. I cannot argue against that. What I am telling you now is not what I believe so much as what I feel. To me it seems that the creative desire that burns in me is a thing different in its nature from the blind Process of matter, is a force running contrariwise to the power of confusion. . . . But this I do know, that once it is lit in a man, then his mind is alight—thenceforth. It rules his conscience with compelling power. It summons him to live the residue of his days working and fighting for the unity and release and triumph of mankind. He may be mean still, and cowardly and vile still, but he will know himself for what he is. . . . Some ancient phrases live marvellously. Within my heart *I know that my Redeemer liveth.* . . .' "

Is not that very like prevarication ? But I prevaricate in the footsteps of a famous exemplar. Have you ever thought over St. Paul's ambiguities in his Epistle to the Corinthians (I., xv. 35) ? Could the resurrection of the body be more ingeniously evaded and " spiritualized " and adapted to all tastes ?

After *The Undying Fire*, God as a character disappears from my work, except for a brief undignified appearance, a regrettable appearance, dressed in moonshine and armed with

Cupid's bow and arrows in *The Secret Places of the Heart* (1922). My phraseology went back unobtrusively to the sturdy atheism of my youthful days. My spirit had never left it. If I have used the name of God at all in the past ten years it has been by way of a recognized metaphor as in "God forbid," or, "At last God wearied of Napoleon." I have become more and more scrupulous about appropriating the prestige of this name for my own ends.

In *What Are we to Do with Our Lives* (1932) I make the most explicit renunciation and apology for this phase of terminological disingenuousness. In spite of the fact that it yielded Peter's dream of God Among the Cobwebs and *The Undying Fire* I wish, not so much for my own sake as for the sake of my more faithful readers, that I had never fallen into it ; it confused and misled many of them and introduced a barren détour into my research for an effective direction for human affairs.

§ 5
War Experiences of an Outsider

THAT THEOLOGICAL EXCURSION of mine was not the only détour I made. I made a still longer détour through the tangle of international politics. I attempted amateurish diplomacies, so to speak, in my writings, and they also need explanation. Everyman almost was imagining diplomacies and treaties in those days, but mine, to a quite exceptional degree, were documented.

Let me return first to the disillusionment about the beneficence of our war-making (1915–16–17) that followed my first attempt in 1914 to find a justifying purpose in "our" war. I did not become "anti-war." I found the simple solution of the conscientious objectors and war resisters generally, too simple for me altogether. My brain was quite prepared for conflict on behalf of the law and order of the world-state. I believe that is necessary to this day. Peace will have to be kept—forcibly. For ages. The distinction people draw between moral and physical force is flimsy and unsound. Life is conflict and the only way to universal peace is through the defeat and obliteration of every minor organization of force. Carrying weapons individually or in crowds, calls for vigorous suppression on the part of the community. The anti-war people made me the more impatient because of the rightness of much of their criticism of the prevailing war motives. I was perhaps afraid, if I yielded to them, of being carried back too far towards the futility of a merely negative attitude. What they said was so true and what they did was so merely sabotage. I lost my temper with them.

And with less stress upon the " perhaps " I was reluctant to admit how gravely I had compromised myself by my much too forward belligerence and my rash and eager confidence in the liberalism, intelligence and good faith of our Foreign Office and War Office in the first month or so of the war. My pro-war zeal was inconsistent with my pre-war utterances and against my profounder convictions. As I recovered consciousness, so to speak, from the first shock of the war explosion and resumed my habitual criticism of government and the social order, I found myself suspect to many of my associates who had become pacificists of the left wing. They regarded me as a traitor who was betraying them to the " war-mongers," while the reactionists in a position of authority, with equal justification and perhaps a nicer sense of my fundamental quality, were extremely suspicious of me as an ally. The hardest line to take is the middle way, especially if one is not sure-footed oneself, and there can be no doubt my staggering course was perplexing to many a friendly observer. Whatever I wrote or said went to an exasperating accompaniment of incredulity from the left, and I felt all the virtuous indignation natural to a man who has really been in the wrong. I was in the wrong and some of the things I wrote about conscientious objectors in *War and the Future* were unforgivable. I turned on the pacificists in *Joan and Peter*, savaged them to the best of my ability, imputed motives, ignored honourable perplexities and left some rankling wounds. Some of those war-time pacificists will never forgive me and I cannot complain of that. I made belated amends in the *Bulpington of Blup*. But that is a minor matter. The thing that occupied most of my mind was the problem of getting whatever was to be got for constructive world revolution out of the confusion of war, and being pro-German and non-combatant, finding endless excuses for the enemy and detracting from the fighting energy of the allies, seemed to me of no use at all towards my end.

I turn over a number of faded and forgotten writings as I try to judge and summarize my behaviour in these crucial years. There is an illuminating sketch of a story " The Wild Asses of the Devil " in *Boon* (1915). In 1915 I find I was already writing about the *Peace of the World* and the *End of the Armament Rings*. In 1916 I produce *What is Coming ?* made up of a number of 1915 newspaper articles. The leaves of my copy of this book are already carbonized, copies of it would be hard to find, if anyone wanted to find them, and if I were to put my reputation before my autobiographical rectitude, I think I should just let this little volume decay and char and disappear and say nothing about it. Most of it is very loose-lipped indeed. In it I am feeling my way about not only among ideas but among what I then thought were insurmountable popular prejudices, in a very blind and haphazard fashion. My propagandist and practical drive was still all too powerful for my scientific and critical disposition.

I wanted something done and I did not want to seem to propose extravagant and impossible things.

Most of these 1915 articles were written with a curious flavour of clumsy propitiation or still clumsier menace, with an evident sense that they might be quoted in Germany, and there is a powerful flavour of ignorance, inexperience and self-importance about them. But I felt it was better to blurt out some things badly than not have them put about at all. I insist in this book that Germany will lose the struggle through exhaustion and that in the final settlement Britain must work closely with the United States (not then in the war). I also forecast the repudiation of the Hohenzollerns by Germany and the establishment of a German republic, but I did not anticipate that this would happen as soon as it actually did. There are some flashes of intuition. It was less widely recognized then than it is now that the way to liquidate a bankrupt world is through a rise in prices and a revaluation of gold. In some way I have got at that in this early war-book, and I am also clear that for any conclusive settlement there must be a grouping of states in larger systems. I talk of some hypothetical combination, which I call the "Pledged Allies," which must pursue a policy in common after the war, and I insist that a republican Germany will be altogether more capable of an understanding with such a combination than a monarchy. The Allies—pledged already not to make a separate peace—ought, I argue, to define a policy *now* before the war ends and pledge themselves to insist upon its realization. The idea of an ultimate Peace Conference becoming a sort of permanent world control is foreshadowed. The boldest paper of all in this amateurish collection of suggestions is a discussion of the possibility of pooling the tropical possessions of the great powers in order to end imperialist rivalries. This particular paper closes with this adumbration of the League of Nations

THE IDEA OF A PLANNED WORLD 681

idea, and it shows how far constructive liberal thought had got at that date (1916):

" And so the discussion of the future of the overseas ' empires ' brings us again to the same realization to which the discussion of nearly every great issue arising out of this war has pointed, the realization of the imperative necessity of some great council or conference, some permanent overriding body, call it what you will, that will deal with things more broadly than any ' nationalism ' or ' patriotic imperialism ' can possibly do. That body must come into human affairs. Upon the courage and imagination of living statesmen it depends whether it will come simply and directly into concrete reality or whether it will materialize slowly through, it may be, centuries of blood and blundering from such phantom anticipations as this, anticipations that now haunt the thoughts of all politically-minded men."

So I was already trying to get the World-State recognized as a war objective in 1916.

In the late summer of 1916 I visited the Italian, French and German fronts. There was a fashion in that year of inviting writers and artists to go and see for themselves what the war was like and to report their impressions. I was kept loafing about in Paris for some week or so, I had a talk with Papa Joffre and was presented solemnly with a set of coloured postcards of all the chief French generals, and very good postcards they made. I went through North Italy by Gorizia to the Carso, returned to France to the front near Soissons and then went at my own request to the British front about Arras, to compare the British and French organizations for aerial photography.

It was an interesting but rather pointless trip. At Arras I met and went about with O. G. S. Crawford, whose ingenious readings of the air photographs delighted me very much—he is now largely responsible for that interesting periodical *Antiquity*, and he has applied all that he learnt in warfare to the nobler uses of scientific survey. At Amiens I was under the wing of C. E. Montague, the author of *A Hind let Loose*, *Disenchantment* and *Rough Justice*. Montague was a curious mixture of sixth-form Anglican sentimentality (about dear old horses, dearer old doggies, brave women, real gentlemen, the old school, the old country and sound stock: Galsworthyissimus in fact), with a most adventurous intelligence. He was a radical bound, hide bound, in a conservative hide. He was a year younger than I, he had concealed his age and dyed his silvery hair to enlist at the outbreak of the war, he had accepted a commission with reluctance and I had been warned he was not the safest of guides. We got on very well together. I remember vividly walking with him across the shell-hole-dotted, wire-littered open towards the front-line trenches. The sun was shining brightly and there was just the faintest whiff of freshness and danger in the air. I doubt if anything was coming over; what shelling was audible overhead was British. We had agreed that blundering up the wet and narrow communication trench was intolerable in such sunshine and we walked bare-headed and carried our shrapnel helmets, like baskets, on our arms. We had confessed to each other what a bore the war had become to us, how its vast inconsequence weighed us down, and we talked as we trudged along very happily of the technical merits of Laurence Sterne.

In the front line although he insisted on my keeping my head below the parapet, he was exposing himself freely, standing up and craning his neck in the hope of seeing a German " out there."

" At twilight sometimes you can see them hopping about from one shell hole to another."

But there was nothing doing that day, there had been some " strafing " overnight but that was over, everyone in the trenches was sleeping and we returned through the tranquil desolation disputing whether there was any reason for anticipating a great outburst of literary activity as a result of the war. He thought that there ought to be and I thought that outbursts of literary activity were due to such secondary conditions as to have no directly traceable relation to the great events of history. . . .

At the time of this pointless sight-seeing I might have been doing extremely useful war-work at home. I was still convinced that the war had to be won by the Allies and I was only too eager to give my time and risk my life and fortune, in any task that used me effectively. But I meant to be used effectively. I refused absolutely to volunteer and drill and acquire the saluting habit for the protection of railway bridges and culverts against imaginary nocturnal Germans in the by-ways of Essex, or for sentinel-go in prisoners camps or anything of that sort. But an old notion of mine, the *Land Ironclads* (published in the *Strand Magazine* in 1903) was being worked out at that time in the form of the Tanks, and it is absurd that my imagination was not mobilized in scheming the structure and use of these contrivances. These obvious weapons were forced upon the army by Winston Churchill against all the conservative instincts of the army; Kitchener had turned them down as " mechanical toys," and when at length they were put into action, it was done so timidly and experimentally and with so inadequate an estimate of their possibilities that their immense value as a major surprise that might have ended the war, was altogether wasted. Later some were bogged in Flanders mud, to the great delight of the contemporary military mind. If the tanks could not be prevented, the next best thing from the old army point of view was to spoil them. " Can't use the damned things. Look at *that* ! " Nowadays things have altered in form but not in essence and the British military intelligence, with its unerring instinct for being two decades out of date, is plainly and dangerously tank-mad.

When I heard about the tanks I felt bitter and frustrated, but that did not save me from getting into conflict later with the rigid intelligence of the professional soldiers.

I was lying snug in bed one night and I could not sleep. My window was open and the rain was pouring down outside and suddenly in an imaginative flash I saw the communication trenches swamped and swimming in mud and a miserable procession of overloaded " Tommies " struggling up to the front line along the wet planks. Some stumbled and fell. I knew men were often drowned in this dismal pilgrimage and that everyone who got to the front line arrived nearly worn out and smothered in mud. Moreover the utmost supplies these men could carry were insufficient. Suddenly I saw that this was an entirely avoidable strain. I tumbled out of bed and spent the rest of the night planning a mobile telpherage system. My idea was to run forward a set of T-shaped poles with an erector wire, so that they could be all pulled up for use or allowed to lie flat and that two tractor wires could then work on the arms of the T. Power could be supplied by a motor lorry at the base of this line.

Either just before this or just after it I met Winston Churchill at lunch in Clare Sheridan's studio in St. John's Wood. I think it was just before. I had aired my grievance about the tanks and so I was able to get going with him about this telpherage project forthwith. He saw my points and put me in touch with capable men to supplement my mechanical insufficiency. Upon his instructions, E. V. Haigh, who was at the Ministry of Munitions, set the Trench Warfare Department in motion, and a temporary lieutenant Leeming—I think from Lancashire—worked out the apparatus with a group of men and made a reality of my dream.

We invented a really novel war accessory—I contributed

THE IDEA OF A PLANNED WORLD

nothing except the first idea and a few comments—and it was available as a perfected pattern before the end of the war, though never in sufficient quantity to produce perceptible effects. The " tin hats " did not like it. It would have saved multitudes of casualties and greatly facilitated the opening phases of the Allied offensive in 1918.

This telpherage of ours was no mere static transport system. It could be run forward almost as fast as infantry could advance; any part could be carried by a single man, it could be hauled up for action and lie when not in use; an ordinary lorry, the lorry that had brought up the poles and wire, could work it from a protected emplacement and it could carry an endless string of such loads as a wounded man on a stretcher or an equivalent weight of food or ammunition. We worked a rough trial length on Clapham Common and then installed, in Richmond Park, more than a mile which behaved admirably. If the line were disabled by a shell it was easy to repair and replace, and it was extremely light to bring up. It was practically invisible from the air, since its use wore no track and it could be shifted laterally and dismantled as easily as it was erected. (A description of the " Leeming " Portable and Collapsible Aerial Ropeway is documented with prints and photographs, under date November 26th, 1917, in the archives of the Ministry of Munitions.)

This work brought me into closer touch with the military caste than I had ever been before. I had known plenty of men, politicians and so forth, who had been in regular regiments for brief periods, but these men I now encountered were the real army and nothing else. They were the quintessence of Service mentality. They impressed me extraordinarily—excessively. My memories of them I am persuaded must be exaggerated. They remain in my memory as an incredible caricature.

I remember vividly a conference we had in a shed upon the Thames embankment. The soldiers came "well groomed" as the phrase goes, in peculiarly beautiful red-banded peaked caps, heavy with gold braid. Crowns and stars, ribbons, epaulettes, belts and bands of the utmost significance, adorned their persons. War was the most important function in life for them and they dressed for it. They sat down, like men who had given some thought to sitting down in the best possible manner. They produced their voices; they did not merely emit audible turbid thoughts as we did. If you had listened only to the sounds they made, you would have felt they were simple clear-headed men, speaking with a sane determination, and yet the things they said were by my standards almost inconceivably silly. Over against them sat my civilian colleagues, and only David Low could convey to you how comparatively ignoble we looked in our untidy every-day costumes, our bowler hats, our wilted collars, our carelessly chosen and carelessly tied war-time cravats. Judged by the way we carried ourselves we might almost as well have had no chests at all. And though our vocabulary was much more extensive there was no click about it. The noises we made came in shambling loose formation—from Scotland and Lancashire and Cockney London.

That contrast stuck in my mind and haunted me. It exercised me profoundly. It set me thinking of the implacable determination of so many types of life—and perhaps of all types of life—not to over-adapt, to make concessions indeed up to a certain extent, but not to make too fundamental concessions,—to perish rather. It made me waver towards the dogma of the class war. Here were these fine, handsome, well-groomed neighing gentlemen, the outcome of some century or so of army tradition, conscientiously good to look at but in no way showy or flashy, and they had clear definite ideas of what war was, what was permissible in war, what was undesirable about war, what was seemly, what was honourable, how far you might go and where you had to leave off, the complete etiquette of it. We and our like with our bits of stick and iron-pipe and wire, our test-tubes and our tanks and our incalculable possibilities, came to these fine but entirely inconclusive warriors humbly demanding permission to give them victory—but victory at the price of all that they were used to, of all they held dear. It must have been obvious to them, for instance, that we hated saluting; we were the sort that might talk shop at mess; we had no essential rigidities, no style; our loyalties were incomprehensible; our effect on "the men" if men had to be instructed, might be deplorable. We had therefore in plain English to be outwitted, cheated, discredited and frustrated; and we were.

It was not a plot against us; it was an instinct. Not one of those soldiers would have admitted, even in his secret heart, that that was what he meant to do. But it was what he did. Damn these contrivances! It was far easier to understand a fellow officer from Berlin or Vienna than these Inventors. It was fundamentally more important for those finished products of our militant sovereign state system to beat us than to beat the Germans; they felt that, even if they did not recognize it clearly. We were trying to get hold of their war and carry it God knows where—it would be the story of those beastly tanks over again. It was a fresh encroachment. At any cost it must not become our war; it must remain theirs. Or it might really turn out to be "the war to end war"—and end all sorts of associated things.

In the behaviour of the War Office and Foreign Office and in the strenuous and intelligent resolve of the Crown to keep itself authoritatively in the limelight, the struggle to keep things in their places and resist novelties became more and more manifest as the war continued. The history of the Great War, regarded as an intensifying clash between old forms and new forces, still remains to be written. And yet that is perhaps the most interesting aspect of all. The war between the Allied Powers and the Central Powers was a war between similars; it was the established proper vertical aspect of the war; it was like any old war except that it was bigger. War had been declared; one side had taken the offensive and the other the defensive according to rule. But within the fighting body of each combatant state, there speedily began this more novel struggle, a horizontal struggle, between class tradition and the insistent need for decisive original inventions and new methods. The soldiers could not invent; it had been drilled out of them. And this struggle again was complicated by the progressive disillusionment of the common man who had neither social nor technical standing. He displayed a deepening dislike to being killed either in the old style or the new. At first he had been fiercely patriotic everywhere and then, as the wilting discipline of 1917 and 1918, the mutinies and refusals showed, more and more desperately recalcitrant. These three elements interacted in different proportions and with varying results in every combatant country, and to trace their interplay would carry me far beyond the region of autobiography into an essay in recent history.

In Britain, as in France, the old order contrived to keep in the saddle and its obstinate loyalty to itself prolonged the struggle through two years of intensified and totally unnecessary waste and slaughter. Radical critics obsessed by Marxist suggestions are apt to ascribe this prolongation of the war simply to the wickedness of armament and financial interests. That is only partially true. It is so much easier to denounce " capitalism " than to denounce real categories and specific governmental institutions capable of reprisal. War industry and financial influences, though unquestionably they were evil influences, could not have worked except through the legal forms of the old order. The steel framework of the obstruction was, everywhere, the self-protective obstinacy of the formal government in control, which would not accept even compromise, much less admit defeat. The profiteers no doubt flattered and used the formal government for their own ends but they were never the masters of it. Much more were they its by-products. They sheltered and did their mischief behind its implacable resistance to efficiency.

To the very end of the war not one of all the generals who prance across the page of history developed the ability to handle the vast armies and mechanisms under his nominal control. Nor was any flexible and effective method of collaboration ever brought into being. The Great War was an All Fools' War. But there was no admission of this fact. The system just went on with the witless slaughter until discipline dissolved, first in Russia and then—luckily for us and the immobilized French—in Germany. And instantly upon the German collapse our populace forgot its gathering doubts. The monarchy, lest there should be any question about the way in which the War to End War had ended, went in state through the beflagged streets of London, unashamed amidst a blaze of uniforms and a great blare of military music, to thank our dear old Anglican Trinity, Who had been, it seems, in control throughout, in St. Paul's Cathedral.

Girls, children, women, schoolboys, undergraduates, unfit, middle-aged and elderly men, indispensables and soldiers from the home front, thronged the streets rejoicing; glad that the national martyrdom was over and quite uncritical already of either Army, Navy or Crown. There were a million of us dead of course, and half of those deaths, even from the military point of view had been sheer waste, but after all *we* had won. And the dead were dead. A Grand Inquest on those dead would have been a more reasonable function, but how disagreeable that would have been!

I remember starting out with Jane during one of these pompous, swarming occasions to get from our flat in Whitehall Court to Liverpool Street Station and so escape to the comparative disloyalty of our home at Easton Glebe. Our cab was held up and we had to abandon it and struggle with our bags through the press as well as we could. We squeezed through at last and caught a later train than we intended. It was one of those occasions when my love for my fellow man deserts me. The happy complacency of survivorship shone on every face in that vast crowd. What personal regrets appeared were richly sentimental and easily tearful. " Poor dear Tommy! How he would have *loved* all this! "

We were going to hang the Kaiser and make the Germans pay. The country was now to be made a country " fit for heroes." God save the King!

" And this," thought I, " is the reality of democracy; this is the proletariat of dear old Marx in being. This is the real people. This seething multitude of vague kindly uncritical brains is the stuff that old dogmatist counted upon for his dictatorship of the proletariat, to direct the novel and complex organization of a better world!"

The thought suddenly made me laugh aloud, and after that it was easier to push along and help steer Jane through the crowd about the Royal Exchange. . . .

But I am digressing and telling things out of their proper order.

Aldershot, I presently realized, was resolved not to have anything to do with this telpherage of ours—at least as we had devised it. It was bad enough for soldiers and gentlemen to be bothered with tanks, but this affair of sticks and string was even worse. After mechanical toys—cat's cradle. It was the sort of contraption anyone might make mistakes about—and then where were you? However, in its earnest desire to keep the business in professional hands, Aldershot produced alternative systems. They were much heavier and clumsier than ours and one, much in favour, required men to walk along the track, so—as we had to explain to these professional soldiers—exposing the system to air photography and air-directed fire. A bugbear we could never banish from these inflexible minds was the dread that our lines—which could be lowered in an instant and cleared away in an hour—would interfere with "lateral movements."

This in no-man's land with its shell holes and old trenches and jungle thickets of cut wire! The thought of a "line," any line, hypnotized these warriors, just as a chalk line will hypnotize a hen.

I was baffled and worried beyond measure by these perverse difficulties. I felt my practical incompetence acutely. I did not know whom to get at and how to put the thing through. I had only a dim apprehension of the forces and instincts that were holding back not merely our little contrivance, but a multitude of other innovations that might have changed the face of the war. Meanwhile on every wet night so many poor lads fell and choked in the mud, and the little inadequate offensives squittered forward beyond their supports and succumbed to the counter-attack. I could not sleep for it. I was so worried and my nerves were so fatigued that I was presently afflicted with *allopecia areata*, well known in the flying corps of those days as an anxiety disease, in which the hair comes out in patches. Ridiculous patches of localized shiny baldness appeared and did not vanish for a year or so, when first they sprouted a down of grey hair and then became normally hairy again. It was not much in the way of a war wound, but in all modesty I put it on record.

I returned from the western front in 1916 with, among other things, a very clear conviction that cavalry was a useless nuisance there. I wrote some disagreeable things about the fodder waggons that choked the roads, about spurs and about our military efficiency generally, in a series of articles which became a book, *War and the Future* (1917). But there was a war Censorship in existence, and an excellent gentleman, Colonel Swettenham—or General I forget which—who had for some obscure reason been put in authority over the mind of England, presently summoned me to his presence and remonstrated with me over the galley proofs of my book. I went home with these proofs considerably emasculated, blue-pencilled and amended in the Colonel's handwriting. I meditated over his alterations. They seemed to me to be intended to save rather the prestige of the military authorities than the country, for if people like I were not to chide the military authorities and tell the public about them, who would? These soldiers would go on with their bloody muddle. Muddle until disaster was assured.

I took another set of proofs, made no material changes in what I had said, sent them to my publisher with my explicit assurance that the Censor had seen a set, and then, though it hurt me greatly to destroy many of the painstaking improvements he had made, I burnt the Colonel's set. The book appeared and he must have read it with a certain astonishment. After some consideration of the situation he wrote me a very nice letter asking me to return the set of proofs that he had corrected. I wrote him an even nicer letter, explaining that that set was not now to be found, and assuring him of my utmost esteem. With quite exemplary civility our correspondence ceased at that point and the censorship troubled me no more.

The chief point of permanent value in that book was my insistence on the fact that the progressive mechanization of war was making war impossible for any countries that did not possess a highly developed industrial organization and adequate natural resources. Five or six countries at most had it in their power to make modern war, and it needed only an intelligent agreement among these powers to end war, if they so wished it, for ever. This is a reality I have never ceased to press upon the attention of people in general. From 1916 to 1933 I have been sprinkling the world with repetitions of this important truth. I was stressing it in the *Daily Herald* in March 1930, in a series of articles " The A.B.C. of World Peace," reprinted in *After Democracy* (1933). The consent of all the sovereign powers of the world to world pacification is quite unnecessary. Indeed, as I point out in the latter series of articles, three or four powers alone could impose an enduring World Pax. This idea will be found very frankly expressed in the Crewe House memorandum I shall presently quote.

War and the Future, however, is a very mixed bag. There is a gusto in some of its war descriptions that suggests that that mighty statesman-strategist, that embryo Hitler-Cromwell (aged 13) who won the various Battles of Martin's Hill, Bromley, was by no means dead in me, even in 1916.

§ 6

WORLD STATE AND LEAGUE OF NATIONS

TO RETURN to my education by the Great War; 1917 is marked in my records by a letter published in the *Daily Chronicle* for June 4th, entitled " Wanted a Statement of Imperial Policy," by a paper in the *Daily News* August 14th, " A Reasonable Man's Peace," and by a third article, in the

Daily Mail, which I was invited to write by the editor, "Are we sticking to the Point? A Discussion of War Aims."

These writings show a very considerable consolidation of my ideas and in that respect they followed the movement that was going on in the general mind. They are collected together in a book called *In the Fourth Year* (May 1918) which is an immense advance upon *What is Coming?*, uncompromising, bolder and more forcible. And in these the idea of a League of *Free* Nations, a plain anticipation of a federal world-state, is stated with the greatest explicitness. One of these papers, " A Reasonable Man's Peace," was twice reprinted as a pamphlet and had an issue, in that form, of about a quarter of a million.

The idea of some supernational Union of States for the preservation of peace is a very old one indeed and its history quite beyond my present range, but the way in which it came into my purview has to be told. The origin of the term "League of Nations" is obscure. Theodore Marburg's *Development of the League of Nations Idea* (1932), is concerned rather with the voluminous participation of that gentleman in the world's affairs than with history—and so the precise facts are difficult to disentangle. His book is essentially an autobiography in the form of letters, and as a general history it over-emphasizes the importance of Theodore Marburg in developing what one may call the Wilsonian notion of a League. A " League to enforce Peace " was certainly begotten in the Century Club in New York in January 1915 and it seems to have owed something to the private propaganda of Sir George Paish. But the term " League of Nations " is of English origin and it seems to have been first used by a small group of people meeting in the house of Mr. Walter Rea and including Sir Willoughby (now Lord) Dickinson, G. Lowes Dickinson, Raymond Unwin, J. A. Hobson, Mrs. Claremont and Aneurin Williams. (E. M. Forster in his life of Lowes Dickinson (1934) gives reasons for ascribing the term to that writer, who may have used it for the two possible "leagues" he sketched in the first fortnight of the war.) These people founded a League of Nations Society, with Lord Shaw as president, early in 1915. L. S. Woolf also was associated with this group but not, I think, at the beginning.

The world was ripe for the lead embodied in such a phrase and it caught on very rapidly. I was late in recognizing its value. I do not seem to have used the term before the end 1916, but then I seem to have taken it up abruptly and noisily; it is all over my war writings in 1917, with a very characteristic emendation for which I think I was wholly responsible, the insertion of the word " Free." I put in that word Free because I hoped then for republics in Russia and Germany and possibly in Great Britain. I did not believe in world peace without revolution and my efforts to keep the revolutionary impulse in touch with the peace-making movement were very persistent. Early writings to which I make acknowledgement in *In the Fourth Year* are Marburg's *League of Nations* (1917–18), André Mater's *Société des Nations* (an excellent French comment first published, I think, about 1917 and translated in its entirety in Sir George Paish's excellent collection of early projects, *The Nations and the League*, 1920), and H. N. Brailsford's *A League of Nations* (1917). Several organizations using the term, " League of Nations " in their titles, were active in 1917 on both sides of the Atlantic. I joined the London society in 1917 and was later associated with a League of Free Nations Association formed in 1918. My mind fixed upon this word League, as being just the needed formula that might give a World-State its first concrete form. It helped pull my outlook together and point it. *In the Fourth Year* is a crystallization of all the incoherent aspirations of *What is Coming?* and of my past generally. It contained a few outspoken phrases about such matters as " The Future of Monarchy," which were at that time considered extremely indelicate. English people have still to brace themselves up to the obvious fact that there can be no world pax without a practical retirement of monarchy, graceful or graceless as royalty may choose.

During these war years my always friendly relations with Lord Northcliffe became closer. I have told already in Chapter the Sixth, § 4 how we first came to know each other and explained how much this remarkable intruder into the British peerage and British public life, had to improvise to meet the colossal opportunities that were thrust upon him. Whenever I met him I talked plainly to him and he respected even when he did not agree with my ideas. He was never at his ease in the old system; his peerage had not bought him; he knew the old social order accepted him, and his newly-titled brothers, by duress and with furtive protest and he felt the continual danger of treacheries and obstructions. There were times when he reminded me of a big bumble bee puzzled by a pane of glass. The Court, the army people, the Foreign Office treated him with elaborate civility but regarded him with hard, defensive eyes. When the first Russian revolution (March 1917) occurred, I created a small scandal by inducing him to print a letter in *The Times* in favour of a more explicit appeal to the Republican sentiment in the world. This gave great offence in the highest quarters. " There goes my earldom," said Northcliffe to me, with a gleam from the ineradicable schoolboy in his make-up. One had a sense of fuss behind the scenes, and the young subalterns of the Third Army, who had been in the habit of playing hockey and taking baths and teas and supper at my house at Easton every Sunday, were suddenly forbidden my now leprous neighbourhood by their superior officers. " King and country " had got them surely enough; it was " *his* war "—it was the war of the " tin hats." The war for world civilization had vanished. But one or two of these

THE IDEA OF A PLANNED WORLD

young men wrote me pleasant notes of apology for this uncivil loyalty imposed upon them.

The government had created two new ministries for the sake of keeping the inquisitive noses of Northcliffe, and his younger competitor Lord Beaverbrook, out of the ancient mysteries of the Foreign Office. This could be done most unobtrusively by busying them elsewhere. The Ministry of Information was devised to prevent Lord Beaverbrook from becoming too well-informed and the Ministry of Propaganda served a similar purpose in occupying and disordering the always rather febrile mind of Lord Northcliffe. Northcliffe asked me to visit him in Crewe House, where the new Ministry of Propaganda was installed, and discussed the general idea of his activities with me.

We sat together in the drawing-room of Crewe House, hastily adapted to the new requirements of ministerial headquarters. " You want a social revolution," he said. " Isn't our sitting here social revolution enough for you ? "

I might have replied that that depended on the use we made of our time while we were there.

The upshot of our conversation was that in May 1918 in collaboration with that excellent scholar, Dr. J. W. Headlam (who afterwards became by knighthood and a change of name Sir J. W. Headlam Morley), I became responsible for the preparation of propaganda literature against Germany. This was almost simultaneous with the publication of *In the Fourth Year* and its exposition of such still admirable common sense as this that follows :

" The League of Free Nations must, in fact, if it is to be a working reality, have power to define and limit the military and naval and aerial equipment of every country in the world. This means something more than a restriction of state forces. It must have power and freedom to investigate the military and naval and aerial establishments of all its constituent powers. It must also have effective control over every armament industry. And armament industries are not always easy to define. Are aeroplanes, for example, armament? Its powers, I suggest, must extend even to a restraint upon the belligerent propaganda which is the natural advertisement campaign of every armament industry. It must have the right, for example, to raise the question of the proprietorship of newspapers by armament interests. Disarmament is, in fact, a necessary factor of any League of Free Nations, and you cannot have disarmament unless you are prepared to see the powers of the council of the League extend thus far. The very existence of the League presupposes that it and it alone is to have and to exercise military force. Any other belligerency or preparation or incitement to belligerency becomes rebellion, and any other arming a threat of rebellion, in a world League of Free Nations.

"But here, again, has the general mind yet thought out all that is involved in this proposition? In all the great belligerent countries the armament industries are now huge interests with enormous powers. Krupp's business alone is as powerful a thing in Germany as the Crown. In every country a heavily subsidized 'patriotic' press will fight desperately against giving powers so extensive and thorough as those here suggested to an international body. So long, of course, as the League of Free Nations remains a project in the air, without body or parts, such a press will sneer at it gently as 'Utopian,' and even patronize it kindly. But so soon as the League takes on the shape its general proposition makes logically necessary, the armament interest will take fright. Then it is we shall hear the drum patriotic loud in defence of the human blood trade. Are we to hand over these most intimate affairs of ours to 'a lot of foreigners'? Among these 'foreigners' who will be appealed to to terrify the patriotic souls of the British will be the 'Americans.' Are we men of English blood and tradition to see our affairs controlled by such 'foreigners' as Wilson, Lincoln, Webster and Washington? Perish the thought! When they might be controlled by Disraelis, Wettins, Mountbattens and what not! And so on and so on. Krupp's agents and the agents of the kindred firms in Great Britain and France will also be very busy with the national pride of France. In Germany they have already created a colossal suspicion of England.

"Here is a giant in the path. . . .

"But let us remember that it is only necessary to defeat the propaganda of this vile and dangerous industry in four great countries. . . .

"I am suggesting here that the League of Free Nations shall practically control the army, navy, air forces, and armament industry of every nation in the world. What is the alternative to that? To do as we please? No, the alternative is that any malignant country will be free to force upon all the rest just the maximum amount of armament it chooses to adopt. Since 1871 France, we say, has been free in military matters. What has been the value of that freedom? The truth is, she has been the bond-slave of Germany, bound to watch Germany as a slave watches a master, bound to launch submarine for submarine and cast gun for gun, to sweep all her youth into her army, to subdue her trade, her literature, her education, her whole life to the necessity of preparations imposed upon her by her drill-master over the Rhine. And Michael, too, has been a slave to his imperial master for the self-same reason, for the reason that Germany and France were both so proudly sovereign and independent. Both countries have been slaves to Kruppism and Zabernism—*because they were sovereign and free!* So it will always be. So long as patriotic cant can keep the common man jealous of international controls over his belligerent possibilities, so long will he be the helpless slave of the foreign threat, and ' Peace ' remain a mere name for the resting-phase between wars. . . .

"The plain truth is that the League of Free Nations, if it is to be a reality, if it is to effect a real pacification of the world, must do no less than supersede Empire ; it must end not only this new German imperialism, which is struggling so savagely and powerfully to possess the earth, but it must also wind up British imperialism and French imperialism, which do now so largely and inaggressively possess it. And, moreover, this idea queries the adjective of Belgian, Portuguese, French, and British Central Africa alike, just as emphatically as it queries ' German.' Still more effectually does the League forbid those creations of the futurist imagination, the imperialism of Italy and Greece, which make such threatening gestures at the world of our children. Are these incompatibilities understood ? Until people have faced the clear antagonism which exists between imperialism and internationalism, they have not begun to suspect the real significance of this project of the League of Free Nations. They have not begun to realize that peace also has its price."

With this much on record I went to Crewe House. I think that Northcliffe knew something of what I had in mind. Or to be more accurate I think that at times—in exceptional gleams of lucidity—he knew something of what I had in mind and sympathized with it and wanted to forward it. But his undoubtedly big and undoubtedly unco-ordinated brain was like a weather-chart in stormy times; phases of high and low pressure and moral gradients and depressions chased themselves across his mental map. His skull held together, in a delusive unity, a score of flying fragments of purpose. He was living most of his time in the Isle of Thanet and rushing to and fro between that house of refuge and the excitements of London. I put it to him that we had no clear idea of the work his Ministry of Propaganda had to do, as a whole, and that to make our exertions effective it was necessary that our objectives should be defined.

Before the creation of the ministry, such propaganda as existed had been a business of leaflet distribution by secret agents and by the air, the forging of pseudo-German newspapers with depressing suggestions and the like, and this was already being expanded very energetically when I took up my duties. Descriptions and details are to be found in the *Secrets of Crewe House*. I did what I could to forward all that and to make such modifications as occurred to me, but these activities did not seem to me to exhaust the possibilities of our organization. Telling lies—and occasionally revealing the concealed truth of the situation—to the German rank and file and the Germans behind the front, " attacking morale " as it was termed, was perhaps a necessary operation in this new sort of warfare we were waging, but it was really much more important now to get to something in the nature of a common understanding between the combatant populations if a genuine peace were to be achieved. The best counter-check to the very vigorous war propaganda sustained by the enemy governments, was honest peace propaganda, and I did my utmost to make Crewe House an organization not merely for bringing the war to a victorious end, but also for defining that end with an explicitness equally binding upon us, our Allies and the enemy.

I had no illusions left about the fundamental wisdom of the British and French Foreign Offices. They were, I realized, in the hands of men of limited outlooks and small motives, whose chief control was their servitude to tradition. They had far less grasp of the world situation than an average intelligent man, and the duty of everyone who had a chance, was to help force their hands towards such a " Reasonable Man's Peace " as was now everywhere defining itself in the liberal mind.

One great desideratum was that there should be a plain statement of " War Aims " to the whole world. Then the combatants would realize the conditions of cessation. I persuaded Crewe House that our work necessitated such a statement of what we were fighting for, properly endorsed by the Foreign Office, and in conjunction with Headlam Morley a memorandum was prepared, submitted to an Advisory Committee and fully discussed. This Committee, by the bye, consisted of the Earl of Denbigh, Mr. Robert Donald (then Editor of the *Daily Chronicle*), Sir Roderick Jones, Sir Sidney Low, Sir Charles Nicholson, Mr. James O'Grady, Mr. H. Wickham Steed (foreign Editor and later Editor-in-Chief of *The Times*), Dr. Headlam Morley, Mr. H. K. Hudson (Secretary) and myself, and the memorandum to which we agreed said among other things :

"It has become manifest that, for the purposes of an efficient pro-Ally propaganda in neutral and enemy countries, a clear and full statement of the war aims of the Allies is vitally necessary. What is wanted is something in the nature of an authoritative text to which propagandists may refer with confidence and which can be made the standard of their activities. It is not sufficient to recount the sins of Germany and to assert that the defeat of Germany is the Allied war aim. What all the world desires to know is what is to happen *after* the war. The real war aim of a belligerent, it is more and more understood, is not merely victory, but a peace of a certain character which that belligerent desires shall arise out of that victory. What, therefore, is the peace sought by the Allies?

"It would be superfluous even to summarize here the primary case of the Allies, that the war is on their part a war to resist the military aggression of Germany, assisted by the landowning Magyars of Hungary, the Turks, and the King of Bulgaria, upon the rest of mankind. It is a war against belligerence, against aggressive war and the preparation for aggressive war. Such it was in the beginning, and such it remains. But it would be idle to pretend that the ideas of the Governments and peoples allied against Germany have not developed very greatly during the years of the war.... There has arisen in the great world outside the inner lives of the Central Powers a will that grows to gigantic proportions, that altogether overshadows the boasted *will to power* of the German junker and exploiter, *the will to a world peace*. It is like the will of an experienced man set against the will of an obstinate and selfish youth. The war aims of the anti-German Allies take more and more definitely the form of a world of States leagued together to maintain a common law, to submit their mutual differences to a conclusive tribunal, to protect weak communities, to restrain and suppress war threats and war preparations throughout the earth.... The thought of the world crystallizes now about a phrase, the phrase 'The League of Free Nations.' The war aims of the Allies become more and more explicitly associated with the spirit and implications of that.

"Like all such phrases, 'The League of Free Nations' is subject to a great variety of detailed interpretation, but its broad intentions can now be stated without much risk of dissent. The ideal would, of course, include all the nations of the earth, including a Germany purged of her military aggressiveness; it involves some sort of International Congress that can revise, codify, amend and extend international law, a supreme Court of Law in which States may sue and be sued, and whose decision the League will be pledged to enforce, and the supervision, limitation, and use of armaments under the direction of the international congress. . . . The constitution of this congress remains indefinite; it is the crucial matter upon which the best thought of the world is working at the present time. But given the prospect of a suitable congress there can be little dispute that the Imperial Powers among the Allies are now prepared for great and generous limitations of their sovereignty in the matter of armaments, of tropical possessions and of subject peoples, in the common interest of mankind. . . . Among the Allies, the two chief Imperial Powers, measured by the extent of territory they control, are Britain and France, and each of these is more completely prepared to-day than ever it has been before to consider its imperial possessions as a trust for their inhabitants and for mankind, and its position in the more fertile and less settled regions of the world as that of a mandatory and trustee. . . .

" But in using the phrase ' The League of Nations,' it may be well to dispel certain misconceptions that have arisen through the experimental preparation, by more or less irresponsible persons and societies, of elaborate schemes and constitutions of such a league. Proposals have been printed and published, for example, of a Court of World Conciliation, in which each sovereign State will be represented by one member—Montenegro, for example, by one, and the British Empire by one—and other proposals have been mooted of a Congress of the League of Nations, in which such States as Hayti, Abyssinia, and the like will be represented by one or two representatives, and France and Great Britain by five or six. All such projects should be put out of mind when the phrase ' League of Free Nations ' is used by responsible speakers for the Allied Powers. Certain most obvious considerations have evidently been overlooked by the framers of such proposals. It will, for example, be a manifest disadvantage to the smaller Powers to be at all over-represented upon the Congress of any such League; it may even be desirable that certain of them should not have a *voting* representative at all, for this reason, that a great Power still cherishing an aggressive spirit would certainly attempt, as the beginning of its aggression, to compel adjacent small Powers to send representatives practically chosen by itself. The coarse fact of the case in regard to an immediate world peace is this, that only five or six great Powers possess sufficient economic resources to make war under modern conditions at the present time, namely, the United States of America, Great Britain, France, Germany, Japan, and doubtfully, Austria-Hungary. Italy suffers under the disadvantage that she has no coal supply. These five or six Powers we may say, therefore, permit war and can prevent it. They are, at present, necessarily the custodians of the peace of the world, and it is mere pedantry not to admit that this gives them a practical claim to preponderance in the opening Congress of the World League. . . ."

This memorandum was sent, with a covering letter from Lord Northcliffe, to Lord Balfour for the endorsement of the Foreign Office. We had all been kept in the dark as to the cramping secret engagements which had been made by our diplomatists, and we had no suspicion that our broad and reasonable proposals were already impossible. We were not enlightened. Dr. Headlam Morley and I were invited for a conversation with Lord Tyrrell who was then Sir William Tyrrell. Possibly he intended to give us a hint about the secret treaties but, if so, he never did as he intended or the hint was too feeble to register upon our minds. Tyrrell was a compact self-assured little man, who tacitly put our memorandum on one side, rested his elbow on it, so to speak, and delivered a discourse on our relations to France and Germany and on the " characters " of these countries, that would have done credit to a bright but patriotic school-boy of eight, and so having told us exactly where we were, he dismissed biologist and historian together unheard. I suppose he had learnt that stuff for gospel from his governess at his knickerbocker stage, and had never had the wit to doubt it. Most upper-class mentality is founded on governesses.

According to such lights as he had acquired in his tender years, he was perfectly honest and patriotic—if a little " pro-French."

It is terrifying to think that these vast powers, the Foreign Offices of the world, are being run to a very large extent by little undeveloped brains such as Tyrrell's, that they are immensely protected from criticism and under no real control from educated opinion. And what they do affects and endangers hundred of millions of lives.

That conversation was the utmost Crewe House got out of the Foreign Office. We assumed rather rashly that our memorandum had been tacitly accepted and pursued our propaganda activities on those lines. That, from the diplomatic point of view was admirable, because in our quasi-official rôle we gave assurances to doubtful Germans, that could afterwards be repudiated. We were in fact decoys. Just as T. E. Lawrence of the " Seven Pillars " was used all unawares as a decoy for the Arabs. And all for nothing ! Plainly I had not learnt the A.B.C. of diplomacy.

There were at that time several small organizations promoting the League of Nations idea. I took part in a successful attempt to consolidate these into one League of Nations Union, which would not merely spread but develop the idea. I put the stress upon the development. It was conspicuously evident that, so far, the idea was lacking in detail and definition ; it was like a bag into which anything might still be put and there were a number of things that I felt were very undesirable as occupants of that bag and others that were vitally important. I was already alive, as that Crewe House memorandum shows, to the danger of a pseudo-parliamentary organization, with an enfeebling constitution, and I felt we had to get ahead of that by working out some clearer statement of the possibilities of the occasion. We evolved therefore a " Research Committee " which could press on with this necessary preliminary work. It consisted of the following members, most of whom, I must admit, did no work whatever upon it ; Mr. Ernest Barker, Mr. Lionel Curtis, Mr. G. Lowes Dickinson, Viscount Grey of Fallodon, Mr. John Hilton, Professor Gilbert Murray, Mr. H. Wickham Steed, Mr. J. A. Spender, Mr. L. S. Woolf, Mr. A. E. Zimmern, and myself, with Mr. William Archer as secretary. It produced only two pamphlets " The Idea of a League of Nations " and " The Way to the League of Nations " before events superseded it.

The former of these pamphlets ends with this passage :

" Negative peace is not our aim. It is something, of course, to have a rest from suffering and the infliction of suffering ; but it is a greater thing to be set free, and peace sets people free. It sets them free to live, to think, to work at the work that is best worth doing, to build instead of destroying, to devote themselves to the pursuit or the creation of the things that seem highest, instead of having to spend all their time in trying to avoid being killed. Peace is an empty cup that we can fill as we please ; it is an opportunity which we can seize or neglect. To recognize this is to sweep out of one's mind all dreams of a world peace contrived by a few jurists and influential people in some odd corner of the world's administrative bureaux. As well might the three tailors of Tooley Street declare the millennium in being. Permanent world peace must necessarily be a great process and state of affairs, greater indeed than any war process, because it must anticipate, comprehend, and prevent any war process, and demand the conscious, the understanding, the willing participation of the great majority of human beings. We, who look to it as a possible thing, are bound not to blind ourselves to, or conceal from others, the gigantic and laborious system of labours, the immense tangle of co-operations, which its establishment involves. If political institutions or social methods stand in the way of this great good for mankind, it is fatuous to dream of compromises with them. A world peace-organization cannot evade universal relationships.

" It is clear that if a world league is to be living and enduring,

THE IDEA OF A PLANNED WORLD 707

the idea of it and the need and righteousness of its service must be taught by every educational system in the world. It must either be served by or be in conflict with every religious organization ; it must come into the life of every one, not to release men and women from loyalty, but to demand loyalty for itself. The answer to the criticism that world peace will release men from service is, that world peace is itself a service. It calls, not as war does for the deaths, but for that greater gift, for the lives, of men. The League of Nations cannot be a little thing : it is either to be a great thing in the world, an overriding idea of a greater state, or nothing. Every state aims ultimately at the production of a sort of man, and it is an idle and a wasteful diplomacy, a pandering to timidities and shams, to pretend that the World League of Nations is not ultimately a State aiming at that ennobled individual whose city is the world."

We got as far as that. And then President Wilson essentially ill-informed, narrowly limited to an old-fashioned American conception of history, self-confident and profoundly self-righteous, came to Europe and passed us by on the other side. Men of my way of thinking were left helpless, voiceless and altogether baffled outside the fiasco of Versailles. What had seemed to be the portal of a World Control standing wide open to us, was shut and slammed in our faces.

My friend Philip Guedalla, discussing this period of memorandum-writing with me the other day, recalled a letter which he declared I had sent to President Wilson, at the President's request, through the hands of Mr. Bainbridge Colby in November 1917. He alleged that through this letter I had contributed materially to the President's "Fourteen Points." I think very poorly of the Fourteen Points and at the time I was unable to recall any communication justifying this accusation. A search was made, however, and finally a copy of the following letter was disinterred. The original was conveyed, with Mr. Guedalla's assistance, past any risks of war-time censorship to Mr. Colby who had gone on to Paris.

I doubt whether this letter was ever actually read by President Wilson though we have Colby's word for it that it reached his hands. I never heard from President Wilson in the matter. Colonel House came to Easton Glebe while the President was in England, but he and Mrs. House were so anxious to hurry on to " see over " Hatfield, the historical mansion of the Cecils, that there was no possibility of any political talk. A chance to see Hatfield might not recur. My letter therefore has no grain of historical importance, but in the light of the concluding passage of the preceding section it has considerable autobiographical significance.

It runs :

Dear Mr. Bainbridge Colby,

You asked me, after our conversation at the Reform Club on the evening of November the fourteenth, to set down on paper my views upon the part America might and should play in this war. It was not the military side of the matter that engaged us, though I feel very strongly that by a bold use of scientific inventions the American intelligence, accustomed to a large handling of economic problems and the free scrapping of obsolescent material and methods, may yet be of enormous service and stimulus to the Allied effort ; it was rather the political rôle of America about which we talked. I warned you that I was perhaps not to be taken as a representative Englishman, that I was scientifically trained, a republican, and " pro-American." I repeat that warning now. Here are my views for what they are worth.

They are based on one fundamental conviction. There is no way out of this war process—there may be a peace of sorts but it will only lead to a recrudescence of war—except by the establishment of a new order in human affairs. This new order is adumbrated in the phrase, *A League of Nations*. It lies behind that vaguer, more dangerous because less definite, phrase, " a Just Peace." We have, I am convinced, to set our faces towards that order, towards that just peace, *irrespective of the amount of victory that falls to us.* We may achieve it by negotiations at any point when the German mind becomes open to the abandonment of militant imperialism. If by a sudden change and storm of fortune we found Germany deserted by her allies, prostrate at our feet, our troops in Berlin and her leaders captive, we could do no more, we should do ourselves and the whole future of mankind a wrong if we did more, than make this same " Just Peace " or set up this League of Nations. There is, I hold, a definable *Right Thing* for most practical purposes in international relations ; there are principles according to which boundaries can be drawn and rights of way and privileges of trade settled and apportioned (under the protection of the general League) as dispassionately as a cartographer makes a contour line.

This I believe is the conviction to which a scientific training leads a man. It is the conviction, *more or less* clearly developed, of rational-minded people everywhere. It is manifestly the idea of President Wilson. It is the conviction that has to be made to dominate the world.

And this conviction of a possible dispassionate settlement is one for which the world is now ready. I am convinced that in no country is there even one per cent of the population anxious to prolong the war. The ninety and nine are seeking helplessly for a way out such as only a dispassionate settlement can give. But they are kept in the war by fear. And by mental habit. Few men have the courage to reach their own convictions. They must be led to them or helped to them. They fear the greed of their antagonists, fresh wars, fresh outrages, and an unending series of evil consequences, if they seem to accept anything short of triumph. No one can read the newspapers of any belligerent country without realizing the overwhelming share of fear in now prolonging the struggle. Germany as much as any country fights on and is helpless in the hands of her military caste, *because there is no confidence in Germany in the possibility of a Just Peace*. There is an equal want of confidence in London and Paris and New York. To create a feeling of confidence in that possibility of a Just Peace everywhere is as necessary a part of our struggle for a right order in the world as to hold the German out of Calais or Paris.

It is easy to underrate the pacific impulse in men and to overrate their malignity. All men are mixed in their nature and none without a certain greed, baseness, vindictiveness. After the strain and losses of such a struggle as this it is "only in human nature" to prepare to clutch and punish whenever the scales of victory seem sagging in our favour. Too much importance must not be attached to the aggressive patriotism of the Press in the belligerent countries. Let us keep a little humour in our interpretation of enemy motives and remember that though a man has still much of the ape in his composition, that does not make him an irredeemable devil. The same German who will read with exultation of the submarining of a British passenger ship, or pore over a map of Europe to plan a giant Germany reaching from Antwerp to Constantinople, founded on blood and dreadfulness and ruling the earth, will, in his saner moments, be only too ready to accept and submit himself to a scheme of general good will, provided only that it ensures for him and his a tolerable measure of prosperity and happiness. The belligerent element is present in every man, but in most it is curable. The incurably belligerent minority in any country is extremely small. There is a rational pacifist in nearly every man's brain, and the right end of the war can come only by evoking that.

It is here that the peculiar opportunity of America and of President Wilson comes in. America is three thousand miles from the war; she has no lost provinces to regain, no enemy colonies to capture; she is, in comparison with any of our Allies except China, a dispassionate combatant. (If China can be called a combatant.) No other combatant except America can talk of peace without relinquishing a claim or accepting an outrage. America alone can stand fearlessly and unembarrassed for that rational settlement all men desire. It is from America alone that the lead can come which will take mankind out of this war. It is to America under President Wilson that I look as the one and only medium by which we can get out of this jangling monstrosity of conflict.

What is wanted now is a statement of the Just Peace, a statement without reservations. We want something more than a phrase to bind the nations together. America has said "League of Nations" and everywhere there has been an echo to that. But now we want America to take the next step and to propose the establishment of that League, to define in general terms the nature of the League, to press the logical necessity of a consultative, legislative, and executive conference, and to call together so much of that conference as exists on the Allied side. *There will never be such a conference until America demands it.* There will never be a common policy for the Allies or a firm proposal of peace conditions, unless America insists. This war may drag on for another year of needless bloodshed and end in mutual recriminations through the sheer incapacity of any Ally but America to say plainly what is in fact acceptable to all.

In addition to the moral advantage of its aloofness, America has a second advantage in having a real head, representative and expressive. Possessing that head, America can talk. Alone in our system America is capable of articulate speech. Russia is now headless, a confusion ; Italy is divided against herself ; in France and Britain politicians and party leaders make speeches that are welcomed here and abused there. No predominant utterance is possible. It will be no secret to an observant American such as you are, that Britain and France are divided in a quarrel between reactionary and progressive, between aggressive nationalism and modern liberalism. All the European allies are hampered by secret bargains and pacts of greediness. They have soiled their minds with schemes of annexation and exploitation in Syria, in Albania, in Mesopotamia and Asia Minor. Russia was to have had Constantinople, and so forth and so forth. This ugly legacy of the old diplomacy entangles our public men hopelessly to-day. Even where they are willing to repudiate these plans to-day for themselves they are tied by loyalty to the bright projects of their allies, and silenced. Their military operations have had no real unity because their policy, their war aims, have been diverse. The great alliance against the Central Powers has been a bargain system and not a unification. The allied statesmen, challenged as to their war aims, repeat time after time the same valiant resolution to " end militarism," free small nations, and the like, standing all the time quite resolutely with their backs to the real issues which are the control of the Tropics, the future of the Ottoman Empire, and international trade conditions. So it seems likely to go on. Any voice that is raised to demand a lucid statement of the Allied aims in these matters is drowned in a clamour of alarmed interests. In Britain and France " hush " in the interests of diplomacy is being organized with increasing violence. Only America can help us out of the tangle by asserting its own interpretation of the common war purpose, and demanding a clear unanimity on the part of the Allies. The war was begun to defeat German imperialist aggression. It is with extreme reluctance that the European powers will accept the one way to salvation, which is the abandonment of all imperialist aggression and the acceptance of a common international method. The League of Nations is a mere phrase until it is realized by a body whose authority is supreme, overriding every national flag in the following spheres, in Africa between the Sahara and the Zambesi, as a trustee in Armenia, Syria and all the regions of the earth whose political status has been destroyed by the war, and permanently upon the high seas and vital channels (such as the Dardanelles) of the world.

America in the last three years has made great strides from its traditional isolation towards a responsible share in framing the common destinies of mankind. But America has to travel further on the same road. The future of America is now manifestly bound up with the peace of Europe, for that peace cannot be secured unless these sources of contention in the supply of tropical raw material and in the transport and trading facilities of the world are so controlled as to be no longer sources of contention. It is easy to argue that America has " no business " in Central Africa or Western Asia, that these are matters for the " powers concerned " to decide. But it is just because America has no " business " in Central Africa and Western Asia that it is necessary that America should have a definite will about Africa and Western Asia. Her aloofness gives her her authority. The " powers concerned " will never of their own initiative decide. They are too deeply concerned, and they will haggle. It is, I fear, altogether too much to expect a generous scheme for the joint settlement of regions by powers who have for a century cultivated a scheming habit of appropriation. But none of these powers can afford to haggle against the clear will for order of America at the present time.

What is suggested here is not a surrender of sovereignty nor a direct " international control " of tropical Africa, but the setting up of an overruling board composed of delegates from the powers concerned : Frenchman, Englishman, Africander, Portuguese, Belgian, Italian and (ultimately) German, to which certain functions can be delegated, as powers are delegated to the government of the United States of America by those states.

Among these functions would be transport control, trade control, the arms and drink trades, the revision of legislation affecting the native and his land, the maintenance of a supreme court for Central Africa, the establishment of higher education for the native, and the systematic disarmament of all the African possessions. A similar board, a protectorate board, could take charge of the transport, waterways, customs, and disarmament of the former Ottoman empire. Only by the establishment of such boards can we hope to save those regions from becoming at the end of this war, fields of the bitterest international rivalry, seed-beds of still direr conflicts. It is in the creation and support of such special boards, and of other boards for disarmament, international health, produce control and financial control, that the reality of a League of Nations can come into being. But Europe is tied up into a complexity of warring and jostling interests ; without an initiative from America it is doubtful whether the world now possesses sufficient creative mental energy to achieve any such synthesis, obvious though its need is and greatly as men would welcome it. In all the world there is no outstanding figure to which the world will listen, there is no man audible in all the world, in Japan as well as Germany and Rome as well as Boston—except the President of the United States. Anyone else can be shouted down and will be shouted down by minor interests. From him, and from him alone, can come the demand for that unity without which the world perishes, and those clear indications of the just method of the League of Nations for which it waits.

There is another area, an area beyond the scope of international controls, which remains an area of incalculable chances because no clear *dominant idea* has been imposed upon the world. This is Eastern Europe from Poland to the Adriatic. The Allies have no common idea, and they never have had a common idea and do not seem to be capable of developing a common idea about this region. They do not even know whether they wish to destroy or enlarge the Austro-Hungarian system. Vague vapourings about the rights of nationality conceal a formless confusion of purposes. Yet if the Allies have no intention of rending the Austro-Hungarian empire into fragments, if they do not propose to cripple or dismember Bulgaria, it is of the extremest importance that they should say so now. There is no occasion to make the

Austrian and Bulgarian fight, as if he fought for his national existence, when he is really only fighting for Germany. All liberal thought is agreed upon the desirability of a practically independent Poland, of a Hungary intact and self-respecting, of a liberated Bohemia, of a Yugo-Slav autonomous state. None of these four countries are so large and powerful as to stand alone, and there are many reasons for proposing to see them linked into a league of mutual protection, mutual restraint and mutual guarantees. Add only to this system the present German states of the Austrian empire, and such a league would be practically a continuation of that empire. But the European Allies lack the collective mental force, lack the mouthpiece, lack the detachment and directness of purpose necessary for the declaration of their intentions in this matter, and they will probably go into the peace conference unprepared with a decision, a divided and so an enfeebled crowd, unless America for her own good and theirs, before the end of the war, gives the lead that will necessitate a definite statement of war aims. Only President Wilson and America can get that statement. To us in Europe our statesmen have become no better than penny-in-the-slot gramophones, who at every challenge for their war aims, say "Evacuate Belgium, restore Alsace-Lorraine to France and Italia Irredenta to Italy, abandon militarism and—*Gurrrrr !* " The voice stops just when it is beginning to be interesting. And because it stops the war goes on. The war goes on because nothing can be extracted from the Allies that would induce any self-respecting Bulgarian, Austrian or democratic-minded German to regard peace as a practicable proposition. They have their backs up against the wall, therefore, side by side with the German militarist—who is the real enemy—because we will not let them have any alternative to a fight to the death.

There, my dear Mr. Bainbridge Colby, are the views you ask for. You have brought them on yourself. You see the rôle I believe America could play under President Wilson's guidance, the rôle of the elucidator, the rôle of advocate of the new order. Clear speech and clear speech alone can save the world. Nothing else can. And President Wilson alone of all mankind can speak and compel the redeeming word.

§ 7
WORLD EDUCATION

MY AWAKENING to the realities of the pseudo-settlement of 1919 was fairly rapid. At first I found it difficult to express my indignant astonishment at the simulacrum of a Peace League that was being thrust upon Europe. I was embarrassed and rather puzzled to find that men I had reckoned upon surely as associates, Gilbert Murray for instance, Zimmern, Ernest Barker and J. A. Spender and that dignified figurehead Grey, were all, it seemed, content with this powerless pedantic bit of stage scenery. In spite of the fact that they had committed their names to the most explicit denunciation of a sham world parliament, of an uncontrolled armament trade and of a weaponless league from which the former enemy states were to be indefinitely excluded, they not only accepted this incredibly defective organization, but became eager apologists for it. I clung to the original demands and promises of Crewe House and the League of Nations Union. This I insisted was not the thing that had to be.

What looked like everyday common sense but was, in effect, sheer imaginative destitution was all against me. I was rather in the position into which a man would have been put by Dr. Johnson if he had talked to him of the possibility of electric lights and air liners. The fact that in the violent passage that would no doubt have ensued, he would have been right and the great Doctor altogether wrong, would not have prevented him from looking and feeling like an egregious fool. I was invited most urgently to feel that my ideas were preposterous and unacceptable. My futile voice mingled feebly with the feeble protests of a few other intelligent men behind the wainscot while the conference rooms reverberated to the feet of the "statesmen" and the pompous expressions of their "policies." I think the first intelligent man to emerge from behind the wainscot and make himself really audible was J. M. Keynes in his *Economic Consequences of the Peace* (1919).

I will not here enter into any discussion of Woodrow Wilson. I never met him, and the quintessence of what I have to say about him is to be found in Book V § 6 of that most discursive novel, *The World of William Clissold*, in which I contrast his triumphant reception in Rome in January 1919 with the funeral of David Lubin, forced to travel obscurely and circuitously to the cemetery through side streets because of the Wilson parade. Nor will I expatiate again upon the strange phase of docility and expectation in the world at the end of 1918, which mocked the limitations of Wilson and Lloyd George and Clemenceau. That I have conveyed (chiefly by quotations from Dr. Dillon and J. M. Keynes) in the *Outline of History* (Chapter XXXIX §§ 3 and 4 in the 1932 Edition). Slowly I realized the full significance of that passage cited from *The Idea of the League of Nations* about the "gigantic and laborious system of labours, the immense tangle of co-operations" demanded of us, and set about seeking how among the new conditions, the still non-existent foundations of a real and enduring World-State might yet be planned and laid.

During the various discussions, committee meetings and conferences that occurred in the course of the consolidation of the earlier League of Nations organizations into the League of Nations Union, I had been very much impressed by the perpetually recurring mental divergences due to the fact that everyone seemed to have read a different piece of history or no history at all, and that consequently our ideas of the methods and possibilities of human association varied in the wildest manner. The curious fact dawned upon me that because I was not a "scholar" and had never been put under a pedant to study a "period" intensely and prematurely, and because I had a student's knowledge of biology and of the archaeological record, I had a much broader grasp of historical reality than most of my associates in this mixture of minds which, as the League of Nations Union, was trying to fuse itself into a directive and controlling public opinion. I began to talk more and more decisively of the need for "general history" and to express opinions such as I embodied finally in a pamphlet *History is One* (1919). I proposed that our Research Committee should organize the writing and publication of a history of mankind which should show plainly to the general intelligence, how inevitable, if civilization was to continue, was the growth of political, social and economic organizations into a world federation.

My idea was at first an outline of history beginning with an account of the Roman and Chinese empires at the Christian era, and coming up to contemporary conditions. It was to be a composite Gibbon, with Eastern Asia included and brought up to date. But it became very speedily plain to me that no such broad but compact historical synthesis by authoritative historians was possible. They lived in an atmosphere of mutual restraint. They would not dare to do anything so large, for fear of incidental slips and errors. They were unused to any effective co-operation and their disposition would be all towards binding together a lot of little histories by different hands, and calling the binding a synthesis ; and even if they could be persuaded to do anything of the sort it would certainly be years before it became available. I was already making a note-book for my own private edification and for use in the controversies that I felt were gathering ahead, and the idea of writing up this note-book of how the present human situation had come about and publishing it—if only to demonstrate that there was some other method possible in history than that of sheer indiscriminate aggregation—became more and more attractive.

It did not occur to me that this Note-Book or Outline of History would be a particularly saleable production. I wanted to sketch out how the job might be done rather than to do it. Before I began it I had a very serious talk with my wife about our financial position. The little parcel of securities we had accumulated before 1914 had been badly damaged by the war. Its value had fallen from about £20,000 to less than half that amount. But the success of Mr. Britling had more than repaired that damage and my position as a journalist had improved. We decided that I could afford a year's hard work on this *précis* of history, although it might bring in very little and even though I risked dropping for a time below the habitual novel reader's horizon. As a matter of fact I dropped below that horizon for good. I lost touch with the reviewers and the libraries, I never regained it, and if I wrote a novel now it would be dealt with by itself by some special critic, as a singular book, and not go into the "fiction" class. I set to work, undeterred by my burning boats, with the *Encyclopaedia Britannica* at my elbow, to get the general shape of history sketched out. It planned itself naturally enough as a story of communications and increasing interdependence. It became an essay on the growth of association since the dawn of animal communities. Its beginning was carried right back before the appearance of viviparous types of life, to those reptiles which shelter their eggs and protect their offspring, and it came on in one story of expanding relationship to the aeroplane-radio-linked human world of to-day. The essay grew beyond expectation, but that stress upon continually more effective communications, upon the gathering co-ordination of lives, is still, as even the reader of the *Outline's* List of Contents can see, the gist of it all.

THE IDEA OF A PLANNED WORLD

I will not here detail how with the *Outline*, as with *Anticipations*, my sense of the importance of my subject grew as I worked upon it. I saw more and more plainly that this was the form, the only right form, in which history should be presented to the ordinary citizen of the modern state, this, and not " King and Country " stuff, was the history needed for general education, and I realized too that even my arrangement of notes, if it was properly " vetted " by one or two more specialized and authoritative helpers, might be made to serve, provisionally at least, for just that general review of reality of which we stood in such manifest need if any permanent political unity was to be sustained in the world. I persuaded Sir Ray Lankester, Sir Harry Johnston, Gilbert Murray, Mr. Ernest Barker, Sir Denison Ross, Philip Guedalla and various other men of knowledge among my friends, to go over my typescript for me ; I got J. F. Horrabin, who makes charts that talk, to help me with some exceptionally eloquent maps, and I suggested to Newnes & Co. the possibility of a publication in parts prior to the publication of the *Outline* in book form by Cassells. In America, Mr. G. P. Brett of Macmillans & Co., was very doubtful about the prospects of the book, but finally he brought it out at the rather odd price of 10 dollars and 10 cents.

The public response was unexpectedly vigorous, both in Britain and America. Edition after edition was sold on both sides of the Atlantic. It made a new and wider reputation for me and earned me a considerable sum of money. Over two million copies of the *Outline* in English have been sold since 1919, it has been translated into most literary languages except Italian—it is proscribed in Italy because it detracts, they say, from the supreme grandeur of Mussolini's Rome —and it continues to sell widely. *A Short History of the World* (1922) has also had an extensive sale. The ordinary man had been stimulated by the war to a real curiosity about the human past; he wanted to be told the story of the planet and of the race, plainly and credibly, and since the " historians " would not or could not do it, he turned to my book. It was quite open to those worthy teachers to do the job over again and do it beyond measure better, but until they could manage to do that, people had either to remain in ignorance of this exciting subject, as one whole, or else go on reading me, or Van Loon, or some other such outsider who had not been sterilized by an excess of scholastic pretension.

Unhappily, though the professional teachers of history could not bar the reading public from access to the new history of all mankind that was now unfolding itself, they were much more successful in keeping it out of the schools. To this day, in school and syllabus, King and Country and Period still prevail and it is still just a matter of luck whether or no an intelligent boy or girl ever comes to the newer rendering of historical fact. Yet beginning history point-blank with mediaeval England is as logical and sensible as it would be to begin chemistry with a study of cookery recipes or patent medicines.

The immense popularity of the *Outline of History* was a very exciting success for me. My self-conceit has always had great recuperative power; it revived bravely now; and I saw a still wider possibility behind the *Outline*, the possibility of giving Mr. Everyman an account not merely of past events, but of the main facts about the processes of life in general and the social economic and political state of the world. I gave this possibility a preliminary airing in some lectures I wrote but never delivered—they were intended for America —and which I reprinted in a book *The Salvaging of Civilization*.

Therein I developed a scheme which I called the " Book of Necessary Knowledge " or the " Bible of Civilization."

That idea was first broached by Comenius, and, some time before me, Dr. Beattie Crozier was insisting that every culture needed its "Bible." I owe the phrase to him. My League of Nations Union experience had enforced my conviction that for a new order in the world there must be a new education and that for a real world civilization there must be a common basis of general ideas, that is to say a world-wide common-school education presenting the same vision of reality. Someone had to begin upon that restatement of educational ideas. I was in no way qualified for such a beginning, yet no one else was stirring, and presently I found myself casting about for colleagues and collaborators in order to complete that first sketch of a world citizen's ideology of which my *Outline of History* was a part. Instead of arguing endlessly about what had to be done, it seemed simpler and more effective to demonstrate, however roughly, what had to be done.

I should have liked to call these books that were taking shape in my mind an *Outline of Biology* and an *Outline of Social and Economic Science*. But following the success of the *Outline of History* a number of so-called " Outlines " of Art—of Literature—of Science—of this and that, had been put upon the market and widely advertised and distributed. They were not really outlines at all ; they were miscellanies of articles by various hands with hardly any common thread of interest, but they exhausted the meaning of the word so completely that when at last after much toil and tribulation I got the books I wanted done, I called them *The Science of Life* and *The Work, Wealth and Happiness of Mankind* respectively.

In organizing the writing of the *Science of Life* I was greatly helped by my early association with biological work and by the facts that my eldest son was a biological teacher and that the able grandson of my teacher Huxley, Julian Huxley, was my friend. He has an extraordinary full and detailed knowledge of the whole biological field. We three got together in 1927 and we made a scheme that covered every division of our immense subject. We worked very harmoniously throughout and, after a part publication, produced the book in 1930.

I had already been casting about for suitable helpers to collaborate in the same fashion upon a summary of social, political and economic science, but in this I was less successful. I entangled my scheme with an inconvenient associate and it had to be disentangled. I need not go into the particulars of my troubles here. The plan I had in mind for this work was bold and more novel than that of either of its predecessors; it was nothing less than an attempt to fuse and recast all this group of " subjects " into one intelligible review of Man upon his planet. It was to begin with a description of his material life and its evolution and it was then to describe the social, legal, political and educational organizations that had grown up as necesssary concomitants of developments. Just as the *Outline of History* was an experiment in analytical history, so this was to be an experiment in synthetic, descriptive economics and politics. The exactest name for such a synthesis would be the Outline of Human Ecology. But I did not call it that because the word Ecology was not yet widely understood.

Hendrik Van Loon, I may note, has done three books which, in an entirely different manner, approach much the same popular conspectus as my own. They are called *The Story of Mankind, The Liberation of Mankind* and *The Home of Mankind*; and if presently he does *The Work of Mankind*, he will have covered practically all my territory, outside the *Science of Life*, and with a very useful and desirable extension into the field of topographical geography. I do my work in my own style and so does he, and for many readers his type of survey may prove to be more attractive and stimulating than mine. *The Work, Wealth and Happiness*

THE IDEA OF A PLANNED WORLD

of Mankind, I have felt for some time, might very well be supplemented by a broad geographical survey.

My trouble with my hastily selected assistant wasted most of my working time for half a year. Two privately printed pamphlets distributed to the members of the committee of the Authors' Society embalmed that tiresome dispute. In the end I brought in a number of fresh advisers and helpers and did the *Work, Wealth and Happiness of Mankind* as I had done the *Outline of History* by " mugging up " the material and writing or rewriting practically all of it myself, and then getting the various part vetted and revised and, in one part, rewritten by specialists. It appeared in 1931 and it has sold very well, but not at all on the scale of the *Outline of History*. It is only now appearing in a popular edition. On the whole considering the greater novelty of the design, I am quite as well satisfied with it as I am with its two companions.

These three works taken together do, I believe, still give a clearer, fuller and compacter summary of what the normal citizen of the modern state should know, than any other group of books in existence. They shape out something that will presently be better done. Clearly there must be some factor, in the relative unsuccessfulness of the later two thirds of the trilogy, which escapes me. They must need further simplification and consolidation. I have not, I think, any extravagant delusions about their quality, but I have perhaps too high an estimate of the value of their general conception.

I am convinced that the informative framework of a proper education should be presented as the three sides of the triangle I have drawn in them ; Biology, History and Human Ecology. A child should begin with Natural History, a History of Inventions, Social Beginnings and Descriptive Geography, that should constitute its first world picture, and the treatment of these subjects should broaden and intensify before specialization. I believe that minds resting on that triple foundation will be equipped for the rôle of world citizens, and I do not believe that a world community can be held together in a common understanding except upon such a foundation. This is not to say that my books are anything more than first exploratory experiments in this foundation work. But they do constitute a very serious first experiment and they foreshadow a new education as it was not foreshadowed until I wrote them.

In this account rendered of the purpose and substance of my life-work I must here insert in a sort of parenthesis one or two other subsidiary books which will otherwise find no place in this story. In 1920 I made a brief visit to Russia, talked to a number of Communist leaders, including Lenin, and published my impressions in a book, *Russia in the Shadows*, and in 1921 I went to Washington to report upon the Disarmament Conference of that year, in a series of newspaper articles which became *Washington and the Hope of Peace*. Since these books were incidents in my development they must be mentioned here, but I need not expatiate upon them.

Here too I must mention, though I need not enter at length into the particulars of it, the Deeks Case which came to an end, after five years of legal proceedings, in 1933. Miss Deeks was a Canadian spinster who conceived the strange idea that she held the copyright in human history. She was permitted and encouraged to sue me, as the author of the *Outline of History*, for infringement of copyright and to produce a manuscript, which she alleged had existed in the form in which she produced it before the publication of my Outline, in support of her claim for £100,000 and the suppression of my book. No evidence of the prior existence of her manuscript, as produced, was ever exacted from her, and she was allowed to carry this silly case from court to court—each court dismissing it contemptuously with costs against her—up to the Privy Council. When finally that court disposed of her conclusively, with costs, she declared her inability to pay a penny of the £5,000-worth of fees and charges that these tedious and vexatious proceedings had entailed upon me. And there the matter ended. Life is too short and there is too much to do in it for me to spend time and attention in hunting out whatever poor little assets Miss Deeks may have preserved from her own lawyers and expert advisers. She has to go on living somehow and her mischief is done. I hope she is comfortable and that she is still persuaded she is a sort of intellectual heroine. I saw her once in court, when I had to give sworn evidence in my own defence, and I found her rather a sympathetic figure. She impressed me as quite honest but vain and foolish, with an imagination too inflamed with the idea of being a great litigant for her to realize what an unrighteous nuisance she was making of herself; there was something faintly pathetic, something reminiscent of Dickens' Miss Flyte, in the way in which she fussed about with her lawyers, with much whispering and rustling of papers, giving her profound and subtle instructions for the undoing of our dire conspiracy; and it is not against her, but against those who encouraged and egged her on, that I am disposed to be resentful.

Since 1914 I had been on very friendly terms with F. W. Sanderson, the headmaster of Oundle, to whom I sent my boys at the outbreak of the war. Sanderson was an original and vigorous teacher, who was feeling his way in a manner all his own, towards a modernized education. He was at the practical end of the business in immediate contact with boys, parents and school governors and I was at the other end in contact with public affairs and the League of Nations, and we converged very interestingly in our talks. My boys, as children at home, had acquired very good French and German and I, just back from my first visit to Russia in 1914 (see *Joan and Peter*), persuaded him to add a Russian teacher to his staff for their benefit, the first Russian teacher, I believe, in any English public school.

Sanderson was a ruddy plethoric man, with his voice in his throat, and always very keen to talk. His mind found its best expression in his very characteristic school sermons; the actual practice of his school and the ideas of his staff lagged far behind his ambitions. He was greatly occupied with the development of a special building at Oundle when he died, The House of Vision, in which boys were to go and think out life. It was to be a sort of museum displaying universal history and the world as a whole; it was to give very much what my three outline books were designed to give, a unified conception of the world drama in which they had to play their parts.

Sanderson was growing mentally and his reach and boldness were increasing to the very day of his death. That came very suddenly and shockingly to me, for I was in the chair at a lecture at University College in the summer of 1922 when—at the end of a rather wandering discourse, his overtaxed and neglected heart stopped beating and he fell dead on the platform beside me.

This lecture was to have opened new ground and he had made great preparations for it. He had added the toil of a sort of mission to Rotarians and people of that sort, to his already heavy work as a headmaster, and this lecture was to have been a key utterance. Apart from my keen sense of the loss of his intimacy and co-operation I was greatly distressed at this abrupt truncation of his work; he was only sixty-five and he seemed full of a panting vitality that might have gone on for years.

THE IDEA OF A PLANNED WORLD

I did all I could to put him on record before his prestige faded. I got together an official *Life* (1923) and, finding myself hampered by the reserves and suppressions customary in such compilations, I also wrote my own impression of him in *The Story of a Great Schoolmaster* (1924). It is so personal and affectionate an impression and it is so expressive of my own educational conceptions as well as his, that if I could I would incorporate it, just as I would like to incorporate my introduction to *The Book of Catherine Wells*, in this already greatly distended autobiography. His successor had none of his distinctive spirit and understanding, and the light of that House of Vision was never lit. In *The Story of a Great Schoolmaster*, I have described how I visited it and found that lantern for the imagination, empty and abandoned six months after his death. Oundle lacked and still lacks the understanding or the piety to carry out his scheme.

I will merely mention here such other incidental books of mine as *A Year of Prophesying* (1924), and *The Way the World is Going* (1929). They are collections of newspaper articles in which I hammer away at my leading ideas, not always very tactfully, and the rare, curious reader who may wander into these volumes will find variations perhaps in the method of approach but nothing of essential novelty.

With this I round off my account of another main mass of my work, my own personal attempt to shape out the informative content of a modern education. Necessarily it is a lopsided account, almost Marburgesque in the way in which the parallel work and thought of other people fall into the background. I have for instance got through this section with no mention of such a book as James Harvey Robinson's *Mind in the Making* or the New History movement in America. But I am not writing a history of modern ideas in the world. I am writing the story of modern ideas in the mind of one sample person, H. G. Wells.

And as I look at the table in my study piled up with my own books and with correspondence and controversial books and pamphlets—quite a little heap for example, including Hilaire Belloc's *Companion to the Outline of History* and *Some Errors of H. G. Wells* by Dr. Downey the Roman Catholic Bishop of Liverpool, I have, except for a passing allusion to Catholic controversialists in Chapter the Eighth, § 3, passed over altogether—I am quite unable to make up my mind how far these millions of printed words are already dead litter and how much is still touching and moving minds. Is all this, and the kindred stuff of similar writers, producing any sensible and permanent effect upon education throughout the world? Much of it has certainly failed, because it was written hastily or just badly, because it was directed at the wrong brains, because it was alloyed with baser metal, prejudices or brief angers that let in corruption. But is it mostly going to be missed? Never in this world will it be possible to make a just estimate of what it has done.

There is a queer little twist in my private vanity, a streak of snobbish imitativeness, which disposes me at times to parallel my lot with Roger Bacon's. I dress up my *persona* in his fashion. This disposition is in evidence in the opening chapter of *The Work, Wealth and Happiness of Mankind*. When I am most oppressed by the apparent lack of direct consequence to all my voluminous efforts, when I doubt whether the modernization of the content of education upon the lines I have drawn in my triple outlines can possibly be done in time to save our present social order, then is it most comforting to me to compare myself with Bacon in his cell scribbling away at those long dissertations of his about a new method of knowledge, which never even reached, much less influenced, the one sole reader, his friend the Pope, in whom he had hope for the realization of his dream. Which nevertheless in the course of a few centuries came to the fullest fruition. I play at being such a man as he was, a man altogether lonely and immediately futile, a man lit by a vision of a world still some centuries ahead, convinced of its reality and urgency, and yet powerless to bring it nearer.

But this is just an imaginative indulgence, a private vice I nurse, and directly I set it down here in plain black and white its absurd unreasonableness is plain. It is only my present preoccupation with my own work that gives me that single-handed feeling. Inflammation of the ego, I begin to realize, is inevitable to any autobiographer in action, and that intensifies this disposition. In truth I am neither solitary nor suppressed. I merely happen to be the one I know best among a number of people who are all thinking very closely upon the same lines. Instead of writing manuscripts that will rest unread or be merely glanced at for centuries, we are printing and scattering our ideas by the million copies.

As I write here there must be between two and three million copies of my own books scattered about the world, and many more millions of other books and newspaper articles, lectures and discourses by other hands, all driving in the same direction. Every day several thousands of fresh minds respond to some part of the suggestions we are making; a teacher here alters his teaching a little; a reader thinks over a point and argues with his friend; a journalist gets a new idea of things and echoes it in an article; an orthodox parson suddenly feels insecure. It was not to be expected that all at once all the schools would experience a change of heart, have a great burning of textbooks and start off at a tangent towards the new learning; nor is it reasonable to complain that even among those who advocate a fresh education for citizenship the apprehension of what we are driving at is usually very inadequate. If the Eric Yarrow Memorial, that House of Vision, stands, misused and abortive, at Oundle, it is only like some gun that has been hit by a shell on the road to victory.

There is no proof that the seed we have already sown has died. On the contrary, the signs of vitality increase. Now it is a series of lessons in some elementary school; now it is a string of broadcast talks like those of Commander King-Hall; now it is a book for children or the newspaper report of a provincial lecture, that comes reassuringly, another fresh green blade forcing its way to the light. The new ideology creeps upon the world *now*. There is nothing in our circumstances to-day to justify this comparison with the spiritual and imaginative isolation of that untimely man who first proclaimed the strange possibilities of experimental science. Our period is far more like the seventeenth than the thirteenth century in its realization of mutation and progressive possibility.

The thoughts of Roger Bacon were like a dream that comes before dawn and is almost forgotten again. The sleeper turns over and sleeps on. All that Roger Bacon wrote was like humanity talking in its sleep. What is happening now is by comparison an awakening. In a dream we can in a flash of time see things complete because what is happening is happening without resistance in a single brain—and then they pass; but the realization of a new day comes to thousands before it comes to millions; at first the illumination is almost imperceptible, everything is touched by it while nothing stands out; there is a slow leisureliness in its manner of approach that belies its steady and assured incessancy.

§ 8
World Revolution

Concurrently with those laborious and troubled efforts to anticipate the necessary informative content of a modern education, my brain was also returning to the problem I had first raised as that New Republic of *Anticipations* which fructified in my *Modern Utopia*, the problem of organizing the coming world-order, in the body and out of the existing substance of the order of things as they are.

The temptation for active men eager for results to shirk this problem, or to stave it off with some immediately workable but essentially evasive formula, has always been very great. The first French Revolution was conducted upon an assumption of " natural " virtue and the American Revolution was essentially a political change and an economic release from an alleged and grossly caricatured " tyranny," a change and release which brought with it scarcely any modification in the liberated system. But Marx did not shirk this fundamental problem. My habitual polemical disposition to disparage Marx does not blind me to the fact of his pioneer awareness of this forest of difficulties in the theory of revolution. He did realize that a movement to reconstruct a society is unlikely to receive the immediate enthusiastic support of the majority of those who fit into and profit by its existing arrangements.

Such people may of course produce profound changes without intending it, as the curiosity of the gentlemen of the Royal Society or the excitement of the South Sea speculators evoked inventions, discoveries and developments of the most world-shaking sort, but they did these things quite unaware of the dangerous dragons they were releasing. It is necessary to find discontent before conscious revolutionary effort is possible ; and, in insisting upon that point, Marx was leading his generation. But it has been the refrain of my lifetime that Marx antagonized property and the expropriated too crudely, and that he confused mere limitation and unhappiness with the rarer and more precious motive of creative discontent. He was himself too energetic and self-centred to realize how meekly human beings can be put upon if they are caught young, how susceptible they are to mass as well as to individual self-flattery and how unwilling to admit and struggle against disadvantages. Most men are ready to sympathize with the under-dog but few will allow they are themselves under-dogs. Nor did Marx realize how acutely people who have wealth and position can be bored and distressed by the existing state of affairs. He looked therefore to the Indignant Proletarian evolved by his own imagination as the sole driving force of his revolution and he stamped the theory of the Class War upon human affairs with immense and fatal determination.

I have pointed out already that the dead impracticability of the Socialism of the opening twentieth century was due to the want of any realizable conception of a Competent Receiver for collectivized property and enterprises. The untutored masses of expropriated people are obviously unable to discharge the functions of an administrative receiver. Something had to be done about it. The " Dictatorship of the Proletariat " of the Communists, is a jerry-built Competent Receiver run up in a hurry to meet this objection. It is not good enough for its job. It is a controversial answer and not a practical solution. But Lenin's reconstructed Communist Party was a much more effective step towards an organized receivership.

To abandon the Class War theory of revolution is to give up the use of a very sustaining opiate and to face an intricate riddle. For many rough immediate purposes, drugged fighters may do better than clear-headed ones, but not in the long run.

One is forced to admit that in periods of tolerable general prosperity (as in America up to 1927) or stabilized repression (as in Hanoverian England), there is little hope for direct revolutionary effort. The illusion of stability must have been undermined in some way before the human

THE IDEA OF A PLANNED WORLD

intelligence will brace itself up to the stresses and vexations of constructive work. In the past the driving discontent has often appeared as a conflict between oppressed and oppressors, either as a class or as a race conflict, and it is still insufficiently realized that the peculiar discontents and instabilities of the present time do not follow that time-honoured formula. The issues are polygonal, they are not two-sided. And it is to mental and not to social classes that we have to appeal.

The other day at the Film Society show (March 11th, 1934) I saw Eisenstein's stirring film *October*, in which noble and enthusiastic proletarians chase corrupt and over-fed imperialists and capitalists and their parasites out of the Winter Palace. The peculiar rôle of a third party in the fight, the Russian Navy, is understressed throughout. Never have I encountered a statement more obstinately misleading. Navies have played a large part in revolutionary history, in Turkey and Germany, notably, as well as in Russia. Every armed technical force is a living weapon with a solidarity of its own, that may turn upon a mentally feeble government which does not use it effectively. The real unorganized proletarians were in fact, if not in film, merely the chorus in the October revolution. That will be their lot in any revolution still to come.

A constructive revolution under modern conditions must begin fragmentarily, it must begin here and there, and it will have associated with it a considerable riff-raff of merely eccentric, extravagant, disgruntled and discredited individuals. These have to be handled with care and discrimination. Revolution begins with the misfits. Every revolutionary process arises out of developing dislocations and disproportions. And the interesting thing about our present situation is the fact that there is no social stratum, no organization, state, nation, school, army, navy, air force, bank, law, industry where the realization among the personnel that things are out of adjustment is not becoming acute. It is a ridiculous travesty of the situation to deal with our western world as a self-complacent "Capitalist System," squatting ruthlessly on masses of enslaved victims who have merely to revolt and evoke a millennium. Russia, after overthrowing the Capitalist System as it manifested itself under the Tzar, has floundered back through several experimental stages to state capitalism, and except that she has rid herself of some very encumbering traditions and types and broached some important experiments, she is still confronted by essentially the same riddles as the western world.

Now, if this is sound, then, I submit, it follows that *everywhere* in the social complex we shall find certain main types of mental reaction dependent upon innate or very intimate personal characteristics. We shall find an originally preponderating number of people carrying on from the phase of apparent stability, hanging on to the current usages to which they are accustomed and trying to the very last to believe that things will go on according to precedent, we shall find an increasing proportion, the resentfully defensive type, disposed to resist, by violence, any change in their habits and we shall also have a number of the open-minded innovating types who will be ready to recognize that something has to be done in the way of adaptation and rearrangement, even if this involves a sacrifice of old customs and privileges and preconceived ideas. As the sense of instability grows, the numbers of both these latter sorts of people, the revolutionaries and the violent reactionaries, will increase at the expense of the first, the contented sort which wants to escape bothers, and the intelligence and will-for-change of the third kind, in particular, will be quickened. In certain social groups dependent largely upon the general liveliness of mind prevailing in them, the tendency to become either viciously defensive or alertly innovating may vary. Such an artificial occupation as that of a stockbroker or a professional betting man naturally attracts people of a narrow-minded smart type and is not likely to turn the mind to any social rearrangements that may threaten the technique of the stock-exchange or the turf, and fewer retired *rentiers* are likely to give their minds to revolutionary reconstruction than public health officials or hydraulic engineers. But in most spheres of interest, in law, public administration, medicine, engineering, industry, education and even the compulsive services, intensifying dislocation is likely to call an increasing proportion of questioning and planning brains into constructive activity. These are the only brains to which we can look for creative drive. For the purposes of revolutionary theory the rest of humanity matters only as the texture of mud matters when we design a steam dredger to keep a channel clear.

These questioning, planning and executive brains which will be stimulated by the realization of social impermanence and insecurity, will start, every one of them, from some fixed system of ideas. Their immediate reactions and activities will be determined at first by the established routines out of which they awaken, and so the early stages of their activities, at any rate, are likely to be not only extremely diverse and chaotic but conflicting. On the other hand the violent reactionaries will have a natural solidarity about the Thing that Is. The primary problem in revolutionary theory is to discover the general formulae, which will reduce the waste through diversity and imperfect apprehension to a minimum, and evoke the most rapid and efficient co-ordination of creative effort.

I have told already of my conception of a New Republic (in 1900) and of my elaboration of this idea in *A Modern Utopia* (1906) and how I tried to make the Fabian Society into an order of the Samurai—to the great excitement of Pease, Shaw, Bland and Sidney Webb, and, to my own effectual discomfiture. I tried to put an acceptable face on my retreat from the Fabian conflict, but that was by no means easy. I had to swallow the dose that I had attempted to do something and failed completely. I had to realize that I had no organizing ability and no gift for leading or directing people. To make up for that, I told myself I would write all the better. But *The New Machiavelli* (1911) with its pose of the deflated publicist in noble retirement is obviously a compensatory production. *The Research Magnificent* (1914) betrays a mind still looking for some method of effective public action. Before it was half written, the livid glares and deepening shadows of the Great War fell across its pages and a new grade in my education began.

I have traced already how the war process stormed across my mind and how my attention was shifted from social structure to international affairs and so to the relation between popular education and international feeling. The idea of doing all I could for the reconstruction of the content of education became so dominant with me that it ruled my intellectual life and shaped my activities for some years. For a time I was so busied with the production of those three books embodying a modern general ideology, that I gave little attention, far too little attention, to the question whether my general idea was being put over to any large number of people. Then I began to feel that I was going on " in the air," that at the best I was producing fairly saleable but, it might be, essentially ineffective books. I might be shooting beside the mark altogether. I became impatient for palpable results.

In some manner the new education had to be got into the education office and the syllabuses and the schools, and since no one else seemed to be doing it, I felt under an obligation to try, however ineffectively, to do something about it myself. I turned my reluctant face towards meetings and committee-rooms again. I had had nothing to do with such

THE IDEA OF A PLANNED WORLD

things since my Fabian withdrawal. I heard with dislike and a sinking heart my straining voice once more beginning speeches. I dislike my voice in a meeting so much that it gives me an exasperated manner and I lose my thread listening to it. I still thought the Labour Party might be the party most responsive to constructive ideas in education, and in order to secure a footing in its counsels I stood as Labour candidate for the London University at the 1922 and 1923 elections. I had no prospect of being returned, but I thought that by writing and publishing election addresses and such leaflets as *The Labour Ideal of Education* (1923) I might impose a modernization of the schools curriculum upon the party policy and so get general history at least into its proper place as elementary school history.

In a speech at the University of London Club, in March 1923, reprinted as *Socialism and the Scientific Motive*, I find I was trying to persuade myself and my liberal-minded hearers of the essential identity of these two things. But I was not really persuaded. I was declaring what ought to be was fact. I was poking about in this political stuff not because I believed it to be the way to my ends, but because I did not certainly know any way to my ends, and this seemed to hold out possibilities. But the older men in control of the Labour Party at that time were quite impervious to the idea of changing education. They did not know that there could be different kinds and colours of education. A school, any school, was a school to them and a college a college. They thought there was something very genteel and desirable about education, just as there was about a municipal art gallery, and they wanted the working classes to have the best of everything. But they did not consider education as a matter of primary importance. They had themselves managed very well with very little.

A phase of great restlessness and discontent came upon

me in 1923–24. I was doing what I felt to be good work in making a digest of modern knowledge and ideas available for the general reader, but this did not fully engage my imagination. I could not subdue myself to the idea that this was the limit of my effectiveness. I made speeches and when I read the reports of them I could not believe I had said so little. I gave interviews and was overwhelmed by a sense of fatuity when they came home to roost. I wrote articles and they seemed to me more and more like the opening observations to something that was never really said. I was oppressed by a sense of encumbrance in my surroundings and of misapplied energy and time running to waste.

In the introduction to this autobiography I have already remarked upon the fugitive element in most intellectual lives, but it is only now as I bring facts and dates together that I realize the importance of fugitive impulses throughout my own story. At phase after phase I find myself saying in effect : " I must get out of this. I must get clear. I must get away from all this and think and then begin again. These daily routines are wrapping about me, embedding me in a mass of trite and habitual responses. I must have the refreshment of new sights, sounds, colours or I shall die away."

My revolt against the draper's shop was the first appearance of this mood. It was a flight—to a dream of happy learning and teaching in poverty. To a minor extent and with minor dislocation this fugitive mood no doubt recurred but it did not come back again in full force until my divorce. Then it is quite clear that it clothed itself in the form of a dream of a life of cheerfully adventurous writing. The concealed element was that my work with Briggs was boring me. That divorce was not simply the replacement of one wife by another ; it was also the replacement of one way of living by another. It was a break away to a new type of work.

I detect all the symptoms of the same flight impulse again about 1909, but then there was not the same complete material rupture with my established life. But *The New Machiavelli* (published in 1911) is quite plainly once more the release of the fugitive urgency, a release completed in imagination if not in fact. I realize now (and the queer thing is that I do realize only now) that the idea of going off somewhere—to Italy in the story—out of the tangle of Fabian disputes, tiresomely half-relevant politics and the routines of literary life, very nearly overwhelmed me in my own proper person, and the story of Remington and Margaret and Isabel is essentially a dramatized wish. I relieved my tension vicariously as Remington. He got out of my world on my behalf—and wrote in lofty tranquillity of politics in the abstract, *à la Machiavelli*, as I desired to do.

We shifted house from Sandgate to London (1909) and from London to Easton Glebe (1910) and there I settled down again. All that is quite sufficiently told in *The Book of Catherine Wells*. The huge issues of the War and the Peace held my mind steady and kept it busy for some years. But in 1924 the same mood returned, so recognizably the same, that I am surprised to realize how little I apprehended the connection at the time. If I did not get to writing in Italy in the pose of the New Machiavelli, I got to the south of France. It was much the same thing. It was the partial realization of my own fantasy after twelve years. What I did I did with the connivance and help of my wife, who perceived that I was in grave mental distress and understood how things were with me. I did not immediately head for France. I went by air first to the Assembly of the League of Nations at Geneva with the idea of going on thence to wander round the world. It was at Geneva that I changed my plans and turned southward to Grasse. I found it was quite possible to get out of things, for some months at least, much as Remington did, establish myself in a quiet corner among the hills, stay there cut off from the daily urgencies of England, sift my thoughts and purposes in peace and presently write.

I began a life in duplicate. The main current of my ostensible life still flowed through my home at Little Easton in Essex; there the mass of my correspondence was dealt with and all my business done, but at the *mas* known as Lou Bastidon near Grasse, I dramatized myself as William Clissold, an industrialist in retreat,—the prophet Hosea could not have been more thorough in his dramatization— and I set this Mr. William Clissold to survey and think out how the world looked to him. For three winters I lived intermittently in that pleasant sunlit corner, living very plainly and simply, sitting about in the sun, strolling on the flowery olive terraces about me, going for long walks among the hills behind, seeing hardly anything of the fashionable life of the Riviera that went on so near to me. And the main thread of my thought and writing for all that time was how to realize the New Republic and bring it into active existence.

I wish that seasonal retirement to Lou Bastidon could have gone on to the end, but obscure difficulties and complications—a craving for an efficient bathroom, electric light and a small car, it may be—presently undid me. I attempted to reproduce Lou Bastidon on a firmer foundation and behold! the foundation became a pitfall. I began to play with house-building and garden-planning. There is a vividness, an immediate gratification of the creative instinct in this amusement, which can distract the mind very readily from reality. Men and women take to building and gardening as they take to drink, in order to distract their minds from the whole round world and its claim upon them, and all the Riviera is littered with villas that testify to the frequency of this impulse. I acquired some land with a pretty rock, vines, jasmin and a stream close by, and I planned and built a house which I called *Lou Pidou*, and after that rash act the cares of house-holding and car-owning and gardening began to grow up about me. The Riviera also got wind of me and reached up sociable tentacles towards my retreat. Lou Pidou was an amateurish, pretty house with a peculiar charm of its own but it insisted upon growing and complicating itself; it became less and less of a refuge and more and more of an irksome entanglement with its own baffling bothers and exactions. I worked there with dwindling zest and energy and stayed less and less willingly and for briefer periods, as those good long sunlit hours in which I could think became rare and ragged and the necessity for management and attention more clamorous, until presently a time came, in May 1933, when I realized I could work there effectively no more.

It was early in 1933 that the opening section of this autobiography was written and the mood of this phase is fully described in that section.

I cast Lou Pidou at last as a snake casts its skin. It needed an effort, but once more the liberating impulse was the stronger. I resolved that I would sell it, or if necessary give it away, and have done with it. I took a farewell stroll in my olive orchard up the hill, said good-bye to my new and promising orange-trees and rose-beds, gave my parental benediction to the weeping-willows and the banks of iris I had planted by my stream, sat for awhile on my terrace with a grave black cat beside me, to which I was much attached, and then went down the familiar road to Cannes station for the last time.

I returned to London by way first of a stormy but entertaining International P.E.N. Congress at Ragusa, over which I presided, and then a holiday in what was altogether new country for me, the fresh green loveliness of Austria in early summer. My flat in London is now my only home. The two small boys who figure at the end of Chapter the Eighth are parents to-day with pleasant households and sons and daughters of their own, and Easton Glebe which is described in *The Book of Catherine Wells* was sold after her death in 1927. It had become too large for me and too empty altogether. I have indeed seen family life right round now from beginning to end. That stage is over. A flat above the rumble of Baker Street and Marylebone Road is as good a place as any to work in and easy to maintain ; I can go away when I please and where I please for as long as I please ; and London, for all my outrageous radicalism, is a very friendly and pleasant city to me. If I have no garden of my own, Regent's Park just outside my door grows prettier every year ; there are no gardens like Kew Gardens and no more agreeable people in the world than the people in the London streets.

The World of William Clissold, the book I wrote in Lou Bastidon, has a rambling manner but it seems to ramble more than it actually does from my main preoccupation. Its gist, to which, after four Books mostly of preparatory novel writing to get the Clissold brothers alive, I came in Book Five, is the possibility of bringing the diffused creative forces of the world into efficient co-operation as an " Open Conspiracy." I am supposing myself to be in the position of an intelligent industrialist with a sound scientific training and this is how I make him see it :

" It is absurd to think of creative revolution unless it has power in its hands, and manifestly the chief seats of creative power in the world are on the one hand modern industry associated with science and on the other world finance. The people who have control in these affairs can change the conditions of human life constructively and to the extent of their control. No other people can so change them.

"All other sorts of power in our world are either contributory or restrictive or positively obstructive or positively destructive. The power of established and passive property, for example, is simply the power to hold up for a price. The power of the masses is the strike, it embodies itself in the machine-breaking, expert-hunting mob. . . . It is only through a conscious, frank and world-wide co-operation of the man of science, the scientific worker, the man accustomed to the direction of productive industry, the man able to control the arterial supply of credit, the man who can control newspapers and politicians, that the great system of changes they have almost inadvertently got going can be brought to any hopeful order of development.

"Such men, whether they mean to be or not, are the actual revolutionaries in our world. . . . I believe that we industrials and the financiers are beginning to educate ourselves and broaden our outlook as our enterprises grow and interweave. I believe that if we can sufficiently develop the consciousness of contemporary business and associate with it the critical co-operation and the co-operative criticism of scientific and every other sort of able man, we can weave a world system of monetary and economic activities, while the politicians, the diplomatists, and the soldiers are still too busy with their ancient and habitual antics to realize what we are doing. . . . We can build up the monetary and economic world republic in full daylight under the noses of those who represent the old system. For the most part I believe that to understand us will be to be with us, and that we shall sacrifice no advantage and incur no risk of failure in talking out and carrying out our projects and methods quite plainly.

"That is what I mean by an Open Conspiracy. . . . Many things that now seem incurably conflicting, communism and international finance for example, may so develop in the next half-century as to come to drive side by side, upon a parallel advance. At present big distributing businesses are firmly antagonistic to co-operative consumers' associations; yet one or two of the big distributors have already made important deals with these large-scale economic organizations from the collectivist side. Both work at present upon very crude assumptions about social psychology and social justice. Both tend to internationalize under the same material stresses.

"I find it hard to doubt the inevitability of a very great improvement in the quality and intellectual solidarity of those who will be conducting the big business of the world in the next century, an extension and an increased lucidity of vision, a broadened and deepened morale. Possibly my temperament inclines me to think that what should be must be. But it is patently absurd to me to assume that the sort of men who control so much of our banking to-day, limited, traditional, careless or doctrinaire, are the ultimate types of banker. It seems as irrational to suppose that such half-educated, unprepared adventurers as Dickon and myself and our partners and contemporaries are anything but makeshift industrial leaders, and that better men will not follow us. Dickon and I are, after all, at best early patterns, 1865 and 1867 models...."

All this was written before anyone was thinking of such an American President as Franklin Roosevelt and his astonishing effort so to regulate a loose capitalist system as to thrust it rapidly towards State Socialism. Where the Clissold version of the Open Conspiracy is least defensible is in its easy disregard of the fact that though privately created productive, industrial and distributive organization is to a large extent capable of direct socialization, *private finance is something absolutely and incurably different in its spirit and conduct from any conceivable sort of public finance*. It is an attempt to extract profit out of what should be a public service, the exchange machinery. It is as anti-social as it would be to attempt to get profits by falsifying the standard yard. That, we have since found out. The industrious reader will find it in course of being found out in the *Work, Wealth and Happiness of Mankind*. The public control of credit and a scientific reorganization of the world's monetary system is the necessary preliminary stage in carrying out a planned world economy. Like myself and our English labour leaders and indeed practically everybody in 1926, William Clissold was still in need of some hard thinking about the relations of money and credit to private ownership.

Furthermore—in an exaggeration of my own aversion from the class-war doctrine—too wide a gap was set by Clissold in his world between the industrial organizer and the technological assistant and skilled artisan. The workers were dismissed as being just workers and the political possibilities and capacity of their better equipped stratum was ignored. I was identifying myself with my imaginary business man almost too thoroughly. I was evidently still sore about the Labour Party as I had found it. In my reaction against the mass democracy that had produced MacDonald, Snowden, Thomas, Clynes and the like as its representative heads, I underrated the steadily increasing intelligence of the more specialized workers and of the ambitious younger working-men. To them at any rate William Clissold is an impersonation to apologize for.

The World of William Clissold was published in 1926. It was published as an important book and it received a very considerable amount of useful destructive criticism. So that I reconsidered this Open Conspiracy almost as soon as it was launched. It was a sound instinct which made me do that book not in my own first person but in the form of a trial personality. I was soon struggling to disentangle myself from various rash commitments of Clissold's and get on to a revised view. I had had this first exercise in general political statement handed back to me with ample corrections—mostly in red ink—and I wanted to profit by them.

In the spring of 1927, I was asked to lecture in the Sorbonne and I chose as my subject *Democracy under Revision*, in which I insisted on the necessity for some such organization as my Samurai to replace the crude electoral methods of contemporary politics. This was, so to speak, Open Conspiracy propaganda adapted to the peculiarly narrow French outlook. My wife, I may note here, was with me in that Paris journey; we were fêted and entertained and very happy together, and neither of us realized that death was already at work in her and that in six months we should be parted for ever. The title page of that printed lecture is the last of all the title pages on which I ever drew a "picshua" for her. I reproduce it here as a reminder of the life-long companionship and the persistent, unassertive help that underlies all this tale of work. Our last half year together I have described in *The Book of Catherine Wells*.

After her death I sat down to alter and explain my conception of the *Open Conspiracy* more exactly—to myself first and then to others. I wrote a little book *The Open Conspiracy: Blue Prints for a World Revolution* (1929) and I was so convinced of its unavoidably tentative quality that I arranged its publication so as to be able to withdraw it, revise it completely and republish it again after a lapse of two years. I did this under the new title of *What are We to Do with our Lives?* (1931). In this, the third version of the Open Conspiracy plan, I began to feel I was really settling down to definitive detail. *The Work, Wealth and Happiness of Mankind*, which was launched after many difficulties in 1932, also contained in its political and educational chapters, and based on a description of current conditions, an even more explicit statement of the Open Conspiracy plan. The definition was still clearer; and the touch surer.

In all this work I was really only cleaning up, working out, and sharpening the edges, dotting the i's and crossing the t's of the problem of the New Republic. The Open Conspiracy was my New Republic plus a third of a century of experience. It was a working plan in the place of Anticipations. I was moving with my generation from a speculative dreamland towards a specific project.

DEMOCRACY UNDER REVISION

Marraine asks Dadda to tell her all about it

In *After Democracy* (1932) I collected together a number of diverse papers, a lecture given in the Reichstag building in Berlin (1928), a lecture given to the Residencia des Estudiantes in Madrid (1932), a memorandum on the world situation prepared at the request of one or two influential people in America in 1932, and at first privately circulated, a lecture to the Liberal Summer School at Oxford (1932) and arising out of the latter, a paper, *A Liberal World Organisation*, in which I gave still further definition from this point of view and that of the same conception. I also tried out my general idea, with very little response, in the *Daily Herald* (December 1932) under the title *There should be a Common Creed for Left Parties Throughout the World*. This has been reprinted as an Introduction to the *Manifesto* of the new Fellowship of Progressive Societies—which is a sort of Fellowship of the New Life fifty years later. The exploratory note in these papers diminished to a minimum as my ideas grew more precise. Each successive change was smaller than the one that went before.

The Shape of Things to Come (1933) is the last important book I have written. It is as deliberate and laborious a piece of work as anything I have ever done and I took great pains to make it as exciting and readable as I could without any sacrifice of matter. There are one or two episodes of quite lively story-telling. I was becoming sufficiently sure of my ground to let my imagination play upon it. The device of a partially deciphered transcription of a fragmentary manuscript got over a multitude of the technical difficulties that arise in an anticipatory history. I think I have contrived to set out in it my matured theory of revolution and world government very plainly.

The World of William Clissold was written during a " boom " phase in the world's affairs, the profound rottenness of the monetary-credit system was still unrealized, and so Clissold turned to social boredom and the irritation of seeing industrial and mechanical invention misused, in order to evoke the discontent necessary for a revolutionary project. But by the time *The Work, Wealth and Happiness of Mankind*, which was, so to speak, the workshop in which was built *The Shape of Things to Come*, was in hand, the artificiality and unsoundness of those boom conditions had become glaringly obvious. The realization was spreading through all the modern categories of workers, the men of science, the men of invention, the big-scale industrial organizers, the engineers, the aviators, the teachers and writers, the social workers, the mass producers, every sort of skilled artisan, every honest and creative-minded man, indeed, everywhere, that if the new mechanical civilization by which they lived was to carry on, they had to be up and stirring. The Open Conspiracy of William Clissold was essentially speculative, optional and amateurish; the Open Conspiracy of De Windt which took possession of a derelict world, was presented as the logical outcome of inexorable necessity. Only through personal disaster or the manifest threat of personal disaster can normal human beings be sufficiently stirred to attempt a revolutionary change of their conditions.

Step by step through that logic in events, the new pattern of revolution has been brought from Utopia and from the vague generalizations of the New Republic, towards contact with contemporary movements and political actuality. I have moved with my class and type, to more and more precise intentions. Small groups and societies to explain and realize the Competent Receiver are springing up; periodicals are being started in relation to it; its phraseology is appearing in actual political discussion. Independent beginnings of a kindred spirit are coming into relations with one another. They are giving and taking. These people are not merely propagandists of an idea. Every one of them according to his or her abilities or opportunities is in training for the civil service, and the industrial teaching and compulsive services of the new order of things. It is from the skilled artisans, the technically educated middle-class, the fraternity of enlightened minds, rather than from the proletarian masses that its energy will come. But it cannot be pretended that constructive revolutionary organization is anything like as advanced as yet even as educational modernization and the spread of cosmopolitan ideas. It is still in the phase of germination. For the reorientation of revolution, just as for the modernization of education, one must accept what the Webbs have called so aptly " the inevitability of gradualness."

Remembering always that "gradual" need not mean slow.

Of the reality of our progress towards constructive world revolution I have no doubt. All revolutionary organizations are snowball organizations. The Open Conspiracy whether under that name or under some other name, or as a protean spirit, will in the long run win schools and colleges to its ends; it will get the worth-while young men, the skilled men and women, the simple and straightforward, the steadfast and resolute. That is to say that ultimately it will get mankind. It supplies the form and spirit of that "competent receiver," the lack of which made the frustration of the earlier socialism inevitable. It is law and order modernized and ennobled. It will find a job for everybody; the sacrifices it demands are temporary and conditional. When it is fully and fairly displayed it is a handsome and hopeful loyalty; the better it is known the finer it appears, the nature of man necessitates loyalty of some sort and there is no other loyalty now that can stand comparison with it.

And there, for a time at any rate, the description of the main arch of my work must end. My brain has been the centre of the story throughout, but just as with the new education, so here also in this conception of the idea of world revolution as the ruling and directive interest in life, similar things have happened and are happening to myriads of brains. I tell how I in particular travelled upon a road along which more and more people are travelling, but my egoism is far more apparent than real. There used to be a popular recitation in my young days telling how Bill Adams won the Battle of Waterloo. Except for a transitory appearance of the " Dook," the victory seemed all the work of Bill. Nevertheless the Battle of Waterloo *was* won by Bill Adams multiplied by some score thousands, and it is small discredit to Bill Adams that he was too busy on his personal front to take much note of what the other fellows were doing.

What is plain to me is that the modern world-state which was a mere dream in 1900 is to-day a practicable objective; it is indeed the only sane political objective for a reasonable man; it towers high over the times, challenging indeed but rationally accessible; the way is indicated and the urgency to take that way gathers force. Life is now only conflict or " meanwhiling " until it is attained. Thirty-four years ago the world-state loomed mistily across a gulf in dreamland. My arch of work has bridged the gulf for me and my swinging bridge of ropes and planks and all the other ropes and wires that are being flung across, are plainly only the precursors of a viaduct and a common highway. The socialist world-state has now become a to-morrow as real as to-day. Thither we go.

§9
Cerebration at Large and Brains in Key Positions

THE PARTICULAR BRAIN whose ups and downs and beatings about in the world you have been following in this autobiography, has arrived at the establishment of the socialist world-state as its directive purpose and has made that its religion and end. This, it has been abundantly apparent, has involved for it very definite and distinctive standards of judgment upon both individual conduct and the conduct of public affairs. It had been perpetually meeting and jostling against other brains, brains in crowds and brains apart, summing them up, learning from them what to attempt and what to avoid; and so it seems worth while to conclude this elaborate description of my own mental growths and reactions, with a few comments upon other mentalities I have encountered at work upon these same intricate challenges and problems that have taken possession of and unified my own.

Social life has presented itself to me at last as a vast politico-educational problem. It is, as it were, a sea of active brains. My individual life is a participating unit in this multitudinous brain-life, the mind of the species. Its general problem is vastly simple, though its individual variations are infinite. It is required to orient all this diverse multitude of brains, about two thousand millions of them at present, in one particular direction so as to bring about a new morale and government of life. It is under penalty to do that. In a measurable time mankind has to constitute itself into one state and one brotherhood, or it will certainly be swept down cataracts of disaster to an ultimate destruction.

It is no novelty that life should present itself in this form

THE IDEA OF A PLANNED WORLD

of a problem of unification. Men have been seeing it more and more plainly so for at least five-and-twenty centuries. Every one of the universal religions, Buddhism, Christianity, Islam, every one in its valiant beginnings, set out to do as much for mankind. All, it is true, failed to attain that universality. They rose like floods and after a time they rose no further. The whole world over never became Buddhist, Christian or Moslem. At first in every case, the onset of the new faith was like the magnetising of an iron bar in an electric coil and many millions of the little individual particles, originally pointing higgledy-piggledy in the general mass, were swung round towards a common objective. Hitherto there has always been a limit set to this process of conversion; the bar was too big for the induction, much of it stretched beyond the influence of the coil, or the inducing current diminished and died out too soon. But that is no reason for declaring that it is impossible to achieve a general peace and a common faith and law for mankind. On the contrary, the success of these pioneer faiths, in spite of philosophical inadequacy and the handicap of local theological associations and unjustifiable miraculous pretensions, started as they were under conditions of tremendous disadvantage by weak individuals and a feeble initial group of disciples, is an extraordinary manifestation of the power of a unifying appeal and of the receptivity of common men to such an appeal. The human animal is more disposed than not for a universal social life, for peace and co-operation, and what has been done during the relatively brief space of twenty-five centuries and a few score generations of men, is merely a first demonstration of what will yet be achieved.

What we have seen in the course of my one brief lifetime has been a great development of our biological and psychological knowledge, and this last science in particular carries still with it almost untouched possibilities of self-restraint, self-direction, mutual sympathy and group and mass co-operation. The art of conduct is in its infancy. Concurrently the advance of physical technique has carried our facilities of mental exchange to undreamt-of levels. We can tell each other and show each other with unprecedented ease. When we consider the beginnings of the great world faiths; the weak voice of the Founder talking in some small dusty market-place to casually assembled crowds, the going to and fro of the undistinguished disciples, the faint and feeble records, the faulty gospels, the obscure epistles, the mis-hearings, the misunderstandings, the distortions of rumour, the heretical blunderings, the difficulties of correction and verification, and compare the ease and clarity with which to-day statements can be made, consistency sustained and co-operation ensured, then the wide prevalence and partial success of these former disseminations become the surest augury for the rapid and conclusive establishment of the new way of living to which not one Founder but myriads of quickening intelligences are awakening to-day. They are not now the disciples of this man or that. This time they are the disciples and apostles of the logic of human necessity. It is not that one man alone has received a revelation and realized the substance of a new and necessary education and planned reconstruction of economic and political relations. The revelation has been prepared by the scientific work and invention of a century, and the call has been broadcast by events.

I have already described some intimate encounters which very importantly affected the final shaping of my *persona* and ideas. Here in a concluding section I think I will set down what I have seen at close quarters and what I have thought of one or two brains which seemed to be exceptionally placed in the world, so that they had apparently unusual directive opportunities. Their conduct was just as much a resultant of innate impulse and suggestion and circumstance as the lives of Gissing or Crane or Bennett or myself, but because relatively they happened to occupy key positions, their reaction on great multitudes of other brains was much more powerful and immediate. Leadership was their rôle. All of them belong to my own generation, the generation of disillusionment, perplexity and mental reconstruction, and all of them are far less lucid, assured and decisive than the men of to-morrow are likely to be.

An outstanding figure in my middle years was Theodore Roosevelt. He had a tremendous effort in his time of masterful direction. He was the Big Noise of America. He was a great release. Political life in America seemed to have become a wholly base technique, and the American outlook upon world affairs, narrowly patriotic, sentimental and selfish, when he broke through and became, by sheer accident, President. He made the liveliest use of his opportunities. His personality became more visible and his voice more audible about the planet than those of any of his predecessors since Lincoln. It was natural for me in my Spade House days, when I seemed only to be talking unheeded beside the flow of events, and quite unable to affect them, to exaggerate the Power he could exercise and to want to meet him. I had still to realise what an obscure and elusive thing political Power is. I had still to doubt whether there are really any powerful individuals now at all.

I went to America to write a series of articles for the London *Tribune* in 1906 and I lunched with the President and walked about the grounds of the White House with him while he talked. He talked easily and frankly, as Mr. Arthur Balfour used to talk. He " stuck through " the formulated politicians of his time. He betrayed none of the uneasiness of the normal politician that any phrase of his might be quoted unfairly against him, and he interested me enormously. I asked him, though in less direct phrases, what he imagined he was "up to" and I think he did his best to tell me.

In those days mental adaptation to the idea of a change of scale in human affairs was still in its opening phases. Nobody had got the thing in its full immensity but everywhere its disturbance was in evidence. His talk was tremendously provisional and speculative. In my book I called him "a complex of will and critical perplexity."

At that time hardly anyone had dared to face up to the conception of a planned world-state. Roosevelt was round about where Cecil Rhodes had been when he died; he probably owed a great deal to the Milner-Kipling-Rhodes school of thought, he was thinking vaguely of a loose combine, an understanding rather than an alliance, of the liberal northern powers to control the next phase of human affairs. He was sceptical of continental Europe, contemptuous of Asia, and oblivious, as we all were then, of the revolutionary possibilities of Russia. And neither of us as we talked that day had the remotest suspicion of the earthquakes that were latent in the monetary system of our world.

Though he had heard of socialism he evidently could not imagine it as an organised reality, as anything more practical than a legal modification of the baronial freedoms of big business by government control. You must remember that in those days there was no such striking evidence as we now possess of the self-terminating nature of the private capitalist system. That possibility was indeed cardinal in Marxist theory but only a very few people knew about it and still fewer understood and believed it. The current system was generally supposed to get along in a looping sort of way by

THE IDEA OF A PLANNED WORLD

trade cycles of depression and recovery, it had the air of a going concern that might jar perhaps at times but could not fail to go ; and it was only after 1928 that any considerable number of people could be made to realize that these alleged trade cycles were not necessarily cycles at all and that there was no reason to suppose that a depression might not go on indefinitely with no effectual recovery at any point. That was outside his imaginative scheme. Such being the limitation of his ideas, it was natural that he should be a hearty individualist, convinced that no man who sought work could fail to find it, that there was room for an unlimited multitude of healthy workers everywhere (so that he passionately opposed " race suicide ") and that all that was needed to keep the world going was strenuous " go." The utmost danger he would admit as threatening the glorious torrent of individualistic life as he saw it about him, was the restraint and choking of competition by the growth of monopolistic combinations, and this could be checked first by very vigorous anti-trust legislation and secondly by a greater wariness in granting public utility and other franchise for the exploitation of natural resources to private lessees. He was in particular the champion of an imaginary citizen farmer—the legendary pioneer Western farmer—and his power of overriding doubts in a sort of mystical exaltation was very great. I tried to insinuate my still not very completely formulated criticism of the current order. I tried to convey my persuasion that all competitive systems must be self-terminating systems. . . .

But here let me quote my very own book :

" It is a curious thing that as I talked with President Roosevelt in the garden of the White House there came back to me quite forcibly that undertone of doubt that has haunted me throughout this journey. After all, does this magnificent appearance of beginnings, which is America, convey any clear and certain promise of permanence and fulfilment whatever ? . . . Is America a giant childhood or a gigantic futility, a mere latest phase of that long succession of experiments which has been and may be for interminable years—may be, indeed, altogether until the end—man's social history? I can't now recall how our discursive talk settled towards this, but it is clear to me that I struck upon a familiar vein of thought in the President's mind. He hadn't, he said, an effectual disproof of a pessimistic interpretation of the future. If one chose to say America must presently lose the impetus of her ascent, that she and all mankind must culminate and pass, he could not conclusively deny that possibility. Only he chose to live as if this were not so.

" That remained in his mind. Presently he reverted to it. He made a sort of apology for his life, against the doubts and scepticisms that, I fear, must be in the background of the thoughts of every modern man who is intellectually alive. He mentioned my *Time Machine*. . . . He became gesticulatory, and his straining voice a note higher in denying the pessimism of that book as a credible interpretation of destiny. With one of those sudden movements of his he knelt forward in a garden-chair—we were standing, before our parting, beneath the colonnade—and addressed me very earnestly over the back, clutching it and then thrusting out his familiar gesture, a hand first partly open and then closed.

" ' Suppose, after all,' he said slowly, ' that should prove to be right, and it all ends in your butterflies and morlocks. *That doesn't matter now.* The effort's real. It's worth going on with. It's worth it. It's worth it—even so.' . . .

" I can see him now and hear his unmusical voice saying, ' The effort—the effort's worth it,' and see the gesture of his clenched hand and the—how can I describe it ?—the friendly peering snarl of his face, like a man with the sun in his eyes. He sticks in my mind at that, as a very symbol of the creative will in man, in its limitations, its doubtful adequacy, its valiant persistence, amidst perplexities and confusions. He kneels out, assertive against his setting—and his setting is the White House with a background of all America.

" I could almost write, with a background of all the world ; for I know of no other a tithe so representative of the creative purpose, the *goodwill* in men as he. In his undisciplined hastiness, his limitations, his prejudices, his unfairness, his frequent errors, just as much as in his force, his sustained courage, his integrity, his open intelligence, he stands for his people and his kind."

I might have written that to-day. " Teddy " was an interesting brain to come up against and it gives a measure of just how much of a constructive plan for the world's affairs there was in the current intelligence of the world twenty-eight years ago. By our modern standards it was scarcely a plan at all. It was a jumble of " progressive " organization and " little man " democracy. Afforestation, " conservation of national resources," legislation against any " combination in restraint of trade " were the chief planks of the platform and beyond that " woosh ! " the emotional use of the " big stick," a declaration of the satisfying splendour of strenuous effort—which, when one comes to think it over, was, on the intellectual side, not so very strenuous after all.

That I suppose was the most vigorous brain in a conspicuously responsible position in all the world in 1906—when I was turning forty. Radical speculative thought was ahead of this, but that was as far as any ruling figure in the world had gone.

A man I never met, who must have been a very curious mixture of large conceptions and strange ignorances, was Cecil Rhodes. Of ignorances—Sir Sidney Low told me once that he never learnt properly to pronounce the name of his protagonist " Old Krooger." I would have liked to have known more about the operations of his cerebral hemispheres, as they rolled about South Africa. Much the same ideas that were running through my brain round about 1900, of a great English-speaking English-thinking synthesis, leading mankind by sheer force of numbers, wealth, equipment and scope, to a progressive unity, must have been running through his brain also. He was certainly no narrow worshipper of the Union Jack, no abject devotee of the dear Queen Empress. The institution of the Rhodes scholarships which transcended any existing political boundaries and aimed plainly at a sort of common understanding and co-operation between all the western peoples and more particularly between all the " Nordic " peoples—he was at just about the level of ethnological understanding to believe in Nordic superiority—indicates a real greatness of intention, though warped by prejudices and uncritical assumptions.

I wish I knew much more about that brain and still more would I like to know about the brain history of Mr. Rudyard Kipling, whom also I have never met. He is to me the most incomprehensible of my contemporaries, with phases of real largeness and splendour and lapses to the quality of those mucky little sadists, Stalky and Co. I do not understand his relation to Rhodes nor Rhodes's attitude to him. He has an immense vogue in the British middle-class and upper-class home ; he is the patron saint of cadet corps masters, an inexhaustive fount of sham manly sentiment, and one of the most potent forces in the shrivelling of the British political imagination during the past third of a century.

The only representative of that Boer War Imperialist group I ever met was Lord Milner. He seemed to me a bold-thinking man, hampered by politic reservations. In 1918 he wrote a preface for a little pamphlet I published, *The*

THE IDEA OF A PLANNED WORLD

Elements of Reconstruction. I came against him in a curious little talking and dining club, the " Coefficients," which met monthly throughout the session between 1902 and 1908 to discuss the future of this perplexing, promising and frustrating Empire of ours. These talks played an important part in my education. They brought me closer than I had ever come hitherto to many processes in contemporary English politics and they gave me juster ideas of the mental atmosphere in which such affairs are managed.

In certain respects our club represented something that seems now, I think, to have faded out from contemporary English life. It had the gestures if not the spirit of free interrogation. It had an air of asking " What are we doing with the world ? What are we going to do ? " Or perhaps I might put it better by saying : " What is being done to our world ? And what are we going to do about it ? "

The club included the queerest diversity of brains. Its foundation was, I believe, suggested by Mrs. Sidney Webb. It was inaugurated by a meeting in the flat of Sir Edward Grey and Mr. Haldane (neither as yet peers) in Whitehall Court and the first assembly included such incongruous elements as Bertrand Russell (now Earl Russell), Sidney Webb (who is now Lord Passfield), Leo Maxse (already in 1902 denouncing the German Peril and demanding the Great War), Clinton Dawkins, who linked us to finance, Carlyon Bellairs, a Big Navy man, Pember Reeves, a New Zealand progressive settled in England, W. A. S. Hewins, L. S. Amery and H. J. Mackinder, all three on the verge of revolt under Joseph Chamberlain against Free Trade. Later on we were joined by Lord Robert Cecil, Michael Sadler, Henry Newbolt (of " Drake's Drum "), J. Birchenough, to strengthen the financial side, Garvin who helped remove the last traces of Encyclopaedism from the *Encyclopaedia Britannica,* Josiah Wedgwood the Single Taxer, Lord

Milner, John Hugh Smith, Colonel Repington, F. S. Oliver, C. F. G. Masterman and others. We found our talks interesting and we kept up a quite high average of attendances. For some years we met in the St. Ermin's Hotel, Westminster, and later in a restaurant which has now given way to a theatre in Whitehall.

Most of these men were already committed to definite political rôles, and Russell and I were by far the most untied and irresponsible members. I had much more to learn than anyone from those conversations and less tradition and political entanglement to hamper my learning. The earlier discussions were the most general and, from my point of view, the best. Could the British Empire be made a self-sustaining system, within a Zollverein? That was at first an open question for most of us. I argued against that idea. The British Empire, I said, had to be the precursor of a world-state or nothing. I appealed to geography. It was possible for the Germans and Austrians to hold together in their Zollverein because they were placed like a clenched fist in the centre of Europe. But the British Empire was like an open hand all over the world. It had no natural economic unity and it could maintain no artificial economic unity. Its essential unity must be a unity of great ideas embodied in the English speech and literature.

I was very pleased with that metaphor of the fist and the open hand—but I did not find it a very contagious suggestion.

As I look back now across a gap of two and thirty years upon that talk among the coffee cups and the liqueur glasses, I see England at a parting of the ways. I was still clinging to the dear belief that the English-speaking community might play the part of leader and mediator towards a world commonweal. It was to be a free-trading, free-speaking, liberating flux for mankind. Russell, Pember Reeves and Webb and possibly Haldane and Grey had, I think, a less clearly expressed disposition in the same direction. But the shadow of Joseph Chamberlain lay dark across our dinner-table, the Chamberlain who, upon the " illimitable velt " of South Africa, had had either a sunstroke or a Pauline conversion to Protection and had returned to clamour influentially for what he called Tariff Reform, but what was in effect national commercial egotism. He was impatient with what he felt to be the impracticable world-liberalism of Balfour, the Cecils and the Liberals. Foreign powers, he thought, were taking an immediate advantage of our longer views. He had no long views. He began a struggle to impose the crude common sense and hard methods of a monopolistic Birmingham hardware-manufacturer upon international relations. More and more did his shadow divide us into two parties. Year by year at the Coefficient gatherings, I saw the idea of the British commonweal being de-civilized and " Imperialized." I was in at the very beginning of the English recoil from our pretensions—and with many they were more than pretensions—to exceptional national generosity, courage and world leadership.

The undeniable contraction of the British outlook in the opening decade of the new century is one that has exercised my mind very greatly, and I fear it would produce an immense bulge in this present already bulging bale of a book if I were to attempt a complete analysis. Gradually the belief in the possible world leadership of England had been deflated, by the economic development of America and the militant boldness of Germany. The long reign of Queen Victoria, so prosperous, progressive and effortless, had produced habits of political indolence and cheap assurance. As a people we had got out of training, and when the challenge of these new rivals became open, it took our breath away at once. We did not know how to meet it. We had educated our general population reluctantly; our universities had not kept pace with the needs of the new time; our ruling class, protected in its advantages by a universal snobbery, was broadminded, easy-going and profoundly lazy. The Edwardian monarchy, Court and society were amiable and slack. " Efficiency "—the word of Earl Rosebery and the Webbs was felt to be rather priggish and vulgar. Our liberalism was no longer a larger enterprise, it had became a generous indolence. But minds were waking up to this. Over our table at St. Ermin's Hotel wrangled Maxse, Bellairs, Hewins, Amery and Mackinder, all stung by the small but humiliating tale of disasters in the South African war, all sensitive to the threat of business recession and all profoundly alarmed by the naval and military aggressiveness of Germany, arguing chiefly against the liberalism of Reeves and Russell and myself, and pulling us down, whether we liked it or not, from large generalities to concrete problems.

These Young Imperialists, as they were then, found it impossible to distinguish between national energy and patriotic narrowness. Narrowing the outlook is a cheap immediate way of enhancing the effect of energy without really increasing it. They were all for training and armament and defensive alliances, and they were all careless or contemptuous of that breadth and vigour of education in which the true greatness of a people lies. I tried to be more fundamental, to trace the secret springs of our inertness. I talked—it was considered a barely pardonable eccentricity —of the crippling effect of the monarchy, of the cultivated suspicion of real capacity in high quarters, and of the monopolization of educational direction by Oxford and Cambridge. I was of opinion that if Great Britain had become a Republic early in the nineteenth century and set up an adequate modern university organization centring in

London and extended throughout the Empire, in the place of those privileged mediaeval foundations and the intensely domestic personal loyalties it has cherished, it would have drawn the United States back into a closer accord and faced the world with an altogether greater spirit than it was now displaying. Our mentality, I reasoned, was still in the great-estate, gentlemen's servants tradition of the eighteenth century because we had missed our revolution. These are all ifs and ans, but that was the disposition of my mind.

Presently Bertrand Russell flung out of the club. There was an argument at which unfortunately I was not present. Hewins, Amery and Mackinder declared themselves fanatical devotees of the Empire. " My Empire, right or wrong," they said. Russell said that there were a multitude of things he valued before the Empire. He would rather wreck the Empire than sacrifice freedom. So if this devotion was what the club meant——! And out he went—like the ego-centred Whig he is—without consulting me. Later the discussion was summarized to me. I said I was quite of his mind. The Empire was a convenience and not a God. Hewins in protest was almost lyrical. He loved the Empire. He could no more say why he loved the Empire than a man could say why he loved his wife. I ought to resign. I said I had no taste for exile ; I never have had a taste for exile ; and so I would not follow Russell unless they threw me out. The more this Imperialist nonsense was talked in the club, the more was it necessary that one voice at least should be present to contradict it. And so nailing my colours to the mast and myself to the dinner table, I remained—and we all continued to get on very well together.

Milner, oddly enough, I found the most satisfactory intelligence among us. He knew we had to make a new world, but he had nothing of my irresponsible constructive boldness. So that he fell into Imperialist Monarchist forms—

which a partly German education may have made easier for him. But upon many minor issues we were apt to agree.

Haldane on the contrary I found intellectually unsympathetic, although his general political attitude was nearer to mine. He was a self-indulgent man, with a large white face and an urbane voice that carried his words as it were on a salver, so that they seemed good even when they were not so. The " Souls," the Balfour set, in a moment of vulgarity had nicknamed him " Tubby." He was a copious worker in a lawyer-like way and an abundant—and to my mind entirely empty—philosopher after the German pattern. He had a cluster of academic distinctions which similar philosophers had awarded him. I used to watch him at our gatherings and wonder what sustained him. I think he floated on strange compensatory clouds of his own exhalation. He rejoiced visibly in the large smooth movements of his mind. Mostly he was very busy on his immediate activities ; his case, his exposition, his reply, his lecture, and it was probably rare for him to drop down to self-scrutiny. When other men lie awake in the small hours and experience self-knowledge, remorse and the harsher aspects of life, crying out aloud and leaping up to pace their rooms, Haldane I am sure communed quite serenely with that bladder of nothingness, the Absolute, until he fell asleep again.

When Einstein came to England and was lionized after the war, he was entertained by Haldane. Einstein I know and can converse with very interestingly, in a sort of Ollendorffian French, about politics, philosophy and what not, and it is one of the lost good things in my life, that I was never able to participate in the mutual exploration of these two stupendously incongruous minds. Einstein must have been like a gentle bright kitten trying to make friends with a child's balloon, very large and unaccountably unpuncturable.

THE IDEA OF A PLANNED WORLD

Haldane found time to produce various books on philosophy. They are still spoken of with profound respect and a careful avoidance of particulars in academic circles, but they mark no turning point in the history of the human mind. They move far away from any vulgar reality in a special universe of discourse. *The Pathway to Reality* was not actually written; it was poured out from notes as the Gifford Lectures in that mellifluous voice, taken down in shorthand and corrected for publication. It is like a very large soap bubble that for some inexplicable reason fails to be iridescent. He also produced a translation of Schopenhauer, omitting an indelicate but vitally important discussion of perversion.

His abundant methodical mind was at its best in formal organization. It is generally admitted that it was his reform of the army in 1905 which made possible the prompt dispatch of the British Expeditionary Force to France in August 1914. His intelligence was certainly better trained and more abundant than that of any of the British professional military authorities, and he might have done great service during the actual struggle. But in a moment of enthusiasm for Teutonic metaphysics he had declared that Germany was his " spiritual home " and Northcliffe, in an access of spy mania, hunted him from office at the outbreak of the war. It was a great disappointment for him, for he was acutely conscious of strategic capacity. But measured against such brains as those of Kitchener and French, almost anyone might be forgiven an acute consciousness of strategic capacity.

I will not speculate about what might have happened if we had had Haldane as war-director instead of the fuddled dullness of Kitchener, the small-army cleverness of French, Haig's mediocrity and the stolid professionalism of the army people throughout. It would lead me far away from this wandering lane of autobiography into a wilderness of entertaining but futile hypothesis, and I have already made some heartfelt observations about the army caste in an earlier section. Moreover after a section on "If Haldane had been at the War Office in 1914," it would be impossible not to go on to what might have happened if we had had Winston Churchill for our war lord—brilliant, I feel sure he would have been, if unsound—and so on to even stranger possibilities. My concern here is simply with Lord Haldane as a man with a voice in human destiny. How was this undeniably big brain concerned with change and the incessant general problem of mankind? I have told how Theodore Roosevelt was touched by that problem. Was Lord Haldane really touched by it at all?

I do not think that between contemporary practicality and the Absolute there was any intermediate level at which the mind of Haldane halted to ask himself what he was doing with the world. His mind was unquickened by any serious knowledge of biology or cosmology, his idea of science was of a useful technical cleverness and not of a clearer vision, and I think it improbable that he brought the conception of unlimited fundamental change into his picture of the universe at all. A legal training directs the mind to equity and settlement rather than progress. And the Absolute is very constipating to the mind. I imagine he just thought that " history goes on—much as ever " and left it at that.

Another of our Coefficients who certainly found a belief in the steady continuity of conventional history a full and sufficient frame for his political thoughts was Sir Edward Grey (who became Viscount Grey of Fallodon). Here again was a brain that I found almost incredibly fixed and unaware of the violent mutability of things. His air of grave and responsible leadership was an immense delusion, for who can lead unless he be in motion? Never had a human being less stimulus for getting on to anywhere or anything. He was a man born to wealth and prominence; he inherited his baronetcy and estates at the age of twenty and he entered parliament with the approval of everyone, the nicest of nice young men, at the age of twenty-three. He was tall and of a fine immobile handsomeness; he played tennis very well and he was one of the most distinguished of British fly-fishers. At the age of thirty-seven in the full tide of his gifts, he wrote an excellent book on the latter art. He was never very deeply interested in internal politics for naturally enough he could see very little to complain of in the condition of the country, but as a matter of public and party duty he was made Under-Secretary for Foreign Affairs when he was thirty, and an opinion grew about him and within him that he understood them. He understood them about as much as Lord Tyrrell, upon whose outlook I have already animadverted in my account of my Crewe House experiences.

I have already said that Tyrrell's mind was governess-made. I would almost extend that to the whole Foreign Office personnel. People of this class are caught young before any power of defensive criticism has developed in them and told stories of a series of mythical beings, France, Germany, England, Spain, with such assurance that they become more real than daddy and mummy. They are led to believe that " Spain " is cruel, " Holland " little and brave, " Germany " industrious and protestant and " Ireland " tragic, priest-led and unforgetting. They think that there are wicked countries and good countries. Once a modernized education has cleared up the human mind in this matter, such widespread delusions will be inconceivable. Readers in those days to come will not believe what I am writing here. But the minds of these people are set in that shape, as the bandaged skulls of the Mangbetu of the Belgian Congo are set in the shape of a sugar loaf, and few so formed ever come round to a sane scepticism about these foolish simplifications. In my *Outline of History* I have done my best to show plainly how the belief in these plausible inventions, as unreal as Baal or Juggernaut, has warped all human life and slaughtered countless millions in the past two centuries. Slowly a clearer vision of the human complex is spreading, but Grey in his grave solemn way talked, just as Tyrrell chattered, of " What France feels in the matter " or " If Germany does so and so, the time will come for us to act."

He would not even disperse these personifications to the extent of saying " They."

I thought Grey a mentally slow, well-mannered, not unpleasantly dignified person until after August 1914. Then I realized what a danger such blinkered firmness of mind as his could be to mankind.

I think he wanted the war and I think he wanted it to come when it did. Sooner or later, on the international chequerboard which he saw in place of reality, Germany would attack. It was better she should attack while her navy was still quantitatively inferior to ours and while the web of precautionary alliances we had woven against her held firm. He would never have taken part in an attack on Germany, a preventive war as they call it in France nowadays, because that was not in accordance with the rules of the game, not at all the sort of thing a gentlemanly country does, but if Germany saw fit to attack first, then, well and good, the Lord had delivered her into our hands.

It is charged against him that he did not definitely warn Germany that we should certainly come into the war, that he was sufficiently ambiguous to let her take a risk and attack, and that he did this deliberately. I think that charge is sound.

His faith in the reality of national personifications outlived the war. When I was working for the creation of a League of Nations Union, it was with a sort of despair that I found that everyone in the movement was insisting on the necessity of having Grey for our figurehead. For him a League of Nations was necessarily a League of Foreign Offices. His intelligence was as incapable of thinking multitudinously of the human beings under the shadow of " France " or " Russia " as a Zoo bear is of thinking of the atoms in a bun.

Another of these governess-moulded minds I encountered was Lord Curzon who was at the Foreign Office in 1920, when I returned from a visit to Soviet Russia. I went to him to suggest a working understanding with the new régime. I tried to explain first that it was now the only possible régime in Russia and that if it was overthrown Russia would come as near to Chaos as a human population can ; secondly that it was a weak régime in sore need of manufactured material, scientific apparatus and technical help of every sort and thirdly, that however strong our objection to Marxist theory might be and however intransigent their Marxism, a certain generosity and understanding now, a certain manifest readiness to help must inevitably force reciprocal concessions. The new Soviet Russia was the best moral and political investment that had ever been offered to Britain. And our Foreign Office turned it down—like a virtuous spinster of a certain age refusing a proposal to elope and bear ten children. Most of this is said quite plainly in my *Russia in the Shadows*.

Lord Curzon listened to me as a man listens to a language he does not understand, but which he is unwilling to admit is strange to him. For him Russia was something as unified and personally responsible as Aunt Sally or the defendant in the dock. When it came to his turn to speak, he began, incorrigibly and with a slight emphasis on his master words, in this fashion : " But so long as *Russia* continues to sustain a *propaganda* against us in *Persia*, I do not see how we can possibly do anything of the sort you suggest...."

I declare that the greatest present dangers to the human race are these governess-trained brains which apparently monopolize the Foreign Offices of the world, which cannot see human affairs in any other light than as a play between the vast childish abstractions we call nations. There are people who say the causes of war, nowadays at least, are economic. They are nothing so rational. They are hallucinatory. Men like Grey, Curzon and Tyrrell present a fine big appearance to the world, but the bare truth is that they are, by education and by force of uncritical acceptance, infantile defectives, who ought to be either referred back to a study of the elements of human ecology or certified and secluded as damaged minds incapable of managing public affairs.

Another outstanding man, of that period before the Great War, with whom I had some mental exchanges was Mr. Balfour—"Mr. Arthur." I used to meet him at Stanway and Taplow Court and in various London houses. He at any rate was high above the governess-made level. There was always an odour of intelligence about him that made his average Conservative associates uncomfortable. He had a curious active mind, he had been attracted by my earlier books and, through him and through Cust, I came to know something of the group of people who centred round him and Lady Mary Elcho, the " Souls." That too was a vague Open Conspiracy, an attempt to get away from the self-complacent dullness and furtive small town viciousness of *fin-de-siècle* England, and to see life freshly. He had grown up in an atmosphere of scientific thought; Francis Balfour, his younger brother, was a brilliant biologist and his *Text-book of Embryology* had been my first introduction to the Balfour family. Arthur Balfour had none of the forceful energy of Theodore

Roosevelt; he was a long-limbed, simple-living but self-indulgent, bachelor man. He was a greater British private gentleman even than Sir Edward Grey. He was so comfortably wealthy, so well connected and so secure that a certain aloofness from the dusty sweaty conflict of life, was in his habit of living.

It is hard to say where, in aloofness, is set the boundary between divinity and cowardice. He could show such courage as he did when as Irish Secretary he was continually under a threat of assassination, because he could not believe that anything of that sort could really happen to him; but when his essential liberalism came face to face with this new baseness of commercialized imperialism, with all its push and energy, he made a very poor fight for it. He allowed himself to be hustled into the background of affairs by men with narrower views and nearer objectives.

He argued sceptically on behalf of religion. His way of defending the Godhead was by asking, What can your science know for certain? and escaping back to orthodoxy under a dust-cloud of philosophical doubts. He anticipated my own remark that the human mind is as much a product of the struggle for survival as the snout of a pig and perhaps as little equipped for the unearthing of fundamental truth. But while that enabled him to accord a graceful support to the Church of England—which might be just as right or wrong about ultimates as anything else—I used my release from rigid conviction for a systematic common-sense interpretation of my world.

In the smooth-water years before 1914 and the subsequent cataracts, I had a great admiration for Balfour. In that queer confused novel, *The New Machiavelli*, one of my worst and one of my most revealing, I have a sort of caricature-portrait of him as Evesham in which I magnify him unduly. (There is also, by the bye, in the same book a remote sketch of the

Coefficients as the "Pentagram Club.") I put various discourses into Evesham's mouth, of which the matter is clearly my own. Here is a vignette, which shows also my own phase of development about 1912.

"Have I not seen him in the House, persistent, persuasive, indefatigable, and by all my standards wickedly perverse, leaning over the table with those insistent movements of his hand upon it, or swaying forward with a grip upon his coat lapel, fighting with a diabolical skill to preserve what are in effect religious tests, tests he must have known would outrage and humiliate and injure the consciences of a quarter—and that perhaps the best quarter—of the young teachers who come to the work of elementary education?

"In playing for points in the game of party advantage Evesham displayed at times a quite wicked unscrupulousness in the use of his subtle mind. I would sit on the Liberal benches and watch him, and listen to his urbane voice, fascinated by him. Did he really care? Did anything matter to him? And if it really mattered nothing, why did he trouble to serve the narrowness and passion of his side? Or did he see far beyond my scope, so that this petty iniquity was justified by greater, remoter ends, of which I had no intimation?

"They accused him of nepotism. His friends and family were certainly well cared for. In private life he was full of an affectionate intimacy; he pleased by being charmed and pleased. One might think at times there was no more of him than a clever man happily circumstanced, and finding an interest and occupation in politics. And then came a glimpse of thought, of imagination, like the sight of a soaring eagle through a staircase skylight. Oh, beyond question he was great! No other contemporary politician had his quality. ... Except that he had it seemed no hot passions, but only interests and fine affections and indolences, he paralleled the conflict of my life. He saw and thought widely and deeply ; but at times it seemed to me his greatness stood over and behind the reality of his life, like some splendid servant, thinking his own thoughts, who waits behind a lesser master's chair."

There is something very youthful in that passage. I have hardened and grown wiser since then. It is easier to be taken that way when one is thirty-eight than in the cooler longer perspective of sixty-eight. Later on I realized that Balfour was letting one thing after another be wrestled from his hands by lesser men. He allowed *The Times* when it was sold, go to the highest bidder ; it fell to Northcliffe and it might have fallen into far worse hands ; Balfour would have done nothing disturbing to himself to prevent it. None of our richer aristocrats seem to have risked any money at that time to keep this public organ in public-spirited hands. Yet the control of that paper was quite essential to their predominance. They trusted to the snobbishness of some *nouveau riche*. So they got Northcliffe who was anything but a snob—and in due course a new mercantile conservatism arose which adopted B.M.G. (Balfour Must Go) as its animating slogan. He could not control these new people but he hampered them and so they turned upon him.

Balfour might perhaps have been a very great man indeed if his passions had been hotter and his affections more vivid. The lassitudes of these fine types, their fastidiousness in the presence of strong appeals, leave them at last a prey to the weak gratifications of vanity and a gentle impulse to pose. He posed. He was aware of himself and he posed—as Mr. Humbert Wolfe has recently told in the *English Review* (June 1934). As the war went on his poses became more and more self-protective.

Amidst the clamour and riot of the war he faded away from power to eminence. I had one queer glimpse of some struggle going on in him and about him. We were at the house of Lady Wemyss in Cadogan Square, talking about the early reactions of the various classes to the war. He had an impulse to tell me something. " The worst behaviour," he began, " has been on the part of our business men." Emphasis. " The *very* worst."

He thought better of it and I was not clever enough or resolute enough to make him say more.

After the war, power left him altogether. He was merely a very eminent person, at last indeed almost the most eminent person in Britain. His last flare of charm and activity was at the Washington Conference of 1924. He helped make it the most amiable conference imaginable and the fund of sympathy between Washington and Westminster was greatly enhanced. There I saw and talked with him but nothing he said has remained in my memory. No doubt he and Grey were very fine gentlemen, but they were expensive to produce and they did not give back to human society anything like an adequate return in mental toil and directive resolution, for its expenditure upon them, for their great parks and houses and the deference that was shown them.

One day—in 1920 or 1921 I think, I went with Jane to the Institute of International Affairs and saw Balfour speaking on the platform. The light fell on his skull and I had a queer impression that quite recently I had seen an almost exactly similar cranium, similarly lit. My mind flashed back to Moscow. I whispered to Jane : " He's got a brain box that is the very pair to Lenin's. . . . It's incredible."

Perhaps it was only a matter of lighting and I will not embark upon any systematic search for correlated resemblances. Lenin by all his circumstances was as insecure, active and aggressive as Balfour was assured and indolent, but both had curious brains with a live edge of scepticism that put them on a far higher level than the blinkered stupidity of Grey and Curzon or the elaborate unreality of Haldane. Neither I think were orthodox minded and Lenin believed in the dogmas of Marx about as much as Balfour believed in the Holy Trinity and both were capable of the most destructive conformity. But while Lenin was using Marxism to make things happen because he was under the urgency of change, Balfour was using Christianity and Christian organization, to resist changes that, whatever else they did, were bound to disturb the spacious pleasantness of his life. I went to Russia as I have recounted in *Russia in the Shadows*, and I had a long talk with Lenin and a number of talks about him.

Now here was a fresh kind of brain for me to encounter and it was in such a key-position as no one had dreamt of as possible for anyone before the war. He appeared to be the complete master of all that was left of the resources of Russia. He was not by any means the master he seemed to be; he had a difficult team of supporters to handle and such an instrument as the Ogpu, which could twist round in his grip and wound him—as it did when it executed the Grand Dukes after his reprieve. And above all he was tied very closely to the sacred text of Marx. A real or assumed reverence for that was what held his following together, and his modification of the sacred Word to meet the great emergencies before him had to be subtle and propitiatory to an extreme degree. He had all these checks and entanglements to hinder him. But the authoritative effect of him was very great indeed.

He had a personal prestige based on his sound advice and lucid vision during the revolutionary crisis. He became then the man to whom everyone ran in fear or doubt. He had the strength of simplicity of purpose combined with subtlety of thought. By imperceptible changes, to an extent that only began to be measured and recognized after his death, he changed Marxism into Leninism. He changed the teachings of a fatalistic doctrinaire into a flexible creative leadership. So long as it was the substance of Lenin, he did not care in the least if it bore the label of Marx. But this year I have seen that his portrait and image in Russia everywhere are quietly elbowing his bearded precursor out of the way. His was by far the more vigorous and finer brain.

Like everybody else he belonged to his own time and his own phase. We met and talked each with his own preconceptions. We talked chiefly of the necessity of substituting large scale cultivation for peasant cultivation—that was eight years before the first Five Year Plan—and of the electrification of Russia, which was then still only a dream in his mind. I was sceptical about that because I was ignorant of the available water power of Russia. " Come back and see us in ten years time," he said to my doubts.

When I talked to Lenin I was much more interested in our subject than in ourselves. I forgot whether we were big or little or old or young. At that time I was chiefly impressed by the fact that he was physically a little man, and by his intense animation and simplicity of purpose. But now as I look over my fourteen-year-old book and revive my memories and size him up against the other personalities I have known in key positions, I begin to realize what an outstanding and important figure he is in history. I grudge subscribing to the " great man " conception of human affairs, but if we are going to talk at all of greatness among our species, then I must admit that Lenin at least was a very great man.

If in 1912 I could call Balfour " beyond question great," it seems almost my duty here to put that flash of enthusiasm in its proper proportion to what I think of the Russian. So let me say with all deliberation that when I weigh the two against each other it is not even a question of swaying scalepans ; Balfour flies up and kicks the beam. The untidy little man in the Kremlin out-thought him—out-did him. Lenin was alive to the last, whereas Balfour ended in an attitude. Lenin was already ailing when I saw him, he had to take frequent holidays, early in 1922 the doctors stopped his daily work altogether and he became partly paralysed that summer and died early in 1924. His days of full influence therefore, extended over less than five crowded years. Nevertheless in that time, he imposed upon the Russian affair, a steadfastness of constructive effort against all difficulties, that has endured to this day. But for him and his invention of the organized Communist party, the Russian revolution would certainly have staggered into a barbaric military autocracy and ultimate social collapse. But his Communist party provided, crudely no doubt but sufficiently for the survival of the experiment, that disciplined personnel for an improvized but loyal civil service without which a revolution in a modern state is doomed to complete futility. His mind never became rigid and he turned from revolutionary activities to social reconstruction with an astonishing agility. In 1920, when I saw him, he was learning with the vigour of a youth about the possible " electrification of Russia." The conception of the Five Year Plan—but as he saw it, a series of successive provincial Plans—a Russian grid system, the achievements of Dnepropetrovsk, were all taking shape in his brain. He went on working, as a ferment, long after his working days had ended. He is still working perhaps as powerfully as ever.

During my last visit to Moscow, in July 1934, I visited his Mausoleum and saw the little man again. He seemed smaller than ever ; his face very waxy and pale and his restless hands still. His beard was redder than I remembered it. His expression was very dignified and simple and a little pathetic, there was childishness and courage there, the supreme human qualities, and he sleeps—too soon for

Russia. The decoration about him was plain and noble. The atmosphere of the place was saturated with religious feeling and I can well believe that women pray there. Outside down the Square there still stands the inscription: "Religion"—which in Russia it must be remembered always means Orthodox Christianity—" is the opium of the people." Deprived of that opium Russia is resorting to new forms of dope. In Moscow I was shown one evening Dziga Vertov's new film: *Three Songs for Lenin*. This is a very fine and moving apotheosis of Lenin. It is Passion Music for Lenin and he has become a Messiah. One must see and hear it to realize how the queer Russian mind has emotionalized Socialism and subordinated it to the personal worship of its prophets, and how necessary it is that the west wind should blow through the land afresh.

In the spring of 1934 I took it into my head to see and compare President Franklin Roosevelt and Mr. Stalin. I wanted to form an opinion of just how much these two brains were working in the direction of this socialist world-state that I believe to be the only hopeful destiny for mankind.

In what has gone before I have done my best to set out before the persevering reader as precisely and plainly as possible the foundations and nature of this picture of the world problem that has been painted bit by bit on my own brain tissues since I played in the back-yard of Atlas House, and I have tried to show the successive phases through which my belief has grown definite, until at last it has become altogether clear to me (as to many others) that the organization of this that I call the Open Conspiracy, the evocation of a greater sounder fellow to the first Communist essay, an adequately implemented Liberal Socialism, which will ultimately supply teaching, coercive and directive public services to the whole world, is the immediate task before

THE IDEA OF A PLANNED WORLD

all rational people. I believe this idea of the planned world-state is one to which all our thought and knowledge is tending. It is an idea that is quietly pervading human mentality because facts and events conspire in its favour. It is appearing partially and experimentally at a thousand points. It does not dismay me in the least that no specific political organization to realize this idea, has yet appeared. By its very nature the formal conflicts of politics will be almost the last thing in the world to be affected by it. When accident finally precipitates it, its coming is likely to happen very quickly. We shall find ourselves almost abruptly engaged in a new system of political issues in which the socialist world-state will be plainly and consciously lined up against the scattered vestigial sovereignties of the past.

I am quite unable to form an opinion how long it will be before this happens and the socialist world-state enters the field of political actuality. Sometimes I feel that it may be imminent. Sometimes I feel that generations of propaganda and education may have to precede it. The war danger and economic stress are both forcing men's minds towards it as the one way out for them. These grim instructors may do much to make up for the negligence and backwardness of the schoolmaster. Plans for political synthesis and economic readjustment seem to grow bolder and more extensive. It was natural therefore, if a little impulsive and premature, that I should go to America and Russia with the question, Is this it already ? What is the relation of the New Plan in America to the New Plan in Russia and how are both related to the ultimate world-state ?

Some readers will object that this is political discussion and not autobiograhy. It is political discussion but also it is autobiography. The more completely life is lived the more political a man becomes. My democratic reading of the rights of man is not so much a matter of voting—usually for candidates put up for me by other people—as asking questions, getting answers and passing judgments on my own behalf. I ask my questions. These two visits are essential events in my life and telling about them is as intimate and personal a rounding off of my story as I can imagine. Modern life is expansion and then effacement. We do not round off, we open out. We do not end with valedictions ; we open doors and then stand aside.

Just before I sailed for America I went to a queer exhibition of futility in the Albert Hall. It was a gathering of Mosley's blackshirts and it would be hard to imagine anything sillier —from the slow pompous entry of this queer crazy creature, dressed up like a fencing instructor with a waist fondly exaggerated by a cummerbund and chest and buttocks thrust out, stalking gravely and alone down the central gangway, to the last concerted outburst confined entirely, I remarked, to his disciplined following, of boyish shouting and hand-lifting : " We *want* Mosley."

I have met Mosley intermittently for years, as a promising young conservative, a promising new convert to the Labour party, with Communist leanings, and finally as the thing he is. He has always seemed to me dull and heavy, imitative in his politics and platitudinous in his speeches, and so I was not greatly interested in what he had to say to this meeting. As his banalities boomed about the hall, without a single flicker of wit or wisdom, their dullness vastly exaggerated by loud speakers, we noted how the habit of mouthing his words was growing upon him—he has for some obscure reason invented a sort of dialect of his own—and then we discussed particulars of his Sandhurst days and his war-record which were new to me. What chiefly held my attention were his supporters and the audience generally. The audience was miscellaneous, curious and little moved, and it did not fully fill the hall. Quite a quantity of pleasant boys and nice young men, and quite a number of others who were not so nice, dressed up in black shirts and grey trousers, were acting as ushers, selling idiotic songs about their glorious Leader, supplying the applause, pervading the meeting, and generally keeping the affair from becoming a complete slump. They seemed drawn chiefly from the middle and upper class. There was something shy about many of them, something either desperately grave and assertive, or faintly apologetic. They were not throwing themselves into their parts as the hairy young Italians they were aping would have done. There was no romantic conviction about them. The thing that really intrigued me was why they did this. What sort of feeble imaginations, I asked, could be flicking about in their nice young cerebral cortices to bring them to this pass?

That question went with me across the Atlantic. Is there really anything we can call education in England at the present time? Or is what passes for education only a sort of systematic softening of the brain? What history had been put before these young men, what vision of life had been given them, that they should start out upon their political life "wanting"—of all conceivable desiderata!—Mosley?

Only after a huge cultural struggle can we hope to see the world-state coming into being. The Open Conspiracy has to achieve itself in many ways, but the main battle before it is an educational battle, a battle to make the knowledge that already exists accessible and assimilable and effective. The world has moved from the horse-cart and the windmill to the aeroplane and dynamo but education has made no equivalent advance. The new brains that are pouring into the world are being caught by incompetent and unenlightened teachers, they are being waylaid by the marshalled misconceptions of the past, and imprisoned in rigid narrow historical and political falsifications. We cannot do with such a world population. We cannot build a new civilization out of two thousand million pot-bound minds. It is all poor, damaged material we have to deal with. Such cramped and crippled stuff might serve well enough for the comparatively unshattered social and political routines of the nineteenth century but it will not serve to-day. It is as dangerous, as catastrophically inert, as loose sand piled high, and always rising higher, over the excavation for a highway.

I prowled round the promenade deck at night thinking how little we were doing for education and how little I had done. I wished I had some virus with which one might bite people and make them mad for education. I was going from one dismally miseducated country to another, and when all was said and done these two were the most enlightened countries as yet in all the world. And I was hoping against my better knowledge to find the seeds of a new way of life already germinating and sending out green shoots.

It is not spring of the world's great year yet.

> *The world's great age begins anew,*
> *The golden years return,*
> *The earth doth like a snake renew*
> *Her winter weeds outworn.*

That was written a hundred years ago and it is still prophetic.

Coming into New York harbour there was fog, a quite appropriate and disturbing fog, with fog-horns about us so like political leaders that you could not in the least ascertain their direction, and the *Washington* in which I was a passenger was as nearly as possible run down by the *Balin* in the Ambrose Channel. The German liner jumped out of the fog abruptly, and passed within ten yards of us on the wrong side. I heard a babble of voices close at hand and looked out of my port-hole into the astonished faces of a group of passengers on the *Balin's* deck within spitting distance of me. She swept by and vanished in the fog and I went up on deck to hear what other people thought of the occurrence. Opinions differed as to how near we had been to a smash ; the estimates varied from six feet to twenty yards. The two boats had sucked in towards each other as they passed. Some of us tried to imagine just what a touch would have meant. Nobody was very much upset about it ; it seemed to be just a part of the general large dangerousness of human affairs at the present time.

When I arrived in New York I began to hear opinions of the " New Deal " from every point of view. I wanted to sample the atmosphere in which the President was working before I went to see him. Various good friends had gathered talk parties of the most diverse composition, and I had written to one or two men I knew would give me first-hand information. Everyone talked freely and it is not for me to document what was said by this individual or that. I found myself sitting next to an unassuming young man whose name I had not quite caught and he began to unfold a view of the world to me which seemed to contain all I had ever learnt and thought, but better arranged and closer to reality. This I discovered was A. A. Berle of the so-called Brains Trust. " And how many more of *you* are there ? " I wanted to ask him—and didn't.

And then, by way of contrast, I heard across the table the distinguished head of a big corporation, a fine grey-headed, rotund-voiced gentleman, denouncing every new thing in America from the President down to the last man in the queue of unemployed, and demanding to be put back forthwith to the happy days of 1924. Or was it 1926? He had observed nothing material since then. "And how many," thought I, "are there of *you*?" His faith in economic anarchism and the eternal succession of trade-cycles was unshaken. Since the present depression was particularly intense and prolonged he argued, the recovery would be all the brighter. He was like a strong infusion of Herbert Spencer and Harriet Martineau in the tradition of that valient optimist, Ambassador Choate—whom I described as Mr. Z, "Pippa's rich uncle" in *The Future in America*.

Between these extremes of understanding and resistance to reality, was an extraordinary variety of types. I had a brush with a delightful couple of New York "Reds," pure Communists, as pure and intolerant as their Puritan forebears. They were of quite wealthy origin, and they recited their belief in Karl Marx, his philosophy, his psychology, his final divine wisdom, as though Lenin had lived in vain, and they were in just as complete and effective an opposition to the New Deal as my grey-haired corporation president. Roosevelt they said was just "bolstering up capitalism." He was trying to sneak past a social catastrophe and cut out their dear dictatorship of the proletariat altogether—contrariwise to Holy Writ. The better he did the worse it would be, for there could be no real blessing on it, said these real right Reds.

In the New Willard, in Washington, I found myself in contact with those fine flowers of American insurrectionism, my old friends Clarence Darrow and Charles Russell. They had been summoned to the capital to report on the working of various codes and they were reporting as unhelpfully and destructively as they knew how. They were "agin the government" all the time and the wildfire of freedom shone in Darrow's eyes.

I have a great affection and sympathy for Clarence Darrow. It is deep in my nature also to be restive under government and hostile to dogma. But he is, by ten years or more, of an older generation, and the American radicalism in which he grew up was very different from the early formative influences I have described in my own case. I believe in the free common intelligence, in freely criticized commonsense, but Darrow believes superstitiously in the individual unorganized free common man. That is to say he is a sentimental anarchist. He is for an imaginary " little man "— against monopoly, against rule, against law—any law.

It is remarkable how widespread among American brains is this fantasy of the sturdy little independent " healthy " competitive man, essentially righteous: the Western farmers, the small shopkeeper, the struggling, saving, hard-working entrepreneur. To this first onset of publicly directed large-scale economic organization in Washington, that New York corporation president I have described and Clarence Darrow, the extreme radical, responded in almost identical terms. " Leave us alone," they said—with passion. The same ideal, of perpetuating a fundamental individualism of small folk, was manifest in the anti-trust legislation of Theodore Roosevelt. It is a dream. The problem of personal freedom is not to be solved by economic fragmentation; that Western farmer lost his independence long since and became the grower of a single special crop, the small shop-keeper either a chain-store minder or a dealer in branded goods, and the small entrepreneur a gambler with his savings, and a certain bankrupt in the end; nevertheless the dream survives. To borrow a phrase from Russia: it is a kulak ideal. I found it still living even among the directors of the A.A.A. in Washington.

In their report upon the codes, Darrow and Russell went so far as to impute motive. That heroic small man of their imaginations was, they said, being deliberately sacrificed to big business—*sold* to big business. But it is not the New Deal and the N.R.A. which are sacrificing the small man to large-scale operations. The stars in their courses are doing that. Nevertheless in this fashion these two anarchistic Old Radicals were able to line up with our wealthy young Communists, who thought Roosevelt was " bolstering up capitalism " and that angry public utility exploiter who declared the New Deal was smashing it. There are manifestly common subconscious elements underlying this amazing unanimity.

What struck me most about the New York atmosphere, and the impression was intensified in Washington, was the mixture of praise and detraction with which the President was mentioned. It had become almost a ritual. There would be a prelude upon his courage, his integrity, his personal charm and then " but——." The varied contexts to that " but," taken altogether, made me realize that Franklin Roosevelt is one of the greatest shocks that has ever happened to the prevalent mental assumptions of the United States. A man's formulated and expressed opinions may be one thing, we have to remember, and his tacit or subconscious assumptions quite another. Premonitions of a new social and economic order which have hitherto seemed the harmless talk of an ineffectual intelligentsia have been broadcast abruptly over vast surfaces of conventional business and political expression. The time-honoured crust of pompous insincerity characteristic of the old order has been broken and has revealed the underlying capacity of the American mind for stark reality. With an air of just giving the old deck of cards a new deal for the century-old game of political poker, the President seems to have taken up a new deck altogether, with strange new suits and altered values, and to be playing quietly and resolutely a different game. What game is he playing ? Does he know himself? Does he realize he is a revolution? Imaginative answers to these perplexing questions, often highly imaginative and experimental answers, furnished the material for all those " buts."

Were they trying to pull him down or trying to make him out? I listened undecided. Principally, I think, they were puzzled about him and, being puzzled, they were alarmed. They did not want to have him—with all due acknowledgements—and they did not know what else they could have. The world of American wealth and enterprise has been so sure of its freedoms, so convinced of its boundless areas and possibilities and so uncritically assured of its own essential goodness and necessity, that it has received the onset of even a certain scrutiny of its operations with a kind of exaggerated claustrophobia. It is disposed to fight and embarrass any form of regulation. It had got itself into the most hideous economic and industrial mess; only a year ago it was scared white and helpless with the terror of immediate catastrophe, but already it is recovering its ancient confidence and declaring, now that the immediate danger is past, that there was never any danger at all. It means to be carping and obstructive—and to the best of its power and ability it will be. In 1906 in my *Future in America* I emerged with the obvious reflection that Americans rich and radical alike had no " sense of the state." Now they are getting a sense of the state put over them rather rapidly, and they are taking it very ungraciously.

This disposition to detract from the President's effort to reconstruct the American front and to hamper him in every possible way, is unaccompanied by any real alternative policy. It is an irresponsible instinctive opposition, a mulish pulling back. There is no going back now for America. If Roosevelt and his New Deal fail altogether, there will be further financial and business collapse, grave sectional social disorder, political gangsterism and an extensive de-civilization of wide regions. And these still wealthy and influential people who are carping and making trouble will be the first to suffer.

The absence of any sense of the state in America, the irresponsible habit of mind fostered by beginning the teaching of history with a rebellion and carrying it on to a glorification of individual push and the mystical democracy of the "Peepul" is the essential difficulty ahead of this eleventh-hour attempt to salvage the immense material accumulations of the past century before they topple over, and to set up an ordered and disciplined direction for the new powers of mankind before it is too late. Order and collective direction means an efficient and devoted Civil Service. The doubt whether America will succeed in making the great adjustments it is facing in time to escape catastrophe, turns largely upon the manifest inadequacy of its present Civil Service to the immense tasks that will necessarily be thrust upon it. Can this Civil Service be supplemented rapidly and effectively? The most momentous question before the United States community is the possibility of improvizing ministers, officials and functionaries sufficiently honest and public-spirited, sufficiently clear-headed, courageous and competent to carry through the inevitable reconstruction.

Now outside the limits of the undermanned and underpaid Federal Civil Service there has long been considerable speculative activity in intellectual circles, among the university professoriate, among writers, scientific and technical workers and mentally active men of leisure, about the constructive defects that were becoming more and more patent in the American community. An intelligentsia has developed—much more considerable altogether than the corresponding strata on the British side. It thinks as a whole more *roughly* than its British equivalents, but more boldly and less deferentially. American business has hitherto ticked

THE IDEA OF A PLANNED WORLD

these people off as "long-haired Radicals" or "parlour socialists" or "cranks" and turned its back on their extending influence. Then, when the crisis was at its blackest, it discovered that these "cranks" might perhaps prove to be "experts." With very mixed feelings it realized that the new President, instead of entrusting himself to the grave and dignified advice of tried "Experience" to heal—or at any rate to go through the motions of healing—at eight per cent let us say, until the ultimate smash—the disaster its routines had made inevitable, was calling these new brains into consultation. Some journalist, not quite sure whether the suggestion of intellectual activity was a curse or a blessing invented the phrase the "Brains Trust," and the report of it went about the world.

It was inevitable after all my broodings upon a possible world-wide Open Conspiracy of clear-headed people, that this report should stir my interest profoundly. I wanted to know just what integrating forces this talk about the Brains Trust might imply, and how they could be brought into relationship with the steady growth of creative revolutionary thought upon the European side.

I have seen enough of this Brains movement to realize that it is no sort of conspiracy; that it is not a body of men formally associated by a concerted statement of ideas. It represents nothing so much in agreement as the radicals who made the republic in Madrid, nothing nearly so close-knit as the pre-revolutionary Bolshevik party. It has indeed scarcely anything to hold it in any sort of unity except that in this miscellany of widely scattered men there is a common determination to bring scientific analysis to bear upon financial and industrial processes, and to make a practical application of the results in the common interest. Its members are miscellaneous both in tradition and in character. It is the President who has drawn them together and it is necessarily from their ranks and associates, rather than from the rascal heelers of the party politicians, grafters by profession, that the supplementing and extension of the Civil Service must be drawn if there is to be any hope for the salvaging of America.

Raymond Moley has interested himself in the history of this Brains Trust movement, and he spread it out very intelligibly to me in a long talk we had in the Hangar Club in New York. He distinguished three main groups of mental influences, the monetary realists, such as Professor Irving Fisher and Professor Rogers, who constitute the rudiments of a scientific monetary control, the economic organizers such as Johnson, Tugwell and Berle, who stand chiefly for an extension of employment and exploitation by the State, and the lawyers—of whom only Felix Frankfurter is known to me personally—who are concerned with the development of legal restraints upon socially destructive speculative enterprise, and upon the use of large scale organization for private aggrandizement. Many of these people have never met each other. The link between them all was first the Executive Mansion at Albany, when Franklin Roosevelt was Governor of New York State and is now the White House. It is the President's notes of interrogation that have drawn them all together into a loose constructive co-operation.

That is the outstanding difference—so far as form goes—between the constructive effort in Washington and Moscow. The one is a receptive and co-ordinating brain-centre ; the other is a concentrated and personal direction. The end sought, a progressively more organized big-scale community, is precisely the same.

I have been four times to the White House, and twice to the Kremlin, to see the man in occupation. But I have never been, and I am never likely to go, inside the gates of Buckingham Palace. Very early impressions may have something to do with that; I have told of my resistance to my mother's obsession about the dear Queen and my jealousy of the royal offspring; but the main reason for my obstinately republican life, as I see it in my own mind, is my conviction that here in England something has been held on to too long, and that nothing is doing here. A constitutional monarchy substitutes a figure-head for a head and distributes leadership elusively throughout the community. This gives the British system the resisting power of an acephalous invertebrate, and renders it equally incapable of concentrated forward action. In war-time the Crown resumes, or attempts to resume, a centralized authority—with such results as I have already glanced at in my account of my war experiences. Quite in accord with the tenacity of an acephalous invertebrate, the empire can be cut to pieces legally, have its South Ireland amputated, see half its shipping laid up and its heavy industries ruined, reconcile itself to the chronic unemployment and demoralization of half its young people, and still, on the strength of a faked budget and a burst of sunny summer weather, believe itself to be essentially successful and invulnerable. So it came about that, almost without thinking it over, as the various League of Nations documents I have quoted bear witness, I had become accustomed to looking westward for the definitive leadership of the English speaking community—and anywhere but in London for the leadership of mankind.

I have told already of my visit to Theodore Roosevelt. It was like visiting any large comfortable, leisurely, free-talking country house. Seeing President Harding had been like attending a politicians' reception in an official building, all loud geniality and hand-shaking, and the protean White House had taken on the decoration and furniture of a popular club. My call upon President Hoover was a sort of intrusion upon a sickly overworked and overwhelmed man, a month behind in all his engagements and hopeless of ever overtaking them, and the White House, in sympathy, had made itself into a queer ramshackle place like a nest of waiting-rooms with hat-stands everywhere, and unexpected doors, never perceptible before or since, through which hurrying distraught officials appeared and vanished. President Hoover did not talk with me at all; he delivered a discourse upon the possible economic self-sufficiency of America that was, I imagine, intended for M. Laval from Paris, who had left Washington a week or so before. I did not find it interesting. After the Harding days there had been a foolish development of etiquette in Washington and instead of going to the President as man to man, the foreign visitor during the Coolidge and Hoover régime was led—after due enquiries—down to the White House by his ambassador. Henceforth America and the English, it had been decided, were to talk only through a diplomatic pipette. Sir Ronald Lindsay took me down, apologetically, and sat beside me during the encounter, rather like a gentleman who takes a strange dog out to a tea-party, and is not quite sure how it will behave. But I respected the trappings of government and nothing diplomatically serious occurred. I just listened and contained myself. Diplomatic usage will, I suppose, prevent Sir Ronald from ever producing his memories of Men I have Chaperoned to the White House.

All this had been swept away again in 1934, I had had some slight correspondence with the President already, I went to him on my own credentials, and found that this magic White House had changed back again to a large leisurely comfortable private home. All the Hoover untidiness had vanished. Everything was large, cool, orderly and unhurried. Besides Mr. and Mrs. Roosevelt, his daughter Mrs. Dall, Miss Le Hand his personal secretary, and another lady, dined with us and afterwards I sat and talked to him and Mrs. Roosevelt and Miss Le Hand until nearly midnight, easily and pleasantly—as though the world crisis focused anywhere rather than upon the White House.

As everyone knows, the President is a crippled man. He reminded me of William Ernest Henley. He has the same big torso linked to almost useless legs, and he lacked even Henley's practised nimbleness with stick and crutch. But when we sat at dinner and when he was in his study chair, his physical disablement vanished from the picture. Mrs. Roosevelt I found a very pleasant, well-read lady; I had been warned she was a terrible "school marm," but the only trait of the schoolmistress about her was a certain care for precision of statement. There was no pose about either of them. They were not concerned about being what was expected of them, or with the sort of impression they were making; they were just interested in a curious keen detached way about the state of the world. They talked about that, in the manner of independent people who had really not so very much to do with it. We were all in it and we had to play our parts, but there was no reason because one was in a responsible position that one should be mystical or pompous or darkly omniscient about it.

Even if my memory would serve for the task, I would not report the drift and shifting substance of our talk. Only one thing need be recorded, the President's manifest perplexity at some recent turns of British diplomacy, and the wonder that peeped out—a wonder we all share—over the question as to what Sir John Simon imagines he is up to, whether he represents any obscure realities of British thought and, if not, why on earth, in the Far East and elsewhere, the two big English-speaking communities seem perpetually discordant and unexpected to each other. My own fixed idea about world peace came naturally enough to the fore. If it were not, I said, for questions of mere political mechanism, stale traditions, the mental childishness of our British Foreign Office and what not, it would be perfectly possible even now for the English speaking masses and the Russian mass, with France as our temperamental associate, to be made to say effectively that Peace shall prevail throughout the earth. And it would prevail. Whatever dreams of conquest and dominion might be in a few militant and patriotic brains outside such a combination, would burn but weakly in the cold discouragement of so great a unison. And what was it—prevented that unison?

But that was only one of the topics we touched upon. What concerns me here is not what was said, but the manner in which it was thought about and advanced. I am not thinking primarily of policies and governmental actions here, but of an encounter with a new type of mind. My own ideas about the coming socialist world-state are fixed and explicit. But they are, I am persuaded, implicit in every mind that has been opened to the possibility of unrestricted change. I do not say that the President has these revolutionary ideas in so elaborated and comprehensive a form as they have come to me; I do not think he has. I do not think he is consciously what I have called an Open Conspirator and it is quite clear his formulae are necessarily limited by the limitations of the popular understanding with which he has to come to terms. But these ideas are sitting all round him now, and unless I misjudge him, they will presently possess him altogether. Events are reinforcing them and carrying him on to action. My impression of both him and of Mrs. Roosevelt is that they are *unlimited* people, entirely modern in the openness of their minds and the logic of their actions. I have been using the word " blinkered " rather freely in this section. Here in the White House, the un-blinkered mind was in possession.

The Roosevelts are something more than open-minded. Arthur Balfour was greatly open-minded, but he lacked the slightest determination to realize the novel ideas he entertained so freely. He was set in the habitual acceptance of the thing that is, church, court, society, empire, and he did not really believe in the new thoughts that played about in his mind. President Roosevelt does. He has a brain that is certainly as receptive and understanding as Balfour's but, with that, he has an uncanny disposition for action and realization that Balfour lacked altogether. This man who can sit and talk so frankly and freely is also an astute politician and a subtle manager of masses and men. As the President thinks and conceives, so forthwith, he acts. Both he and his wife have the simplicity that says, " But if it is right we ought to do it." They set about what they suppose has to be done without exaltation, without apology or any sense of the strangeness of such conduct. Such unification of unconventional thought and practical will is something new in history, and I will not speculate here about the peculiar personal and the peculiar American conditions that may account for it. But as the vast problems about them expose and play themselves into their minds, the goal of the Open Conspiracy becomes plainer ahead. Franklin Roosevelt does not embody and represent that goal, but he represents the way thither. He is being the most effective transmitting instrument possible for the coming of the new world order. He is eminently "reasonable" and fundamentally implacable. He demonstrates that comprehensive new ideas can be taken up, tried out and made operative in general affairs without rigidity or dogma. He is continuously revolutionary in the new way without ever provoking a stark revolutionary crisis.

Before I visited Washington, I was inclined to the belief that the forces against such a replanning of the American social and political system as will arrest the present slant towards disaster, the individualistic tradition, the individual lawlessness, the intricate brutal disingenuousness of political and legal methods, were so great that President Franklin Roosevelt was doomed to an inevitable defeat. I wrote an article *The Place of Franklin Roosevelt in History* (Liberty Magazine, October, 1933) in which I made my bet for his overthrow. But I thought then he was a man with a definite set of ideas, fixed and final, in his head, just as I am a man with a system of conclusions fixed and definite in my head. But I perceive he is something much more flexible and powerful than that. He is bold and unlimited in his objectives because his mental arms are long and his courage great, but his peculiar equipment as an amateur of the first rank in politics, keeps him in constant touch with political realities and possibilities. He never lets go of them and they never subdue him. He never seems to go so far beyond the crowd as to risk his working leadership, and he never loses sight of pioneer thought. He can understand and weigh contemporary speculative economics, financial specialism and international political psychology, and he can talk on the radio—over the heads of the party managers and newspaper proprietors and so forth—quite plainly and very convincingly to the ordinary voting man.

He is, as it were, a ganglion for reception, expression, transmission, combination and realization which, I take it, is exactly what a modern government ought to be. And if perhaps after all he is, humanly, not quite all that I am saying of him here, he is at any rate enough of what I am saying of him here, for me to make him a chief collateral exhibit in this psycho-political autobiography.

On July the 21st I started from London for Moscow in the company of my eldest son, who wished to meet some Russian biologists with whose work he was acquainted, and to see their laboratories. We left Croydon in the afternoon, spent the night in Berlin and flew on by way of Danzig, Kovno and Welikye Luki, reaching Moscow before dark on the evening of the 22nd. We flew in clear weather as far as Amsterdam, then through a couple of thunderstorms to Berlin. We were late in reaching the glitter of illuminated Berlin; the raining darkness was flickering with lightning flashes and our plane came down to make its landing with flares burning under its wings along a lane of windy yellow flame against the still red and white lights of the aerodrome. The flight next day from Welikye Luki to Moscow, flying low and eastward in afternoon sunshine, was particularly golden and lovely.

In 1900, when I wrote *Anticipations*, this would have been as incredible a journey as a trip on Prince Houssain's carpet; in 1934 it was arranged in the most matter of fact way through a travel agency, it was a little excursion that anyone might make; and the fare was less than the railway fare would have been a third of a century before. In a little time such a visit will seem as small a matter as a taxi-cab call does now. It is our antiquated political organization and our retrograde imaginations that still hold back such a final abolition of distance.

Moscow I found greatly changed—even from the air this was visible; not set and picturesque, a black-and-gold barbaric walled city-camp about a great fortress, as I had seen it first in 1914; nor definitely shabby, shattered and apprehensive as it had been in the time of Lenin, but untidily and hopefully renascent. There was new building going on in every direction, workers' dwellings, big groups of factories and, amidst the woods, new *datchas* and country clubs. No particular plan was apparent from the air; it looked like a vigorous, natural expansion such as one might see in the most individualistic of cities. We came down over a patchwork of aerodromes and saw many hundreds of planes parked outside the hangars. Russian aviation may be concentrated about Moscow, but this display of air force was certainly impressive. Twenty-two years ago, in my *War in the Air*, I had imagined such wide fields of air fleet, but never then in my boldest cerebrations did I think I should live to see them.

I confess that I approached Stalin with a certain amount of suspicion and prejudice. A picture had been built up in my mind of a very reserved and self-centred fanatic, a despot without vices, a jealous monopolizer of power. I had been inclined to take the part of Trotsky against him. I had formed a very high opinion, perhaps an excessive opinion, of Trotsky's military and administrative abilities, and it seemed to me that Russia, which is in such urgent need of directive capacity at every turn, could not afford to send them into exile. Trotsky's autobiography, and more particularly the second volume, had modified this judgment but I still expected to meet a ruthless, hard—possibly doctrinaire—and self-sufficient man at Moscow; a Georgian highlander whose spirit had never completely emerged from its native mountain glen.

Yet I had had to recognize that under him Russia was not being merely tyrannized over and held down; it was being governed and it was getting on. Everything I had heard in favour of the First Five Year Plan I had put through a severely sceptical sieve, and yet there remained a growing effect of successful enterprise. I had listened more and more greedily to any first-hand gossip I could hear about both these contrasted men. I had already put a query against my grim anticipation of a sort of Bluebeard at the centre of

Russian affairs. Indeed if I had not been in reaction against these first preconceptions and wanting to get nearer the truth of the matter, I should never have gone again to Moscow.

This lonely overbearing man, I thought, may be damned disagreeable, but anyhow he must have an intelligence far beyond dogmatism. And if I am not all wrong about the world, and if he is as able as I am beginning to think him, then he must be seeing many things much as I am seeing them.

I wanted to tell him that I had talked to Franklin Roosevelt of the new prospect of world co-operation that was opening before mankind. I wanted to stress the fact upon which I had dwelt in the White House, that in the English-speaking and Russian-speaking populations, and in the populations geographically associated with them round the temperate zone, there is a major mass of human beings ripe for a common understanding and common co-operation in the preparation of an organised world-state. Quite parallel with that double basis for a world plan, I wanted to say, there is a third great system of possible co-operation in the Spanish-speaking community. These masses, together with the Chinese, constitute an overwhelming majority of mankind, anxious—in spite of their so-called governments—for peace, industry and an organized well-being. Such things as Japanese imperialism, the national egotism of the Quai d'Orsay and of Mussolini, the childish disingenuousness of the British Foreign Office, and German political delirium, would become quite minor obstacles to human unity, if these common dispositions could be marshalled into a common understanding and a common method of expression. The militancy of Japan was not so much a threat to mankind as a useful reminder for us to sink formal differences and spread one explicit will for peace throughout the world.

Japan, with a possible but very improbable German alliance, was the only efficient reactionary menace left for civilization to deal with. France was inaggressive in spirit; Great Britain incurably indeterminate. I wanted to find out how far Stalin saw international matters in this shape and, if he proved to be in general agreement, to try and see how far he would go with me in my idea that the present relative impotence of the wider masses of mankind to restrain the smaller fiercer threats of aggressive patriotism, is really due not to anything fundamental in human nature but to old inharmonious traditions, bad education and bad explanation; to our failure, thus far, to get our populations clearly told the true common history of our race and the common objective now before mankind. That objective was the highly organized world community in which service was to take the place of profit. The political dialects and phrases which were directed towards that end were needlessly and wastefully different. Creative impulses were being hampered to the pitch of ineffectiveness by pedantries and misunderstandings.

Was it impossible to bring general political statements up to date, so that the real creative purpose in the Russian will should no longer be made alien and repulsive to the quickened intelligence of the Western World, by an obstinate insistence upon the antiquated political jargon, the class-war cant, of fifty years ago? All things serve their purpose and die, and it was time that even the passing of Karl Marx, intellectually as well as physically, was recognised. It was as absurd now to cling to those old expressions as it would be to try to electrify Russia with the frictional electric machines or the zinc and copper batteries of 1864. Marxist class-war insurrectionism had become a real obstacle to the onward planning of a new world order. This was particularly evident in our English-speaking community.

This ancient doctrine that the proletariat or the politician temporarily representing him, can do no wrong, estranged the competent technologist, who was vitally essential to the new task, and inculcated a spirit of mystical mass enthusiasm opposed to all disciplined co-operation. I wanted to bring it plainly into our talk that Russia was now paying only lip service to human unity and solidarity ; that she was in actual fact drifting along a way of her own to a socialism of her own, which was getting out of touch with world socialism, and training her teeming multitudes to misinterpret and antagonize the greater informal forces in the West making for world socialization and consolidation. Was it not possible, before opportunity slipped away from us, to form a general line of creative propaganda throughout the earth ? . . .

It was typical of the way in which mental interchanges lag behind the swift achievements of material progress that Stalin and I had to talk through an interpreter. He speaks a Georgian language and Russian and he does not even smatter any Western idiom. So we had to carry on our conversation in the presence of a foreign-office representative, Mr. Umansky. Mr. Umansky produced a book in which he made a rapid note in Russian of what each of us said, read out my speeches in Russian to Stalin and his, almost as readily, to me in English, and then sat alert-eyed over his glasses ready for the response. Necessarily a certain amount of my phraseology was lost in the process and a certain amount of Mr. Umansky's replaced it. And our talk went all the slowlier because I was doing my best to check back, by what Stalin said, that he was getting the substance, at least, if not the full implications, of what I was saying.

All lingering anticipations of a dour sinister Highlander vanished at the sight of him. He is one of those people who in a photograph or painting become someone entirely different. He is not easy to describe, and many descriptions exaggerate his darkness and stillness. His limited sociability and a simplicity that makes him inexplicable to the more consciously disingenuous, has subjected him to the strangest inventions of whispering scandal. His harmless, orderly, private life is kept rather more private than his immense public importance warrants, and when, a year or so ago, his wife died suddenly of some brain lesion, the imaginative spun a legend of suicide which a more deliberate publicity would have made impossible. All such shadowy undertow, all suspicion of hidden emotional tensions, ceased for ever, after I had talked to him for a few minutes.

My first impression was of a rather commonplace-looking man dressed in an embroidered white shirt, dark trousers and boots, staring out of the window of a large, generally empty, room. He turned rather shyly and shook hands in a friendly manner. His face also was commonplace, friendly and commonplace, not very well modelled, not in any way " fine." He looked past me rather than at me but not evasively; it was simply that he had none of the abundant curiosity which had kept Lenin watching me closely from behind the hand he held over his defective eye, all the time he talked to me.

I began by saying that Lenin at the end of our conversation had said " Come back and see us in ten years." I had let it run to fourteen, but now that I had seen Franklin Roosevelt in Washington I wanted to meet the ruling brain of the Kremlin while my Washington impressions were still fresh, because I thought that the two of them between them indicated the human future as no other two men could do. He said with a quite ordinary false modesty that he was only doing little things—just little things.

The conversation hung on a phase of shyness. We both felt friendly, and we wanted to be at our ease with each other, and we were not at our ease. He had evidently a dread of self-importance in the encounter; he posed not at all, but he knew we were going to talk of very great matters. He sat down at a table and Mr. Umansky sat down beside us, produced his notebook and patted it open in a competent, expectant manner.

I felt there was heavy going before me but Stalin was so ready and willing to explain his position that in a little while the pause for interpretation was almost forgotten in the preparation of new phrases for the argument. I had supposed there was about forty minutes before me, but when at that period I made a reluctant suggestion of breaking off, he declared his firm intention of going on for three hours. And we did. We were both keenly interested in each other's point of view. What I said was the gist of what I had intended to say and that I have told already; the only matter of interest here is how Stalin reacted to these ideas.

I do not know whether it illuminated Stalin or myself most penetratingly, but what impressed me most in that discussion was his refusal to see any sort of parallelism with the processes and methods and aims of Washington and Moscow. When I talked of the planned world to him, I talked in a language he did not understand. He looked at the proposition before him and made nothing of it. He has little of the quick uptake of President Roosevelt and none of the subtlety and tenacity of Lenin. Lenin was indeed saturated with Marxist phraseology, but he had a complete control of this phraseology. He could pour it into new meanings and use it for his own purposes. But Stalin was almost as much a trained mind, trained in the doctrines of Lenin and Marx, as those governess-trained minds of the British Foreign Office and diplomatic service, of which I have already written so unkindly. He was as little adaptable. The furnishing of his mind had stopped at the point reached by Lenin when he reconditioned Marxism. His was not a free impulsive brain nor a scientifically organized brain; it was a trained Leninist-Marxist brain. Sometimes I seemed to get him moving as I wanted him to move but directly he felt he was having his feet shifted, he would clutch at some time-honoured phrase and struggle back to orthodoxy.

I have never met a man more candid, fair and honest, and to these qualities it is, and to nothing occult and sinister, that he owes his tremendous undisputed ascendency in Russia. I had thought before I saw him that he might be where he was because men were afraid of him, but I realize that he owes his position to the fact that no one is afraid of him and everybody trusts him. The Russians are a people at once childish and subtle, and they have a justifiable fear of subtlety in themselves and others. Stalin is an exceptionally unsubtle Georgian. His unaffected orthodoxy is an assurance to his associates that whatever he does would be done without fundamental complications and in the best possible spirit. They had been fascinated by Lenin, and they feared new departures from his talismanic directions. And Stalin's trained obduracy to the facts of to-day in our talk simply reflected, without the slightest originality, the trained and self-protective obduracy of his associates.

I not only attacked him with the assertion that large scale planning by the community, and a considerable socialization of transport and staple industries, was dictated by the mechanical developments of our time, and was going on quite as extensively outside the boundaries of Sovietdom as within them, but also I made a long criticism of the old-fashioned class-war propaganda, in which a macedoine of types and callings is jumbled up under the term bourgeoisie. That is one of the most fatal of the false simplifications in this collective human brain-storm which is the Russian revolution. I said that great sections in that mixture, the technicians, scientific workers, medical men, skilled foremen, skilled producers, aviators, operating engineers for instance would, and should, supply the best material for constructive revolution in the West, but that the current communist propaganda, with its insistence upon a mystical mass directorate, estranged and antagonized just these most valuable elements. Skilled workers and directors know that Jack is not as good as his master. Stalin saw my reasoning, but he was held back by his habitual reference to the proletarian mass—which is really nothing more than the " sovereign Peepul " of old fashioned democracy, renamed. That is to say it is nothing but a politician's figment. It was amusing to shoot at him, with a lively knowledge of the facts of the October revolution, an assertion equally obvious and unorthodox, that " All Revolutions are made by minorities." His honesty compelled him to admit that " at first " this might be so. I tried to get back to my idea of the possible convergence of West and East upon the socialist world-state objective, by quoting Lenin as saying, after the Revolution, " Communism has now to learn Business," and adding that in the West that had to be put the other way round ; Business had now to learn the socialization of capital—which indeed is all that this Russian Communism now amounts to. It is a state-capitalism with a certain tradition of cosmopolitanism. West and East starting from entirely different levels of material achievement, had each now what the other lacked, and I was all for the planetary rounding off of the revolutionary process. But Stalin, now quite at his ease and interested, sucked thoughtfully at the pipe he had most politely asked my permission to smoke, shook his head and said " Nyet " reflectively. He was evidently very suspicious of this suggestion of complemental co-operation. It might be the thin end of a widening wedge. He lifted his hand rather like a schoolboy who is prepared to recite, and dictated a reply in party formulae. The movement of socialization in America was not a genuine proletarian revolution; the "capitalist" was just saving himself, pretending to divest himself of power and hiding round the corner to come back. That settled that. The one true faith was in Russia; there could be no other. America must have her October Revolution and follow her Russian leaders.

Later on we discussed liberty of expression. He admitted the necessity and excellence of criticism, but preferred that it should be home-made by the party within the party organization. There, he declared, criticism was extraordinarily painstaking and free. Outside criticism might be biased. . . .

I wound up according to my original intention by insisting upon the outstanding positions of himself and Roosevelt, and their ability to talk to the world in unison. But that came lamely because my hope for some recognition, however qualified, on the part of the man in control of Russia, of the present convergence towards a collective capitalism in the East and West alike, was badly damaged. He had said his piece to all my initiatives and he stayed put. I wished I could have talked good Russian or had an interpreter after my own heart. I could have got nearer to him then. Normal interpreters gravitate inevitably towards stereotyped phrases. Nothing suffers so much in translation as the freshness of an unfamiliar idea.

As I saw one personality after another in Moscow, I found myself more and more disposed to a psycho-analysis of this resistance which is offered to any real creative forces coming in from the West. It is very marked indeed. In a few years, if it is sustained, we may hear Moscow saying if not "Russia for the Russians," then at least "Sovietdom for the followers of Marx and Lenin and down with everyone who will not bow to the Prophets," which, so far as the peace and unity of the world is concerned, will amount to the same thing. There is a strong incorrigible patriotism beneath this Russian situation, all the more effective because it is disguised, just as there was an incorrigible French patriotism beneath the world-fraternization of the first French Revolution.

A day or so later I discussed birth control and liberty of expression at considerable length with Maxim Gorky and some of the younger Russian writers, in the beautiful and beautifully furnished house the government places at his disposal. Physically Gorky has changed very little since 1906 when I visited him, an amazed distressful refugee, upon Staten Island. I have described that earlier meeting in *The Future in America*. I stayed with him again in 1920 (*Russia in the Shadows*). Then he was a close friend of Lenin's but disposed nevertheless to be critical of the new régime. Now he has become an unqualified Stalinite. Between us also, unhappily, an interpreter had to intervene, for Gorky, in spite of his long sojourn in Italy, has lapsed back to complete mono-lingualism.

Some years ago John Galsworthy helped to create an international net of literary societies called P.E.N. Clubs. At first they served only for amiable exchanges between the writers of the same and different countries, but the violent persecution of Jewish and leftish writers in Germany, and an attempt to seize and use the Berlin Pen Club for Nazi propaganda, raised new and grave issues for the organization. Just at that time Galsworthy died and I succeeded him as International President. I was drawn in as President and chairman to two stormy debates in Ragusa and Edinburgh respectively. The task of championing freedom of expression in art and literature was practically forced upon this weak but widespread organization. It had many defects, but it had access to considerable publicity, and in these questions publicity is of primary importance. Small local battles to maintain the freedom and dignity of letters were fought in the Berlin, Vienna and Rome P.E.N. Clubs, and I now brought to these new Russian writers the question whether the time had not come to decontrol literary activities in Russia, and form a free and independent P.E.N. Club in Moscow. I unfolded my ideas about the necessity of free writing and speech and drawing in every highly organized state; the greater the political and social rigidity, I argued, the more the need for thought and comment to play about it. These were quite extraordinary ideas to all my hearers, though Gorky must have held them once. If so, he has forgotten them or put them behind him.

We wrangled for an hour or so at a long tea table, which had been set in a high sunny white portico, with fluttering swallows feeding their young above the capitals of the columns. About half a dozen of the younger Russian writers were present and the Litvinovs came in from their equally beautiful villa on the far side of Moscow to join in the discussion. To me the most notable things by far about this talk was the set idea of everyone that literature should be under political control and restraint, and the extraordinary readiness to suspect a " capitalist " intrigue, to which all their brains, including Gorky's, had been *trained*. I did not like to find Gorky against liberty. It wounded me.

I must confess indeed to a profound discontent with this last phase of his. Something human and distressful in him, which had warmed my sympathies in his fugitive days, has evaporated altogether. He has changed into a class-conscious proletarian Great Man. His prestige within the Soviet boundaries is colossal—and artificial. His literary work, respectable though it is, does not justify this immense fame. He has been inflated to a greatness beyond that of Robert Burns in Scotland or Shakespeare in England. He has become a sort of informal member of the government, and whenever the authorities have a difficulty about naming a new aeroplane or a new avenue or a new town or a new organization, they solve the difficulty by calling it Maxim Gorky. He seems quietly aware of the embalming, and the mausoleum and apotheosis awaiting him, when he too will become a sleeping Soviet divinity. Meanwhile he criticizes the younger writers and gathers them about him. And he sat beside me, my old friend, the erstwhile pelted outcast dismally in tears whom I tried to support and comfort upon Staten Island, half deified now and all dismay forgotten, looking sidelong at me with that Tartar face of his, and devising shrewd questions to reveal the spidery " capitalist " entanglement he suspected me of spinning. One sails westward and comes at last to the east, and here in Russia after the revolution, just as in Russia before the revolution, all round the world to the left, we have come to the worst vice of the right again, and literary expression is restricted to acceptable opinions.

It does not matter to Gorky, it seems, that our poor little P.E.N. organization has fought for a hearing for left extremists like Toller, and that all its battles so far have been to liberate the left. In this new-born world of dogmatic communism, he insisted, there was to be no recognition for White or Catholic or any sort of right writer, write he never so beautifully. So Maxim Gorky, in 1934, to my amazement made out a case for the Americans who had hounded him out of New York in 1906.

I argued in vain that men had still the right to dispute the final perfection of Leninism. Through the media of art and literature, it was vital that they should render all that was in their minds, accepted or unorthodox, good or bad. For political action and social behaviour there must be conventions and laws, but there could be no laws and conventions in the world of expression. You could not lock up imaginations. You could not say, "Thus far you may imagine and no further." Socialism existed for the dignity and freedom of the soul of man, and not the soul of man for socialism. There were sceptical smiles as the translator did his best to render this queer assertion. Perhaps I made things too difficult for him by speaking of the soul of man.

Gorky, the reformed outcast, wagged his head slowly from side to side and produced excuses for this control of new thought and suggestion by officials. The liberty I was demanding as an essential in any Russian P.E.N. that might be founded, might be all very well in the stabler Anglo-Saxon world; we could afford to play with error and heresy; but Russia was like a country at war. It could not tolerate opposition. I had heard this stuff before. At Ragusa, Schmidt-Pauli, speaking for the Nazis, and at Edinburgh, Marinetti, the Fascist, had made precisely the same apologies for suppression.

I was inspired to produce an argument in the Hegelian form. I asserted that nothing could exist without the recognition of its opposite and that if you destroyed the opposite of a thing altogether the thing itself went dead. Life was reaction, and mental processes could achieve clear definition only by a full apprehension of contraries. From that I argued that if they suppressed men who sang or painted or wrote about the glories of individual freedom, the picturesqueness of merchandising, the mysteries of the religious imagination, pure artistry, caprice, kingship, sin or destruction and the delights of misbehaviour, then their Leninism also would lose its vitality and die. This was I think translated correctly to these exponents of the orthodox Russian temperament but they contrived no sort of reply.

Litvinov cut across their indecision with a question whether I wanted to have the exiled White writers come to Moscow. I said that was for him to decide, it might do them and Russia a lot of good to have them back and listen to what they had to say, but anyhow the principle of the P.E.N. Club was that no genuine artist or writer, whatever his social or political beliefs and implications might be, should be excluded from its membership. I had brought them my proposal and I promised I would leave a written version of it to put before the approaching Congress of Soviet Writers. If they chose to enter into the liberal brotherhood of the P.E.N. Clubs, well and good. If they did not, I should do my best to make their refusal known to the world. In the long run it would be the Russian intellectual movement that would suffer most by this insistence upon making its cultural relations with the outside world a one-way channel, an outgoing of all that Russia thought fit to tell the world and the refusal of any critical return. Mankind might even grow bored at last by a consciously heroic and unconsciously mystical Soviet Russia with wax in its ears.

Later on I found a rather different atmosphere in the household of Alexis Tolstoy at Detskoe Selo (which is Tsarskoe Selo rechristened). There too I met a number of writers and propounded this idea of a thin web of societies about the world associated to assert the freedom and dignity of art and literature. There has always been very marked mental, temperamental and political contrast between Leningrad and Moscow. The bearing of the two populations is very different, and the former place has a large cold seventeenth-century dignity and a northern quality which compares very vividly with the disorderly crowded street bustle, the bazaar animation of Moscow. Even the religiosity of the new faith has a different quality. There is nothing in the northern city with the emotional value of Lenin's tomb, and the anti-God museum in the great church of St. Isaac opposite the Astoria Hotel is a mere argumentative brawl within the vast cold magnificence of that always most unspiritual fane. Christianity never was alive in

Leningrad as it was at the shrine of the Black Virgin in Moscow and neither is the new Red religion as alive.

Perhaps I put my case to the Leningrad writers with better skill after my experience in Gorky's villa, but I encountered none of the suspicion and rigid preconceptions of that first meeting. They were quite ready to accept the universalism of the P.E.N. proposal, and to assert the superiority of free scientific and artistic expression to considerations of political expediency. They promised to support my memorandum to the approaching Congress of Soviet Writers, proposing the constitution of a Russian P.E.N. centre, open to every shade of opinion, and I shall await the report of their clash with the definite intolerance of the Moscow brains with a very keen interest. But at the time of writing this Congress has still to meet.

I argued with Gorky also about birth control, because he, with many others of these Russian leaders, in a confusion between subconscious patriotism and creative optimism, is all for a Russia of four hundred or five hundred millions, regardless of how the rest of mankind may be faring. Russia may want soldiers to defend its Russianism, which is exactly on the level of Mussolini's reasons for damning the thought of birth control in Italy. In the old days Gorky was a dire pessimist with a taste for gloomy colours, but now his optimism has become boundless. Under the red ensign the earth can support an increasing population, he seemed to argue, until standing room is exhausted. To the Proletariat under the new régime, as to God under the old, nothing is impossible. Where it gives mouths it will give food. The Soviet men of science, he imagines, can always be instructed and, if necessary, disciplined to that effect.

In Gorky's study was a great book of plans which he thrust upon me. They were the plans of an almost incredibly splendid palace of biological science. It outdid the boldest buildings of the Tzardom. Five hundred (or was it a thousand?) research students from abroad were always to be working there. Among other activities. Where *is* this? I asked. He produced a plan of Moscow and indicated the exact spot. I said I would like to go and see it. But, he smiled, it was not yet completed for me to see. I had a flash of understanding. I would like to go and see the foundations. But they have not yet begun the foundation! You shall see it, said Gorky, when you come again. It is only one of a group of vast research and educational establishments we are making. You need have no anxiety about the quality of scientific work in Soviet Russia or of its capacity to meet whatever calls are made upon it. In view of these plans.

From Gorky evoking biology in a land of controlled literature by waving an architect's drawing at it, it was an immense relief to go and see some of the most significant biological work in the world actually in progress, in Pavlov's new Physiological Institute outside Leningrad. This is already in working order and still being rapidly enlarged under its founder's direction. It is the least grandiose and most practicable group of research buildings in the world. Pavlov's reputation is an immense asset to Soviet prestige and he is now given practically everything he asks for in the way of material. That much is to the credit of this government. I found the old man in vigorous health, and he took me and my biological son from one group of buildings to another at a smart trot, expounding his new work upon animal intelligence with the greatest animation as he did so. My son, who has always followed his work closely, plied him with lively questions. Afterwards we sat in the house over glasses of tea and he talked on for a couple of hours. He is ruddy and white-haired; if Bernard Shaw were to trim and brush his hair and beard they would be almost indistinguishable. He is eighty-five and he wants to live to a hundred-and-five just to see how the work he has in hand will turn out.

My son and I had visited him in 1920 in *Russia in the Shadows*, when Gip was still a Cambridge undergraduate, and so it was natural that a comparison of Russia in 1920 and Russia in 1934, should get into the stream of the discourse. He talked down his two Communist assistants who were at the table with us. He talked indeed as no other man in Russia would be permitted to talk. So far, he said, the new régime had produced no results worth considering. It was still a large clumsy experiment without proper controls. It might be a success in time, it was certainly a considerable nuisance to decent people with old-fashioned tastes, but at present there was neither time nor freedom in which to judge it. He seemed to see very little advantage in replacing the worship of the crucified by the worship of the embalmed. For his own part he still went to church. It was a good habit, he thought. He delivered a discourse quite after my heart on the need for absolute intellectual freedom if scientific progress, if any sort of human progress, was to continue. And when I asked him what he felt about dialectical materialism, he exchanged derisive gestures with me, and left it at that. He will not be bothered by minor observances; he sticks to dating by the old weekday names, and his always very simple way of living has carried over, just as his magnificent researches have carried over, with scarcely a modification, from the days before the great change. There was, by the bye, a nursery with a real governess for his two grandchildren! I doubt if there is another governess in Soviet territory. As we came away my son said to me: "Odd to have passed a whole afternoon outside of Soviet Russia."

That I thought was a good remark. But if we had been outside Soviet Russia, where had we been? That was not so easy. It wasn't the Past. It was a little island of intellectual freedom ? It was a scrap of the world republic of science ? It was a glimpse of the future ? But in the end we decided that it was just Pavlov.

If I had to talk to Stalin and Gorky and Alexis Tolstoy and Pavlov through a sort of verbal grille, there were other people about who could talk English, and who wilfully or inadvertently exposed some acutely interesting minor aspects of the new Russia. It seems beyond disputing that while the political controls incline to be excessive and oppressive, the lay-out of the material scheme, as one sees it in Moscow at least—for I saw nothing whatever of the planning of Leningrad—is hasty, amateurish and often shockingly incompetent. Disproportion is visible everywhere and all sorts of ineffectivenesses forced themselves on my attention during my ten-day stay quite without my looking for them; there is for instance still a shortage of paper to print even the books in greatest demand, and the paper used is often like thin packing paper; vitally important educational work is held up in consequence; the street traffic again in Moscow, although it has nothing like the volume of the traffic in London or Paris, is disorganised and dangerous, and if one does not belong to the automobile-using class—there are still classes of that sort—getting about is toilsome and tediously slow; the distribution of goods through a variety of shops with different prices and using different sorts of money is preposterously inconvenient. Moscow is growing very rapidly and the replanning and rebuilding seemed to me poorly conceived. Since other great cities have their tube system, Moscow also is making an imitative tube system, although its alluvial water-bearing soil is highly unsuitable for the tubes they are making at the inadequate depth of thirty feet or so. It will be the least stable " Metropolitan " in the world, and it is plain the problem should have been approached from some other and more original direction. I was told by various apologists that what is being done in Moscow is not representative of the real Russian effort; that at different points, usually they are remote points, marvellous things are being achieved. But I suppose there are the same sort of people there as here in Moscow, and in Moscow as planners and constructors they are anything but marvellous.

The outstanding achievement of the new régime, when all is said and done, is the great change in the bearing of the new generation, which has cast off altogether the traditions of serfdom and looks the world bravely in the eye. Coupled with this, an integral part of it indeed, is the " liquidation of illiteracy." But are either of these advances unprecedented? The common folk of the United States of America were as free, equal and confident in the days of simplicity a hundred years ago. And they had their common schools. It is really nothing so very miraculous to be almost the last country in Europe to respond to the need for a common citizen who can read. These people do not know anything of the rest of the world. But wait and see what *these* young people will *do*, interpolates my Bolshevik guide. A hundred years ago America was just such a land of promise.

Still more similar to this Russian change in manners, was the swift establishment of equalitarian phrases and attitudes after the first French Revolution. Neither American nor French democracy prevented a subsequent development of inequalities of power and fortune. Plutocracy succeeded Aristocracy. " This time," say the Bolsheviks, " we have guarded against any similar relapse." But though they may have abolished profiteering and speculation they have not abolished other sorts of advantage. Their defensive obscurantism makes just the shadows in which fresh infringements of human dignity can occur. As the initial revolutionary enthusiasm dies away, officialdom, protected from independent criticism, is bound to find its way to self-indulgence and privilege. All over Moscow and Leningrad you can bribe with foreign currency because of the absurd *Torgsin* system, and the population everywhere is learning to hop quickly and deferentially out of the way of an aggressively driven Lincoln car. The Communist propaganda is altogether too self-satisfied about the intensity and uniqueness of its revolution.

The perpetual reference of those who showed me about to something away over there or coming to-morrow, recalled the Spanish *mañana*. " Come and see us again in ten years' time," they say, at every revelation of insufficiency. If you say that a new building is ramshackle or flimsy they assure you that it is merely a temporary structure. " We don't mind tearing things down again," they explain. The impulse to shift things and pull them about seems to be stronger than the impulse to make. They are transferring the Academy of Sciences from Leningrad to Moscow for no reason that I can understand. Possibly it is to render the control of general scientific thought more effective. One Pavlov is enough for them ; they do not want any revival of that old world radical mentality with its unrestrained criticism, its scepticism and its ridicule. They want their men of science to be industrious bees without stings and live in Gorky's hive.

When Bubnov, the Commissar of Public Education, parted from me outside a charming exhibition of original paintings by little children, very like the original paintings by little children exhibited in every other country in the world, he broke out into happy anticipations of the lives this new generation would lead in a reconstructed Russia. "All this," he said, pointing to a disorderly heap of builders' muck which had submerged a little garden before us, " is temporary." The constructors of the new Metropolitan had, it seems, just made this dump and then gone away for a bit. " This used to be a pretty park," said Bubnov. But it would be all right ten years hence.

Bubnov and Stalin are now among the last survivors of the leaders who did the actual fighting of the revolution, and he said they both meant to live to be a hundred just to see the harvest of Russian prosperity coming in at last. But besides the children in the model schools there are plenty of unaccountable little ragamuffins flitting about the streets. If Stalin and Bubnov live to be two hundred, I feel, Russia will still remain the land of half fulfilled promises and erratic wanderings off to new beginnings.

I came out of Russia acutely frustrated and disappointed in my dream of doing anything worth while to define an understanding between the essentially revolutionary drives towards an organized socialism in America and Russia respectively. They will certainly go on apart and divergent with a maximum of mutual misunderstanding, at least until there is a new type of intelligence dominating the intellectual life of Communism. If I could have talked Russian, or if I had been clever enough to pervert the Marxist phraseology in Lenin's fashion, I might perhaps have come near to my intention. I might have got into real contact with a mind here or there, if not the leading mind. I was fairly beaten in an enterprise too big for me.

As I thought it over in the homeward aeroplane, I felt that Russia had let me down, whereas I suppose the truth of what has happened is that I had allowed my sanguine and impatient temperament to anticipate understandings and lucidities that cannot arrive for many years. I shall never be able to imagine that what is plain to me is not plain to everyone. I had started out to find a short cut to the Open Conspiracy and discovered that, by such abilities as I possess, there is no short cut to be found to the Open Conspiracy.

I had expected to find a new Russia stirring in its sleep and ready to awaken to Cosmopolis, and I found it sinking deeper into the dope-dream of Sovietic self-sufficiency. I found Stalin's imagination invincibly framed and set, and that ci-devant radical Gorky, magnificently installed as a sort of master of Russian thought. There are no real short cuts perhaps, in the affairs of men, everyone lives in his own world and between his blinkers, whether they be wide or narrow, and I must console myself, I suppose, as well as I can, for my failure to get any response out of Russia, with such small occasional signs of spreading contemporary understanding as may appear in our own western life. There has always been a certain imaginative magic for me in Russia, and I lament the drift of this great land towards a new system of falsity as a lover might lament estrangement from his mistress.

The truth remains that to-day nothing stands in the way to the attainment of universal freedom and abundance but mental tangles, egocentric preoccupations, obsessions, misconceived phrases, bad habits of thought, subconscious fears and dreads and plain dishonesty in people's minds—and especially in the minds of those in key positions. That universal freedom and abundance dangles within reach of us and is not achieved, and we who are Citizens of the Future wander about this present scene like passengers on a ship overdue, in plain sight of a port which only some disorder in the chart-room prevents us from entering. Though most of the people in the world in key positions are more or less accessible to me, I lack the solvent power to bring them into unison. I can talk to them and even unsettle them but I cannot compel their brains to see.

§ 10
Envoy

I WENT BY THE TRAIN called the "Red Arrow," the Soviet echo of the *Flèche d'Or*, from Moscow to Leningrad and thence I flew to Tallin. I am finishing this autobiography in a friendly and restful house beside a little lake in Esthonia....

I have done my best now to draw the outline and development of a contemporary mind reacting freely to the disintegrating and the synthetic forces of its time. Copious as this book has become I have still omitted a great bulk of comment and detail that did not seem to me to be of primary importance in this story of the awakening of world citizenship in a fairly normal human intelligence. It has not always been easy to disentangle irrelevant matter without desiccating the main argument. But in a life of eight-and-sixty years there accumulates so great a miscellany of memories and material that, but for some such check upon discursiveness as my design has given me, my flow of reminiscence might have gone on for ever. I confess to an uneasy realization now as I draw to my conclusion that I have not done any sort of justice to the keen interest of countless subsidiary happenings, to the fun of life and the loveliness of life and to much of the oddity of life, beyond the scope of its main essentials. I feel I have been so intent on my thesis, particularly in this very long concluding chapter, that I may have failed to convey my thankfulness to existence for being all else that it so incessantly and generously is. My generalizing impulses have perhaps ruled too much and made my picture of life bony and bare. In my effort to combine the truthful self-portrait of a very definite individual with an adequate reflection of the mental influences of type and period and to keep my outlines firm and clear, I have deliberately put many vivid memories and lively interludes aside, ignored a swarm of interesting personalities I have encountered, cut out great secondary systems of sympathy and said nothing whatever about all sorts of bright, beautiful and pleasant things that have whirled about me entertainingly for a time and then flown off at a tangent. I could write gaily of travels, mountain tramps, landfalls, cities, music, plays, gardens that have pleased me. . . .

What remains is the story of one of the most pampered and irresponsible of " Advanced Thinkers," an uninvited adventurer who has felt himself free to criticize established things without restraint, who has spent his life planning how to wind up most of them and get rid of them, and who has been tolerated almost incredibly during this subversive career. Exasperation there has been, bans and boycotts from Boots to Boston ; public schoolmasters and prison chaplains have intervened to protect their charges from my influence, Nazis have burnt my works, the Catholic Church and Italian Fascism have set their authority against me, and dear old voluble indignant Henry Arthur Jones in *My Dear Wells!* and many better equipped writers—Hilaire Belloc and Archbishop Downey for example—have been moved to write vehement controversial books. But refusals to listen and cries of disagreement are not suppression, and it would ill become an advanced thinker to complain of them. They are recognition. If they are not recognition of the advanced thinker himself, they are recognition of his supports and following, and of the greater forces of which he is the expression. I take it, therefore, as a fair inference from the real immunity I have enjoyed, that such revolutionary proposals as mine are anything but unique and outstanding offences. What I have written openly and plainly is evidently in the thoughts of many people. In spite of much sporadic repressive activity, this new ferment of world-state ideas is spreading steadily throughout the world. Repression, even violent and murderous repression, there is, no doubt, in Germany, in Italy and elsewhere but, where it occurs, it has a curiously forced and hysterical quality ; it is no longer whole-hearted repression by assured authority, it is indeed not so much the result of intolerant counter-conviction as resistance to conviction. It is on the defensive against itself. Its violence, in more cases than not, is the convulsive tightening of a slipping grip. The supporters of the thing that is, seem everywhere touched by doubt. Even more plainly is that the case with reactionaries. We advanced thinkers owe our present immunity, such as it is, very largely to the fact that even those of our generation who are formally quite against us, have nevertheless been moving, if less rapidly and explicitly, in the same direction as ourselves. In their hearts they do not believe we are essentially wrong ; but they think we go too far,—dangerously and presumptuously too far. Yet all we exist for,—our sort,—is to go too far for the pedestrian contingent. . . .

I began this autobiography primarily to reassure myself during a phase of fatigue, restlessness and vexation, and it has achieved its purpose of reassurance. I wrote myself out of that mood of discontent and forgot myself and a mosquito swarm of bothers in writing about my sustaining ideas. My ruffled *persona* has been restored and the statement of the idea of the modern world-state has reduced my personal and passing irritations and distractions to their proper insignificance. So long as one lives as an individual, vanities, lassitudes, lapses and inconsistencies will hover about and creep back into the picture, but I find nevertheless that this faith and service of constructive world revolution does hold together my mind and will in a prevailing unity, that it makes life continually worth living, transcends and minimizes all momentary and incidental frustrations and takes the sting out of the thought of death. The stream of life out of which we rise and to which we return has been restored to dominance in my consciousness, and though the part I play is, I believe, essential, it is significant only through the whole. The Open Conspirator can parallel—or, if you prefer to put it so, he can modernize—the self-identification of the religious mystic: he can say, " personally when I examine myself I am nothing "; and at the same time he can assert, " The Divinity and I are One "; or blending divinity with democratic kingship, " The World-State, c'est Moi."

There is a necessary parallelism in the matured convictions of all intelligent people, because brains are made to much the same pattern and inevitably follow similar lines of development. Words, colourings and symbols can change very widely but not the essential forms of the psychological process. Since first man began to think he has been under a necessity to think in a limited number of definable shapes. He has to travel by the roads his ancestry made for him and their fences are well nigh insurmountable. So mystical Christianity, Islamic mysticism, Buddhist teaching, in their most refined and intense efforts towards distinctive penetration, have produced almost identical and quite easily interchangeable formulae for their mysteries. The process of generalization by which the mind seeks an escape from individual vexations and frustrations, from the petty overwhelming pains, anxieties and recriminations of the too acutely ego-centred life, is identical, whatever labels it is given and whatever attempts are made to establish exclusive rights in it. All these religions and every system of sublimation, has had to follow the same route to escape, because there is no other possible route. The idea of creative service to the World-State towards which the modern mind is gravitating, differs widely in its explicitness, its ordered content and its practical urgency, from the All of Being, the Inner Life, the Ultimate Truth, the Personal Divinity, the Friend who sticketh closer than a brother, who is nearer than breathing and closer than hands and feet, and all those other resorts of the older religions, but its releasing and enveloping relation to the individual *persona* is, in spite of all that difference in substance, almost precisely the same.

The difference between our modern consolation systems on the one hand and their homologues in the religions and conduct-philosophies of the past on the other, lies almost entirely in the increasingly monistic quality of the former. They imply an abandonment, more or less tacit or explicit, of that rash assumption of matter-spirit dualism, which has haunted human thought for thousands of generations. The change from egoism to a larger life is consequently now entirely a change of perspective; it can no longer be a facile rejection of primary conditions and a jump into " another world " altogether. It is still an escape from first-hand egoism and immediacy, but it is no longer an escape from fact. And the modern escape to impersonality is all the more effective and enduring because of this tougher, unambiguous adhesion to exterior factual reality. The easy circuitous return through shadowy realms of abstract unreality to egoism on a higher plane is barred; the Life of Contemplation and receptive expressionism, are no longer possible refuges. The educated modern mind, constrained to face forward, is systematized but not abstracted. For all his devotion to larger issues, for all his subordination of lesser matters, the Open Conspirator like the Communist or the positivist man of science, remains as consistently *actual* as blood or hunger, right down to the ultimates of his being.

So ends this record of the growth and general adventure of my brain, which first squinted and bubbled at the universe and reached out its feeble little hands to grasp it, eight and sixty years ago, in a shabby bedroom over the china shop that was called Atlas House in High Street, Bromley, Kent.

THE END

INDEX

Ackroyd, Dr. W. R., 64
After Democracy, 693, 748
Alexander, Sir George, 536, 542
Allen, Grant, 193, 194, 476, 546 *et seq.*, 650
America, present-day politics in, 785
Amery, Rt. Hon. L. S., 102, 501, 761, 764, 765
Angell, Sir Norman, 331
Ann Veronica, 470, 482, 498, 548, 638
Answers to Correspondents, 316, 327
Anticipations, 332, 475, 638, 643, 719, 731, 799
Archer, William, 672, 706
Arlen, Michael, 645
Arnold House, 594, 597
Astor, W. W., 372, 514, 517
Atlas House, Bromley, 60 *et seq.*, 108, 192
Austen, Jane, 47, 506
Autocracy of Mr. Parham, The, 501
Aveling, Dr., 347

Bacon, Roger, 728
Bagnold, Enid, 602
Balfour, Francis, 772
Balfour, Lord, 507, 635, 704, 755, 763, 772 *et seq.*, 797
Balzac, Honoré, 503
Baring, Maurice, 635
Barker, Ernest, 706, 715, 719
Barker, Granville, 541
Barrie, Sir J. M., 374, 509, 533
 visit to Wells, 454, 596
 When a Man's Single, 371
Barron, Oswald, 602
Baxter, Charles, 533
Beaverbrook, Lord, 697
Beerbohm, Max, 521
Bellairs, Carlyon, 761, 764
Belloc, Hilaire, 728, 823
Benham, Sarah, 43, 44, 57
Bennett, Arnold, 307, 410
 books of, 628
 correspondence with Wells, 625
 source of success of, 626
 personality of, 629
Benson, Mgr. R. H., 602
Bentham, Jeremy, 600
Berle, A. A., 785, 792
Besant, Mrs. Annie, in the socialist movement, 238, 248

Bierce, Ambrose, 612
Biology, Textbook of, 344, 351
Birchenough, J., 761
Birkenhead, Lord, 522
Blake, William, 241
Blanchamp, Mr., 357, 520
Bland, Hubert, 265, 601 *et seq.*, 661
Bland, Mrs. Hubert, 601 *et seq.*, 624
Bleak House, 47
Bomb, The (Harris), 525
Book of Catherine Wells, 462, 727, 739, 746
Boon, 679
Bottomley, H., 522
Bottomley, J. H., 479
Bowkett, Sidney, 100, 105, 597, 614
Boys, Prof. C. V., 211
Bradlaugh, Charles, 236
Bradlaugh-Besant trial, 184
Brailsford, H. N., 695
Brett, G. P., 719
Briggs, Dr. William, 335 *et seq.*, 340 *et seq.*
Brownlow, Earl of, 373
Bubnov, 819
Bullock, Miss, 49, 52, 109 *et seq.*, 135
Bulpington of Blup, The, 499, 624, 679
Burney, Fanny, 47
Burton, William, 234, 250, 306
 as analytical chemist, 302
 declares himself a socialist, 238
 edits *Science Schools Journal*, 240
By the Ionian Sea (Gissing), 575
Byatt, Horace, 140 *et seq.*, 156, 171 *et seq.*, 172, 188, 339

Campbell, Mrs. Patrick, 542
Candy, Arabella, 278, 279, 283, 288, 315
Card, The (Arnold Bennett), 628
Carlyle, Thomas, 99, 241
Caroline, Queen, 46
Casebow, Mr., 152
Cassell's *Popular Educator*, 168
Causation, Wells on, 222, 223
Cecil, Lord Robert, 761
Certain Personal Matters, 374
Chamberlain, Rt. Hon. Joseph, 761, 763
Chambers' *Encyclopaedia*, 168
Chapman, Mr., 523
Chesterton, Cecil, 602
Chesterton, G. K., 471, 538, 602
Choate, Ambassador, 786

Christian Socialism, 246
Christina Alberta's Father, 477, 499, 624
Chronic Argonauts, The, 309, 339, 516, 643
Churchill, Rt. Hon. Winston, 102, 635, 683, 684
Claremont, Mrs., 695
Clayton, Mrs., 523
Clodd, Edmund, 567
Clynes, Rt. Hon. J. R., 745
Coefficients Club, 761
Colby, Bainbridge, 707, 708
Cole, Martin, 313
Colefax, Lady, 635
College of Preceptors, 87, 91, 334
Collins, Sir William J., 302, 303, 307, 356, 369
Comédie Humaine, 504
Comic Cuts, 328, 329
Communist Socialism, 264
Cone, The, 309
Conrad, Joseph, 615 *et seq.*, 625 *et seq.*
Contemporary Novel, The, 495
Cooper, Mr., 40, 41, 108
Cooper, Fenimore, 78
Courtney, W. L., editor of *Fortnightly Review*, 645
Covell, Mr., 40
Cowap, Mr., 138
Crane, Cora, 612 *et seq.*
Crane, Stephen, 612 *et seq.*, 620, 623
Crane, Walter, 238, 618
Crawford, O. G. S., 681
Crewe, Lady, 635
Crichton-Browne, Sir James, 636
Crowhurst, Mr., 115
Crown of Life (Gissing), 577
Crozier, Dr. Beattie, 721
Currie, Sir James, 172
Curtis, Lionel, 706
Curzon, Lord, 532, 635, 771, 772
Cust, Harry, 33, 471, 474, 525, 772
    appoints Wells dramatic critic, 534
    edits *Pall Mall Gazette*, 373, 374, 512
Cyclic Delusion, The, 224

D'Abernon, Lord, 532
Daily Mail, the, 328
Dall, Mrs., 794
Darrow, Clarence, 786
Darwin, Charles, 202
Davies, A. M., 234, 250, 296
Davies, Morley, 511
Dawkins, Clinton, 761
Deeks Case, 724
de Lisle, Lord, 51, 53
Denbigh, Earl of, 701
Desborough, Lady, 635
Deschanel, 174
de Soveral, Marquis, 635

Dickens, Charles, 47, 92, 506
Dickinson, G. Lowes, 694, 706
Dickinson, Lord, 694
Discovery of the Future, 636, 648
Dixie, Lady Florence, 124
Donald, Robert, 701
Downey, Archbishop, 728, 823
Doyle, Sir A. Conan, 552
Dream, The, 499, 500
Dream of Armageddon, A, 645
Drummond's *Natural Law in the Spiritual World*, 162
Duke, John, 62

Education Act of 1871, 84, 93, 327, 507
Educational Times, 350, 353, 374
Einstein, Prof. Albert, 29, 221, 766
Eisenstein's film, *October*, 733
Elcho, Lady Mary, 471, 635, 772
Elements of Reconstruction, 761
Englishman Looks at the World, An, 657, 666
Euclid's *Elements*, 140, 154
Evans, Caradoc, 147
Evening News, the, 328

Fabian Society, 238, 247 *et seq.*, 251 *et seq.*, 661
    association with Labour Party, 255
    attitude towards education, 262
    mission of, 262
    New Heptarchy Series of, 259
    Wells' efforts to reorganize, 660
    Wells resigns from, 661
Fabianism and the Empire, 260
Faults of the Fabian, The, 661
Fellowship of Progressive Societies, 748
Fetherstonhaugh, Lady, 52, 53, 109
Fetherstonhaugh, Miss, *see* Bullock, Miss
Fetherstonhaugh, Sir Harry, 52, 137
Field, Mr., 160, 162
First Men in the Moon, The, 472
Fisher, Prof. Irving, 792
Five Year Plan in Russia, 264, 778 *et seq.*, 800
Food of the Gods, 260, 654
Forde, Captain, 49
Forster, E. M., 694
Forsyte Saga, The (Galsworthy), 504
Foucault, Léon, 174
France, Anatole, 668
Freethinker, The, 162, 164, 184
French, Lord, 767
Freud, Sigmund, 301
Frewen, Morton, 612
Future in America, 789, 809

INDEX

GALL, JANIE, 272, 273, 277
Galsworthy, John, 498, 809
Garvin, J. L., 761
Geology, Wells on, 226
George IV, King, 43, 46, 52
George, Henry, 168, 177, 179
Gertz, Elmer, 522
Gissing, George, 563, 634
    career and work of, 567 et seq.
    death of, 581
Gladstone, Rt. Hon. W. E., 46, 78, 92
Glimpse, The (Arnold Bennett), 629
God and Mr. Wells (Archer), 672
God the Invisible King, 673, 674
Gorky, Maxim, 809 et seq.
Gosse, Edmund, 520, 596
Graham, Cunninghame, 521
Grahame, Kenneth, 557
Great Good Place, The, 21
Green, J. R., *History of the English People*, 99
Gregory, Maundy, 522
Gregory, Sir Richard, 236, 371
Grein, J. T., 521
Grey of Fallodon, Viscount, 706, 715, 761, 763, 768, 770, 772
Guedalla, Philip, 502, 707, 719
Guest, Haden, 661
Gulliver's Travels, 138
Guthrie, Professor, 210 et seq., 220, 227, 231

HAIG, EARL, 767
Haigh, E. V., 684
Haldane, Lord, 761, 763, 766 et seq.
Hamilton, Lady Emma, 52
Hamilton, Sir William, 52
Harding, President, 793
Hardy, Thomas, 152
Harmsworth, Alfred, 326
Harmsworth, Alfred C, *see* Northcliffe, Lord
Harmsworth, Geoffrey, 330
Harmsworth, Harold, *see* Rothermere, Lord
Harmsworth, Lester, 330
Harris, Frank, 214, 285, 513, 645
    career of, 522 et seq.
    takes over *Saturday Review*, 520
    Wells visits, 356
Harris, Mrs. Frank, 526, 527
Harris, usher, 171, 181, 190
Hawthorne, Nathaniel, 305, 309
Headlam, Dr. J. W., *see* Morley, Sir J. W. H.
Headlam, Stuart, in the socialist movement, 238
Healey, Elizabeth, 234, 291, 295, 305, 374, 444
Henley, W. E., 373, 513, 515, 532, 795
Henley House School, Kilburn, 317

Hewins, W. A. S., 761, 764, 765
Hick, Henry, 577, 584, 586
Hilton, John, 706
Hind, Lewis, 514, 515
History is One, 717
History of Mr. Polly, 499
Hitler, Adolf, 100, 102
Hobson, J. A., 694
Holmes, Judge, 635
Holt Academy, Wrexham, 292
Honours Physiography, 371
Hoover, President, 793
Horder, Lord, 347
Horrabin, J. F., 719
Horsnell, Horace, 602
House, Colonel, 708
Housman, Laurence, 602
Howes, Prof. G. B., 201
Hudson, H. K., 701
Hudson, W. H., 194
Hueffer, Ford Madox, 473, 615, 617, 622
Hueffer, Oliver Madox, 617
Human Origins, 476
Humboldt's *Cosmos*, 98, 173
Huxley, Mrs., 176
Huxley, Prof. Julian, 29, 351, 721
Huxley, Prof. T. H., 173, 201, 202, 209, 227, 228, 350
Hyde, Edwin, 147, 152
Hyndman, H. M., 249

IMPERIAL COLLEGE OF SCIENCE AND TECHNOLOGY, 208, 231
    Debating Society of, 214, 234
Imperial Palace (Arnold Bennett), 628, 629
In the Days of the Comet, 477, 480, 500, 654
In the Fourth Year, 667, 694, 695
Invisible Man, The, 543, 561
Irving, Sir Henry, 114
Irving, Washington, *Bracebridge Hall*, 197

JAMES, HENRY, 488 et seq., 503, 538, 596, 615, 634
    activities of, 20
    and expressionism, 611
    character of, 535
    novels of, 537
James, William, 493, 538
Jeans, Sir James, 42
    on causation, 224
Jefferies, Richard, 193
Jennings, A. V., 204, 214, 313, 347
Jepson, Edgar, 602
Jerome, J. K., 557

INDEX

Joan and Peter, 492, 500, 503, 674, 679
Joffre, Marshal, 681
Johnston, Sir Harry, 172, 719
Jones, Mr., of Wrexham, 294 *et seq.*, 322
Jones, Henry Arthur, 823
Jones, Sir Roderick, 701
Joynson-Hicks, Mr., 479
Judd, Professor, 227, 231, 232
Jude the Obscure, 152
Jung, definition of *persona*, 24

KEY, JOHN, 152 *et seq.*
Keynes, J. M., 716
King, Miss, 114, 119, 131
King, Sir William, 110, 111, 146
Kingsley, Charles, 249
Kingsmill, Ethel, 423
Kingsmill, Hugh, 521, 522, 523
Kipling, Rudyard, 508, 533, 626, 760
Kipps, 155, 472, 492, 499, 586, 638, 639
Kirk's *Anatomy*, 174
Kitchener, Lord, 767
Knott, Mrs., 74

Labour Ideal of Education, 737
Labour Party, association with socialism, 255
Lady Frankland's Companion, 306, 311
Land Ironclads, 683
Landseer, Sir Edwin, 55
Lang, Andrew, 193, 547
Lankester, Sir Ray, 471, 719
Laval, M., 794
Lawrence, D. H., 464
Lawrence, T. E., 705
League of Nations, Wells on, 694 *et seq.*
Lee, Vernon, 493
Leeming, Lieut., 684, 685
Le Gallienne, Richard, 552
Le Hand, Miss, 794
Lenin, Nicolai, 94, 95
  comparison with Balfour, 776; with Stalin, 805
  reorganization of Communist Party, 264
Let Us Arise and End War, 668
Liberal World Organisation, 748
Life and Loves of Frank Harris, 529
Life of Bernard Shaw (Harris), 528
Lindsay, Sir Ronald, 794
Lippmann, Walter, 599
Little Wars (Wells), 102
Litvinov, 351, 812
Lloyd George, Rt. Hon. David, 29, 333
Loewenstein, 522
Love and Mr. Lewisham, 171, 200, 410, 411, 458, 467, 473, 477, 557, 582, 586

Low, Barbara, 354
Low, David, 499, 502, 686
Low, Frances, 354
Low, Ivy, 355
Low, Sir Maurice, 354
Low, Sir Sidney, 354, 557, 701, 759
Low, Walter, 350, 353, 355, 363, 512, 520
Lowson, J. M., 370
Lucy, Sir Henry, 635
Lyell, Sir Charles, 228
Lytton, Bulwer, 508

MACCOLL, D. S., 521
MacDonald, Rt. Hon. Ramsay, 256, 522, 745
Macguire, Mrs., 635
Mackinder, H. J., 761, 764
McLaren, Mrs. Christabel, 172
McTaggart, 635
Man of the Year Million, 514, 643
Mankind in the Making, 257, 262, 638, 649, 654
Mansfield, Katherine, 462
Marburg, Theodore, 694, 695
Marriage, 489, 496, 498, 500
Martineau, Harriet, 786
Marx, Karl, 180, 247, 249
  and English Trade Unionism, 255
  and problem of revolution, 731
  association of socialism and democracy, 254
  unimaginativeness of, 263
Mason, A. E. W., 613
Masterman, Rt. Hon. C. F. G., 102, 471, 762
Mater, André, 695
Maurice, F., 249
Maxse, Leo, 761, 764
Meanwhile, 478
Men Like Gods, 501
Meredith, Annie, 196
Meredith, George, 481, 634
Meynell, Alice, 514
Midhurst Grammar School, 140, 171, 242
Mill, John Stuart, 250
Milne, A. A., 324, 326, 500
Milne, J. V., 318 *et seq.*, 329
Milner, Lord, 761, 762, 765
Mitchell, laboratory instructor, 216, 217
Mitchell, Sir Chalmers, 273, 521
Modern Utopia, 185, 260, 261, 332, 436, 469, 638, 649, 656, 731, 735
Moley, Raymond, 792
Mond, Mrs. Alfred, 636
Mond, Mrs. Emile, 636
Monkey Island, 113
Montagu, Rt. Hon. E. S., 347

Montague, C. E., 682
Montefiore, A. J., 327
Moore, Doris Langley, 601, 604, 605
Moore, George, 617, 626
More, Sir Thomas, 246
More's *Utopia*, 180
Morley, Sir J. W. Headlam, 697, 701, 704
Morley, Miss, 90
Morley, Mrs., 86, 90
Morley, Thomas, 293
  Geoffrey West on, 92
  school of, 83, 85, 242
Morris, William, in the socialist movement, 238, 244, 247, 249, 265, 597
Morrison, Arthur, 532
Mosley, Sir Oswald, 649, 782
Mr. Blettsworthy on Rampole Island, 501
Mr. Britling Sees it Through, 492, 500, 503, 670
Munday, Mr., 40, 41, 108
Municipilisation by Provinces, 259
Murchison, Sir Roderick I., 228
Murphy, James, 221, 224
Murray, Prof. Gilbert, 706, 715, 719
Mussolini, Signor, 649
Myers, F. W. H., 635
Mysterious Universe, The (Jeans), 224

NASH, MR., 123
Neal, Elizabeth, 44, 49
Neal, George, 43, 44, 57
Neal, John, 43, 44
Neal, Sarah, *see* Wells, Mrs. Joseph, 43
Nelson, Lord, 52, 55
Neo-Malthusianism, 436, 475, 483
Nesbit, E., *see* Bland, Mrs. Hubert
New Machiavelli, 472, 473, 477, 482, 548, 638, 662, 736, 739, 773
New Statesman started, 260
New Vagabonds Club, 557
New Worlds for Old, 481
Newbolt, Henry, 761
Nicholson, Sir Charles, 701
Northcliffe, Lord, 323, 663, 704
  buys *The Times*, 775
  career of, 328
  friendship with Wells, 330, 696
  mentality of, 330
  on his success, 329
  produces school magazine, 326
Nothing to Pay, 148
Novels, "character" in, 494
  dialogue, 500
  Henry James on, 489 *et seq.*
  objectives of, 493
  of the future, 502
  Wells on, 488 *et seq.*
  with a purpose, 496

Old Wives' Tale, The (Arnold Bennett), 628
Oliver, F. S., 762
Olivier, Lord, 471, 600
  as a Fabian, 598
  in the socialist movement, 238
Origin of the Idea of God (Allen), 547
Orr's *Circles of the Science*, 55
Ostrogorski, Professor, 599
Oundle School, 323, 726, 729
Outline of History, 716 *et seq.*
Owen, Robert, 180, 246, 249

PAINE, TOM, 138
Paish, Sir George, 694, 695
Paley's *Evidences*, 188
Pall Mall Gazette, 373
Passfield, Lord and Lady, *see* Webb, Mr. and Mrs. Sidney
Passionate Friends, 477, 551
Pavlov's Physiological Institute, 815
Payne, James, 546
Payne, Jim, 611
Pease, Edward, 608, 661
P.E.N. Clubs, 809
Pennicott, Clara, 113, 115, 130
Pennicott, Kate, 113, 119, 131
Pennicott, Thomas, 103, 112 *et seq.*, 123, 131
Petrography at South Kensington, 230
Physical Society, 211
Physics, riddles of science of, 219
Physiological Aesthetics (Allen), 547
Pinero, Sir Arthur, 542
Pinker, J. B., 410, 614
Planck, Max, 221, 222, 226
Plato's *Republic*, 139, 177, 185
Platt, Mr., 153, 155, 168
Poe's Narrative of A. Gordon Pym, 97
Popham, Mr. and Mrs., 597
Porter, Mr., 234
Powell, Professor York, 610, 611
Private Life of Henry Maitland (Roberts), 567
Private Papers of Henry Ryecroft (Gissing), 575
Proudhon, *La Propriété c'est le Vol*, 249
Proust, Marcel, 463

RALEIGH, SIR WALTER, 635
Rasselas, 138
Raut, M., 293, 294
Rea, Sir Walter, 694
Rediscovery of the Unique, 223, 356
Reeves, Pember, 761, 762
Reid, Capt. Mayne, 78
Reinach, Madame, 509
Repington, Colonel, 762
Research Magnificent, 498, 624, 736

Rhodes, Cecil, 756, 759
Rhondda, Lady, 485
Riceyman Steps (Arnold Bennett), 628
Richardson, Dorothy, 557
Ridge, W. Pett, 508, 514
Riley, Miss, 45, 64
Robbins, Amy Catherine, at Woking, 542
  at Worcester Park, 557
  in Italy, 567, 572
  joins Wells in London, 375, 426
  life with Wells, 461 *et seq.*, 509
  literary work of, 462
  marries H. G. Wells, 438
  Wells' letters to, 384, 386 *et seq.*, 392
  death of, 742, 746
Robbins, Mrs., 394, 396, 512, 516
Roberts, Adeline, 362, 369, 386, 388
Roberts, Morley, 567, 578
Robinson, James Harvey, 727
Rodgers and Denyer, Messrs., 116, 117, 124, 151
Rogers, Professor, 792
Rolfe, Frederick, 602
Romney, George, 52
Roosevelt, Mrs. Franklin, 794, 795
Roosevelt, President Franklin, 515, 744, 780
  policy of, 785 *et seq.*
Roosevelt, President Theodore, 755 *et seq.*, 793
Rosebery, Earl, 764
Ross, Sir Denison, 719
Rossetti, Christina, 618
Rothenstein, Sir William, 567
Rothermere, Lord, 328
Rouse, Mr., 295
Royal College of Science, 175, 201, 207 *et seq.*
Ruck, Berta, 602
Runciman, J. F., 521
Ruskin, John, 286
  as socialist, 238, 247, 249
Russell, Bertrand, 761, 762, 765
Russell, Charles, 786
Russia, experimental state capitalism in, 264
  Wells' visits to, 726, 771, 779, 799
Russia in the Shadows, 724

SADLER, MICHAEL, 761
Saintsbury, Professor, 520
Salmon, Miss, 74
Salvaging of Civilization, The, 720
Samurai Order, 658 *et seq.*, 735, 745
Sanders, W. Stephen, 259
Sanderson, Cobden, in the socialist movement, 238
Sanderson, F. W., 323, 725, 726
Sassoon, Sir Edward and Lady, 635
Saturday Review under Harris, 520

Scepticism of the Instrument, 224
Science of Life, 351, 721
Science Schools Journal, 240, 302, 309, 374
Sea Lady, 468, 473, 477, 498, 597
Secret Places of the Heart, The, 478, 677
Secrets of Crewe House, 700
Select Conversations with an Uncle, 374, 511
Shape of Things to Come, 262, 501, 643, 748, 749
Sharp, Clifford, 602
Shaw, G. Bernard, 471, 522, 620
  and the theatre, 541
  at the Fabian Society, 239, 661
  brain of, 29
  contributes to *Saturday Review*, 521
  first meeting with Wells, 539
  friendship with Frank Harris, 528
  in the socialist movement, 238, 244, 249, 265
  meeting with Conrad, 621
Shaw, Lord, 695
Shelley, Percy Bysshe, 185, 240, 305
Sheridan, Clare, 612, 684
Short History of the World, 719
Shorter, Clement K., 514
Sickert, Walter, 532
Silk, Mr., 357, 520
Simmons, A. T., 234, 239, 291, 321
Simon, Sir John, 795
Sitwell, Edith, 462
Sladen, Douglas, 557
Slip under the Microscope, A., 100
Smith, E. H., 234, 238, 239, 250
Smith, John Hugh, 762
Smith's *Principia*, 140, 154
Snowden, Philip, 745
Socialism, as practical Christianity, 246
  association with democracy, 254
  condemnation of profit motive, 249
  defects in nineteenth-century, 251, 653
  development of, 245
  early adherents to, 238
  essential unfruitfulness of, 265
  foreign, 248
  influence of Marx on, 263
  marriage under, 481
  progressiveness of Communist, 264
  repudiation of planning by, 262
  unprogressiveness in Western, 251
  Webb theory of, 253
  Wells' impression of, as student, 244
  Wells' Utopian, 657
  without a competent receiver, 252, 732
Socialism and Sex Relations, 480
Socialism and the Family, 478
Socialism and the Middle Classes, 478
Socialism and the Scientific Motive, 737
Soul of a Bishop, 498, 674

INDEX

Sparrowhawk, Mr., 115
Spencer, Herbert, 238, 250, 412, 664, 786
Spender, J. A., 706, 715
Squire, Sir John, 602, 674
Stalin compared with Franklin Roosevelt, 780; with Lenin, 805
    Wells' interview with, 800 *et seq.*
Steed, H. Wickham, 701, 706
Stevenson, Bob, 533, 611
Stevenson, R. L., 193, 305, 611
Stolen Bacillus, 515
Story of a Great Schoolmaster, 500, 727
Story of Days to Come, 645
Story of Tommy and the Elephant, 584
Strachey, Lytton, 502
Strachey, St. Loe, 471, 495
Street, G. S., 532, 542
Sturm's *Reflections*, 48
Sue, Eugene, *Mysteries of Paris*, 114
Surly Hall, 113 *et seq.*, 131
Sutherland, Miss, 52, 53
Sutro, Alfred, 602
Sutton, Mrs., 76, 77
Symons, Arthur, 521
Swettenham, Colonel, 692
Swinnerton, Frank, 567, 633

TAYLOR, MISS, 386
Taylor, Mr., 234
Tennyson, Lord, 506
Terry, Ellen, at Surly Hall, 114, 283
Thackeray, W. M., 506, 507
Thomas, Rt. Hon. J. H., 745
Thomas, Owen, 511
Thomson, Sir Basil, 533
Tilbury, Mr., 561
Time Machine, 214, 309, 339, 518, 530, 625, 645, 758
Times, The, 328, 329
Times Book Club, lecture to, 495
Tit Bits, 316, 327
Tobin, A. I., 522
Tolstoy, Alexis, 813
Tolstoy, Count Leo, fugitive impulse of, 21
Tomlinson, H. M., 623
Tono Bungay, 53, 158, 492, 499, 503, 638, 639
Trevelyan, Rt. Hon. Sir George, 102
Trollope, Anthony, 506
Trotsky, Leon D. B., 94, 95, 173
Trotter, Wilfred, 658
Tutton, A. E., 240
Tyndall, 552
Tyrrell, Lord, 704, 769, 770, 772

UMANSKY, MR., 803
Undying Fire, The, 499, 658, 674, 675

Universe Rigid, The, 214, 223, 356
University Correspondence College, 335 *et seq.*
University Correspondent, The, 353, 361
Unwin, Raymond, 694
Up Park Alarmist, 135

VAN LOON, HENDRIK, 720, 722
Vathek, 138
Veranilda (Gissing), 578
Verne, Jules, 508
Vertov, Dziga, 780
Victoria, Queen, 46
Vincent, Edgar, *see* D'Abernon, Lord
Vincent, Mr., 517
Vision of Armageddon, A, 567
Voltaire's books, 138
Voysey, C. F. A., 638

WALKER, SIR EMERY, in the socialist movement, 238
Wallas, Graham, 238, 244, 258, 265, 597
Walton, Mrs., 171, 183
War and Peace, 504
War and the Future, 679, 692, 693
War in the Air, 666
War of the Worlds, 472, 543
Ward, Mrs. Humphry, 507
Warwick, Lady, 433, 526, 527
Washington and the Hope of Peace, 724
Watson, H. B. Marriott, 517, 533
Watts, Arthur, 602
Way the World is Going, The, 727
Webb, Sidney, 598, 601, 761, 762
    at the Fabian Society, 661
    in the socialist movement, 238, 249, 252, 258, 265
Webb, Mrs. Sidney, 252, 253, 258, 265, 598, 600, 661
    originates Coefficients Club, 761
Wedgwood, Josiah, 761
Weismann, 200
Wells, Charles Edward, 53, 57
Wells, Edward, 53
Wells, Elizabeth, 53
Wells, Fanny J., 63, 64
Wells, Francis Charles, 195, 311
    apprenticeship of, 115
    at Nyewoods, 366
    in boyhood, 103
    in employment, 108, 109
Wells, Frederick Joseph, 195, 197, 304
    birth of, 63
    boyhood of, 104
    apprenticeship of, 115
    goes to South Africa, 369
    loses his job, 365
    on Wells' divorce, 426
    school of, 74
    starts work, 109

INDEX

Wells, Frederick Joseph, Wells' letters to, 379, 384, 390, 391, 393, 401, 403, 408
Wells, G. P., brain of, 29
  collaborates with his father, 351, 721
  visits Russia, 799, 816
Wells, Hannah, 54
Wells, Henry, 53
Wells, Herbert George, birth of, 64
  accident to, 76
  apprenticeship of, 116 et seq.
  as a lover, 422
  as a teacher, 173
  as dramatic critic, 534
  at Bromley Academy, 83
  at Henley House School, Kilburn, 317
  at Holt Academy, 292
  at Midhurst Grammar School, 141, 171
  at the New Vagabonds Club, 557
  at Up Park, 135, 175, 183, 302
  at Worcester Park, 557
  attends the Y.M.C.A., 160
  becomes a pupil teacher, 126
  believed to be consumptive, 299
  builds Spade House, 638
  class feeling of, 93-5
  comparison with Roger Bacon, 728
  conception of the world in youth, 95
  confirmation in Church of England, 187; preparation for, 188
  contributes to Debating Society, 234; to the *Daily Mail*, 663, 665; to the Fabian Society, 478; to the *Saturday Review*, 359
  declares himself a socialist, 238
  description of his mother, 44 et seq.; of his father, 53 et seq., 192
  early ideas on religion, 160 et seq.
  early reading of, 76, 138, 167
  early years of, 38, 64
  edits *Science Schools Journal*, 240
  efforts to reorganize the Fabian Society, 660
  Fabian report of, 255
  failure as science student, 231, 233; in drapery trade, 157
  first schools of, 74
  first start in life, 112
  first-class pass in zoology, 204
  friendship with A. V. Jennings, 204; with Catherine Robbins, 363; with Northcliffe, 330, 696; with Rebecca West, 106
  friendships in boyhood, 105
  health undermined as a student, 237
  idea of a planned world, 643 et seq.
  impressions of socialism as student, 244
  in Italy, 567, 572
  in literary journalism, 352
  in love with Isabel Wells, 283

Wells, Herbert George, in Southern France, 740
  in Woking, 542
  interest in Henry George, 179; in Plato, 177, 178
  interview with Cust, 512; with Stalin, 800 et seq.
  invents telpherage system, 684
  is joined by Catherine Robbins, 375, 426
  lack of sympathy with his first wife, 360
  leaves his first wife, 375, 426
  leaves school, 91
  leaves Wookey, 129
  letters to his brother, 379, 384, 390, 391, 393, 401, 403, 408; to his father, 381, 395, 400, 408; to his mother, 120, 169, 383, 394, 395, 398, 400, 409; to Miss Robbins, 384, 386 et seq., 392
  life as a student in London, 266 et seq.
  life with Catherine Robbins, 461 et seq., 509
  liking for Latin, 140, 154
  marriage, first, 337; second, 439
  matriculates, 215
  meeting with his first wife, 432, 433
  obtains diploma of College of Preceptors, 334, 345
  obtains Doreck scholarship, 345
  on acquisitiveness, 196
  on adolescence, 143
  on Allen (Grant), 546; on Allen's *Woman Who Did*, 549
  on America's part in the war, 708
  on apprentices, 147
  on Aryans and Jews, 100
  on Balfour, 772
  on Bennett (Arnold), 625 et seq.
  on biographies, 25
  on biological education, 346, 348 et seq.
  on biological science, 220
  on Boys (Prof.), 211
  on Catholicism, 165, 573
  on Conrad, 615, 618
  on constructive revolution, 731 et seq., 742
  on Curzon, 771
  on Darwin, 202
  on educational methods at College of Science, 207
  on emancipation of women, 483
  on fear of death, 301
  on Foreign Office personnel, 769
  on free love, 435, 436, 480, 483
  on Gissing (George), 567 et seq.
  on Grey (Viscount), 768
  on Haldane, 766
  on Harris (Frank), 522 et seq.

INDEX

Wells, Herbert George, on higher education, 339 et seq.
- on his *Anticipations*, 645
- on his *Discovery of the Future*, 648
- on his early writings, 291, 305
- on his letters, 376
- on his *Modern Utopia*, 656
- on his *Outline of History*, 717 et seq.
- on his *persona*, 24
- on his visit to President Franklin Roosevelt, 794 et seq.
- on Hitler, 100, 102
- on Hueffer (Ford Madox), 617
- on Huxley, 202
- on individuality in causation, 222 et seq.
- on James (Henry), 488 et seq., 535
- on jealousy, 476
- on Judd (Prof.), 227
- on Lenin, 777
- on Leningrad and Moscow, 813, 817
- on life as a draper, 149
- on literary criticism, 507
- on literary style, 622
- on literature in the nineties, 506
- on London houses, 274
- on making of scientific apparatus, 212
- on measuring vibrations of a tuning fork, 216
- on Montague (C. E.), 682
- on Northcliffe, 330
- on novels, 488
- on origin of modern culture, 136
- on private school education, 321
- on psycho-analysis, 30, 79
- on quality of brains, 29, 752
- on reason for leaving his wife, 421 et seq.
- on relations of the human mind to physical reality, 226
- on reverie, 75
- on Roosevelt (Theodore), 755
- on Sanderson of Oundle, 726
- on school system, 84
- on science in relation to the world, 200
- on science of physics, 218, 219
- on sex consciousness in children, 79
- on sexual awakening, 181
- on Shaw (G. B.), 539
- on social life, 752
- on socialization in relation to municipal organization, 257
- on stopping education at 14, 132
- on the Blands, 601
- on the "Brains Trust" in America, 791
- on the British Empire, 762
- on the Coefficients Club, 761 et seq.
- on the Communist idea, 178
- on the educated mind, 619, 620, 628

Wells, Herbert George, on the Fabian Society, 238, 247 et seq.
- on the failure of socialism, 653
- on the framework of education, 723
- on the Harmsworths, 326 et seq.
- on the Imperial College of Science, 207, 208, 232, 237
- on the Jewish question, 353
- on the League of Nations, 694 et seq.; 716 et seq.
- on the "New Deal" in America, 785
- on "the New Republic," 652, 663
- on the "Open Conspiracy," 742 et seq.
- on the theatre, 541
- on the World-State, 651
- on top hats, 284
- on use of tanks in war, 683
- on value of work accomplished, 26
- on Wallas (Graham), 598
- on war, 665 et seq., 677 et seq.
- on Wilson's "Fourteen Points," 707
- on world change, 242 et seq.
- on written examinations, 142
- ostracized owing to *Ann Veronica*, 471
- physical appearance of, 280
- pre-Marxian socialism of, 179
- prepares propaganda literature against Germany, 697
- present home of, 742
- President of P.E.N. Clubs, 809
- produces *Up Park Alarmist*, 135
- reading in sociology and economics, 240
- reads the *Freethinker*, 162, 164
- relations with his brothers, 103; with his father, 193
- religious views of, 66, 67
- resigns from Fabian Society, 661
- rewrites the *Time Machine*, 518
- school holidays, 113
- source of success of, 626
- stands as Labour candidate, 255
- studies under Huxley, 175, 199; under Guthrie, 210
- study of geology, 227; of German, 215; of Marxism, 180; of physics, 210; of science, 173; of zoology, 201
- sued for infringement of copyright, 724
- takes B.Sc. degree, 233
- talk with Lenin, 95
- theological views of, 671 et seq.
- University career, 112
- Utopian theories of, 657 et seq.
- visit to America, 755, 782; to the Burtons, 306; to Frank Harris, 357; to Russia in 1914, 726, in 1920, 724, 771, in 1934, 779, 799 et seq.; to the war zones, 681
- war game of, 102

Wells, Herbert George, works in chemist's shop, 138; in draper's shop, 146; for University Correspondence College, 335
  writes for *Pall Mall Gazette*, 374
  writings about sex, 467 et seq.
Wells, Isabel Mary (Mrs. H. G.), 280, 283, 315, 334
  lack of sympathy with Wells, 360, 426
  marriage of, 337
  runs a poultry farm, 431
  second marriage of, 432
  death of, 434
Wells, Joseph, as a reader, 193
  as cricketer, 62
  at Atlas House, 192
  at Liss, 197, 376
  early years of, 53 et seq.
  first meets Sarah Neal, 51
  is lamed for life, 108
  marriage of, 57
  moves to Nyewoods, 110, 303
  sets up in business, 60
  Wells' letters to, 381, 395, 400, 408
  death of, 198
Wells, Joseph, senr., 53
Wells, Joseph, of Redleaf, 54, 55
Wells, Mrs. Joseph (Wells' mother), 43
  becomes housekeeper at Up Park, 109
  early years of, 44
  first meets her husband, 51
  is dismissed from Up Park, 365
  love affairs of, 50
  marriage of, 57
  moves to Nyewoods, 366; to Liss, 376
  plans for her son, 115, 138, 146
  religious beliefs of, 48, 176
  Wells' letters to, 120, 169, 383, 394, 395, 398, 400, 409
  death of, 197
Wells, Lucy, 53
Wells, William, 53, 276
Wells, Mrs. William, 272, 278, 283, 288, 315, 356, 427
Welsh, James, 552

Wemyss, Lady, 776
West, Geoffrey, 168
  biography of Wells, 303 et seq., 311, 420
  on Morley's school, 92, 93
West, Rebecca, 551
Whale, James, 561
What Are We to Do with Our Lives?, 677, 746
What is Coming?, 679, 694, 695
Wheels of Chance, The, 499, 543, 624
When the Sleeper Awakes, 557, 582, 645
Where is Science Going?, 221
Wife of Sir Isaac Harman, The, 477, 485, 498, 548
Wilberforce, Bishop, 203
Wilde, Oscar, 359, 524, 542
Wilderspin, Mr., 171, 191
William IV, King, 46
Williams, Aneurin, 694
Williams, Bertha, 374, 461
Williams, Cousin, 128
Williams, "Uncle," 126 et seq.
Wilson, President Woodrow, 333, 666, 707, 716
Wolfe, Humbert, 775
Woman Who Did, The (Allen), 548
Wonderful Visit, The, 472
Wood's *Natural History*, 77
Woodward, Martin, 204
Wookey, Wells at, 126
Woolf, L. S., 695, 706
Woolf, Virginia, 462
Work, Wealth and Happiness of Mankind, 197, 226, 252, 262, 501, 600, 622, 721 et seq., 728, 744, 746, 749
World of William Clissold, The, 478, 500, 501, 716, 740, 742, 745
World Set Free, The, 666
Wyndham, George, 507, 532, 635

Year of Prophesying, A, 727
Young Man's Companion, 55

ZAHAROFF, 522
Zimmern, Alfred, 599, 706, 71